EXPOSÉ

EXPOSÉ

LAURA VAN WORMER

MIRA®

ISBN 1-55166-526-3

EXPOSÉ

Copyright © 1999 by Laura Van Wormer.

Visit us at www.mirabooks.com

Printed in U.S.A.

For Chris

With grateful thanks to my talented editor and publisher, Dianne Moggy, and her editorial assistant, Miranda Stecyk, and the whole terrific group at MIRA Books.
I also wish to thank Lynn Goldberg for her wisdom and expertise, and too, of course, my longtime friend and agent, Loretta Barrett, and her associates, Kirsten Lundell and Nick Mullendore.

Finally, a special word of thanks to the community of Meriden, Connecticut. It's a wonderful place.

I
Connecticut

1

I am the reporter at the Castleford *Herald-American* who argues the most with our editor, which means said editor has more or less assigned Crazy Pete Sabatino and his conspiracy theories permanently to me.

"And you know those kids on the milk cartons?" Pete is whispering as he leans forward in my cubicle at the paper.

"You mean the missing children?"

"Yes," he answers solemnly. "They're taking them. The Masons are."

The linchpin of Pete's conspiracy theory is that George Bush and six other Masons secretly rule the world. I must confess, this theory does not frighten me the way it's supposed to, no doubt because I am White Anglo-Saxon Protestant myself, descended from a long line of New England Republicans. (Though it should be noted that my voting record sometimes wildly strays from ancestral patterns.)

"The Masons are taking the children to the aliens for genetic research," Pete continues. "Remember the alien vortex I told you about?"

"In Long Island, near the Brook Haven labs," I say patiently. "Where you said we shot down the TWA flight because we were shooting at an alien ship coming into the vortex."

"Right. That's where they're taking the children." When I don't say anything, he stresses, "Look, Sally, I've read about this, I've talked to people about it, and I've seen evidence. I know. I *know*."

Crazy Pete has not always been this way. My neighbor, who used to take piano lessons right after Pete at Mrs. Fothergill's when they were young, said it was only after Pete turned sixteen and refused to play anything but "Tara's Theme" from *Gone with the Wind*—over and over and over—that people began to suspect he might be slipping a cog or two. At eighteen he went off to the University of Connecticut at Storrs for three weeks and then came back home to live with his parents, where he has been ever since. He is a bright man, and feeds his insatiable curiosity about conspiracies and the new world order through a series of books and pamphlets and videos he orders from rural-route post office box addresses in Texas and California. Pete also watches TV programming that can only be brought in by the enormous satellite dish he has built on top of his father's house, and listens to radio shows received by his forty-foot shortwave radio tower, also located on his father's roof.

If I'm thirty, Pete's got to be around forty. His mother's dead now, but his father's still around, a retired construction worker who seems oblivious to his son's role as the earth's savior from George Bush and the aliens. Pete has a part-time job at the library, cataloging historical documents on microfiche, and everyone agrees he is nice enough, clean enough and bright enough, if only he didn't start in on the aliens. (Conspiracy theories regarding the Republican party are usually okay in Castleford, since the populace is overwhelmingly Democratic.) And then there's Pete's habit of slipping into the library's community room after hours to play—what else?—"Tara's Theme" on the piano, but with great and mighty flourishes that come only from decades of practice and that frankly give everybody the creeps.

"What kind of genetic research," I ask Pete, pencil poised over paper, "are the aliens doing with these children?"

"They're still trying to perfect our race so we'll stop destroying the planet."

At that moment my editor, Alfred Royce Jr., appears from around the corner. Al is sixty-one, but is still a junior because his father is still going strong at ninety. And since his father holds majority ownership of the paper, Al is running it, although popular opinion often leans toward lynching him. This opinion is most often expressed by his sister, Martha, who has lately been barred from the executive suite under charges of treason.

"Hey, Pete, how are you?" Al says.

Pete just nods, looking a bit sullen.

"Is our star reporter, Sally Harrington, getting it all down right?"

"Yes. She's good, Al, but you never seem to print anything."

"When we get the facts exactly right, when we get the substantiation we need," Alfred promises, "the stories will run." He has been saying this for the three years I've been here. "So listen, Pete, tell me what you've got on Dudleytown."

I look at my boss. Dudleytown is the ruins of a community on a mountaintop between Cornwall and Litchfield in northwest Connecticut. It was a settlement founded by the Dudley family in the 1700s, which died out altogether by 1900, with several stories of violent and dreadful deaths attached to it. The area residents today, of course, hate ghost hunters trespassing on their property to get up to the ruins of the town, so they have begun a vigilant campaign to pretend that no such place exists, which in turn has only accelerated interest in the area.

"Oh, yeah, Dudleytown," Pete says seriously, nodding, "that was a genetic experiment that didn't work out. You know that we...us...mankind...is on its fourth attempt. The first three combinations didn't work. We are a combination of thirty-two alien species bred with the ape."

"But do you think it's really haunted?" Al asks him, ignoring the biology lecture.

"The Masons don't want anyone up there, you know," Pete says. "They're trying to pretend Dudleytown never existed."

"Why?" I ask.

"Because there's still evidence of the alien landings up there, where the ships used to come in. The Masons killed everyone in the town because they threatened to develop into a superior race. A race that would threaten the Masons' world domination."

"Well that's good enough for me," Alfred announces. "Sally, I want you to take Devon with you to Dudleytown and find out what's what. Get lots of pictures."

I look at him. "When?"

"Why not today?"

"Because," I answer, "I'm in a suit and heels and going to the special meeting of the city council regarding the HUD investigation into the downtown housing project."

"Don't worry, I'll send Michelle," he tells me.

Michelle is an intern who will not dare object if Al cuts out all of the salient facts from her story since she'd do anything to get a job that has a paycheck attached. (It should be explained that the staff of the Castleford *Herald-American* is actually very good at reporting the news of our four-town area of two hundred thousand people—that is, as long as an unfavorable news story doesn't affect one of Al's fraternity brothers from Dartmouth or anyone serving on the executive golf committee at the Castleford Country Club.)

"Oh, well, if you're sending an ace reporter, how can I object?" I turn to Pete. "Perhaps you'd like to come with us to Dudleytown. So we can take some pictures of that evidence of alien landings."

He looks horrified. "My God, they'd get me for sure. There's no way I could go up there without them knowing."

"Well, what about us?" I protest, looking innocently up at my boss. "Who's going to protect us?"

"Oh, they won't do anything," Pete assures me. "Since you haven't done anything about them yet, they think you don't know."

"Don't know what?" I ask.

"That they murdered your father," Crazy Pete says.

2

It wasn't that I believed Crazy Pete's claim that the Masons killed my father, but it was the way he said it, the abruptness of it, that got to me.

I was nine and my brother was five when Daddy died in the great Castleford flood. He had been volunteering with the rest of the city to save what they could after the reservoir dam broke, and while my father was examining the new high-school gymnasium, part of the wall gave way and fell on him.

My father was a self-employed architect who did not carry as much life insurance as he should have. But then, he had only been thirty-four years old, his business had only just hit its stride (people said that if he'd survived the flood, he would have been a millionaire, thanks to the rebuilding that followed), he was healthy and strong, and thoughts of death had been very far from his mind. My mother, I'm pretty sure, had no idea the extent (or lack) of life insurance Daddy had been carrying. She never said anything to us about finances, but simply went back to teaching grade school to keep body and soul together. My maternal grandparents helped us when they could and we managed to hang on to the house.

My father had been born and raised in Castleford, a small city in central Connecticut that began as a farming village, grew into a town and, after the railroad came through in the 1800s, boomed into an industrial city. My father's full name was Wilbur Kennett Harrington, but everyone called him "Dodge," because he was a star running back, first for Castleford High and then for Yale in nearby New Haven. Dad's family had once been extremely well-to-do but my grandfather, a hopeless gambler and big-time drinker, had destroyed the family's fortune. Over a period of fifteen years he managed to squander all of the wealth his ancestors had accumulated over two centuries, and the day before the sheriff came to repossess the estate, Granddad figured the best way to deal with the problem was to simply shoot himself in the pool house after dinner.

The Castleford my father knew as a child was chosen by a national news magazine as one of the best places to live in the entire United States during the late 1940s and 1950s. Good jobs at the factories, excellent schools, ample land, inexpensive housing and gorgeous parks and lakes and mountains earned Castleford its reputation as a residential nirvana. By the time I was a kid in the 1980s, however, Castleford was being cited as a victim of poor city planning, an industrial dinosaur. The plants and factories had cut way back—many had actually shut down or moved south—working-class neighborhoods staggered downward into welfare slums, school test scores fell, the housing market tanked, and litter began to blow over the community's once-regal Victorian streets. The worst humiliation was a new highway that enabled travelers to bypass the city entirely.

I wasn't even allowed to go downtown, not that I wanted to. The movie theaters of my father's day had closed, and so had the restaurants, the hotels, the skating rink. Buildings were boarded up. There was nothing to do in Castleford except "go to the mall" on the new highway, which my mother wouldn't let me do, either, that is, until I was sixteen and got a job at the Gap.

The economy of central Connecticut has improved as new technology moved in, and Castleford has vastly changed for the better. It still has a bad rap, though. A recent headline read "1/3 Castleford on Welfare or SS."

I love Castleford. Even during the worst time. Much of the Castleford my father introduced me to is still very much alive. There are beautiful urban and suburban neighborhoods, stunning churches and classic New England farmland scenes. And, always, always, Castleford has those splendid mountains, the Hanging Hills they're called, and we have thousands upon thousands of acres of parkland left to us by our ancestors.

There's still even some old money in town, *big* money.

Our house—where my mother still lives—was a wonderful place for a child. On one side was, and still is, a working farm, on the other, the mansion my father grew up in, which, in subsequent years, became a convent.

My mother, the former Isabel "Belle" Ann Goodwin of Newport, Rhode Island, met my father at a dance while she was a coed at Mount Holyoke. They married the day she graduated. As a wedding present, my maternal grandparents bought this five-acre parcel of the old Harrington estate that my parents desperately wanted, and also gave them the down payment to build a small home my father designed. Made of stone, the house looks as though it's been there for two hundred years. That was Daddy's thing, adapting historic designs for homes and buildings by using modern materials and technology. He built our house as the first stage of what he hoped would one day be the center portion of a new Harrington mansion.

As children, Sarah Goodwin Harrington, aka Sally (that's me), and Robert Wilbur Harrington, aka Rob (that's my little brother), had free reign. We roamed the hills and pastures and woods, paddled a canoe in the pond, fished, built tree houses and had adventures galore.

It's true, though, that my mother was very sad for a very long time. I remember that. How, around us, she was all smiles and hugs and enthusiasm, and how, when she was not looking, I saw the worry and heard the deep, sorrowful sighs.

Once, when I was ten, I heard my mother crying. I got out of bed and saw her in the kitchen, her head down on the table, crying, asking my father to tell her what to do.

I didn't go to her that night, but I never forgot it. And every time I thought things were really great, I'd look carefully at my mother and then, yes, I could see that the pain was still there. And then after a while I knew that the quiet sadness in me and my brother might never ever go away, either.

We missed Daddy very much. We still do.

"Sally," Devon is shouting. "Sally!"

"*What?*" I finally answer, whipping around and nearly poking my eye out with a tree branch. It's the middle of a hot July afternoon and I am, at this point, tired and very cranky. We've been tramping around for hours, and to my knowledge, no Pulitzer prize has ever been awarded to a journalist looking for ghosts and aliens.

"I hate to say it, Sal..." Devon begins, looking up from the map in his hand.

I just stand here, waiting. I stopped at home to change into khaki shorts on the way here, and a T-shirt and hiking boots. I've pulled my hair back in a ponytail.

Devon nervously fingers the strap of his camera case. Not a good sign. "I think we're on the wrong mountain. I think Dudleytown's over there somewhere." He's pointing across the ravine that has just taken us two hours to climb. At the bottom is a rushing stream; on the other side, a ravine wall as steep as this one was.

I sigh, shaking my head in defeat, wiping the perspiration from my forehead and then swatting at the gnats that are buzzing my head despite a generous application of Cutter's. "Look, Devon," I finally say, pointing, "can't you just take a picture of that rock and make it look spooky so we can call it a day?"

"Sally!"

"I'll write the whole article," I say. "The history of Dudleytown, the mysterious deaths, I won't lie. I'll just—" I hear something, a voice. Far off. I cock my head in that direction. "What was that?"

We listen.

"I can't hear anything but the stream," Devon says.

"I do. I did." I take a few steps over to a ledge. There it is again, a voice in the distance. A woman. I throw my hand out. "Over there. Did you hear that?"

"No."

"Somebody's calling. From over there, down there somewhere."

"But the car's the opposite way, Sal. If you go that way, who knows where—"

I hear the woman's voice again and it sounds terrified. "I think somebody's in trouble." I start sliding down the embankment, a small torrent of rocks and shale coming down with me.

"It's probably just some kids—" Devon begins, but then he evidently hears it, too, for I glance over my shoulder and see that he's following.

* * *

"*Help!* Someone please help us!" a woman cries minutes later.

"*He-e-elp!*" a child's voice screams in a dreadful high-pitched voice of terror. "*He-e-elp!*"

"We're coming!" I call, crashing through the underbrush, following the sound of their voices.

I dash over the rise, panting, and come upon three figures: a man doubled over on the ground, a woman jumping up and down beside him, and a child squatting on the ground next to the man, covering his eyes with his hands and screaming "*He-e-elp!*"

"Oh, thank God!" the woman gasps. "My husband's having a heart attack!"

I am already down on one knee, gently bringing the man's face toward me. "Hi, what's your name?" I ask while loosening his collar. Beneath his tan, I can see the man's face is ashen, but not the blue or gray color usually associated with heart attacks.

The man is trying to focus on me. He is gasping, nearly hyperventilating. "Corbett," he manages to get out.

"Corbett," I repeat, smiling. "I'm Sally. Corbett, I want you to try and control your breathing, to let it out slowly and draw it in slowly."

The little boy is still screaming.

I glance over at the woman. "Perhaps you could comfort your son."

The woman nods and walks over to draw her child—who still has his eyes covered—into her arms.

I feel the man's pulse. "That's it, slowly in, slowly out. That's it. In-n-n, ou-u-ut, in-n-n, ou-u-ut." I am counting. I get his heart rate; it's high, but nowhere near catastrophic. "Corbett, do you have any pain?"

He looks confused.

"Is there a pain in your chest? Or in your neck? Your arm?"

When he hesitates, I say, "Or is your heart just pounding like it's going to burst. Racing, hard, taking your breath away?"

"Yes, that's it," he says.

"That's it, keep breathing—slowly." I look over my shoulder to see Devon has arrived. "Put your fanny pack under his head," I direct, turning back to the patient. His color is returning to normal, as is his breathing. "This is Devon," I explain as we ease the man's head onto Devon's pack. "That's good, your breathing's getting back to normal. Now, try to sip some water," I suggest, holding my water bottle to his mouth. Gingerly he does, and then settles back on the ground again.

"That's very good," I say, feeling his wrist again. "Your pulse is almost normal." I look at him intently. "Any pain yet? Anywhere?"

He shakes his head, looking less scared now.

"I knew we should have brought the cell phone," the woman says. "I could have called Medivac. I must have been mad to drag Corbett up here. It's all my fault." She speaks with an English accent. "But somebody told us about some wretched ghost town and Corbie wanted to see it."

"Dudleytown," Devon supplies.

"Poor Dad," the woman says to her son, rocking him.

"I don't think you've had a heart attack," I tell Corbett. "But we'll call EMS just in case." I glance back at Devon, who takes out his cell phone and punches in 911, pulling his map out and walking away a few steps.

I smile. "I think you're going to be just fine, Corbett. That you *are* fine."

"I'm not having a heart attack?" he says in a completely different tone of voice, propping himself up on his elbows.

"Sally knows about CPR and heart stuff," Devon calls.

"You do? Is he all right?" the wife asks anxiously. "What's the matter with him?"

"Have you been under a great deal of stress lately?" I ask him.

"Yes, he has been," the woman says eagerly, moving back over, now half dragging the child.

The man nods.

"Have you been on any new medications?" I ask. "Tranquilizers, anti-anxiety drugs?"

He nods. "Yes, as a matter of fact." He looked to his wife. "Verity? What's it called?"

"I can't remember, darling. It's one of those tranquilizers—but he was acting so strangely," she adds to me, "I asked him to stop taking it."

"And you did?"

He nods. "Yesterday."

I nod. "I think what you had was a panic attack. It feels like a heart attack, but it's an adrenaline thing, you can't turn it off and it's frightening."

"Are you a doctor?" the woman asks.

I have to laugh a little. "Only a reporter, I'm afraid. With lots of unwanted medical experience."

"Thank God," the woman says, squatting to hug her son and reach for her husband's hand. "Thank God you came along. I don't know what we would have done."

Only then does the little boy dare look at me. "Is Dad okay?"

I smile. "I think your dad's going to be just fine."

He smiles shyly at his father, although he does not let go of his mother.

"Thank God, Corbett," the woman says, touching the side of the man's face. "I'm sure this woman's right. You look so much better already."

"I feel like a horse's ass," he quietly admits.

Click. I've finally realized who these people are. The stylishly attractive woman in her forties, the English accent, the name Verity; the older man, Corbett; and the young child.

This has to be Verity Rhodes and Corbett Schroeder. She is the glamorous editor of *Expectations* magazine; he is the business tycoon enjoying his second or third marriage.

"Ah," the woman says, studying my face, "I see that you've figured out who we are."

Perhaps, I think, her mother should have called her Vanity.

3

I wish I could say I'm just like my mother. I wish I could say that I'm gentle and patient and attentive and emotionally stable the way genuinely stoic people always are. Unfortunately, I'm afraid I'm sometimes a bit of a trial. Smart like my mother, yes; honest, to a fault; but there is a compulsive streak in me that definitely comes from somewhere else. I have been known to swing into blissful, confident highs, and then to drop into seemingly inexplicable mires of melancholy blues. Thank heavens I physically resemble Mother, because it is those looks, I'm keenly aware, that have often allowed me to get away with what I do in those compulsive moments between the highs and the lows.

Everybody says Mother looks a lot like the actress Lee Remick used to: wide, startling blue eyes; honey-blond hair and a round face that seems to gain more cheekbone every year. Add a few inches, darken the hair slightly—actually, fade all of Mother's looks a shade or two—agitate her aura, and that's me. (My little brother, Rob, used to say that Mother is like Lee Remick in *The Omen* and I'm just like Damien, the evil offspring.)

The irony that my mother resembles an actress who died of cancer is not lost on any of us, for Mother very nearly died of it, too. But that was over four years ago and Mother is still very much alive, and she has a new light in her eyes and a spring in her step.

She is out back in her vegetable garden when I drive up. It's late, almost eight-thirty, but it's still light outside. She has been keeping a huge vegetable garden in the back as long as I can remember, and there are flower beds all over the yard and along three sides of the house. There is a small potting shed where she stores her tools, which is actually a smokehouse from the 1850s that my father dragged over from the old estate and converted for her. I always say the property looks very English and Mother always says, no, dear, it's very New England.

Mother is on summer break from teaching. She is kneeling in the vegetable garden on a stadium seat cushion from Yale (which someone dutifully replaces each year at Christmastime), wearing a cotton print dress and a big straw hat that is secured with a scarf. At her side is a wicker basket, in which she is carefully placing green tomatoes. I smile to myself, thinking how Mother has missed her time by half a century or two.

My dog, Scotty, runs ahead to say hello. He is a collie-shepherd-retriever from the Humane Society. He sneaks up on Mother and licks her cheek twice before she can get away. "Hello, baby," my mother says softly, talking to Scotty or to me or to both of us. Scotty, feathery tail wagging, wanders off into our neighbor's vast cornfield to look for my mother's dog, a sleek golden retriever named Abigail.

"You'll never guess who I met in the hills around Dudleytown today," I say.

"The editor of *Expectations* magazine and a corporate raider named Corbett," Mother says, looking up. She laughs. "Devon stopped by to pick some beans."

"So much for my big news."

Mother stands up and takes her gardening gloves off. "He said you were wonderful, dear, that you calmed those poor people down and did all the right things."

I shrug. "I don't know about that."

"I do," she says, stepping toward me. "My little girl has the best bedside manner of any doctor I know."

She should know, I guess, since she was stuck with me during her cancer ordeal.

I walk over to scoop up her basket for her.

"You're just in time to help me make relish," she says. "Otherwise these will rot and go to waste.

Mother says "to-mah-toes." So do I. So did Rob until he got to high school and said it was too faggy and that he was going to get his head kicked in by less-genteel members of the Castleford football team if he didn't cut it out.

"Isn't it kind of late for you?" I ask as we walk toward the house. Mother almost always gets up at five every morning, and she likes to be in bed with a book by nine.

"It's such a beautiful night," she says, "I felt like being outside." It is a lovely July evening, warm, but with a slight breeze. Everything is lush and green, the heron is on the pond, the crickets have begun to chirp. The dogs are dashing somewhere around in our neighbor's cornfield because we can hear them and occasionally we see telltale jiggles of the stalks that are already over eight feet high. It's cattle corn this year, though, not sweet corn. Darn.

"I went to a little soiree tonight with Mack," Mother says, climbing the stairs to the deck.

"Really," I say, following. Mother has never been without admirers over the years, but the poor guys (usually just divorced, just widowed or just awful, period) rarely got anywhere with her and gave up (or were, I suspect, quickly and politely dismissed). My friends always said not to worry, Mother would remarry when she was ready, but I still wonder. When I was younger, I figured she refrained from dating out of fear of ensuing violence from Rob and me, or because it was genuinely difficult to find a man who could stand up to my father's memory. Whatever, Mother didn't even go out on a date until I was fifteen, and even then the most death-defying dating situation she ever embarked on was something like a history lecture at the Castleford Public Library.

It certainly wasn't as if Mother hadn't been approached and propositioned. She had been—big-time. In fact, the loneliest aspect of her early widowhood, she would say, was not being able to freely socialize. Mother was simply too young and too good-looking, and the husbands of her friends would try to get her alone to profess their love, or worse yet, simply make sexual advances. I know because I witnessed it firsthand, once even with a neighbor down the road, Mr. Geister. The furnace had gone dead one very cold winter Sunday morning and Mother had called him in desperation because the furnace man hadn't appeared.

I was about to go downstairs when I heard a scuffle—Mr. Geister had physically cornered Mother in the little furnace room off the basement—and Mr. Geister gasp, "I'm sorry, Belle, but I love you."

"I—I need to get by, Paul," I heard Mother say.

"I won't ever let you go," he whispered.

"Let go of me." Mother's voice could have cut steel.

"Belle," he pleaded.

"Mom!" I called from the stairs. "Mrs. Geister's on the phone. Is Mr. Geister here?"

"Hello? Hello?" Mr. Geister said into the kitchen phone a few moments later. He sighed and replaced the phone into the receiver. "I guess she hung up." He looked at my mother. "I better get home."

"Give Carla my best," Mother said. "And thank her for loaning you out." As soon as he left, Mother whirled around. "Young lady, that telephone never rang." And then she grabbed me and hugged me so hard I couldn't breathe.

We never discussed those episodes, mostly because I think my mother found them somewhat humiliating, as if she thought the men thought she had invited their attentions in some way. (Some prefeminism myths die hard in my mother's group.) When I was at UCLA I used to wonder how she was managing, since my brother could get hit with a brick before he'd ever realize what was going on.

But attending a soiree with Mack—this *Mack*—was news. I had met him twice and this was maybe the tenth time she had mentioned him since. He had been widowed for about three years. He'd been a research physicist—with a Ph.D.—at Pratt Whitney for years, and now was teaching at Wesleyan University in Middletown.

"So what kind of swinging soiree was this?" I ask, following Mother into the kitchen.

"I didn't say it was swinging," she laughs, avoiding my eyes. "It was just a little garden party at the university to welcome the new faculty."

I raise my eyebrows but say nothing. This is a big deal for Mother—her first appearance with Mack at an official function where he works. She wouldn't have done it unless she expected to be seen there again.

Mack Cleary is a good candidate for Mother. He is gentle, courteous, physically active and nice-looking. He has one son that is grown and married and living in Atlanta. Mack is terribly shy, though, so most of what I know about him comes from Mother. He likes art and music and history, interests that my mother shares. He also moors a sailboat in East Haddam on the Connecticut River, and until my mother married my father and moved to Castleford, she had always kept a sailboat moored in her parents' backyard in Rhode Island.

I wonder at the small pang of jealousy I suddenly feel on my father's part. After all, he's been dead for twenty-one years.

As if to ward off my snooping into her personal life, Mother washes the tomatoes in the sink and asks me how things are going between me and Doug.

"I don't really feel like talking about it, if you don't mind."

"You need to decide what you're doing, Sally," she says for the twentieth time this year.

Doug has the same complaint. He says he doesn't know what is going on between us and he's *in* the relationship. I don't know what to say; I love him, but how much, I don't know. Enough to get married? I don't think so. But maybe. But maybe not.

Hell if I know. I wonder if other women feel this way when the subject of marriage comes up and they feel as though they have never really experienced a genuine love affair where they felt as though they loved someone with all their heart.

"Oh, Mother, by the way," I say at the back door after whistling for Scotty, "I had Crazy Pete in my office this morning."

"Oh, that poor soul."

"Well, he seems okay, Mother. His conspiracy theories keep him very busy and he has his job at the library. And he has that big house to live in with his father, where he can set up all his equipment and listen to Radio Free Martian Land."

Mother looks out the window over the sink. "I think they're coming out," she says, referring to the dogs. "Oh, there they are!" and she laughs, for Scotty is being pursued by Abigail and the two have shucks all over their fur, as if they're camouflaged.

I slide the screen door open to let them in and pluck the remaining pieces of corn shucks off. "Anyway," I continue, "Pete said something about Daddy and the Masons." I am not about to tell her that he thinks maybe they killed him.

"Your father was a Mason," she says, petting the dogs and moving to fill the water bowl.

"He was?"

She nods. "And his father. And his grandfather, and your great-grandfather's father, and on and on back to Lancashire in merry old England, I believe."

"Huh."

She glances over. "Why? What did he say?"

"Oh, nothing, really. I just didn't know Daddy belonged."

Mother puts the water bowl down and both dogs go for it. "Your father was a Mason and a Rotarian."

"How about an Elk?"

"Hmm," she says, putting her hand on her hip, thinking. "No. He was something else, though. What was it? Unison Club! That's it. Thursday lunch. Rotary was Tuesday, the Masons at night."

We chat a little more until I look at the clock. Time to get home. Mother walks me to the front door and Abigail walks Scotty. "I'm really glad you have Mack in your life," I tell her.

She smiles a little, embarrassed. "Thanks, dear."

"You're supposed to say you're glad Doug's in my life," I prompt her, opening the door.

"I was when you were a senior in high school," she offers. It's not that she doesn't like Doug, Mother just doesn't understand how I can be thirty and not married, and so she blames Doug for the situation.

"Good night, Mother," I say, kissing her cheek. "Talk to you later."

"Good night."

When I get into my Jeep, I take out my cell phone and call Crazy Pete. The answering machine picks up and I hear Pete's voice say, "Choose carefully the message you leave."

"I'm choosing carefully, Pete," I assure him. "Listen, I want to talk to you some more about my father. Call me, will you?" I leave the number. The more I think about it, the more irritated I am. Crazy or not, Pete can't just go around saying stuff like that.

When we get home, Scotty jumps out of the car and goes racing around the house—around and around and around—to chase off all real and imaginary enemies. I go inside and find a very long message from Verity Rhodes.

4

"I like *Vanity Fair* better than *Expectations*," Doug comments while turning his blue Volvo sedan onto Route 202 in Litchfield.

My boyfriend—or as my mother says, beau—Doug Wrentham, is an assistant district attorney in the criminal courts of New Haven. This is important to know if only to understand that even when making an idle comment, Doug can make it sound very serious. And since we are about to arrive at Verity Rhodes's house, the editor of *Expectations* magazine, I'm hoping this is not a sign that he is itching to misbehave. He doesn't want to be here tonight. He could have gone to the Yankees game, and they're playing the Mariners tonight, his team of all teams.

"Perhaps you'll keep that observation to yourself for a little while," I say without resentment in my voice, for that would be fatal. Resentment is a form of resistance, implying conflict, and the lawyer in Doug simply cannot let any conflict go by unless he has won it. Or thinks he has. I look at him. "I'm very nervous, Doug. And I really appreciate you coming with me."

"I'm nervous, too," he murmurs, taking another turn.

"Really?"

"For you, I guess."

"Dinner at our home in the country," Verity Rhodes had said in an English accent that made me want to sit up straight and throw my shoulders back, "you must come. As a small thank-you for what you did for us."

It became quickly and awkwardly clear in my telephone conversation with Verity Rhodes that she was inviting me to dinner but had no intention of extending the invitation to Devon, the photographer. And so when she asked me if there was someone I'd like to bring, I didn't feel as though I could say Devon. In fact, when I mentioned Doug there was a short silence, as if Verity were disappointed in my response. But she quickly said, "Then you must bring your Doug, by all means."

So, here we are, on Saturday night, *my* Doug being a good sport and coming to dinner with me.

"Don't you think it's weird they didn't just send you some flowers?" Doug asks out of the blue. "Or give you a free subscription to the magazine? Why are they making you drive halfway across the state to eat with them?"

I don't mind Doug being somewhat skeptical (because I have been, too, ever since the invitation was extended), but the timing of this is a hell of thing since we are very nearly there.

"I don't think it's odd," I say, smoothing my skirt. "Given the circles they travel in, I'm sure they think entertaining us in their home is a very special gift."

"Oh, well then," he says sarcastically.

I don't say anything. Whenever Doug's sarcastic I can't help but remember that our relationship has ended twice already in the past two years, and then started up again despite our best intentions.

"You think she might offer you some kind of a job, don't you?" Doug says. After a moment, he glances over. "I do, too."

"Don't be ridiculous," I say, but my heart is pounding. Oh, God, after all this time, to have a shot at mainstream journalism. To finally get my act together and get out of Castleford and back into the swing of things. Not back to Los Angeles, but to something a little less foreign, like New York, only ninety miles away. Manhattan. I can handle that.

But what kind of job could it be? Fact-checking probably, copyediting possibly. Nothing terribly exciting, I'm sure.

"Okay, where now?" Doug says, stopping at a stop sign.

"Are we at...? Ah, okay, we go left here," I say, reading the directions, "onto Grass Gate Meadow." I take a deep breath and let it out, trying to relax. "And then we should see it."

"What's the number?"

"No number."

"Holy smokes," Doug says on an intake of breath, "you don't suppose that's it, do you?"

About a half mile away, built into the side of a rolling hill, is what looks to be a Victorian palace. White, with twin turrets, gingerbread and several porches.

"She said take the first left."

Doug lets out a low whistle, turning into the drive. "This kind of house in Litchfield…"

"They're pretty rich," I acknowledge. "They've got a house in Palm Beach, a house in Aspen, a flat in London. What I don't understand is how she ever has any time to go to any of them."

"So you've done your due diligence."

"Of course." I don't have to supply Doug with possible topics of conversation because as soon as people find out that he works in criminal justice, they ask endless questions about every heinous crime they can think of.

"Whoa! What's this?" Doug says, slamming on the brakes.

We have come upon a gate. It is made of white wood rails, stretching across to fences on either side, but it is a gate, nonetheless, and it is locked. There is an intercom box on a short pole in front of it.

Doug rolls down his window. "Hello?"

"Hello!" a voice hails back. It's a woman and she sounds Irish.

I undo my seat belt and scoot over to lean past Doug. "Hi, it's Sally Harrington and Doug Wrentham."

"Mr. and Mrs. Schroeder are expecting you. You may drive straight up to the front door, please."

"Thank you."

It is a gorgeous home as only Litchfield can offer, although I strongly suspect the Schroeders have added quite a bit to the original house. I've never seen a Victorian home of this size in New England—certainly not one that has two spires. San Francisco maybe, but even then I would doubt its authenticity.

There is one car in the circular drive, a silver Range Rover with Connecticut plates. The driveway branches off behind the house.

The last time I brushed elbows with people like this—people whose names were standard fare in the columns—was in Los Angeles, more specifically, Beverly Hills, when I worked at *Boulevard* magazine. The name of the magazine is a reference to Sunset Boulevard, which runs through Brentwood, Bel Air,

Beverly Hills and West Hollywood. *Boulevard* is a high-gloss chronicle of high society in Los Angeles (i.e., anything or anybody with lots of money). When I first started there I was but a mere flunky, typing letters and taking phone calls, but by my second year I had graduated to ghost-editing on behalf of my boss, the new features editor, who hated to edit and, in fact, was not very good at it. She was so very good at getting to people, however, that no one seemed to care—so long as someone got the job done, i.e., me.

I definitely became the trusted servant at *Boulevard*. Once I was sent to deliver a Harry Winston diamond necklace and earrings to a photo shoot with Sharon Stone. Another time I was dispatched in a limo to find the Duchess of York, Sarah Ferguson, in a Santa Monica boutique and deliver her to a party in Malibu. And then, by my third year, the big secret was out—Sally Harrington was the emergency rewrite person, the one who could make a publishable interview out of the worst garbled mess. This led me to ghostwriting the celebrity guest-writer essay every month. (This feature was cooked up with movie publicists; I'd write the piece, the celebrity in question would okay it, and the magazine would hawk it.) By my fourth year, I was skulking around most major events in L.A. trying to make some kind of earthly sense of this house-of-mirrors lifestyle I was writing about. The problem was, even when I did make any sense of it, *Boulevard* was the last place I could write about it. I was only to write about what I saw in the mirrors that were so very carefully positioned.

So by my fifth and final year at *Boulevard*, one could say I was jaded. Or sick, in the way one always is after eating a lot of sweets and little nutritious food. I wanted to be a journalist, but my skills and personality were making me a very successful "magazine person." There was a big difference.

That's why I greatly admire what Verity Rhodes has done with *Expectations* magazine. Like *Vanity Fair*, *Expectations* runs major articles by major writers, but also manages to have a lot of fun with gossipy items and columns. When they do run a celebrity interview, which they do each month, they do it very well, most often amazingly evenhanded, the writers (or editors) balancing the puffery of the publicity machine with less-flattering facts from reality. The pictures are always great, too. In the old days, it was the kind of magazine I dreamed of writing for.

The problem is, after writing for the newspaper these past couple of years, I've come to love straight journalism. The process feels entirely different. If my writing at *Boulevard* was like painting a picture to order, then my writing at the *Herald-American* is like printing a picture of a finished jigsaw puzzle, one whose five hundred pieces require that I first make the necessary connections between them before assembling the whole.

What is so strange right now, though, is how I thought I had gotten over my attraction to celebrity. Driving up to this mansion is telling me differently. The sense of excitement is familiar and maybe even more exhilarating because the last place I ever expected to find high glamour was out here in Connecticut.

The greetings at the door are warm and I feel the nervousness drain out of me. Verity and Corbett are gracious hosts and I can see that Doug is relaxing, too. I scarcely recognize Corbett, he is so laid-back and alive-looking in his casual slacks and sport shirt. (He looked so old and little out there in the woods.) A mother's helper brings young Corbie out to say hello (his freshly combed hair is damp from, we are told, a bath in our honor), and then we are ushered through the house to the back, to a brick patio where, Verity announces, Corbett is going to cook for us, "on the hideously expensive grill he never uses."

Verity is not a classically pretty woman, but she is so perfectly put together—lightened hair; perfect makeup; tight, shapely body—one feels as though she is. As good as Corbett looks tonight, most people, upon first meeting I should think, would mistake him for Verity's congenial father.

The gardens in back of the house are the kind I see in *HG*, elaborate and intricately designed, the way one expects the queen's private garden to be at Windsor Castle. Not even my mother's gardener friends who are retired have such gardens; the flowers here are far too expensive and impossible to maintain without strong men in regular attendance.

Corbett pours us drinks from a glass cart on wheels (that I know I could never keep clean), and then Doug goes off with him to study the grill.

Verity and I sink into overstuffed chintz cushions in teak chairs. I murmur how beautiful the house is, but what strikes me most are the gardens.

"Thank you," she says, smiling, "I work very hard at them."

She must see the surprise in my expression, for she adds, "I have a man who comes to do the heavy labor, but I do the pruning, fertilizing and, believe it or not, most of the weeding. My gardens are why I could never be the editor of *Vogue*." She laughs, holding up her hands, showing short manicured nails. "I live for them. And for little Corbie, of course."

I've been wondering to whom the Irish voice over the intercom belonged, and I find out when a young woman appears at my side with a tray of hors d'oeuvres. "Miss," she says to me with a slight curtsy.

"Hi."

"This is Meghan," Verity says. "Who takes care of us."

"Madam." Meghan slightly curtsies again.

"She does. She wakes us, feeds us, organizes us, everything. I would be utterly at a loss without her."

The due diligence I have done on our hosts filled me in on Verity's rise from modest beginnings in the East End of London, her academic achievements as a scholarship student at a posh public school, the style and flair and brilliant editorial instincts she showed even at Cambridge, and then at her first job at *Je Ne Sais Quois* in Paris. I knew of Verity's vault to editor of *Country Elegance* in London, her discovery by magazine magnate Seymour Rubin, who brought her to New York to take the helm of the then-faltering *Expectations*. I read how she met Corbett Schroeder through Donald Trump and married Corbett six months later, and how she had delivered Corbett Junior by cesarean on her fortieth birthday. I know that Verity loves to write and eat and ride horses, the latter a dream that she saw come true as soon as she began to make money.

As for Corbett Schroeder, his story is impressive in a different way. The son of a Massachusetts car salesman, he nearly flunked out of the University of Massachusetts, was fired from Kinney Parking by Steve Ross, married the heiress to the Stridely Soda empire, shot up the executive ranks and then spun off a company of his own. He ditched the first wife for a second, the ex-wife of Senator Boswell from California (heiress to the Barney Films Studio), went into communications and later ditched that wife (who subsequently married her exercise instructor) to marry Verity. He has four children. The oldest is forty-eight, two years older than Verity, and the youngest, Corbie, is six.

Corbett's conglomerate, Vision Lights Unlimited, Inc., is known for film production and cosmetics, but its real money is made, I know, in industrial lubrication and waste management. (In other words, grease and garbage.)

"What part of Ireland are you from, Meghan?" I take a stuffed mushroom from the tray.

"Oh, the west coast, Miss. Ennis."

I tell her I know it, that my mother and I visited there a couple of years ago.

Meghan suppresses the urge to talk more of her homeland and moves on with her tray to the men.

"Before we get settled for the evening," Verity says, glancing back over her shoulder and then back to me, "there's a little business I'd like to discuss with you."

I take a sip of wine from a glass I suspect is made of fine Belgian crystal.

"Since we last met—under such *interesting* circumstances," the editor continues with a sly wink, "I've had a chance to read quite a bit of your work. Your writing."

I am surprised. "At the *Herald-American?*"

"Yes," she says, nodding. "You're rather good, you know."

"Thank you."

"And I had a rather interesting chat with your former employer on the West Coast."

"At *Boulevard?*"

"Yes. Actually, I talked to several people since it seems your immediate supervisor, the features editor, did not last long after you left."

I smile slightly. I can't help it.

"It would seem you had been doing a great deal of her work."

I shrug, noncommittal. "I don't think that's true."

"Well," Verity says, "everyone else evidently does. The associate publisher sent me a pile of tear sheets he swears you wrote but were never given credit for. Interviews, articles, entire columns."

The associate publisher was an old friend, God bless him. I nod once as an acknowledgment. "I did a lot of last-minute editing."

Verity laughs. "Oh, is that what you call it?"

She sips her wine and lofts one perfectly plucked eyebrow. "So how would you like to try your hand at writing a profile for *Expectations?*"

I think I might either shout or die right there.

"I would be floored," I manage to say, "and flattered and terrified—and the happiest person on earth, I think."

She smiles. "Good. Now, let me ask you, have you ever heard of a woman named Cassy Cochran?"

I think for a minute. The name sounds familiar.

"She is the president of the Darenbrook Broadcasting System, the television division of Darenbrook Communications," Verity says.

"Oh, right! Of course, I do. She married Jackson Darenbrook, the guy who started DBS."

"Good, you know who she is," Verity says. "Because that is whom I wish you to profile for *Expectations.*"

I beam, I can't help it. This is unbelievable.

"I'd like you to swing by my office next week to go over the assignment," Verity continues, her voice sounding rather businesslike now. "Off the top of my head, we'll be paying twenty for ten thousand words. Twenty-five hundred, maybe four thousand in advance, a kill fee if we don't use the piece, expense account for travel and primary interviews. We get world rights. The thing is, I want it for our February issue, so it has to be finished by September. If you want to do it, you'll have to sign a contract immediately and get on it. Leave me a number where I can fax you a copy of our agreement and you can have your lawyer look it over."

"That gives me about five," I calculate.

"Five weeks," she confirms. "So what do you think?"

"I think it's the opportunity of a lifetime."

Verity smiles knowingly. "Indeed, that is how I hoped you would see it."

I lean forward in my chair. "You're kidding, right."

She laughs again. "No, indeed I am not, Sally. You are going to write a big piece for us and it will be great."

I am not with it at all for the rest of the evening. My mind is racing with how to get time off from the paper, how to get started on the piece, and what this can lead to if I pull it off. Corbett happily carries on the dinner conversation. He is polite to me, but with the courtesy of one who assumes I am not listening. He talks to Doug about a true-crime movie his studio has under option and Doug is explaining to him the judicial process. This is a topic that makes both men happy. I don't think Verity is quite so taken with the subject, for she winks at me once, as if her mind is elsewhere, too.

Dinner, incidentally—the steaks—had to be cooked by Meghan in the kitchen because the men never did figure out how to use the grill.

5

"You're kidding!" Doug exclaims in the car. "Twenty thousand bucks for five weeks' work!"

"It's not the money," I begin.

"Quit!" he urges. "Sign the contract and tell Royce to shove it. Better yet, pick a fight with him and make him fire you so you can apply for unemployment after you hand the piece in. No, I guess you can't do that. That would be illegal."

One of the things I love about Doug is his criminal mind. He thinks up crimes and then quickly jumps to his prosecutor's role to figure out how to catch the crook he has just created.

"So you think I should do it?" I ask him.

"Are you kidding? Of course you should! You've been waiting for a chance like this ever since you came back to Castleford."

"But—" I'm not sure if I should say what I'm thinking.

"But?" he repeats, glancing over from the road.

"I mean, what if this leads to other things?"

He shrugs. "Then it leads to other things. What's the big deal?"

This is what I hate about Doug. In one moment he can demand that I vow commitment to him, and in the next, indicate that I'm nothing to him and I can go on my way, no skin off his teeth. Of course, I feel exactly the same way about him, which is probably why our sex life tends to be rather good. We're always making love like it's the last time—or maybe the first—depending if we're about to split up again or are unexpectedly back together.

I know, I know. You would think we could act like adults by now. We love each other and trust each other in so many vital ways, but every time we settle down to get serious, one or both of us shy away. I don't know if this is a sign that it's not a match, or that we each have a nervous trepidation about absolute commitment. Perhaps it has something to do with the way my father died so suddenly when I was young. Or how Doug's wife declared her vows on the altar with all sincerity, only to bolt three years later.

"Won't it be a big deal," I say to Doug, "if I end up moving to New York or something?"

He shrugs. "So you move to New York."

"Okay," I shrug, "fine, I'm moving to New York."

After a few moments, Doug says, "Scotty will just love being locked up in a New York City apartment all day."

Creep.

"And, of course, your mother will be devastated."

"She will not!" I protest. "She'll be relieved I'm living my life. She still thinks I'm hanging around here because I'm scared she'll get sick again."

"And you're not?"

"I'm not," I say firmly.

After about a mile, he speaks again. Quietly. "If we're meant to be together, and you move to New York, I could apply for a job in the D.A.'s office and move there, too. Or maybe I could transfer to the Stamford courts and we could live in Greenwich or somewhere."

"Greenwich? I don't have a million dollars," I say, irritated by the thought of having my wings in New York clipped quite so fast.

"But you might," he laughs.

"Right now I don't have much of anything," I complain. "I've got a car that's not paid for, a computer that's not paid for—"

"You've almost finished your student loans—"

"But they're not finished yet. I don't have any clothes—"

"Ha!"

"Not the kind of clothes I need to do this story."

"You'll go to the outlets with your mother and you'll be fine."

"What am I going to do about Scotty?"

"Leave him with your mother. Leave him with me."

"To live in a high-rise in downtown New Haven?"

"You're looking for excuses, Sally."

"I'm looking for excuses," I confirm, nodding, looking at the sun setting behind the hills of Connecticut.

Doug reaches over to pat my knee. "It's okay to be a little scared. In fact, it's preferable. It means something new is finally happening."

Doug doesn't stay the night. By the time we reach my house I am far too excited about the profile for *Expectations* to do anything but start on it. So he drives me down the long gravel drive of Brackleton Farm & Stables, and then turns off onto the rutted dirt road that serves as my driveway. We wind deep into the woods, far from the main house, and emerge at a large clearing where my one-bedroom fieldstone carriage house stands.

For over a century the house was inhabited by a series of overseers for the Brackletons, who for generations were gentlemen farmers and horse breeders. Within the last decade, however, the farm has been inherited by a son who prefers Boston, so while he leases most of the fields to other farmers, he is allowing some guy to dynamite one of the bigger fields to strip-mine the stone and gravel and then sell the earth for topsoil, an exercise that is supposed to, in the end, create a beautiful man-made lake (which, incidentally, is part of the heir's plan to ultimately convert his ancestral property into an eighteen-hole golf course).

At any rate, my little house is beyond the woods, away from the strip-mining, and I have ample privacy and quiet. If I had the money (dream on), I would buy as much of the Brackleton farm as I could and run it as a proper farm again. I would go in big for cash crops of tobacco. (A lot of people don't know that Connecticut tobacco leaves are used for the outside wrappings of good cigars.) I'd go into dairy and goats—goat cheese, that's big. Maybe I'd make ice cream that has so much butterfat in it that everybody would line up for miles. I'd grow asparagus, because I love it, and I would probably grow some grains, and if I did that, I would probably want to build a small distillery, where people could come on tours, and where I would make some kind of rare whiskey or vodka that costs like a hundred dollars a bottle.

(Mother says I'm a lot like my father in this regard, that I'm a dreamer. Perhaps I should start off with fresh vegetables like everyone else and ship them to New York.)

If there was a drawback to renting the carriage house, it was the necessity of having to buy a four-wheel-drive vehicle to reach it. If the snow and ice in this mountain region is not tough enough to handle, our muddy spring seasons are. This is how I have come to own a Jeep Cherokee when what I really want is a Miata, not that I can afford either one.

Doug kisses me good-night and waits in the car until I have unlocked the door and am nearly knocked over by Scotty's greeting. I wait until Doug has turned around and made the far corner of the drive before I let Scotty go, and then he is off into the night.

I immediately head toward the corner of my living room that doubles as an office and turn on the computer. Then I go into the kitchen to start some coffee and pick up the phone to call a lawyer friend in California whose firm, I know, represents a lot of Los Angeles writers. Would he look over an agreement for me, for a piece in *Expectations?* Just make sure it was all right? I'd pay him of course.

"*Expectations!* Sally!" he says. "One day you're working for the *Joe Schmo Gazette* in Nowhere, Connecticut, and the next, *Expectations?*" I tell him he's a big-city jerk—who's out of touch with America. What the hell does he mean the *Joe Schmo Gazette?* At least we report the news, not who is sleeping with animals or renting hookers like most of his clients do. I thank him and promise to fax the agreement as soon as I get it.

I go into the bedroom to change into an extra-large T-shirt, then into the kitchen to let Scotty in the back door and give him a large Milk-Bone. Then, finally, I am able to sit down at my computer and travel the Internet to www.dbs.com to see what the network itself might have to say about its president.

I find Cassy Cochran with very little problem. And I am somewhat startled by how beautiful she appears to be. It's the kind of beauty that usually demands a career in front of the camera, and I can see how a profile of her will work well in *Expectations.* She gives great face, as they say.

While I'm waiting for my printer to spew all the on-line material on Cassy Cochran and on the network itself, I jump up to consult an old *Who's Who in America* I took home from the office when they got the new ones. Cochran.... Got it.

Huh. I'm a little surprised, because according to this, she's recently turned fifty.

Fifty. This is what fifty looks like? Well, it is a press photo, no doubt retouched, and the definition over my computer is not the best.

In the next three hours I hop, skip and jump around to all the usual Internet resource databases paid for by the paper, and by two in the morning I have compiled a great deal of background information on my subject.

Cassy Littlefield was born in Cedar Rapids, Iowa. Her father died when she was eleven. She graduated Northwestern University cum laude and immediately married Michael Cochran. They both worked at a TV station in Chicago, where her husband excelled. They had one son, Henry, and then the Cochrans moved to New York where Michael flew up the news ranks to become executive producer of WWKK. Cassy's ascent in TV was much slower but steady, and by age forty she had risen past the news division to become the first female station manager in New York, at WST. A year later, Michael was fired from WWKK and he went into independent production.

Three years later Cassy was lured over to the newly formed DBS group to build the network's national news division. Within six months she was named president of the entire network and, for all intents and purposes, proceeded to invent DBS. She built—and sold—DBS to the affiliates largely around a talk show, *The Jessica Wright Show,* and *DBS News America Tonight with Alexandra Waring.*

During her first year at DBS, the Cochrans divorced and Michael moved to Los Angeles. Eighteen months later Cassy married the flamboyant CEO of Darenbrook Communications, Jackson Darenbrook, who had been widowed young and had been one of the media's favorite eligible bachelors for years. He is only a year or two older than Cassy.

Huh.

I look over my notes again and frown. There certainly isn't much bite in this story. And stories in *Expectations* always have bite. Maybe there was something in the divorce proceedings that would jazz it up.

Maybe Verity is interested in doing this profile because Cochran is so beautiful and her husband is so rich. Or maybe this is a puff piece to lure advertising from all the Darenbrook companies, which include hundreds of newspapers, at least fourteen national magazines, six printing plants, a couple of satellites, the TV network and a group of electronic-information companies.

Well, the only thing I can do is talk to Verity and see what it is she's looking for. And then maybe I can find a couple of people who can tell me some interesting things about Cassy Cochran, like her ex-husband. Stepchildren. Or executives at competing networks...

The telephone rings and I snap it up. "Hello?"

"Hello," Doug says.

"Hi."

"Hi."

"Well," I begin, "what do you want?"

"You."

I look at the clock. "It's almost three. Aren't you tired?"

"Not if it means I can see you," he says. "I thought maybe you'd be through with what you're doing by now."

This is strange. Very unlike Doug. "What's the matter?"

A pause. "I don't know. I guess I was just thinking about your magazine thing. And I guess I figure I better spend as much time with you as I can—now. You know, because I may not be seeing a whole lot of you in the near future."

I have to smile. "That's very sweet."

"Does that mean yes, I can come over?"

"That means yes."

"Hooray!" he cries in a very unlike-Doug fashion (which I love him for) and hangs up. He'll be here pretty quick.

I turn off my computer, give Scotty a scratch behind the ears and go into the bathroom to draw a hot bath.

Life is good.

6

I first got my good look at Doug Wrentham in an elective English course in my junior year of high school. He was new. His father was in the insurance business and had received a huge promotion, which meant he was transferred from Portland, Oregon, to the home office in Hartford. (The Wrenthams hated it here, and moved back to Oregon the day after Doug's younger sister graduated from high school.)

Doug was about five foot ten, with dark brown eyes and dark brown hair. He was very handsome (more so back then, I'm not sure why) and—as hard as it is to imagine today—very, very shy. He was smart and a natural athlete, and had made the football team in August, no problem, so that first fall he had quickly gotten to know a lot of the jocks and the cheerleaders.

I enjoyed sports but wasn't a jock, I was good-looking, but not elastic enough to ever dream of doing splits as a cheerleader. (Also, I think I was just too cool, frankly, even back then, to be properly cheery.) I don't know what the heck I was, frankly, since I wasn't even an aspiring journalist because I thought the kids on the newspaper were weird. I did like the literary magazine, though, and I dabbled in student politics, not because I cared all that much about the issues, but because I enjoyed winning elections. I also liked making speeches and kissing up to the faculty, only to cut school the next day to go upstate and drink beer.

At any rate, back to Doug. The elective class we took that semester was called General Semantics and it had to do with the effect that language has on human behavior. One of the mysterious exercises we did in this mysterious class (because, truly, I'm not sure any of us got what we were doing, not until years later when we could see how language could incite, for example, race riots), was to go up to a selected student and, in confidence, say something nice about him to his face. Poor Doug was selected as the student—we knew the teacher picked him because he was so shy—and was made to stand in the corner. Well, his face was scarlet in no time, and when it was my turn to go up to him, I did not hesitate, but looked him straight in the eye and said, "You are the best-looking guy in this whole school."

He smiled, bowed his head and laughed slightly in response, and I think I walked away feeling more embarrassed than Doug.

Fast-forward to our senior year when, as seniors, we got a small cafeteria-study room separate from the rest of the school. I saw Doug that first day back at school and I saw his face brighten at the sight of me. He said hi and I said hi, slightly amazed that this year he could speak.

And I realized he liked me.

Because I had run in so many student elections over the years, my classmates were accustomed to voting for me for anything, and so when nominations were made for homecoming queen, a lot of misguided souls automatically put my name forward and I found myself one of five candidates. I was horrified. Also nominated were the two co-captains of the cheerleading squad, our class valedictorian and a beautiful girl from the South who had the most spectacular breasts of anyone at school. I was neither spirited nor rah-rah nor ooh-la-la.

My responsibilities were to get dressed up and drive around town in a convertible in the homecoming parade, and then be trotted out at halftime of the football game when the homecoming queen would be announced. And then, that night, I was supposed to go to one of the cheerleader's houses for a dinner and then on to the homecoming dance where we would all be introduced yet again. I found this whole exercise mortifying because I knew I was not going to win, and I made a point of only running in elections where I knew I would. On the other hand, I realized that as a member of the homecoming court, I would be an excellent date for Doug to take to the dinner and dance that night, seeing as he was on the football team and knew all of the boys who were going out with the other girls nominated.

But would he ask me? I thought not, because when I crossed

paths with him again and again in the senior commons he would just turn red, say hi and walk away.

"So who's your date for the dance?" one of the cheerleader captains asked me. "I need to know, because if you don't have a date, I can get one for you."

Well, that did it. I had turned down two offers already in hopes Doug would ask me, but he hadn't, and the idea that someone was going to have to fix *me* up was simply too much to bear. Doug, at that moment, was getting a soda out of the Coke machine and so I walked right over and tapped him on the shoulder. "Doug, will you take me to the homecoming dance? Because if you don't they're going to make me go with somebody else and I'd rather go with you."

"Um," he said, eyebrows rising high in surprise. He bent down to get his soda from the dispenser and turned back to face me. "Yeah, okay. Sure."

"And I'm afraid we'll have to go to Susie's before the dance, for dinner."

"Oh, yeah, I was invited."

"Great! Thanks," I said, and I walked back across the senior commons to Susie. "I'm going to the dance with Doug Wrentham."

"*Really?*" she said, openly surprised. "You and Doug?"

"What's the matter with that?"

"I didn't even know you *knew* him," she confessed. (I suspected something then that would be confirmed months later, when Susie got loaded after graduation and cried on Doug's shoulder that she had always loved him.)

Anyway, that was that and it was great and I was happy. This would be, I swear to God, the first time I ever went out on a formal date with a guy I actually liked. Before, I'd always had a crush on one guy and then ended up dating his friend. Or I would find out that the object of my crush was in reality a jerk, and as soon as I wasn't interested in him anymore, he would suddenly decide to pursue me.

Doug showed up at my house to pick me up in his family's station wagon and mumbled something in reply to my mother's questions that were meant to relax him, but which utterly failed. And so Doug and I drove over in his family's station wagon to Susie's, where we did not speak to each other or even look at each other for the entire party. Then everyone started to leave and so we kind of headed toward each other and walked out to the car. We got in and he cautiously turned to me and asked, "Would you—maybe—want to, um, have a beer before the dance?" and I looked at him with wonder and awe. There seemed to be more to shy Doug than I thought, and he drove us to the parking lot of the Castleford Country Club and reached for a cooler from the back that had some "pony boys" (seven-ounce bottles of Miller beer) in it. We each had one. It was icy and good, and we were on our second when the security guard from the club came out to talk to us.

We were on private property and I was about to freak, for this is where all the rich people in Castleford belonged and I was certainly not one of them. But Doug, cool as could be, rolled down his window and said, "Hi."

"Are you a member of this club?" the guard asked.

"Yes," Doug said.

"The name?"

"Wrentham," he said. "W-R-E-N-T-H-A-M."

"Okay, but you shouldn't stay here long. And don't let anyone see you with those beers." And he walked away.

Doug started the car.

"I didn't know you belonged here," I said.

"I don't," Doug said, backing the car out, "but if you act like you own the place, people usually think you do."

And that's when I realized that there was a whole lot more to this shy, good-looking boy.

I slip on a silk robe and go back out to the living room to wait for Doug. Scotty sits at my feet as I sort all the material from my printer and start labeling files.

Cassy Cochran
Catherine Littlefield (mother, alive)
Henry Littlefield (father, deceased)
Michael Cochran (first husband)
Jackson Darenbrook (second husband)
Henry Cochran (son)

I'm slipping a copy of an interview Cassy Cochran did with *Media Women* into her file, when Scotty's head jerks up. In an instant, he's on his feet and at the door, barking. I open the door to look out and Scotty gets past me and charges off into the night. No sign of Doug or his car.

I call Scotty. He won't come but continues to furiously bark. Not a good sign; this means he's treed a possum or raccoon or, oh please no, has cornered a skunk. (Anyone who assumes the boxes and boxes of Massengill Feminine Douche powder in the linen closet are mine are wrong. They're for the dog.) "Scotty," I say sharply, "knock it off and come here."

Miraculously, he does come so I gave him a Milk-Bone.

It took Doug three dates to kiss me, and then after six months, he tried to go straight from kissing lying down to intercourse. That was so Doug. Too shy to put a hand under my blouse, too scared to even touch the snap of my jeans, but so overwhelmed with desire that after a while he thought maybe if he just started undoing his belt as a sign that he wanted to...

I burst into tears. Because by this time I was in love with Doug and his shyness and his obvious excitement had me terribly aroused, and yet night after night he hadn't been able to bring himself to do anything. Except this one night, that is, and I guess I kind of freaked because I did not want to deny Doug anything—he had been such a gentleman for so long. When I look back, I don't even know what it was that he had intended to do that night, whether he had thought well, let's try and go all the way, or maybe he had something else in mind. I never knew. Certainly I had given him every signal that I was available to him in a way I had never wished to make myself available to another boy, but it never occurred to me he would skip second and third base altogether and try straight for home.

"I'm not on the Pill or anything," I wailed, crying into his shoulder. "I'm sorry, Doug, but we can't."

"It's all right, it's all right," he whispered, upset.

And then we sat up and had what I thought was a very adult discussion, one-sided of course, about how I would call Planned Parenthood and make an appointment and get some kind of birth control. Until then, no way José. (In a town like

Castleford, with an alarming number of unplanned pregnancies, my mother had made darn sure I understood how a woman got pregnant and that the best way to avoid such a fate was not to engage in sex! But, if I ever… Well, there was a place, she reluctantly admitted, though she preferred I came to her before… In other words, my mother knew my temperament and she knew that if she lectured me too much, I would simply push my sexual life totally underground.)

I went to Planned Parenthood in New Haven and went through all the counseling they make you do and then they sent me in for my first gynecological exam. The doctor came in, an older woman, and she looked at my chart to see that I was eighteen years old and had come to find out about birth control. She looked at me over the top of her glasses. "You have never had sexual intercourse before? You are a virgin?"

I nodded my head. I was also shaking from head to toe.

"Really?"

"I've never," I whispered, looking down.

When we got to the actual examination, there came a very pleased-sounding announcement from behind the sheet. "Ah, and so you are!" The doctor peeked up at me over the sheet. "This is very, very good. You make me very happy, young lady."

It wouldn't be until years later that I would understand how nice it had been for the doctor to see that sex education actually sometimes worked.

At any rate, I chose birth control pills, although the clinic people didn't seem so thrilled about it. Their concern, the counselor explained, was that they would not protect me from venereal disease. And then we went into all of that. And when I stuttered and stammered I had every reason to believe Doug was a virgin as well, she gave me that same look the doctor had when I claimed I had never had intercourse before.

But they sent me off with pills and condoms and good information. And I told Doug that I had to wait until after my next period before I could start taking the pills, and then I had to wait two months after that before we could—

"You know, so then we can…"

"Oh," he said enthusiastically.

That was a long time to wait. From March to the end of May. So for two months we didn't spend a whole lot of time alone. (There were alternatives to intercourse, I knew, but it seemed all too embarrassing to even approach them with Doug.)

Then Doug asked me if I'd like to go out to dinner. To a nice restaurant. And I had to smile because he had the timing down just right. I had been on the Pill for two complete months.

Well, wouldn't you know, that night we had none of our usual places to go. My house was full of people, so was Doug's, so were the houses of our friends. Someone had borrowed my key to the school auditorium, where we used to slip in and climb up to a windowless storage room behind the stage. So after dinner we drove around and around and we ended up going to the high school parking lot. Why we thought this was a good idea, I'll never know, but someone was watching over us because no police rounds interrupted us.

We drove around to the back of the school and had a beer. We didn't kiss, we just drank and talked about heaven knows what. And then he said it was ten o'clock and so I assumed it was time.

So I said, "Well."

And he said, "We can go in the back. I brought a blanket."

And so we climbed into the back of the station wagon, put the seat down and then lay together and kissed a while.

He still didn't touch my breasts or anything. Not even then! He just said, "Do you want to try?" and I said, "Yes," and so I took off my panty hose and my underpants and he undid his belt and unzipped his pants. I have to admit that I was very excited because Doug was never out of control, always so shy, so to have him want something of me physically, so badly that he was prepared to go to these embarrassing lengths (I knew he was scared, for he was shaking as much as I was) was a turn-on. We struggled a bit with clothes and then he rolled on top of me and kissed me and I felt him kind of poke around and so finally I reached down to guide him toward me.

"Ow!" I said as he tried to press forward.

Immediately he recoiled, breathlessly asking, "Are you all right?"

"It hurts," I whimpered.

I don't know what got into Doug then, but instead of backing off, which I thought he would, he took hold of me and pushed again and I cried again, but he didn't pull back, he just kept pushing and I yelped again and then suddenly, he was through and inside of me and we both froze a moment, not believing it. And then he moved ever so slightly and there was no resistance, and then he moved again a little, and I was just getting into it, thinking, I might get to like this, when I felt all kinds of warmth spilling out of me.

By the time I left for UCLA and Doug left for Amherst, we felt like sexual conquerors, although, I've got to tell you, he never did get very good at foreplay. So when we got together at Christmastime and he wanted me to sit on top of him, I knew that he had slept with someone else. I just knew. I didn't say anything about it, but I went back to California thinking I was free to see whomever I liked.

I was into LaLa Land big-time. My roommate was the daughter of a producer whose movie had made a hundred million dollars the summer before (she was hardly the postman's daughter, in other words) and her family simply *loved* me because, well, compared to Morning (I swear that was her name; can you imagine?), I knew how to behave and they knew their daughter. In other words, I started to move in a very fast, very rich crowd. But still, you know what? I never did more than kiss another boy (or man) for the duration of my relationship with Doug. I would say no to more than a few beers, violently resist cocaine and say, "Are you kidding?" whenever the drug ecstasy was pushed on me.

My mother should get a medal. She did something right.

On spring break I got a ride to Missouri to meet Doug—halfway for both of us—and Doug said there was something different about me. I said no, it wasn't me, it was him. He was kind of a wise ass, I said, although what I meant, I think, was that he was more sure of himself, cocky even, and I didn't like it. But we spent five days together, a lot of it in bed, and I grew progressively more alarmed. And yet I loved Doug. I knew I did, and I trusted him, and we still had fun, which was bizarre since everything in his behavior should have told me he wanted to spread his wings, get out there and get around, be a man, you know.

When I came home from school in May there was a letter waiting for me saying that Doug was very sorry, but our relationship just wasn't what he wanted anymore.

I was devastated. And shocked at how devastated I was.

I saw him once that summer, in August, by mistake, at one of his buddies' houses where he was visiting, and we had too much beer and I slept with him. Then I kind of came to, slapped him, grabbed my clothes and walked out. I wouldn't see or speak to him again for nine years.

I see the headlights of Doug's car bounce around the bend of the drive and Scotty's back on his feet, barking. I hold Scotty's collar and open the door. Doug gets out of the Volvo and slings his overnight bag over his shoulder. Gravel crunches under his feet as he makes his way toward the house.

"Hi," I say.

"Hi." His voice is quiet, depressed.

I open the screen door. "What's the matter?"

He comes in and lets the bag slide off his shoulder to thump to the floor. "I don't want you to get rich and famous and leave me."

"Oh, Doug," I sigh, laughing and taking him in my arms.

I heard about Doug through the grapevine. He graduated from Amherst and went on to Boston University Law School, and married some gal who was getting her MBA at Harvard. When he graduated, he went to work for a prestigious Boston firm that specialized in corporate bankruptcies. Doug and his wife were a very glamorous couple, I was told, and were making their way quickly in Boston. At the time, I was sitting around watching my mother cry from the aftereffects of chemotherapy, so I wasn't particularly impressed by this news one way or the other. I was, however, lonely and angry that other people had gone on with their lives and were living happily ever after.

And then we had our tenth high school reunion. I was told that Doug was not coming to the reunion so I made a point of going. The first person I saw was Susie the cheerleader, who was married and living in Cheshire. Her beautiful porcelain skin had already started cracking, no doubt in part due to the three children she had already given birth to. "You mean, Sally, you haven't *heard?*"

"Heard what?"

"That Doug's wife left him," she whispered. And then her eyes widened in delight. "For her stockbroker!"

I don't know why, but it didn't surprise me. My only question was whether or not his wife had sat on him in bed.

"Were there any children?" I asked.

"No."

And then I knew, deep down, that in that moment I had forgiven him of any sins I perceived he had committed.

The world beyond Castleford, I knew, was a very confusing place.

"I love you," Doug whispers in my ear.

And we go into the bedroom.

7

"You can't have tomorrow off and that's it," Alfred Royce Jr. says, turning to his computer to dismiss me from his office.

"Fine," I shrug, and turn to go.

"What do you want the day off for?"

I turn back. "Al, you're supposed to ask me that first and then say no."

He squints dangerously at me. "Don't tell me what I'm supposed to do."

"Fine," I say again, turning around again.

"What do you want the goddamn day off for?" he shouts.

"What do you care?" I sass back, wheeling around. (There is a method to my madness.) "Maybe I'm sick, maybe I have malaria or something and I have to go into New York for some special treatment. Maybe I'm not telling you to spare your feelings, Al, because I don't want you to worry yourself sick."

"How could you possibly be related to your mother?" he wants to know.

"I don't know! But I'm going to her house and get a note from her so you'll let me take the day off. You only owe me about thirty-two vacations days, Al. I haven't had a vacation since I started working in this place."

He wags a finger at me. "I told you, you cannot roll those days over."

"All I want is one day off!" I cry. "Okay—" I back off, holding my hands up in surrender "—make it half a day. I'll be in by two and stay until midnight."

"Okay," he says, swiveling back to his computer. "But you'll be back here by one."

Rolling my eyes, I walk across the newsroom toward my cubicle.

"Sal!" Joe Bix, the reporter in the cubicle next to me, calls. "I signed for a package for you from WSCT. It's over there, in your in-box."

I hurry to open it. WSCT is a formerly independent TV station in New Haven that became a DBS affiliate a few years ago. A friend of mine there has dug up some tape from a broadcast I read about over the Internet this weekend. It's from the night their talk-show star, Jessica Wright, was found after a kidnapping ordeal. The rescue happened so suddenly and DBS was so anxious to break the news first, that Cassy Cochran had thrown together a makeshift crew of executive staffers in the studio and went on the air herself to break the story until the regular DBS anchor, Alexandra Waring, could be located.

I hurry to the conference room on our end of the floor and luckily it is vacant. The TV there, as it always is, is tuned into *CNN Headline News.* I turn the VCR on, push the tape in and wait.

The black screen turns to a test pattern and then suddenly there is the DBS "News Special Bulletin" logo with an urgent soundtrack. And then there is Cassy Cochran.

Fifty or not, the woman is an absolute knockout. A combination of the wrong makeup and terrible lighting illuminates every line in her face in only the way television can, but anyone can plainly see this woman possesses the kind of natural blond, blue-eyed looks that have been a national obsession for a century. Her long hair is loosely pinned up on the back of her head, the way my mother used to wear hers in college.

It is very hard to believe this woman has had such a brilliant career in such a male bastion without any funny business going on. It is sad, but this is the way I have been trained to think, to look twice as hard at the credentials of great-looking women.

"Good morning, I'm Cassy Cochran," she says evenly into the camera, "with a special news bulletin from DBS News. DBS talk-show host Jessica Wright has been found in an abandoned mental hospital in Buffalo, New York. Jessica Wright is alive and has sustained some injuries but is expected to make a full recovery."

She touches her right ear, squinting slightly, and is obviously listening to something or someone through an earphone. "Ladies and gentlemen, we have a special eyewitness report from Alexandra Waring, who is on the scene where Jessica Wright was found less than one hour ago. To recap, Jessica Wright has been found, she is alive, has sustained injuries, but is expected to make a full recovery. And now to Buffalo, New York.''

The tape then jumps to a shot of the dark-haired anchorwoman of DBS, who is standing in front of a dragonesque-looking castle ablaze in spotlights and the flashing lights of police cars, fire trucks, emergency vehicles and ambulances.

That was it, Cassy Cochran's sixty seconds of national broadcasting, but it has an effect on me. There is something about her that is appealing, a quietly heroic quality, or maybe it's some kind of sincerity that one rarely—if ever—sees in newspeople after about three years on the air. No matter what anybody says, people who appear on camera for a living get off on it, and after a while, that high changes to something else, a kind of craving for power and control. This isn't bad, it's just the way it is. Anchors want things done their way, and the effort to make it happen does a lot toward eroding that initial zeal and exhilaration that got them in the chair in the first place.

I rewind the tape and bring it back to my desk to shove into my briefcase. Then I drop into my chair and pick up the telephone to hear my voice mail.

A snitch from the Castleford school board wanting to tattle.

My lawyer friend from L.A., confirming he has received the fax of the proposed agreement with *Expectations*.

A Castleford resident whose exotic parrots escaped from his house, thanking me for getting his plight into the paper. One of them has been found.

Pete Sabatino whispering that it's urgent, I can reach him at the following number.

The *Herald-American* archivist, letting me know she has found what I had requested.

The last message is the first I respond to since she has found an extensive interview with Cassy Cochran from an old Northwestern University alumni magazine from the 1980s.

I return the other calls, edit two pieces for the paper written by other reporters and then finally break down and call Crazy

Pete Sabatino. I am furious with him. It's been days since I left a message for him to call me.

"Hello?" a woman's voice says. There is the sound of dishes in the background. Voices, too.

"Hi, it's Sally Harrington calling. I was left this number to reach Pete Sabatino."

Immediately the woman's voice gets confidential. "He said for you to go to the bridge at Kaegle's Pond at noon. It's really important. You're to go alone." And then she hangs up!

I run the number through my address-finder on my computer. It belongs to Casey's Diner on Route 70.

I have more important things to do today—like figuring out what I'm going to wear to Verity Rhodes's office tomorrow morning. I don't have time to go chasing after Crazy Pete. Kaegle's Pond is halfway to Southington.

I sigh.

Because I know I will go.

"Pete?" I ask tentatively, squishing my way through the smelly mud bank in the pair of Wellingtons I always keep in the Jeep. Thank heavens I had thought to spray Cutter's on me, too, because the gnats are swarming around here.

I look at my watch. Two minutes to noon. I dial my office on my cell phone to see if Pete has left a message. No message.

I keep going until I'm standing under the old railroad trestle. Years ago a train ran twice a day to and from the quarry to deliver stone to the main line. That's why the mountains on this side of town look so odd; about a fifth of the mountainsides can be seen in the form of elegant, turn-of-the-century brownstone houses on the west side of Manhattan.

I look around. There are the remains of fires and beer cans. Graffiti is spray-painted on the concrete reinforcements of the trestle.

And then I see it. A body. Lying on the other side of the trestle.

8

I don't recognize the dead man. He looks to be around forty-five, heavyset, black hair with a little gray. His eyes are brown; I can see that because they are wide open.

Someone shot him in the chest and left him there, on his back, eyes wide open, staring up at the sky. He is most definitely dead.

I call Devon and tell him to get up here. Then I call the police.

One of the more gruesome aspects of writing for the paper of a small city is that death is big news and so we are sent to any unnatural deaths the city desk hears about. You can't imagine how much mangled human carnage I've seen in the last two years on the interstate highways that run through Castleford—91, 15 and 84—and so, in an odd way, looking at this dead body is a lot easier because it's at least intact. (I miss working at *Boulevard*, where the closest we ever got to death was the photo morgue.) At this point, I guess, a dead body doesn't upset me the way it should. It is, to me, the mere shell left behind after the spirit has moved on to the next phase. (I do believe that; I sense my father "living" on another level somewhere.)

I respect the police enough not to touch anything, but I do take a very good look at the man while I debate whether or not I should tell the police who it was that told me to come here. Why Pete would have killed this man, I can't imagine, but I have a horrible inkling that maybe one of his conspiracy theories finally went terribly awry.

The guy is wearing a short-sleeved sport shirt; his upper arms are straining the sleeves. He is wearing, like everybody else these days, khakis. He is stocky and strong. He has a gold chain around his neck and is wearing a large gold signet ring with a diamond in it.

And then I experience a scare. A young voice from behind me gasps and says "Wow!" and I wheel around to see two boys, maybe twelve years old, who have fishing poles over their shoulders. I immediately step between them and the body, holding my arms out, trying to make them back away.

"This is not something you want to see," I plead, grabbing the T-shirt of the more curious of the two and yanking him back in front of me so he can't see.

"Is he dead, is he murdered?" he wants to know.

His friend, pale beneath his freckles, turns around and is voluntarily walking away.

"There's been some kind of accident," I say. "I'm afraid he is dead and the police are coming, boys, so we need to go over there and wait for them."

"Oh, come on, can't I see?" the one kid persists, trying to get around me again.

"You can ask the police," I say, pulling him back.

His friend is now retching in the bushes.

Gore does not faze the curious one, but the sight of his friend throwing up does, and so, in sympathy, he suddenly bends over and starts throwing up, too.

So when the police arrive, among the muck and mire and gnats and vomit and blood, we have quite a bit of sorting out to do about who saw what and when and why any of us are at the pond. Devon also arrives and manages to get some pictures before the officers shoo him away; he happily runs back to the paper to develop them.

The police officer in charge is Detective Buddy D'Amico. I know him very well, for we not only went to school together, but he kissed me once in first grade behind the supply-closet door during reading. I tell Buddy the truth immediately, that Pete Sabatino left a number for me to call and when I did, somebody at Casey's Diner told me I was to come here at noon. I came and this, the body, is what I found.

Buddy looks at me funny and asks me if I'm sure. I say yes.

By now the police have quarantined the area with yards of yellow police crime scene tape; the state police arrive with the county coroner. The boys are taken home, but Buddy holds on to me and I make some notes while Buddy alternately ignores me and then asks me the same questions over and over again. An assistant D.A. from Doug's office, Patricia Murray, arrives from New Haven. I actually know her fairly well. She asks me some questions.

It's nearly five o'clock when Buddy lets me go, and only then with a warning that I am not to leave town. Remembering my appointment in New York tomorrow, I beg for permission to go and he gives it, but says he will be checking to make sure I'm back in town by two. Relieved, I walk off, but then Buddy calls my name again and trots over.

"Look, Sally, if you hear from Pete—"

"I'll tell him to contact you."

He smiles slightly. "No, you call me, and we'll come get him."

"Ah," I say, and I think, *Oh, Pete, what have you done?*

I go back to the office and report in to Al, who has already assigned Joe Bix to another angle of the story. I go into my cubicle to bang out my version of events. Here I am, right in the middle of the biggest story of the year in Castleford, and I am having trouble concentrating because a packet of information about Cassy Cochran is sitting in my in-box. I finally stick it in my briefcase and return to the story at hand.

It doesn't take long for me to get back into the murder piece. After all, I am a player in this one. Devon stops by and slides an envelope across my desk.

"The victim?" I ask.

He nods.

"Don't tell Al we have it yet," I murmur, and he nods again, salutes and slides off. I call Buddy D'Amico. "If you had your wish, Buddy," I say, "how much about the dead guy would you want in tomorrow's paper?"

"The least amount possible."

"And what will I get in return if, say, we don't print that he's five foot ten, has black hair with a little gray, is about forty-five, has brown eyes, is stocky and is wearing a gold chain and a gold signet ring with signature diamond in it? And we don't run a picture of the body?"

"Come on, Sally."

"Come on, Buddy," I say.

He sighs. "How about I'll release his identity to you first. And a picture of him in better days."

"I'm not sure that's enough, Buddy."

"You'll be the first to know when we make an arrest?"

"Done," I tell him. I hang up and revise tomorrow's piece to read, "I found the man's body. At the request of the police, this reporter will withhold a description of the victim until he is identified and his family is notified of his death."

I'm finally done about seven, my story is put to bed and I am able, at long last, to head home. I have retained a retired neighbor, Mr. Quimby (it is always Mr. Quimby, for he is a proper gentleman from Maine and I dare not ask his first name since he has never offered it), to let Scotty out twice a day. If I am going to be very late, he comes over and feeds Scotty and often stays with him for a while, watching TV and allowing the deliriously happy dog to snooze on the couch with him—where Scotty is otherwise never allowed.

Scotty goes romping outside and I quickly read the fax my lawyer friend has sent me back from L.A. The agreement with *Expectations,* he says, is fine as worded and far more generous than their standard contract. He wants to know who I'm sleeping with.

After I let Scotty back in the house I sit down at my desk and start reading through the new research packet I have on Cassy Cochran and make some notes. I still haven't decided whether I will risk driving into Manhattan tomorrow morning for my meeting with Verity Rhodes or take the train.

The phone rings and I answer. "My God, Sal," Doug's voice booms, "you *found* that body over in Castleford? Why didn't you call me?"

"Oh, I meant to," I say lamely. I am still digesting an article that says Cassy Cochran's first husband, Michael, had been fired from his job in New York because of excessive drinking. I have also made a note about her father's early death, and the fact that in everything I have read thus far, the cause has never been given.

"Does anyone know who the victim is?" I ask absently.

There is a pause and then he says, "What is the matter with you? *You're* supposed to be finding out who he is!"

"I don't have time," I say. "Joe's on it."

"The biggest story of the year and you're focusing on some crap for *Expectations?*"

The hostility and sarcasm wake me up. I guess he's changed his mind about wanting me to work in New York after all. Okay then, I change mine.

"That's right, Doug," I say, and I hang up on him.

A little after eleven o'clock, while I am laying out my clothes for tomorrow's appointment, someone knocks on the kitchen door and Scotty goes nuts. I know it isn't Doug (he always comes in the front door) and only as I cross the kitchen do I remember that there is a murderer running around Castleford and perhaps I should be a little bit careful.

Well, if Crazy Pete Sabatino murdered the guy in the woods today then I should be *extremely* nervous, since it is Pete who is pressing his nose against the glass in my kitchen door.

"Pete," I say, holding Scotty by the collar. Pete pushes the door open and rushes past me to shut off the lights.

"Can you close your drapes?" Pete whispers loudly. "They may be watching."

I think a second. "Sure," I finally say, dragging Scotty with me into the living room and pulling the curtains closed over the picture window and the smaller windows in the dining nook that serves as my office. "It's okay, Pete, you can come out now."

He darts out from the kitchen, looking around. "Let the dog go."

"But—"

"He won't bite me."

I let Scotty go and, sure enough, after barking furiously for a few moments, he suddenly runs over to the hand Pete offers him and licks it, tail wagging.

Pete does not look so hot. He is sweaty and pale and dirty. Of course, he is a fugitive from the law. I ask if I can get him something to eat and he is grateful, so I tell him to relax and I go back into the kitchen to fix him a ham-and-cheese sandwich and potato chips and a tall glass of water. I bring it back in and urge him to eat first, and while he does, I'm afraid (the creep that I am) I start my voice-activated tape recorder and stick it in the bookcase behind him where he can't see it.

When he has finished eating, I say, "Well, you've had quite a day. Have you seen the police yet?"

He shakes his head vigorously and then scoops up the glass of water to drink thirstily.

"They're looking for you. I'm afraid I had to tell them I was out there at Kaegle's Pond to meet you."

He puts the glass down. "I didn't kill him."

"I didn't think you did. I just wondered how it happened."

"They killed him," he says with a straight face. "You know that."

"Who?"

"The Masons."

"Ah." I nod. "Do you know how he was killed?"

He nods. "Shot with the same gun he was going to use on me. He came to find me at home this morning, only I ducked him."

"Who?"

"A man."

"Can you describe him?"

"Not really. He was big, though, you know, fat with muscles. I only got a glimpse. He came in a white Dodge Ram van, though, no front plate. That's all I saw before I got out the back of the house."

"How old was he?"

"I don't know. But young, beefy."

"Was your father there?"

"No, he was at the senior center. It's War Day."

War Day was when older veterans went to the senior center to talk about World War II or Korea, watch a film or listen to a speaker and then have lunch. There were quite a few WACs and WAVs and Red Cross babes who also attended. It was a lively weekly event.

"So who do you think the victim is?"

"I don't know!"

"And what do you think he was doing there?"

"Obviously he was waiting to kill me!" he nearly wails.

"So who killed him?"

"The guy! Because he couldn't find me and knew he could get me out of the way by framing me for the murder."

I'm not so sure about that. From his description of the man who came to his house this morning, I strongly suspect that he ended up being the victim, not the assailant. "Okay, Pete," I say patiently, "let's slow down and go over all of this. First of all, why is anyone after you?"

"Because I know too much, and as long as I didn't say anything to anyone that could hurt them, they didn't care."

"Do you know who any of these people are? I mean, the actual individuals?"

He thinks for a moment, frowning slightly. "Well I know George Bush is one of the heads of the whole thing."

Inwardly I groan. "I mean locally, Pete. Are there any individuals you can identify by name?"

"Well, the Masons," he insists. "The Masonic Temple is right there in the middle of town."

"Pete," I say, suddenly tired of this, "my father was a Mason and—"

"I know," he says, interrupting me, "that's why it was so bad when they killed him. Those people know something about that."

"What people?"

"The ones looking for me."

I stare at him coldly. "Pete, look, my father died in the flood when the wall of the high-school gym collapsed."

Pete leans forward. "That's what they want you to think."

Now I am mad. "And how the hell do you know that?"

"I just do," he insists. "I've heard things."

"From who?"

"Just around," he says.

I rub my eyes, trying not to lose it. "Okay," I say, lowering my hand, "let's start again. Who came to find you at your house this morning?"

"A big beefy guy I've never seen before."

"And who is the dead guy in the woods?"

"I don't know."

"Why not?"

"Because I haven't seen the body!" he cries.

"So you never went to the woods today?"

"No."

I look at him. "So Pete, you sent me out to the woods to meet with the big beefy guy who was chasing you?"

"No! Yeah." He is perplexed.

"You wanted me to meet him," I offer. "And find out who he was, and what he wanted, right?"

He nods vigorously. "Yes. I called you because I knew he would be there. I thought you could talk to him and get to the bottom of this."

Do I dare ask? I have to. "Get to the bottom of what?"

"He knew a lot," Pete tells me.

"Did he know something about my father? Is that why you wanted me to see him?"

"He knew a lot," Pete whispers, nodding. "I think he knew about the Swissair crash. They couldn't find the bodies in the wreck, remember? I knew where they were. I think he knew, too."

I narrow my eyes. "The alien vortex."

"Yeah," he whispers.

9

By five-thirty the next morning I have talked Crazy Pete into meeting one of New Haven's better criminal attorneys at the police station. In the meantime he has napped, eaten again and I have filed another story on the murder for the *Herald-American*, based on the more sensible things Pete has told me about the victim appearing at his house. I shower and dress for my interview with Verity Rhodes. I drive Pete downtown, park in front of the police station, escort him into the lobby, introduce him to his attorney, introduce Pete and his attorney to the sergeant on desk duty and announce I will be available to answer Detective D'Amico's questions at the paper after one o'clock. Then I jump in my car, stop at Quik Mart for coffee and a *Herald-American* (that has my face plastered across the front page: Reporter Finds Murdered Man) and hit the road.

Driving into New York in the summer is a pain in the neck because it doesn't matter what road you take in Connecticut or New York, all of them are always under construction, night and day, and somebody invariably has an accident and a thousand people always have to stop and look at it. This morning is no exception, and I end up having to call Doug on my cell phone to have him coach me through the surface roads of White Plains, Yonkers and the Bronx to get into Manhattan. (Doug has season tickets to the Knicks and never gets there late.) I nose the Jeep into a parking garage (that I cannot believe is twenty-four dollars for two hours!) on Fifty-third Street, walk over to a coffee shop where I order bacon and eggs and then call Castleford for messages.

"Dear," my mother's voice says, "I hate to sound like a spoilsport, but do I have to read the paper to learn that my daughter's found a murdered man in the neighborhood?" Pause. I can visualize Mother reading and shaking her head over Devon's pictures of the crime scene. "This is ghastly, just ghastly. How awful. That poor man." Pause. "That poor man's family." She clears her throat. "Well, I just wanted to check on you, Sally, and find out how you are after your ordeal." Pause. "Your brother used to play hockey on Kaegle's Pond. I love you."

"Mother," I say moments later to her answering machine, "I am just fine. I'm sorry about not calling you, but I'm actually in New York this morning talking to Verity Rhodes about writing that piece for her. I'll be back in Castleford around one and I'll call you. And I love you, too."

I open my briefcase and try to reread my notes on Cassy Cochran.

It is not easy to refocus when I am nearly sleepless and my head is churning with visions of murderers and aliens. ("Of course," Doug said to me earlier, "your friend Pete may have simply freaked out and killed the guy.")

Security at the entrance of the Bensler Building directs me to a large man sitting behind a desk. When I respond to the gentleman's query regarding who it is I am here to see by saying, "Verity Rhodes," I swear the guard straightens up a little and smiles. "I'll check," he promises, and after a quick call he tells me it's okay, I am to go to the thirty-fourth floor, and he slaps a badge into my hand that has my name and a number on it.

The reception area of *Expectations* is elegant, with thick beige carpeting, light-colored wood furniture, a chintz sofa and wing chairs. On the wall are splendid covers of *Expectations* from yesteryear. There is a magnificent vase of irises and snapdragons.

I am surprised to find a real, live receptionist sitting behind a massive desk. These days most executive suites in publishing look great but offer a single pathetic telephone on a coffee table as a way of welcome. I tell the receptionist who I am and who I am here to see.

"Ms. Harrington?" a voice inquires shortly thereafter. It belongs to an older woman, somewhere in her sixties. "I'm Doris Black, Verity's executive assistant."

We shake hands.

"Will you come with me? She's taking part in a phone conference that has run over, but she didn't want to keep you waiting." Doris Black is in slacks, silk blouse and flats, and I wonder if I am overdressed in my Donna Karan skirt and jacket (a deal from my last outlet-mall shopping trip.) When she shows me into Verity's office, though, and I see that Verity is in an Armani suit and heels, I am glad I have dressed exactly the way I have.

Still on the phone (wearing a delicate headset), Verity waves hello to me from behind her desk and then shrugs, as much as to say, *I don't know who these people are and why I have to talk to them?* Doris shows me to a chair at a small conference table in the corner of the office. "Can I get you something to drink?" she whispers. "Coffee? Tea? Mineral water? Orange juice?"

I say water is fine and sit back, ostensibly taking my notes out of my briefcase and reviewing them, but in reality using the motions as a cover to case the joint. It is very nice digs. The first thing I notice is that the rug appears to be a genuine Oriental silk. At twelve by eighteen, I can't imagine how much it cost. Thirty thousand, maybe? How could Verity let people walk on it? And then I remember that her husband is a kazillionaire and has no doubt bought it for her. She has a remarkable desk, too, a massive, turn-of-the-century piece that looks like walnut. There are several plants along a windowsill that spans the length of the office and the view of the East River is spectacular.

"At last!" Verity cries, ripping the headset from her head and springing up. "And you're here—on time, may I add, looking fantastic and well rested."

She gives me a hug of sorts, clasping my arms and simultaneously brushing her cheek against mine while holding the rest of my body at bay, and then whirls us over to the conference table where she flings a copy of the contract onto the table.

"Did you get my fax?" she asks, sitting down.

"Sunday. I was impressed."

"Good," she says absently, slipping on glasses and scanning the papers. "How long is it going to take you to review the agreement?"

"Oh, I already have."

She looks at me over the top of her glasses.

"I had a literary lawyer review it."

The side of her mouth hitches up slightly in an approving smile. "And?"

"And he tells me this agreement is not only fair, but more generous than your standard one."

She sits back in her chair. "Any changes?"

I shake my head. "He wanted to know who I was sleeping with at *Expectations*."

She throws her head back to laugh. "Ah, supportive of our hard work."

I guiltily think of my own skepticism about beautiful women who rise quickly in the ranks.

"So he said you could sign it?"

"Yes."

"Great!"

She slides the contract over and I take a moment to make sure it's the same agreement she had faxed.

"You sign there and there, and then I'll sign, too." We complete this part and she shuffles through more papers, pulls out a check and hands it to me.

It is for five thousand dollars and it is made out to me.

"That is also the kill fee," Verity explains. "The money you get to keep if, for some reason, we don't run the piece. Although I can't imagine why we wouldn't."

"Thank you," I say. The check should say *quit money* on it, because I am afraid this is what it might take to get time to write this piece.

Verity slides over an American Express card. "And sign the back of this, please. At the completion of the assignment I'll expect that back—or, who knows, maybe you'll write something else for us."

I feel a wave of excitement pass through me.

"You are to use it for your out-of-pocket expenses, airline tickets, hotel, car rentals, meals, et cetera, but I have to warn you, it's only for five thousand and that can go very quickly when working on a story. And no, what you don't spend, you don't get to keep, so use it in good health and get that story."

I sign the back of the credit card and let it lie there to dry.

"Now, the story of Cassy Cochran," Verity says, sitting back in her chair. "Tell me what you think. I'm sure you've done some kind of research on her since Saturday."

"Truthfully?" I ask. "I think this piece is going to be tricky."

She looks interested. "How so?"

"To all appearances, Cassy Cochran seems too well balanced and too well liked to make very interesting reading."

Verity nods. "Indeed, we should all suffer from that—too nice of a reputation." She leans forward to rest her elbow on the table. "But I'm interested in the way you said, 'to all appearances,' as if there might be something more."

"I don't know that there is," I admit.

"So how would you make this piece interesting reading?"

"Well, she's very beautiful and so the photo shoot would be wonderful. I mean, she's a woman, you know, 'of a certain age,' and yet, wow, she looks great."

"Agreed. And we will be making the most of it. She's agreed to do a shoot with Ryder for us."

I let out a whistle. He is one of the top-five glamour photographers.

"But what about your piece?" Verity asks. "How are you going to make that more interesting? How are you going to get behind the appearances?"

"Well, of course, I think it'll liven things up to have interviews with famous people, like Alexandra Waring and Jessica Wright—"

"Yes," she says in a deeper voice, "but what else?"

"Well, to be honest, I think the more interesting stories may lie with her husbands."

Verity's eyes light up.

Encouraged, I race on. "The first husband evidently had a bad drinking problem, and the second, Jackson Darenbrook, well, his history is so extraordinary—his eccentric millionaire father who is suspected of having killed his first wife, his half siblings born by four different women, his rise to power in the family business, his own beautiful first wife dying in the country club pool, his years outdoing Warren Beatty on the dating scene, his hiring Cassy to run DBS News and then promoting her to president of the network and then getting romantically involved with her—" I gesture with one hand. "I think it's going to be her relationships with these men that are going to be the most interesting."

Verity is nodding, thoughtful.

"Also," I continue, "her father died when she was young and

I can't seem to find out the cause of death, which makes me wonder if there might be something there. Something, perhaps, that would tie in with her future relationships with men. And when I say relationships, I don't just mean romantic, or sexual, I mean with all the male bosses she's had. It's hard to believe a woman who looks the way she does didn't get hit on every five minutes, particularly twenty-five years ago."

Verity waits for me to continue, and when I don't, she says, "Anything else?"

"Not that I wish to share right now."

A subtle smile appears on the editor's lips. "Keep your cards close to your chest, eh? Well, that's good. But you'll check in with me? Maybe come by for a progress report in the next week or two?"

I nod. "If you'd like."

She starts gathering the papers. "What about your job at the paper? This story's going to take the full five weeks, you know that."

"I'm getting a leave." *One way or another.*

"All right, that's it then," she says. "Except—" She rises and walks over to her desk and comes back with a business card and a thick manila folder secured with a rubber band. She gives me the card first. "This is my personal line here at the office, my number at home and my cell phone number. You may call me anytime."

Instantly I am reminded that I have been given this chance not because of my brilliant writing career, but because Devon and I stumbled on the Schroeders in the middle of nowhere when they needed help.

"And this is a copy of our file on Cassy Cochran," she explains. "Addresses, phone numbers, pertinent facts, some interviews. I am going to make a courtesy call to her this morning and introduce you as the writer, but I will let you set up your own appointments. I'll tell her to expect your call this afternoon."

I nod. "Thank you."

"Also, Doris will show you an office you can use when you're in town. It's more like a cubicle, really, as other writers need space, too—but you will have a phone and a desk and a PC you can call your own for the next five weeks."

"This is unbelievable," I marvel.

"You did me and my family a great service, Sally, and now I only wish to do one for you. Although," she adds, "I'm sure you would have moved on to bigger things on your own, anyway—rather, returned to the bigger things you were doing before your mother got ill."

The surprise I feel at the mention of Mother's illness evidently shows on my face, for Verity smiles while edging me toward the door. "Surely you don't think I hand out twenty-thousand-dollar assignments willy-nilly to just anybody? I did some checking."

I hastily smile. "Yes, of course."

She sees me out the door, does that sort-of-hug thing again and hands me over to Doris. As the executive assistant leads me away, I glance over my shoulder to see that Verity is still watching me from the doorway of her office. She offers a little wave, and I smile and give her a little wave, too.

10

As soon as I am clear of Manhattan and speeding along the Bruckner Expressway toward Interstate 95, I call my voice mail at the *Herald-American* to find out what's happening. Doug called and Joe Bix, the other reporter on the Kaegle's Pond Murder, wants to touch base. The last message is from my boss. "Call me as soon as you get this if not before."

"I'm on my way back," I tell Al when he comes on the line.

"It's a very good thing," he says pleasantly, "because in order to wring your neck I need you in front of me."

"Oh," I say.

He loses it. "What is this about you harboring the prime murder suspect at your house last night? That you got him a lawyer, brought him to the police station and then friggin' left town without saying a goddamn thing!"

"I'm on my way in."

"How can you possibly justify—"

"Helping someone you know damn well is not up to defending himself, Al? Is that what you're going to ask me?"

"What the hell kind of reporter *are* you? You work for me. Get it?"

"Yeah, well, maybe we better talk about that," I say, clicking the phone off.

I drive for another ten minutes on 95 before punching in the numbers for the paper again. I get our electronic switchboard and I punch in Joe's extension. He's there.

"Hi, Joe, it's Sally. Do they know who the victim is yet?"

"Not that they're telling."

"No surprise there. Where's Crazy Pete?"

"Still downtown."

"They taking care of him, you think?"

"Yeah. He's okay. Actually, it's probably better he's down

there, because the popular theory is that whoever killed that guy may want to kill Pete."

"Whose theory is this?"

"That's why I was calling you," he laughs. "I thought it sounded like a rumor you might have started."

"Well, I didn't."

"Did you really give Crazy Pete a place to stay last night?"

"Uh-huh."

"Was Doug there?"

"No."

"Well... Would you care to give a guy a quote about last night for his story?"

Now I laugh. "When I get in, I'll show you what I've got, okay?"

Zipping along 95 at a good clip now, I make another call.

"Attorney Wrentham," Doug says after snapping up his phone. On TV prosecutors have big offices and secretaries. Well, in Doug's outfit, they have one secretary and a whole lot of prosecutors at a whole lot of desks in one big room.

"Hi," I say.

"How did it go?"

"Great. Really good. I start now. She gave me a check for five thousand dollars and an American Express card for expenses with a ceiling of five thousand."

He gives a low whistle. "Have you talked to Royce yet?"

"I'm on my way into work now."

There is a pause in the conversation. "Come on, Sal," Doug finally says, "renew my faith and tell me you were going to mention the fact that you were harboring a fugitive last night. Or were you just going to let it slide?"

I smile. "I was just going to let it slide. The truth is, I didn't know what else to do with him. He was scared to death and I wanted to get ready for my interview."

"Earth to Sally," he says, "he could be a murderer."

"No, not Pete." I change lanes as I change the subject. "So, you guys know who the victim is yet?"

"Yep."

I wait. "Well?"

"Sorry. Murder's not your thing anymore, anyway, Sally."

"Oh? What is?"

"Glamorous celebrities in the big city."

"Yeah, right. Any chance of a hint about the identity of the victim?"

"Talk to D'Amico. Any chance of dinner tonight?"

"No dinner, but you can sleep over. And I'm going to sleep, big-time. And Scotty wants you to come over because you throw sticks a lot farther than I can, particularly when I've had no sleep."

"It's going to be late," he warns me.

"Me, too. So I'll call you," I promise, hanging up.

I drive for the next forty-five minutes in silence, thinking things over, most of all about how I am going to handle the demands of the job I have and the chance of a lifetime I have just received.

I am also thinking about the bills I can pay off with that five-thousand-dollar check in my purse.

It's not until I am taking the connector in Milford between 95 and the Merritt Parkway that I realize the big red Chevrolet pickup truck with blackened windows has been behind me for quite some time. As I approach the split in the connector I remain in the right-hand lane, as if I'm going to go north on the Merritt. At the very last second I veer into the left lane to go south, causing the driver of the car I've cut in front of to quite rightfully lean on the horn.

The red truck swerves to follow suit and swings in behind the car honking at me. The truck accelerates suddenly onto the shoulder, starting to pass that car on the right. Going around the curving ramp, I pull to the left of the car in front of me on the other shoulder. Now several cars are honking. The truck speeds up even with the car that is between us in the proper lane. I slow. He slows.

I turn on my flashers and slow way down and then floor it, shooting onto the Merritt, swerving into the passing lane and flying over the iron-grid Sikorsky Bridge at seventy. After passing a couple of cars, I swing into the right lane, exiting the Merritt at Shelton, where I barely slow down to run the red light at the end of the exit ramp before turning right on Route 110.

Within seconds I hear a siren and, relieved, see a cop car

speeding to catch up. I pull over and wait for the officer to approach my car. "License, please," he says.

I lean out the window to look back down the road. "Do you see a big red Chevrolet truck with blackened windows, officer?"

"I would like to see your license," he says from behind his sunglasses. His partner remains in the patrol car and I bet she is radioing in my plates.

Seeing no truck, I hand the officer my license. He examines it carefully and looks at me again. "Registration?"

I get it out of the glove compartment and pass it to him as requested.

"Insurance card?"

I hand it to him.

He examines them all in silence, shuffling them over and over like he's in some sort of a card game, and looks up. "What kind of driving do you call that? That you were doing?"

"Defensive," I say. "I'm being followed. A red Chevy pickup with darkened windows. It has a combination plate, but I couldn't read the numbers. It started tailing me on 95, maybe as far back as Westport, and then he made his move on the connector and I was doubling back, trying to shake him."

There is a hint of a smile. "By whom are you being followed?"

Great, a literate cop. "I don't know, officer, but I do know that yesterday I discovered the body of a murdered man in Castleford and so the next day when some truck with dark windows starts tailgating me on a highway, I want to get away from him."

He looks back down the road behind us. And then back to me. "You're the reporter?"

I nod. "For the *Herald-American* in Castleford."

He nods. "Heard about that." He looks back down the road again. "So where's this truck that was tailgating you?"

"Back on the bridge, I should think," I say, "looking for me."

"And why would anyone be looking for you, do you suppose?"

"I didn't want to find out." I look at my watch.

"In a rush?" he asks.

"I promised the police I'd be back in Castleford by one."

"You know," the officer says, "this is a very impressive story of yours, Ms. Harrington. But even so, I'm afraid your ticket is going to be just plain vanilla, running a red light. I'm going to overlook the speeding, though. Which I shouldn't, because you were going fifty in a twenty-five-mile-an-hour zone. Wait here."

He takes his time writing out the ticket in the patrol car. While watching in the rearview mirror for a glimpse of the truck I know the officer thinks I've made up, I call into the paper and tell Al's assistant I am slightly delayed. Finally the officer comes back to hand me the ticket. Only then does he take off his sunglasses. "I hope everything works out for you," he says. "It sounds like you're leading a complicated life."

"Thank you, officer." I take the ticket and pull out onto the road. I turn into a commuter parking lot to turn around and, heading back to the Merritt, I give the officers a wave as I ride by. I turn onto the entrance ramp for the northbound Merritt, picking up speed as I round the bend of the ramp. As I come up to the Merritt, I see that the red truck is waiting.

11

I can stop or make a run for it. I take another look at those darkened windows and make my decision. And floor it. But not before I memorize the back plate.

What's great about my Jeep is that its acceleration system hauls A. And so I haul myself past the Chevy onto the Merritt, zoom across the grill of the Sikorsky Bridge again and by the time I reach the other side, I am dialing the Castleford police. "Sally Harrington for Detective D'Amico, it's an emergency."

They patch me through to wherever he is, but by that time I see the Chevy truck in my rearview mirror again. "Buddy, I've got a red Chevy pickup that's been chasing me all over 95 and the Merritt." I recite the plate number to him. "I can't give you a description of the driver because the windows are darkened, but the truck's one of those big things with the four wheels in the back."

The truck is gaining on me. Since I'm doing ninety, he's got to be doing a hundred. Damn it, why can't I be on 91? Budget constraints in our county have translated into fewer state police on the roads and the only place the troopers ever set speed traps, for some unknown reason, seems to be on 91.

There is increasing traffic and there is no way I am going to continue playing this high-speed game around all these people. "I'm getting off on 22 in North Haven!" I yell to Buddy and fly off the exit. What to do, what to do? I slow for the stop sign and then turn east on 22. As I approach the intersection with 91, I take a left for the entrance ramp and keep bearing left onto a service road, hoping the truck will take the highway. I don't know where he is, but I keep going until I see a driving range-batting cage place. I veer off the road, kicking up clouds of dust as I bounce across the parking lot before I illegally park near the front of the building. I grab my purse and jump out of the car and, as I'm hobbling in my high heels up the sidewalk to the en-

trance, I see the Chevy come tearing in. I run inside past a baf-
fled-looking woman at the desk, twist my ankle and then limp
into the batting cages area. I put on a helmet, grab a bat, go into
one of the cages and slam the gate closed behind me.

I'm as ready as I'll ever be.

The guy in the next cage says, "Lady, are you okay? Do you
need some help?"

"Please," I gasp. He is a kid, maybe fifteen, but a big kid. He
comes into my cage to explain to me how things work. I keep
looking over my shoulder to see who comes in. But no one
does. The cell phone in my bag is ringing.

"Sally, where are you?" Buddy says. "The plate number you
gave me belongs to a truck stolen from Bridgeport."

The young man tells me the name and address of the place,
which I pass on to Buddy.

"Stay where you are, stay with people—I've got a North Haven cruiser less than a mile from you."

The police are here within minutes and the officer finds me in
the batting cage. The Chevy's in the parking lot, he says, but no
one's inside. I take my helmet off and hand the bat to the young
man before I limp off with the officer, leaving the kid open-
mouthed.

We walk to the parking lot, where the officer's partner is
standing by their patrol car. They've parked behind the Chevrolet to block it in. The manager of the place is out there wanting to know what is wrong; another squad car pulls in and
comes to a stop near the truck as well.

I review the last hour with the police. No, I don't know who
was following me. "Look at the windows!" I keep saying. "I
thought windows like this were illegal!"

They are black as night.

I explain about the murder in Castleford and that I can't help
but wonder if this has something to do with that.

We look around; there are several people, mostly men, hitting balls at the range. The police ask the attendant who was the
last one to come. "I think the one on the end," she says, pointing to an older man.

"He's got a bag of clubs with him," the officer observes.

"What about that guy?" I ask, pointing to a burly fellow with dyed hair who is wildly hacking left and right with a driver from the tee. The guy is no golfer.

The officer approaches the man to talk. The man points, takes out his license and something else from his wallet and gives it to the officer.

My cell phone is ringing again. "Ms. Harrington?" a voice says. "This is Doris Black from Verity Rhodes's office calling. Verity asked me to pass along word that Cassy Cochran will be expecting your call at three o'clock this afternoon. She'll be at her office at DBS."

I look at my watch. It's ten minutes after one. "Great, thank you. I will be sure to call her."

"You have the number?"

"Yes, thank you."

"Who was that?" the officer wants to know.

"It's unrelated to this," I mumble, looking around. It is hot and I am a perspiring mess. I suspect my shoes and suit may be beyond repair. "Look, the Castleford police expect me back there—like now."

"Just give us your name and address and phone number," the officer says, "and we'll follow up. But are you sure you didn't see the driver?"

"I didn't see anything. Look at the windows!"

"Tell Detective D'Amico we'll be in touch," he instructs me.

"When I see him," I say, moving toward my car.

"You're to see him as soon as you set foot in Castleford," the officer warns me.

I climb into my car and in a few minutes I'm back on the Merritt and the air-conditioning is blasting and I am gulping water from the bottle I always keep in the car. I look around for menacing cars, but there are none. My blood pressure slowly descends and I feel better.

My reception at the Castleford police station is amazingly formal. I am ushered into D'Amico's office immediately, where I find the detective on the phone. "Well!" he says, hanging up, "if it isn't Typhoid Mary, causing calamity wherever she goes."

"I think that's a mixed metaphor with Calamity Jane," I sigh, taking my compact out to check my face. I look like hell, with mascara smeared every which way. Yuck. I snap the compact shut and look at him. "So has North Haven found him?"

He purses his lips slightly and shakes his head. Buddy is a very nice-looking man. In high school he went out with the same cheerleader all four years and we thought for sure they would marry. They didn't. He went to Southern Connecticut as a day student, she went off to William and Mary. The next thing we knew, she was the wife of a bond broker and living in Darien. Buddy only married Alice a year and a half ago. Alice was a year behind us in school.

"They went through everybody at the driving range," Buddy says, "matching car to driver, all the way through the lot, and guess what they found?"

"What?"

"The manager's car was missing." He shakes his head. "Whoever stole the Chevy stole his car. They found it in a parking lot off the Long Wharf exit on 95." He squints at me. "Sally," he says, his voice growing in awe and amazement, "you managed to get a moving violation while this guy was chasing you?"

"In Shelton. I tried to explain, but the cop wasn't buying. So I turned around to get back on the Merritt and there he was."

"Only you, Harrington," he murmurs, sifting through some folders in the stand on his desk. He selects one, pulls it out and opens it, glancing over the contents. "So why do you think someone was following you?"

"You tell me." I remember something. "I've got to call Al!"

"It's okay, he knows you're here," Buddy tells me.

"Oh." I look at him uncomfortably, as if I am in the principal's office and I'm not exactly sure for which activity I have been caught.

"Let me repeat my question, Sally. Why do you think someone was following you?"

"I have no idea. Truly." I turn the tables. "I understand you know the identity of the victim now." I have no idea if he does, but it's been over twenty-four hours since the murder. He might.

"And how do you know that?"

Bingo. I smile. "Confidential sources."

He studies me for a moment. "Yeah, we do," he says, sitting back in his chair. He props his elbow on the arm and rests the side of his face on his closed hand. "You know him, too."

"Me? Buddy, I swear, I have no idea who the dead guy is. I stood there looking at him for ten minutes. I've never seen him before."

"You don't remember seeing him? Not around town?"

I shake my head. "No, and I have a good memory for faces."

He looks me squarely in the eye. "He worked for your father."

"My father's been dead for twenty-one years."

"He worked for your father," he says again. "Tony Meyers."

I look away, trying to think. "No, don't know the name."

"He would have been around nineteen."

I frown. "That guy did not look like an architect."

"Exactly." He sits there, waiting for me to say something.

"The only person who might know something about him would be Mother."

"I was just about to go over there." He pauses. "Your mother said she'd prefer to have you there, too."

I smile again. Mother wants to make sure I get all the inside information.*Tony Meyers, Tony Meyers...*

"I'm holding you to our agreement," Buddy says. "Nothing in the paper until I say so."

"Agreed."

As I walk through the station house, following Buddy, I glance at my watch and see that it's past three. I have no choice but to call Cassy Cochran here and now.

"Yes, hi," I say into my cell phone, "it's Sally Harrington of *Expectations* magazine. I believe Ms. Cochran is expecting my call."

Buddy turns around to frown at me. "What are you doing?"

I press my finger to my mouth, silently pleading.

"You have one minute," he tells me, holding up one finger.

Cassy Cochran quickly comes onto the line. "Hi!" she brightly greets me.

"Hi, how do you do?" I ask politely.

A patrolman walks by and his walkie-talkie squawks loudly

and another officer is yelling that he can't find someone's address.

"Please excuse the noise," I say.

"What's the address again?" the patrolman yells across the room to the dispatcher.

The dispatcher starts yelling back.

"I don't mean to be nosy," Cassy Cochran finally says, "but where in Sam Hill are you?"

"Um, well, a police station. I'm just finishing up a story for our local paper here in Connecticut."

"Does this have to do with the murder victim our newsroom tells me you found yesterday?"

I am surprised. But then, she's probably checked me out since I'm going to be writing about her.

"Yes, actually, it does."

"Sally Harrington!" a sergeant bellows from the doorway. "Detective D'Amico's waiting!"

"Sounds tantalizing," Cassy Cochran says. "Any chance you'll give a scoop to our affiliate in New Haven?"

"Only after we print it," I say automatically.

She laughs.

"Sally Harrington, get your ass out to the garage! Now!" the sergeant yells.

Cassy Cochran laughs again. She sounds very nice. "You've got to go. Listen, take my home number and call me tonight." After writing her number down and hurrying out to the police garage, I wonder if Cassy Cochran can possibly be as nice as she sounds given the cutthroat nature of her business.

I follow Buddy over to Mother's and we find that she's dragged a box down from the attic that she says contains summaries of my father's business affairs at the time of his death. "Give me a receipt," she tells Buddy, "and you may take it with you."

"Thanks, Mrs. Harrington. This will save a lot of time."

"Why don't you come into the kitchen?" Mother suggests, leading the way. "I've made fresh scones."

When we walk into the kitchen I can see that Mother's beau, Mack Cleary, is out back, working on the part of the stone wall that has fallen. He is wearing shorts and a polo shirt and looks very fit. And bigger than I remember. At least, his shoulders are. He doesn't look much like a professor today.

"I didn't see Mack's car," I can't help but say.

"It's over at Art's getting the brakes relined."

We settle around the table and Mother serves us coffee and scones.

"So, Mrs. Harrington, do you remember Tony Meyers?"

She looks down into her coffee for a moment. Then she nods. "He was the young man who worked for Dodge—my husband. Way back. He couldn't have been more than seventeen. He lived on Pratt Street with his mother. The father left and I remember Dodge saying he needed the work. Besides," she adds, looking up at Buddy, "Dodge said he had an aptitude for building. I think his father had been in construction."

Buddy is taking notes. "What exactly did he do?"

"Oh, everything. He did all of Dodge's deliveries—you know, delivered bids and specs of plans to clients, snooped around to find out about new building plans, checked on the construction sites of buildings or homes my husband had designed." She laughs. "Spy a little on the competition, see what they were up to."

"Kind of a jack-of-all-trades."

"Yes." Mother is thinking about something and I know she is wondering whether she should say it or not.

"Go ahead, Mother."

"I was just thinking..." She closes her eyes and holds the bridge of her nose for a moment, and then opens them. "His name wasn't Tony. It was John. John Meyers."

Buddy frowns. "Are you sure?"

"I'm positive," Mother declares. "Dodge called him Johnny. Johnny Boy. No, I know that for a fact, that's right—Johnny Boy Meyers."

I look at Buddy. "And the name you have is Tony Meyers?"

Buddy nods. "Could be a brother." He makes a note. He asks Mother a few more questions and gets ready to leave. I know he is anxious to check through the box of my father's papers. Frankly, if I didn't have the *Expectations* piece looming, so would I.

"Sally," my mother whispers, gently touching my shoulder.

She is a wise woman to use this approach since she knows by experience I am not a happy camper when awakened.

I struggle to open my eyes. I feel drugged. I remember sitting on the couch in Mother's den and putting my feet on the ottoman for a minute, and then...

"It's Alfred Royce, Sally," Mother whispers. "He's wondering where you are. I told him you're working on the murder story."

"What time is it?" I ask. My mouth feels like I have paste in it. I also have a headache and, after I notice the light outdoors, a sinking feeling in my stomach. It is no longer afternoon, I strongly suspect.

"Six forty-five. You were just so tired, Sally, I put Al off as long as I could."

I murmur something about how can you put off the inevitable and take the phone from my mother. "What the hell is going on with you?" Al yelled. "What are you doing at your mother's? Why aren't you here? You said—"

"Oh, shut up, Al," I say irritably.

My mother's eyes grow quite large.

"What did you say?"

"I said, 'Shut up.' You've got your story for tomorrow's edition. I'm coming in to put the finishing touches on it."

"No," Al says, "I'm putting the finishing touches on you. You're fired."

"Ha!" I say.

"Do you understand me? You're fired. You've missed the whole story and if it wasn't for Joe we wouldn't have any copy at all for tomorrow's edition."

"I know who the murdered man is," I say, yawning. "What story could be bigger than that?"

"That Crazy Pete Sabatino's the murderer," Royce says, "and that Crazy Pete's on the run again."

12

I'm trying to park my car behind the *Herald-American*—somebody's Lincoln is in my space at seven-thirty at night, thank you very much—when my cell phone rings and I find myself talking to, for the second time today, Cassy Cochran.

"From what I hear in our newsroom," the network president says, "this may not be the best time for you to try to freelance a piece for *Expectations*."

"Why?" I ask, getting out of the car and locking it. "What do you hear?"

"That you sheltered the primary murder suspect in your home last night, that you were followed by someone in a stolen car on the way home from New York and that the dead man found in Castleford might have a connection to your family."

I am impressed. "I am impressed," I say.

"We have our ways," she says modestly. "Seriously, I was calling to find out if maybe we should just postpone the article. I'm willing if you're willing. There's nothing I'm trying to publicize except our new magazine show and that will be up and on the air in September, anyway. In fact, with more time, maybe we can come up with something more interesting for you to write about."

"Really? You're serious?" I let myself into the building with my security card and hit the staircase.

"Absolutely."

"Well then, let me check with Verity," I say, "because you're right. This may not be the best time for me to leave Castleford. I mean, I'm not a suspect or anything—"

I like how Cassy Cochran laughs. It is light, friendly.

"You're a funny kind of person to be assigned to a story like this," she tells me. "Verity usually has some pretty tough characters working for her."

I have to laugh out loud, and the sound echoes up and down

the staircase. I've heard plenty of stories about what it takes to be on an annual retainer with *Expectations.* The fainthearted need not apply. And I must confess, I have been wondering how they will photograph me as a contributing writer. Will I look like I eat nails for breakfast, too? Before going to Kenneth's to get my hair done?

"Give Verity a call and see what she says," Cassy suggests. "And then let's talk. That is, if you're not in jail by that time."

"I still get one phone call, Ms. Cochran, and know that it will be made to you."

She laughs again. "You know, this might even end up being a little fun."

"Have you been dreading it?"

"Are you joking?" she nearly cries. "Good Lord, I've been in this business for thirty years and surely you've noticed that I've managed to keep my face out of the press."

"Except," I point out as I walk onto the third-floor landing, "the night Jessica Wright was found."

She makes a sound of approval. "You've seen that already, have you?"

"You betcha," I say just as Alfred Royce Jr. appears at the other end of the hallway.

"Where the *fuck* have you been!"

"Uh-oh," Cassy Cochran says. "Talk to you later."

I fold up my phone and walk right past Al. "Why don't you come and have a seat?" I have half a mind to tell him how he has just distinguished himself within earshot of the president of DBS. I throw my stuff down in my cubicle and pull out my chair to sit.

"Where have you been?"

"Al!" somebody yells from the other side of the newsroom. "I finally got the mayor on the phone!"

Al points a finger at me. "I'm not through with you."

"I'll be here," I say. I pick up the regular phone to call Verity at *Expectations.* Her office voice mail says she has left for the day. I try another number she gave me this morning and she picks up.

"Verity Rhodes," she says in a brisk British accent. There is the hubbub of people in the background.

"Verity, it's Sally Harrington calling. I'm so sorry for bothering you already—"

"It's quite all right. What's up?"

I explain about Cassy Cochran suggesting we postpone the piece, about my being in the middle of a murder investigation, Cassy wanting to think about a more interesting angle, and that we thought the story could be pushed back a couple of months—if Verity is willing.

"I am not willing," she says matter-of-factly. "Either the story is ready in five weeks or there is no story."

"Oh," I say, a little taken back. "All right."

"Of course she's going to want it postponed!" she continues. "Because she doesn't want it written at all, which just goes to show, Sally, there is a story waiting for you to write about. And the sooner the better. I am standing in the middle of a cocktail party at the Four Seasons and I am anxious to conclude this conversation."

I hear some laughter. Verity has an audience.

"Okay. Thank you, Verity. Goodbye."

Hmm. Well, at least this Verity sounds more like the editors I have known.

I turn to my computer and start writing when Al reappears. "I told you, you're fired."

"Before or after I tell you who the dead man is?"

"You know who the dead man is?" a woman's voice says before Martha Royce Kellem's face appears around my cubicle wall. Martha is only a year younger than Al but has had a very good face-lift and is slim, whereas Al is getting pretty fat. She has been suing their father for years to make him put her in charge of the paper; her current status as a board member doesn't really allow her to do anything. For a while, in protest, Martha wrote a column for a competing Hartford paper, but old man Royce threatened to cut her out of his will altogether. I assume there is a board meeting tonight because that would explain why our parking lot is full of brand-new Continentals—and why someone has parked in my assigned spot.

"Stay out of this, Martha," Al growls.

"Well you can't fire her *now*," she says.

"I can do what I like. It's my paper."

"It's our paper," she says sweetly. "Besides, you'll never fire her—you're still sweet on the mother."

At this, I look up, suppressing a smile. It's true. Al does have a thing for Mother.

"Not only do I know who the dead man is, Al, but I've got a high-speed car chase for tomorrow's edition, involving me and a stolen pickup truck from Bridgeport and the North Haven police.

"*Joe!*" Al yells.

Joe Bix's head pokes around the corner.

"Do you know who the dead man is yet?"

"Not yet."

"Don't fire her," Martha advises him, walking away. "I'll be with the others in the conference room, Al."

After she leaves, Al turns to me, raising an eyebrow. "How do you know who it is?"

"The important thing is that I do," I reply. "But the question is, Al, will you give me a five-week unpaid leave, effective tomorrow, in exchange for that information? I should explain that if you say no, then I will simply quit this god-awful job. If you say yes, however, then Joe gets the scoop and all my information now and access to me for the next five weeks. *Joe* does," I add, "not you."

"What the hell are you talking about?" Al shouts.

"Okay, make that one-week *paid* leave and four weeks' unpaid. You heard me, Al. I need the time and you better agree, or the price is going up."

"You wouldn't dare withhold that information from your paper!"

"*Two* weeks' paid leave—you owe it to me for all the vacation I never got last year, anyway. And three weeks' unpaid leave. I'll be back by Labor Day." I look at my watch. "You've got ten seconds before I start packing and go to the *Courant*." The *Hartford Courant* is our major competitor in the area.

"Cripes!" Al says, looking at Joe.

"Do it, Al," Joe urges quietly. "She'll feed us everything." He looks at me. "Right? And whatever ties this has with your family?"

I nod and look back to Al.

"Damn!" he fumes.

I cross my arms over my chest and start to hum, as if I have all night.

"All right!" he says.

"Good."

"But no paid leave!"

I pick up the picture of my mother and brother off my desk and put it in my briefcase as if packing to leave.

"Okay, one week," he says.

"Effective tomorrow?"

He glares at me and then nods.

"Deal," I say, putting out my hand. "You won't regret it."

"Fuck you, Harrington," he says, walking away.

Joe rolls his chair into my cubicle and we set to work.

I don't get home until almost ten to let Scotty out. I am tired, confused and my house is a mess. I never know how it gets this way, but one or two hasty mornings a week usually does it. The dog food cans, rinsed, are still sitting by the sink next to the soda cans, bottles, empty yogurt containers—all waiting to be taken outside to the recycle bin in the back. Eight days of newspapers are stacked up on the counter, waiting to be put in another recycle bin. The mail, most of which is still unopened, lies on the kitchen table next to the mess of unread magazines I always vow I will someday cancel. Laundry is overflowing from the clothes hamper; Scotty's hair is gathering in wisps around the edges of the kitchen floor; dust is everywhere in the living room from the windows being open and the rock-blasting at the Brackletons'; in my bedroom a pile of cleaning that never got dropped off is on the floor (I think Scotty's been sleeping on it); the bed needs changing; there are the piles of my winter clothes that never got put away stacked on my dressers; and piles of books are stacked in every room, all in danger of toppling over.

At least, I think, I can put my winter snow boots away somewhere. It is July.

But I never seem to have time. It is wonderful to have a house and a dog, but part of me longs for the days in Los Angeles when I had my spiffy efficiency in the Valley. Back then I simply dropped my cleaning off at the complex's front desk on my

way to work and a cleaning lady—an illegal alien, of course—
came every two weeks to overhaul my apartment while I struggled up the ladder of success at the magazine. And then, too, I
had kept my job from college—at least the best part of it—
which was bartending at a trendy nightclub on Santa Monica
Boulevard in Beverly Hills on Saturday nights. I could make up
to two hundred dollars in cash tips, a necessity to keep my car
and my cleaning lady going, to say nothing of keeping me in
Lean Cuisine frozen dinners.

The magazine had given me a membership to a health club,
too. I used to work out three days a week. Now I feel lucky if I
see the Y once a week.

"Scotty," I inform my big love of a dog, whom I describe as a
collie mix, but my mother secretly thinks is a police mutt. I
know this because she wrote as much on the back of a photograph of Scotty and Abigail. "Abigail (golden retriever) and
Scotty (police mutt)." "Come on, boy, you and I are going out
for a walk."

His eyes light up, his mouth parts in a smile, his tail starts
that special wide swing and he begins to dance. *Yippee! We're
going for a walk; you and me!*

Truth is, my Scotty's big teeth make him look like a junkyard
dog and people are scared of him. He's got a deep barrel-
chested bark, too, but he is my gentle giant—a sweetheart, a little lamb masquerading as a ferocious police mutt.

To heck with the house! The newspaper! The magazine! With
sleep! I need air! I need my dog! So I change into gym shorts, an
athletic bra, T-shirt and running shoes while Scotty goes to the
mud room to get his leash. "We're outta here, baby!" I tell him,
skipping out the back door and stopping in the backyard to do
a few stretches. And then off we go down the drive, Scotty's
fluffy collie tail high and wagging.

Still in Castleford after all these years, I think.

No one asked me to come home when Mother got ill. But I
knew how shaky Mother's finances were with Rob at school,
and I frankly wasn't sure what her health benefits as a teacher
would cover in terms of care at home. Mother had cancer, but
not the horribly progressive kind; hers came in the form of a tu-
mor attached to her lung—my mother had not smoked, ever—

the kind of cancer that hundreds of thousands of people discover they must take on every year and, if discovered early, can be successfully treated. So Mother had surgery, followed by chemotherapy treatments, which made her very ill, and so I never regretted my decision to come home to be with her.

I thought I'd be home for a month, maybe two. When Mother's reluctant call came with the bad news, I had just found out my boyfriend in L.A. was two-timing me and I was thinking about getting away for a while to get him out of my system, anyway. I was also severely disenchanted with my career at *Boulevard.* In other words, my reasons for coming home to Castleford were not nearly as pure as people thought.

But, as my mother says, I came home, which was ultimately all that mattered.

To this day I don't think I did anything for my mother except prepare a few odd meals here and there and do the heavier work around the house. And cut the grass, weed, rake, that kind of thing. We started her garden together and Mother was quietly amazed at my clumsiness and stupidity. She would say things like, "I'm sorry, I thought you might remember how to..." and I would say, "The last time I did this I was seven years old, Mother." And so, certainly for the first two months, I more or less had a vacation. I'd stay up to watch old movies or go out on the town—as much as one could "go out" around Castleford after frequenting clubs in L.A. for years—sleep in, do some chores around the house, go for a run and do lots and lots of reading.

The worst thing was that while ·Mother was getting chemo, which just took everything out of her for almost a week before she'd have to go back and get it again, our dog was dying. Murphy, a springer spaniel, was almost seventeen and could barely move. And I just could not face telling my mother what the vet had advised. I just couldn't do it. So I went to the mall in town and blew every cent I had left on a golden retriever puppy who was on sale because she had kennel cough. I called the vet and he assured me Murphy had had kennel cough vaccines and I brought the puppy home.

Mother was taking a nap upstairs and so I just went up and

put the puppy on her bed; it fell soundly asleep because it didn't feel well.

At first Mother was angry. I mean really angry. The puppy would upset Murphy, and how did I think Murphy would feel if this puppy got all the attention? And then Mother's eyes suddenly welled up with tears and she hung her head and brought a hand up to her eyes and said, "Dr. Kardowski said we should put Murphy down, didn't he?"

And so I started to cry and sat down on the edge of the bed and the puppy woke up and licked my mother's hand and I said, yes, he said Murphy was in a lot of pain, and had a kidney infection and arthritis and the lumps on him were cancerous and—

And then the puppy had diarrhea on the carpet and so our discussion ended.

Mother asked me to keep the puppy with me, downstairs, for a while. She tried to take Murphy for a walk, but he just couldn't go farther than the stairs. And so, as weak as Mother was, she picked Murphy up in her arms and took him upstairs to her room for the day. And at four o'clock, she called me upstairs and asked me if I would take him to Dr. Kardowski. "He is expecting him."

And she hugged the dog and kissed him and told him she loved him so much, that he was the best dog in the world. As her eyes blinded with tears, she turned away and I scooped Murphy up and took him downstairs to the car.

I'm not going to go into how difficult it was to let them take Murphy. I will just say I never cried so much in my life, not even when my father died, because I knew what was going to happen and it seemed so awful. But what else could we do? And what else could I do but hold Murphy as she went to sleep?

My God, I don't know what we would have done without Abigail. That little face, that little puppy, so sick and so in need of love. Caring for her brought a new energy to my mother; it was as if Abigail reinforced her own treatment. Good food, lots of rest, warmth, a little gradual exercise, a lot of love. Mother had something to look forward to every single day.

Somehow, with the arrival of Abigail, I knew I wasn't going

back to Los Angeles to live, at least not for a while. Mother said something about Al Royce mentioning I should stop by the paper, just to talk. And one day I did and he had a slot open temporarily and I heard myself say I'd be pleased to take it. A month later, Mother was given her first really good news about her future, and she mentioned that the cottage on Brackleton Farm was coming up for rent and perhaps, for a little while, I might consider renting it. That is, if I was staying on.

This was a nice way of saying that by this time I was driving Mother crazy and she wanted nothing more than to get back to her life, which did not include having me and my junk all over the place.

After two weeks of working at the *Herald-American*, Al took me to a local pub for a drink to discuss my staying on permanently. While we were there, Doug came in to meet a friend, and I sort of sat there in stunned silence. I had not seen him in nine years. I had no idea he was in the area. I thought he was still in Boston.

He just sort of stood there, blinking, looking across the pub at me sitting in the booth. Al was talking a mile a minute about something and I just sat there, looking back at Doug. Finally I smiled a little and gave him a wave.

"I don't believe it," Doug said, coming over. "What are you doing here? I thought you were in L.A."

"Doug, this is Alfred Royce, the editor of the *Herald-American*. Al, this is Doug Wrentham, who grew up here in Castleford."

"I know your father," Doug said. "He was on the golf committee with my dad."

Al shook his hand. "How is your father?"

"Pretty good."

"Good."

"Um, listen," Doug said to me, "when you're through here, maybe...?" He shrugged. "Could we have a drink or bite to eat or something and catch up?"

"Our business is almost concluded," Al told him. "Give us another ten minutes and I'll release her."

Doug nodded, smiled at me and backed away to the bar to talk to whoever it was I assumed he was there to meet.

"So, Sally," Al said, "are you going to be a fly-by-night and take off in a couple of months, or are you going to dig in and get some solid work experience with us here at your old hometown paper? Hmm? Can we induce you to stay?"

"The money stinks, Al," I said honestly.

"We're in a recession," he pointed out. "It's dirt cheap to live in Castleford right now."

"Well, I'm not sure that's a reason to want to work for dirt cheap."

"Look, you and I know your mother wants you to stay awhile, so why don't you just stay and do some good writing and reporting and learn everything right here? Then you can go back to L.A. as a first-class, grown-up journalist and not a glorified secretary."

When we broke up our meeting, I sauntered over to Doug, glad I was wearing a particularly flattering skirt and heels. His friend said something and Doug whirled around expectantly. "Hi." He took a step forward and, wincing slightly, said, "Al doesn't have some kind of claim on you, does he?"

I poked him in the diaphragm. I couldn't help it. I felt better, actually, having made physical contact. "That's what you think I would be doing? Dating some old, fat, married guy?"

"I didn't know!" he pleaded, holding up his hands.

"Ugh! God!" I slapped him on the shoulder. "You should know, you jerk!"

His friend leaned over. "And you haven't seen each other in nine years?"

"And not for another nine if he keeps this up," I muttered, looking past him to the bartender. "Amstel Light, please." I got a bottle and motioned to the bartender that he could keep the glass. My mother would have had a stroke, but I was reverting to high school behavior and drinking out of the bottle seemed just the thing to do with Doug.

"So I thought you were in Boston."

"Just moved back to New Haven. I got a job in the D.A.'s office there, specializing in securities fraud."

I looked at his hand, which had no ring. "I thought you were married." Too late I remembered what I'd heard at the reunion.

"So did I," he said quietly. Then he turned away to reach for the dish of peanuts and I realized that Doug had been hurt. Badly.

"My mother," I began, "had a cancer scare. I mean, she had cancer."

He turned quickly. "Oh, I'm so sorry—"

"Well, she's just coming out of it. She's really done amazingly well with surgery and chemo, and she actually just got a clean bill of health last week. We're going to go to Ireland for a week to celebrate."

"That's wonderful. Tell her I said hello, will you? That I asked about her?"

I ignored this comment because it sounded like he wouldn't be around to see her himself and suddenly I wasn't keen on that. Suddenly I was so glad to see him, so excited he was here. Back in Connecticut. And that so was I.

"Royce was just trying to convince me to accept a full-time position at the paper."

"But I thought you were in L.A."

"I was. I was working at *Boulevard* magazine. And then I came home when Mother got ill." I noticed his expression.

"But Mother's terrific. Really. I think she's going to be one of those survivors who's going to be better than before."

"That's great, Sally."

"Excuse me, you guys," Doug's ignored friend said, "but I gotta see a man about a horse," and he headed off to the men's room.

"Who's that?" I asked.

"You don't recognize Castleford High's former star quarterback?"

"That's not Red!"

"The one and the same."

"Oh, my God, he looks terrible! And he's been sitting here and I didn't even recognize him."

"He is terrible."

"Really?" I looked over to see the empty Scotch glass at Red's seat.

"And he's living with his parents again."

"Oh, boy, that's not good." And then I had to laugh. "I've

been living with my mother, so I don't know why I'm being critical."

"That's different, Sal."

"I just found a place, actually. Remember the old Brackleton farm?"

"The one with the stables."

"The cottage is up for rent. And it's not bad. So I was thinking if I stayed awhile, I might rent it."

He looked at me seriously. "Is that a possibility?"

I felt dizzy, the attraction came back so strongly. *I love him,* I heard myself say in my head. *I want him back.*

And so here I am, still in Castleford, dating my high-school sweetheart.

The honking is coming from the Cadillac Seville, which has just pulled onto the side of the road. The driver's window rolls down. "Well, Sally Harrington, I haven't seen you in a million years. How are you?"

It is Mrs. O'Hearn, a neighbor. "I'm good, thank you. How are you?" I look both ways and then walk Scotty across the street to talk to her.

"Good, good," she coos. Then she smiles, lofting an eyebrow. "I hear your mother's keeping company with a professor these days."

My back stiffens. Mother would hate the idea that people are talking about her. "Well, after being a widow for twenty-one years, I think it's time she went on a date, don't you?"

"Well now, who is he? Someone told me he teaches at Quinnipiac."

"Wesleyan. He teaches physics."

"Oh, he's an intellectual." Her eyebrows go up. "And he's divorced, or…?"

"He's a widower. For three years, I think."

"Ah-ha. I see. And his name?"

His name is none of your business. "Um, Malcolm Cleary. They call him Mack."

"And you like him?"

"Yes, very much."

"I just find this such extraordinary news, after all these years," she marvels.

"Well, he's certainly not the first man to ask her out," I say, thinking of how Mr. O'Hearn's eyes sometimes trailed after my mother. Mr. O'Hearn is the richest man in town now, a multi-millionaire who built a huge estate up in the hills. It's hard to believe that twenty-four years ago he was struggling to get started in building and demolition, and that it was my father who gave him his first job. It had been strange watching the O'Hearns get so rich while we got so poor. (Rather, while we were "without money." Mother has always insisted on the distinction. "Poor means you have no money and no prospects for ever getting it. Being without money is simply a transitional period until your hard work pays off." The longer I live, the more I think Mother is right.)

"Well," Mrs. O'Hearn says, "I suppose it's time Belle thinks about the later years."

I frown and Scotty pulls at the leash as much as to say, *Let's get away from this dame, I don't like her.*

"It's so difficult to be alone at our age," Mrs. O'Hearn says. "I know you young people don't mind it, but it's really— Well, let's just say there are advantages to having a good marriage." She smiles. "And are you seeing anyone special? How old *are* you now, Sally?"

"Um, yeah, I'm seeing someone," I say casually, backing away from the car as if Scotty's pulling is too much for me to handle. "Things are very good in our family, Mrs. O'Hearn. I'll tell Mother you were asking about her."

"Oh, do, bye-bye!"

As she roars off, I wonder if she knows that people in town say Mr. O'Hearn keeps a former waitress in the apartment over the antique store he bought for his daughter.

"So what do you say, boy?" I ask the dog. "Do we run home now?"

Scotty dances.

"Okay, but take it easy, I'm really out of shape." And we start to jog homeward.

Nothing is more beautiful in summer than central Connecticut as night falls. The sky above the mountains glows pink, red and orange, and the rest of the horizon turns a royal blue, darkening quickly toward velvet black. The stars twinkle, and the moon, if it is around, kindles a quiet, almost holy light.

Suddenly it is dark, but we can still see in the shadow-light. I let Scotty off his lead. As we jog along, winding off on Bafter's Lane, toward home, I become acutely aware of the smell of summer—that green smell of central Connecticut. It is the trees and the grasses and the wildflowers and the earth that make this smell. When I lived in Los Angeles, even on the most beautiful nights, I always smelled clay in the air, and I suspected the air was never clean, not even right after a rainstorm.

You'd think I was a farm girl.

Well, maybe in ways, I am. On the Harrington side we had two hundred years of gentlemen farmers; on Mother's, three hundred years of farming, but nothing too gentlemanly about it until about sixty years or so ago when Mother's father was the first to go to college.

Scotty and I make good time on the lane and I say, what the heck, let's take the back trail, and we cross the field where the strip-mining is going on. Here the air is heavy with the smell of stone. Fieldstone, gravel, granite—the massive deposits have been hiding under four feet of topsoil that in itself had produced enough rocks in the 1700s for the Brackletons to build a wall around their entire farm. That same rich, fertile topsoil, which grew hundreds of thousands of bushels of corn and beans and squash and tomatoes and cucumbers is now gone. It's been sold by the ton and is now growing a lawn, I hear, at a high-ticket condo complex over in Cheshire.

Scotty and I veer away from the mining, taking the trail through the woods, through the pine forest, over the soft needles, around the spiky remains of the pine branches that have fallen, down through a swampy bit and then up through the woods proper. It is spooky now. Halfway through the trail I nearly wipe out, turning my ankle on a rock, and so I slow to a walk and Scotty doubles back to make sure I am all right.

"Uhhh!" I utter. "Geez, Louise, Scotty, I'm a basket case," I say, chest heaving. "I've got to do something. I'm going to be like Lardo the Water Buffalo if I don't do something."

I smile then. The outside lights of the cottage are on. That means Doug is here and I'm glad. I need to talk over the events of the day with him. And, with any luck, I might be able to talk him into making me his specialty, a ham and mushroom and spinach and cheese omelette.

Scotty runs ahead to investigate, leaving the woods and loping across the yard. Doug's Volvo is parked out front. Scotty runs around to the back of the cottage; I hear him bark twice and then he is quiet. I walk around the cottage, trying to normalize my breathing.

And there is Doug, sitting on the backstairs, and next to him is Crazy Pete Sabatino, the fugitive wanted for murder.

13

—▶ ◀—

"I found him behind the woodpile," Doug says.

Pete is hunched up on the stairs, balancing a bowl of chicken noodle soup on his lap, which he is trying to eat while keeping his eyes on me at the same time.

"Hello, Pete," I say, doing some stretches. I can't see Doug's face clearly in this light, but I can imagine his expression. *Why does this guy keep coming to you?*

"I'm on the lam again," Pete says breathlessly between slurps of soup.

I nearly burst out laughing, it sounds so melodramatic.

"He hadn't eaten," Doug says. "I found the soup. That's all he wanted."

"Pete," I say gently, sitting down on the stair below his. "This is my friend Doug Wrentham."

The spoon in Pete's hand stops in midair. "I know." He shoves the spoon into his mouth, making a metallic clicking noise as the spoon hits his teeth.

"Doug is an assistant D.A. in New Haven. In other words, he's an officer of the court."

"Technically," Doug adds, "all lawyers are."

"Yes," I say, "but Pete, this one's a lot more an officer of the court than most. So be careful what you say. Because he'll tell."

"I have that lawyer you got me," Pete says. He puts the spoon down on the step with a clatter and drinks right out of the bowl to finish the soup. Then he lowers the bowl to look at me. "He got the police to release me this morning, but then they got to the police and sent them back to my house to get me again."

"Who got to the police?" Doug asks.

Pete wisely does not answer. Instead he places the bowl carefully on the step beside him.

"You think they told the police something?" I ask Pete. "Something that made the police want to arrest you?"

Crazy Pete nods. "See, they want the police to put me in jail. Because then they can get me like they got James MacDougal."

"The Whitewater guy?" Doug says. "He died of a heart attack."

Pete lowers his voice. "They withheld his medication and it killed him."

Doug looks first to me and then back to Pete. "Who withheld his medication?"

I am cringing in anticipation of his answer—*The Masons*—but Pete fools me.

Pete shakes his head. "You don't want to know. It's better you steer clear of this." He nods in my direction. "It's too late for her."

The telephone is ringing in the house and I get up, grateful for the diversion. I've told Doug about Crazy Pete and his conspiracy theories, but now that Pete and I are involved in a real-life murder, it doesn't seem so funny anymore. Any real information he has needs to be carefully sifted from all the chaff he carries in his head.

I glance at the kitchen clock as I pick up the wireless phone. Nine twenty-five. "Hello?"

"Sally? It's Cassy Cochran calling. I'm sorry to bother you, but I knew you were going to try to call me later and I'm stuck here at a function with my husband and we're going to be a lot later than I thought. So I wanted to try and reach you and find out what's what with the piece for *Expectations*."

"Oh, that," I say, trying to refocus.

The woman laughs. "You sound utterly sick of it already."

"Oh, no," I say quickly. "It's just that it's been a long day and—" I drop my voice and turn away from the open window, moving toward the living room. "I just got home from a run to find a suspect on my doorstep talking with my boyfriend—who happens to be an assistant D.A."

"You're joking!"

"No," I whisper in all seriousness.

"Your boyfriend's not working on the case, is he?"

"No."

"Well," she says, "what are they doing, the suspect and the assistant D.A.?"

"Doug gave him some chicken noodle soup." I start laughing. I can't help it.

She is laughing, too.

"And the strangest thing is, Cass...Mrs....Ms. Cochran—"

"You were right the first time—Cassy—please, call me Cassy."

"Well, the strangest thing is, Cassy," I say, "is that nothing, I mean *nothing* this big has happened in this town for two and half years. And then the second I have this big chance to do a great piece for *Expectations,* all hell breaks loose and I can't seem to get rid of this story. It's following me!"

"Did you get a chance to talk to Verity?"

"Yes. And she was not pleased. I called while she was at some cocktail party at the Four Seasons—"

"Oh, right," Cassy Cochran murmurs. "Her husband's celebrating. He's, uh, taking over Clarendon Cosmetics."

"Oh," I say. "I didn't realize that was Corbett."

"No one was supposed to," she says.

Do I detect disapproval in her voice? "Did they want to be taken over?"

"Well—frankly, no." A pause. "I have a friend who's worked there a long time. It's not necessarily a good thing. But, you know, their stock's been way down because of global trade problems...."

I look over my shoulder and see that Doug is standing in the doorway. "I'll be there in a second," I promise. "Sorry about that," I say back into the phone.

"Are you talking to the suspect or the boyfriend?"

I laugh. "So where are you? You said you were at a function."

"I'm just outside the coatroom at the Pierre Hotel. My husband's brother is launching a new magazine and we're having a post-party dinner that's going on forever. It's family, you know, difficult to duck. Besides, he's a good guy."

"Which brother is this? Norbert?"

"Heavens no!" she nearly cries. "No, it's Beau."

"Ah, the one in California," I say, to show her I've been doing my research. "You must have a very hectic life," I continue.

"What with the network and all of your husband's responsibilities."

"We don't have to harbor fugitive killers or anything, though," she says.

I really like this woman and feel like I could talk with her for hours. Unfortunately, this is not the time.

"So—Cassy—I better tell you what Verity told me."

"Yes, do."

"She says she's counting on the piece for the February issue. So we have to get to work now. Which, when you think about it, is very flattering to you, since February's the big advertising issue after Christmas, presumably the one everyone reads."

"Oh, you shouldn't tell me that," she groans. "Nothing against you, Sally, but I'm starting to get nervous about this."

"I should think there'd be something wrong with you if you weren't."

A sigh on the other end.

I'm trying to visualize this big-shot executive sighing in the coatroom of the Pierre Hotel, but I've never been there so I can't imagine it. All I know about the Pierre is that Rose Kennedy had an apartment there for years.

"Well," I say, "I got leave from the paper. So I'm free to meet with you whenever you are available."

"Are you sure? What about the convict?"

"Oh, he'll be fine. As a matter of fact, I'm seriously considering packing my bags and coming into the city for a few days to get away from all this nonsense."

"What is today?" Cassy asks herself. "I've got my book here.... Let's see, tomorrow's Wednesday. A nightmare. Thursday's... Well, not so bad. I've got some time in the early afternoon. And Friday, I've something in the morning, but... Listen, Sally, if you're serious, I can do an hour on Thursday, say one-thirty. And then two hours on Friday. That will at least get us started."

"Great!" I declare, suddenly feeling very excited. This would be so cool. "And you want to do it at DBS?"

"Well, come in on Thursday to the office and let's see how it goes."

Which means, I know, *Let's see if we get on, if I trust you, or if I decide I'd really like to keep you as far away from my home as possible.* I don't blame her. It's a little disconcerting how well we get on together, but I remind myself Cassy is not a movie star or anything, whose ego I'm used to, she's a self-made professional woman.

"I've also worked up a preliminary list of people I'd like to talk to," I say.

"Let me guess," Cassy says. "My ex-husband."

"Well, uh, yes."

She laughs. "I figured. Well, look, tomorrow, why don't you fax your list to my office and I'll go over it before you come? I'll prepare some numbers and addresses for you."

"That would be great."

"And if you want to talk to anybody here at DBS, we can check and see if they're going to be around the next couple of weeks."

"That would be great."

"So, let's see—I assume you might want to talk to Alexandra."

It is so weird to hear the name of the national anchorwoman, Alexandra Waring, said so casually.

"Yes. That would be great."

"Well, I know she's around. I'll see what her schedule's like. And what about Jessica?"

"Jessica Wright? That'd be fabulous."

"Okay. She's a little tougher right now, only because she's doing a special series and she's doing some of it out of town."

"Oh, I can go there. To wherever," I say quickly.

"Ah," Cassy says approvingly, "so Verity has actually assigned a budget to this piece."

"Yes. Seriously, I think this is a big issue for them."

"Huh. Well, that *is* flattering. Okay, so who else do you want to talk to?"

"Kyle McFarland? He was your executive news producer?"

"Who's moved on," Cassy says. "He's in London." She laughs. "Which might be fun for you."

"London, eh? Well, I just might talk to him on the phone then, if that's all right."

"Okay. Who else?"

"Your CEO, Langley Peterson."

"No problem."

"Your husband."

She laughs. "Oh, are you in for it. He'll talk your ear off. But no problem, Jackson will be around."

"Your son, Henry."

"He's in Chicago, but sure."

"And I've got your mother written down."

"Ugh. I was afraid of that. Well, let's talk about that one on Thursday, Sally. Of course you can talk to her, but perhaps I should explain a little about where my mother's coming from before you do."

I put a star next to Catherine Littlefield's name and then circle it three times. She would be key. "Your old boss at WST in New York."

"Fine."

"Your old boss in Chicago?"

"Going back to the prehistoric ages, are you?"

"And then I've got a list of others I wanted to ask you about," I say. "Your roommate in college, and some of your friends, new and old. High-school boyfriend, people like that."

"Hmm. Sounds ghastly, but we'll talk about it on Thursday. Fax me the list." And she recites the fax number before we get off the phone.

I have a lot to do before the day after tomorrow. But most of all, right now what I need is sleep.

I jot down some notes on my desk and walk back to the kitchen to hang up the phone. Doug is waiting there, leaning against the counter. "He's gone," he says. "He took off into the woods."

I sigh. "Poor guy." I put the phone back and turn around. "You know he didn't do it. He's utterly harmless."

"Sally, I've got to report that he's been here."

"Yeah," I say dejectedly. I walk over and take his hands in mine. "But if I get him to come back—in the house—could you maybe tell the police he's in your custody? So he can at least get some sleep and I can get his lawyer again? For the morning? You know what that jail is like."

"Sally—"

"Please? He won't go anywhere. Really. And then we could just drop him off in the morning. And I can call his dad tonight and tell him he's safe. His dad's old. You don't want him to have to go down to the jail tonight. Let him get a good night's rest, too."

Doug sighs heavily. "All right, I'll call Buddy. But you have to get him in here."

I go outside and call Pete's name. No response. Scotty walks over to stand next to me. "Pete, come on, it's late and we're all tired. Come inside and take a hot shower. I'll give you some pajamas and I'll pull the bed out for you in the living room again." No response. "Doug and I will sleep in the bedroom, but Scotty will sleep in the living room with you. That way he can keep watch while you sleep." *That way Scotty can keep tabs on you so Doug can sleep.*

Suddenly Crazy Pete steps out of the darkness. "Thanks," he whispers. And then he hurries past me into the house.

II
Manhattan

14

I left Castleford the next morning.

I fixed breakfast for Doug and Crazy Pete, waved goodbye as they drove off to the police station, packed my bags, dropped Scotty off at Mother's and took off for New York.

Mother is clever with money and she called one of her wild last-minute hotel numbers to book three nights at the Sheraton Center for me on Fifty-seventh Street (less than six blocks from the West End Broadcasting Center, headquarters of DBS) for only $85 a night when the real rate is more like $245). I can't tell you how luxurious it feels to drive into downtown Manhattan, hand over the Jeep to the valet, waltz up to the front desk to check in and then unpack all my stuff in the room as if this is the way I've always lived.

I am mad about hotels. Even motels, if it means a clean room and room service. The point is, I can't get over the wonderfulness of having someone else clean up after me. A hot bath, room service dinner with wine, lounging in bed, a good movie on the TV and a bunch of magazines and newspapers spread out before me is my idea of heaven.

And so, I am in heaven. I am also in New York!

Mother knows how to reach me and so does Doug, but otherwise no one else does. And since I have shut off my cell phone, I have the added luxury of calling in to find out what is going on without having anyone being able to call me back. So what shall I do first?

The Sheraton obviously caters to a business clientele because my steal-of-a-deal room has a large writing desk, two telephone lines and a fax machine. I set up my desk, organizing my files on Cassy Cochran, and run through a checklist of my tools: computer, computer battery, computer charger, adapter, portable printer, ream of paper, steno pad, voice-activated tape recorder, backup recorder, ten AA batteries, pens, pencils, Hi-Liter markers. Okay, I am ready for work.

I change into slacks and a linen blazer and low heels and walk over to the *Expectations* offices. At the reception area in the lobby, I find out that Doris Black came through: my name is on the security-pass list and I can go right up to the thirty-third floor.

There is, I find, no receptionist on the floor beneath Verity's; this floor is shared with various departments of other magazines owned by Seymour Rubin. I wander down the hall, still half waiting for someone to throw me out of here, and find my way to the room of carrels for visiting writers. No one else is here. I walk over to the cubicle I think Doris said is mine and I smile because there is a little sign on it that has my name.

I dump my briefcase on the floor and turn on the computer. I'm dying to see what kind of reference systems the magazine has, but my excitement is short-lived because I find that without a password I can't access anything more than simple word processing. I pick up the phone and ask the operator for Doris Black.

"Doris Black," she says.

"Doris, hi, it's Sally Harrington, the writer working on—"

"I know who you are," Doris says congenially.

"Well, I'm here, downstairs in my carrel—"

"Verity will be very glad to hear it," Doris says approvingly. "You waste no time, Sally, and Verity is particularly interested in getting the Cochran piece done."

"Yes," I say.

"Can you hold the line, please?"

She's gone before I can say yea or nay and then, just as fast, Verity is on the line. "Sally, bravo! And to think last night I was nervous you might not get to work on this story until next week. I knew I picked the right writer."

I don't know what to say, so I just say, "Thank you."

"Look, I'm canceling my luncheon date. You're going to be my luncheon date! How's that? I'll pick you up in twenty-five minutes."

The next thing I know, I am walking down Park Avenue with Verity. She is keeping a fast pace, talking a mile a minute about something somebody did at the Groucho Club in London and how funny it was. We sweep into the side entrance of a building on Park and in short order I realize I'm in the famous Four Seasons Restaurant. We walk past the coat check and up a staircase and straight ahead. "I prefer the Grill Room," Verity says as a handsome man approaches. "Julian, darling, what a party last night!" Verity exclaims, doing that simultaneous kiss-and-restrain thing she does. "Julian, do you know Sally Harrington?" she asks, as if the maître d' might know all *Herald-American* reporters from Castleford, Connecticut.

"No, I don't believe I've ever had the pleasure," he says, holding out a hand. "How do you do?"

He leads us around the floor of tables in what I assume is the Grill Room, although I don't see a grill, to another set of stairs that lead up to a balcony overlooking the first level. We are shown to a table that is evidently Verity's usual hangout, because Julian refers to it as "hers."

Julian pulls my chair out for me and then Verity's. I notice the table is set for three. I don't say anything, though; I just look around.

"The woman at that table below us," Verity says quietly, "is Betty Prashker. She's edited everybody from Stephen King to Dominick Dunne. She's a legend in book publishing. At the next table is Michael Anderson of the *Times.* I don't know who that attractive woman is with him. I like her dress. Looks French." She shifts her eyes. "And that, of course, is our former mayor, Ed Koch." Her eyes move on. "That what's-his-name from Bears, Stern. They bought the old American Brands building, you know. And over there, in the corner, of course you recognize Jane Pauley." Suddenly Verity's eyes light up and she waves at a younger-looking man who has come up from the coatroom level and is talking to Julian. "Here he is!"

The young man circles the floor and takes the stairs up to the balcony. As he approaches the table I can see he is somewhere in his thirties, and if he is not handsome, then he is simply so smooth and well-turned-out he gives the impression of being so. "Verity," he says happily, holding out his hand, "I'm so glad you called."

Verity doesn't rise but clasps his hand with both of hers. "I'm so glad you could make it on such short notice." She turns to me. "Sally, I want you to meet one of my favorite people in the world, Spencer Hawes. Spencer, Sally Harrington, the writer I told you about."

"Sally," he says, holding his hand out to me.

"Spencer's an executive editor at Bennett, Fitzallen & Coe," Verity explains as he sits down in the chair across from me.

It is a very strange lunch, and for the life of me I can't figure out why I was invited. Verity and Spencer do nothing but gossip about the book publishing industry. A few names I have heard of, but most not, and frankly, after a while I can feel myself getting edgy, wanting to get out of there to get back to work. The food is splendid, though—smoked trout appetizer and medallions of veal as an entrée—and I enjoy it. And then, as we are all sipping coffee, suddenly all attention focuses on me.

"I've got to go to this opening of a play tonight at the Joe Papp Theater," Spencer says. "One of my authors helped on the script. I was wondering if you might care to join me."

I suppose he mistakes my surprise for deliberation, for he adds, "It's supposed to be pretty good. Curtain's at eight. We could have an early bite and then go."

"Do you have to go back out to Connecticut?" Verity asks, and suddenly I am relieved that I'm staying in Manhattan because after the conversation these two have been having, it would seem positively homespun if I were to say I did.

"Oh, no," I say, "I'm staying in town." (Like I'm a Jane Austen character or something.)

"Well then!" Verity says brightly.

"I should go over my notes for tomorrow," I say. "My first interview session with Cassy is tomorrow."

"Oh, go to the theater!" Verity urges. "It will give you something for polite chitchat with Cassy tomorrow."

I look at Spencer and he looks at me as if he is hoping against hope I will say yes, although I cannot imagine why. I am sure he can get almost anybody to go with him anywhere. I have noticed he wears no wedding band, but that could mean anything, couldn't it? This whole lunch could mean anything since

I am at sea as to why I am here in the first place. "I didn't really bring appropriate clothes," I begin.

"What you're wearing is fine," Verity assures me. "It's only the Papp."

"I think you look great," Spencer tells me. "So what do you say?"

"Okay," I nod. "That would be very nice, thank you."

He and Verity discuss where we should meet for our "quick bite" at six-thirty and Spencer writes out the address for me. He also writes down his office number and asks me where I am staying. I tell him.

By the time we leave the Four Seasons, I am convinced that if I am to get any work done in New York, the last place I should ever go is to the magazine offices. A very large part of Verity's job, I am beginning to realize, is schmoozing around town, and I am guessing that Spencer is her contact at Bennett, Fitzallen & Coe. It is one of America's oldest book publishers; it was also one of the largest independent publishing houses in the country until it was sold to an international conglomerate and underwent drastic restructuring and turmoil in the 1980s. The publishing house was sold yet again a few years ago to a German publisher.

Bennett, Fitzallen & Coe, however, is still an awe-inspiring name in America, and thus, as an executive editor, Spencer holds an impressive and prestigious job. If nothing else, I gathered over lunch that he knows what and who the house is publishing these days, what and who they're bidding for, or what and who they are besmirching because they *aren't* publishing it or them.

I think Verity made him ask me to the theater. The question is, why?

I return to the hotel and call Castleford for messages.

"I'm sorry to bother you, Sally," my mother says on my voice mail, "but what on earth did you say to Gisela O'Hearn?"

"Nothing, Mother," I report, dutiful daughter I am who calls her mama back immediately. "She asked me if you were seeing anyone and I said yes and she asked me Mack's name and so I told her."

"When did you see her?"

"Last night when I was jogging."

"Well, she certainly works fast, I'll give her that," Mother mutters. "I was just at the grocery store, where I learned that I've run away with a scientist who works on nuclear bombs."

We both laugh. Mother is so far out of the circles of gossip in Castleford I am amazed she's even heard this.

"Why would Mrs. O'Hearn say something like that?"

"Oh, sweetie, she's just not a very happy person."

I suspect there is more to it than that. I think Mrs. O'Hearn is terribly jealous of my mother, even if she's very rich and Mother is not. But I am in New York supposedly working on the career opportunity of a lifetime and there is no reason I should get sidetracked by everyday Castleford nonsense, so I don't say anything.

"The irony is, Sally, when you were a baby," Mother continues, "Gisela and I were almost close. She had her baby, I had mine, and our husbands were up-and-coming in the construction business. And later, when your father went out on his own, you know he gave Phil his first contractor's job."

Yeah-yeah-yeah, Mother, I've got a world to conquer, can we please move this along?

As if Mother hears me, she says, "Enough about that, dear, *how* is it going? How is the room?"

I feel guilty I didn't call her immediately, because the room is terrific and she had gone out of her way to find it for me, and I tell her that, and tell her she's the greatest and I will let her know how things are going. And then I blurt out that I am going to the opening of a new play at the Joe Papp Theater tonight. She asks, "With whom?" and I say an editor at Bennett, Fitzallen & Coe I met at lunch today at the Four Seasons, and Mother is just laughing and laughing, happy, saying that I certainly don't waste time but soar right to the top, that's her girl!

My next call is to Joe Bix's beeper number and against my better judgment, I leave the number of the hotel.

Then I call Doug's office.

"Attorney Wrentham," he says.

"Hi, it's Sally," I say, as if my five hours in New York have changed me so much that I need to identify myself because he won't recognize my voice.

"A lot of excitement around here," he says under his breath. "Carter's moving your friend Pete to a safe house." Carter is an assistant D.A. in the office who works on murders.

"Whose house, my house?" I can't resist saying.

"No," Doug says. "Listen," he whispers, "I can't talk now." He raises his voice. "So how goes it in the Big Apple?"

"Great!" I say. "Verity took me to the Four Seasons for lunch and tonight I'm going to an opening at the Joe Papp Theater."

"Oh, so it's Joe Papp now, is it? First-name basis?" he says. "It's the *Joseph* Papp Theater."

I burn a little because he's right. I just picked up the slang version from Spencer and Verity.

"So who are you going with, Verity?"

Suddenly I feel guilty, because suddenly I don't want to tell Doug who I'm going with. I guess because this is supposed to be my little adventure away from Castleford and I also guess, in the back of my head, I want tonight to seem a little like a date—for the sake of livening things up back home or something.

"A friend of Verity's had an extra ticket," I say. "So I'm taking it."

"Well that's nice. Are you all set for tomorrow?"

No, I think. *I haven't done a damn thing all afternoon.* "Yes," I say. "But Doug, won't you tell me why you're hiding Pete?"

"No." And he means it.

The other line is ringing on the hotel phone and I tell Doug I have to go, I just wanted him to know I'd be at the theater tonight so I wouldn't be talking to him later. I take the other call.

"Man-oh-man, Sal, are things jumping around here," Joe Bix reports. The line is not the greatest and from the background noise I realize he is on his car phone.

"What's going on?"

"The dead man at Kaegle's Pond, Tony Meyers," Joe says. "He's some sort of toxic-waste-disposal king from Long Island. Out of Riverhead. Has a lot of government contracts."

"What was he doing in Castleford?"

"Nobody knows, although he grew up here. His mother's in Arizona somewhere—no other family here."

"Where'd you get this?"

"I gotta friend at *Newsday.* But Sally, I need you to talk to

D'Amico again. Yesterday Crazy Pete was wanted for murder, today he's persona non grata, no one's talking, no one knows where he is. His father's packed up and left for his sister's house in Florida. Claims it's too dangerous."

"Why?"

"Thinks whoever nailed this Meyers guy might go after them, I guess."

"But why?"

"I'm asking you!"

"If Buddy's hiding him," I say, knowing full well, of course, that it's the county D.A.'s office that is, "then I'd focus on the dead man and the toxic-waste angle. Toxic-waste disposal and Long Island smells like the Mafia to me."

"That's an ethnic slur," Joe says.

"Okay then," I say, correcting myself, "smells like organized crime. I'd focus on him and his business. What did Buddy say about us running his ID?"

"We're okay."

"Great, then do it."

"He wants us to ask people to come forward if they saw Meyers, if they know what he was doing here. But I still gotta keep tabs on Crazy Pete, you know that. I'll be damned if we get scooped by an out-of-town paper. What if he gets killed or something and we miss out?"

Why do I suspect Joe is not very concerned about Pete's well-being? "I'll see what I can find out," I promise, hanging up and punching in Doug's number again.

"Attorney Wrentham."

"So it was a Mafia hit, huh?" I say. "And you guys are scared Pete will be next?"

"The Mafia?" Doug says. "No one says the Mafia anymore."

Bingo. So they *are* looking into the possibility of an organized-crime hit on Meyers. "Maybe I will call you later," I say.

"No way, snoopy reporter lady," he says. "Bye."

15

I amaze myself at how nervous I am. I've showered and changed into a skirt and blazer and walk the blocks to the restaurant where I am to meet Spencer Hawes. I am a little early, but he is already there, sitting at the bar. "Hey," he says, smiling, sliding off the stool to greet me, "you look great," and he warmly shakes my hand.

We are seated at a small table and I order a glass of house chardonnay. We spend some time with small talk—he is from Maine, originally; his father owns a marina; he went to Brown University and briefly attended graduate school at Columbia; took a job at Time-Life Magazines; jumped over to Warner Books, then over to Simon & Schuster and then, three years ago, to Bennett, Fitzallen & Coe. Likes it a lot. I share a brief sketch of my life-to-date, including the fact that I am seeing Doug.

"I'm sorry if I'm coming on too strong," he suddenly says, looking down into his glass of Scotch. He looks up. "It's been a long time since I've spent time with, well, you know—a New England kind of woman. Work ethic and all that."

I'm dying to ask what kind of woman he has been spending his time with, but I decide he'll tell me if he wants to.

"It's nice to know that I'm not too far gone to remember how nice women can be." He smiles slightly, a tinge of color coming to his cheeks. "And attractive. With no secret fangs."

Oh, my, I think. Vampires, snakes, mad dogs; what kind of woman has secret fangs?

I don't know what to say to any of this, so I smile slightly and sip my wine.

Our dinner arrives and I comment on how good my spinach ravioli is.

"Do you know how long it's been since I've seen a woman eat?" he asks. "Not eat-eat, but eat anything but lettuce and carrots and a cookie? Ugh!" he suddenly cries, vehemently shaking his head. "Enough. No more, I promise," he says, opening his hands in a forward motion, as if releasing a bird. He picks up his fork and tastes the ziti he ordered, sautéed with tomato, garlic and black olives. "You think I'm neurotic, right?" he asks me.

I hesitate a moment and then say, "Well, I think you may be overly bright, overworked and were probably recently, well, overturned—shall we say?—by a person who's not very healthy." When he doesn't say anything but simply stares at me, I add, "And, you know, when you hang out a lot with somebody who's not well, after a while you start thinking like them, particularly if you think you're in love with them. You want to *understand* them. Gain their trust, their innermost thoughts. So later, when you come up for air and relate to the real world, you feel like you're not well in the head, either, and you're not, because you've been trained to think like the person who's not well, the one you might be in love with." I smile. "Fortunately it doesn't take years of cognitive therapy to reverse it. You just feel like hell for a while. Like the Incredible Hulk after the change back."

Spencer places his fork carefully on the edge of his plate and picks up his water glass to drain it. He puts the glass back down and, hand still on it, says, "You are a bright and lovely person."

"Thank you," I say lightly, resuming my dinner.

"And you don't sound like anybody who ever worked for Verity before," he continues, leaning forward slightly. "Where did she find you?"

"In the woods," I remind him.

He watches me eat a minute and then leans forward again. "How do you know so much? Have you been, like, in therapy for a million years or something?"

I laugh, covering my mouth with my napkin. Lowering it, I say, "No. I've just been there, where you are. And I have a very cool mother. Who knows everything. She explained it all to me."

"What was he like, this guy, who made you think like an unwell person?"

"Not terribly unlike the woman who's in your life, I suspect."

"Was," he says.

"Was in your life," I say, getting the message loud and clear. I am flattered. And nervous. And excited. He is smart, well educated, very successful, but vulnerable in ways I find refreshing. Doug's idea of vulnerability is asking me to give him a massage on his neck and shoulders—and nowhere else. "Anyway—Bill. You asked about Bill."

"That was his name?"

I nod. "I met Bill when I was working at *Boulevard* magazine. He was an aspiring actor—"

"Oh, brother," Spencer groans in anticipation.

"Right. And he was working as a waiter. I was still moonlighting on Saturday nights as a bartender at this same place. And one night Bill came over after we had closed and sat at the bar and rested his chin on his hand, his elbow on the bar, and I remember thinking, *This is the best-looking man I've ever seen in all my life.* And he was charming, with a smile to die for. And for whatever reason, although we'd worked together for months, that particular night Bill zeroed in on me as if I were the love of his life, that he had suddenly come to his senses and realized that he was wild about me, that he couldn't live without me."

Spencer is nodding, mesmerized. "What did he look like?"

"Blond. Blue eyes that were beyond belief. Chiseled features, à la Charlton Heston. Six foot, body hard as a rock—" I think of something else that usually was, too, and I know I am blushing.

"A real Adonis," Spencer encourages me.

"Yes." I take a sip of wine. "Next thing I knew, he had moved in with me and I was handling his career, writing releases, posing as an agent with casting directors, all kinds of stuff."

"Did you bring him to parties? I mean, did *Boulevard* have parties and stuff like we do?"

"We got invited to everything. Screenings, cocktail parties, openings, all that stuff, and anything my boss didn't go to, she always passed the invitations on to me. And so, yes, I took Bill to everything."

"So you tried to advance his career."

I look down at the table, taking a deep breath. "Yeah." I bring my eyes back up. "How could I have been so stupid? I swear, I thought he loved me."

Spencer holds out his hand to me across the table. Instinctively I put mine in it before thinking it through. He simply squeezes it and says, "I'm sure he did love you, as much as a person like him was capable of loving someone else."

I take my hand back. "Thanks," I murmur, embarrassed. I pick up my fork again, but I have no idea why because I now have zero appetite. Thinking about Bill still makes me feel stupid, humiliated, ridiculous—and heartbroken. For a while I really thought he was it.

"Mine was an actress-turned-aspiring-writer," Spencer says.

I look at him and immediately feel better, because in an instant I realize he has been even stupider than I was with Bill.

"I thought she would have loved me even if I were a shoe salesman," he says, not laughing but trying to. He sighs. "How did your relationship end?"

"I found out he was cheating on me, so I threw him out."

Spencer nods slowly.

"And then I came back to Connecticut."

"So you haven't kept in touch?"

"Heavens no."

Spencer considers this while signaling to the waiter. With his eyes fixed on the waiter's approach, he says matter-of-factly, "She moved out of my apartment and right into a movie producer's apartment. I guess she'd rather be an actress after all. I think writing was too much work."

I hazard a guess. "She was gorgeous."

"Oh, Sally, you have no idea."

"But I do."

We don't talk much after that. We skip coffee and dessert.

We walk over to the theater and I can't imagine how a woman could use a man like Spencer so casually. But then, as he explained to me, he has very little free time in his life and the ex always resented that fact. Oh, yes, she liked the parties and dinners, but those were not frequent. What was frequent was that he worked his rear end off with administrative junk from nine to five and then read manuscripts and edited from five to nine. She did like the economy of paying no rent while she lived with him, which gave her a lot more money for facials and shoes from Joan&David.

How long had she stayed?

Not even a year.

"She did you a favor by getting out when she did," I say when we reach the theater. "Which means," I add in his ear as we make our way through the lobby, "that she probably loved you to the extent she could love anybody."

He turns to look back at me over his shoulder. His smile is frozen. He pulls me up next to him and I find myself slinging my arm through his, and that is the way we enter the theater.

"I don't want to be a fool anymore," he whispers.

I am not quite sure what has happened to me. One minute I'm Sally Harrington from Castleford, Connecticut, preparing for the interview of a lifetime, and then the next I find myself laughing and feeling carefree and excited by a man I scarcely know. We are an enviable couple: we are good-looking people; we are young and successful and obviously, at least for tonight, on top of the world. After the play, we go backstage to meet the actors. Then we move on to the Algonquin to sip champagne, talk and smile. Soon we are holding hands as we walk up Fifth Avenue, talking and laughing as we look in the windows of all the fabulous stores, the Manhattan dazzle of lights making it all seem unreal.

In the Barnes & Noble window Spencer proudly points out the books that are published by Bennett, Fitzallen & Coe. At Tiffany's we decide the jeweler's windows are losing their touch. At Bergdorf's we raise imaginary glasses in a salute. At FAO Schwartz he tells me how he rocked his rocking horse right out of his room and down the stairs once as a kid, landing him in the hospital with a concussion.

At the Plaza, we have decaffeinated coffee and pastries. And then we have a brandy. And then we have another. And I realize we are getting snockered.

And then we are walking again, hand in hand, along Central Park South, toward my hotel. When we pass what is the old Ritz, Spencer suddenly turns to me and sweeps me back up against the building and gives me the most wonderfully romantic, passionate kiss. We are in a clinch. And he feels absolutely marvelous and all I want is to be there, with him, feeling him hold me, his passion welling up against my hip.

He pulls back to look at me. And brings his hands up to hold my face. He looks at me as if he is in pain. He kisses me again and holds my face again. "Who *are* you?" he whispers.

I can't talk. I lower my head on his shoulder and hang on to him, wondering what has happened, what is happening.

"I want to make love with you," he whispers in my ear, hoarse.

I nod into his shoulder. His breathing is ragged. I hear people and cars going by, but I'm never going to move. I am going to stay right here for as long as I can.

"I want to make love with you," he whispers again, holding me closer, and I feel his erection and it makes me feel weak. "I want every part of you," he says, kissing my hair.

I feel desperate, but I can't move. I swear to God all I want to do is to wrap my legs around him and do it right here. I just want him in me, here, now. I hold him more tightly, my face still buried in his shoulder, waiting for him to move us, to think of something. He can't wait for me to consent, because I won't give it. We have to just do it.

He grabs my hand and abruptly pulls me to the hotel lobby. The lights blind me. He releases my hand and strides to the front desk, pulling out his wallet and tossing a credit card onto the counter. I am stunned, standing there, positive everyone in the lobby knows exactly what is happening. And then Spencer is back and he takes my hand firmly and marches me to the elevator. We don't speak, not even in the elevator; he only holds my hand so tight it almost hurts. The elevator stops, he hesitates, wondering which way to the room, and then he pulls me down the hall over the thick carpeting. He slides the card key in and the door swings open and I go inside and he comes in and closes the door.

We are at each other, kissing, grappling right there, not even turning on the light, and I fall to the floor, pulling him down with me. I go after his belt and he pulls my panty hose down and I swear to God, I cannot believe it, but we just do it right there, like that, with our clothes on. He's desperate to push inside me and when he does, I go through the roof, clinging to him, and I wrap my legs around him and squeeze, hard, and he pushes and pulls, in and out, in and out, and I'm losing my mind. I grab at the carpet, moaning, rising higher and higher as he shoves and thrusts and pushes and twists and it is so good, so good, so good—

I shudder and gasp, shudder and gasp again, clenching my thighs, and then I shake, shake like I'm coming apart, and I make an urgent noise because I *am* shaking apart. And then I collapse and Spencer grabs me more firmly and moans the most guttural, primitive sound, and thrusts two, three more times—freezes—and then roars "Sally!" in my ear and collapses, holding on to me, gasping for breath.

I feel the wet trickling down my thigh. It is hot. Warm. Soon to be cold.

We say nothing but only lie there, holding each other. We can't say anything, we can't do anything; he stays inside me until he starts growing large again, which is not a very long time away.

And we do it again.

16

A vacuum cleaner outside my hotel room door awakens me and for one split second I feel happy, warm and relaxed, and then in the next…

Oh, my God.

The guilt and fear twists deep into my stomach and I wonder how I could have done what I did last night. And then crept back here at four in the morning.

But I know how, because the memory floods warmth through—

The guilt comes back and I am frightened. This is not me. This is not admirable behavior.

I love and respect Doug.

What have I done? How could I do it?

But I remember why I did it—I remember how it felt, how I felt—and I cannot keep thinking like this because in a while I won't regret what I've done in the least, but will only want more of it.

I glance at the clock. It's after eleven! My interview is at one-thirty!

I vault out of bed to survey the papers it seems like I laid out weeks ago on the desk. I call room service for coffee and yogurt and notice the message light is flashing. I dial in for voice-mail messages but there are none, so I call the hotel operator.

"There is a package for you at the front desk," he says. "Would you like us to send it up?"

"Sure," I say, wondering what it could be.

I start skimming my notes and I don't feel quite so panicked about the interview anymore. I know this material on Cassy Cochran pretty well. When the bellhop knocks on the door, I jump up to open it. In his hand is a manila envelope addressed to me. I give him a dollar and close the door. There is no return address, simply my name.

I sit down on the bed with a funny feeling in my stomach. I open the envelope and slide out a small leather-covered book that has no title on it. I open it. The title page says 1904. *Selected Poems of Emily Dickinson.*

I look in the envelope and see a folded piece of paper. I open it and read the bold handwriting.

Thursday, 7:30 a.m.

Dear Sally,

I am so scared and yet so happy this morning I don't know what to do.

I don't know why I'm giving you this small volume, except maybe because I love it and I want you to have it. You have given me a kind of joy and release I have never felt before.

Spencer

P.S. If you don't want to call me, I'll understand. (Not really, but it sounds like the right thing to say. Please call. I want to see you.)

There is another knock at the door. It is room service. I direct the waiter to put the tray on the desk, sign the bill after wincing at it (five-fifty for the same plastic container of Dannon's I get at the grocery store? Four twenty-five for a cup of coffee? Eighteen percent gratuity? Sales tax?) and send him away.

I pick up the telephone.

"Spencer Hawes's office," an efficient-sounding young woman says.

"Hi, it's Sally Harrington returning his call."

"Oh! It's you!" she says, excited. "Spencer said to find him wherever he is if you called. Can you hang on? I think he's over in the art department."

"Certainly," I say. I can't help but smile. I just wish the fear in my stomach would settle down.

After a few minutes, Spencer comes onto the line. "You called," he says with awe.

"How could I not?" My stomach flip-flops as I say it.

"Oh, God, Sally," he murmurs. "I just don't know what to

say except I must see you. Tonight, tomorrow, the next day—and the next and the next—"

I laugh, wishing he was not quite so effusive, but I suspect this is the way he is when he's happy.

"I know," he says. "I know I shouldn't say stuff like that right off the bat, but—I mean—Sally, have you ever? I mean, here I thought I've done just about everything, and yet this morning I feel like I just started living last night."

"I know," I acknowledge.

"Can I see you? I'm supposed to go to this thing at the Metropolitan, but I can send someone else."

"I've got to do this interview—"

"I know, I know, you have to work. Well, how about you get your work done and then we have dinner? I don't want to—I mean, we don't have to—you know. I just want to see you, Sally."

I know exactly how he feels. And I am shaken by it.

The West End Broadcasting Center is home to the Darenbrook Broadcasting System, and it is a very impressive facility. It's not far from my hotel, located on Twelfth Avenue at Fifty-sixth Street, all the way over on the Hudson River. At one time, I have read, the facility stood all by itself, but now the Riverside Park South project rises around it. Still, the network offices have a commanding view of the river. West End, as the facility is known, is a three-story building constructed in a gigantic U, facing the Hudson, and in the center is a gorgeously landscaped park. One wing of the complex is broadcasting, the opposing wing houses the print and electronic divisions, and the middle is home to the executive suite, a company cafeteria and a day-care center on the ground floor that opens onto the park. The actual DBS studios and newsroom are part of the complex that is built below ground.

Security is extremely tight. The cab is allowed through the front gates only after the guard has called ahead, and when the cab swings around the circle of the receiving area, a security guard is waiting on the sidewalk to meet me. He hands me a badge, which has a little electronic screen showing my name in digital letters. He watches carefully as I clip it onto the lapel of my blazer. "How does my name appear like that?" I ask him. "Is this a little computer?"

"It's a receiver," he says. "It's programmed from our central security office."

"Ah," I say. "This wouldn't happen to be a tracking device as well, would it?"

"Actually, yes." He smiles. "And I wouldn't take it off, if I were you, to see what happens."

"Well that sounds ominous," I say, laughing.

He doesn't respond, which I guess means that his statement was supposed to sound ominous. Of course all I want to do now is take the badge off to see what happens. Given the kidnapping of Jessica Wright last year, however, I suppose it would be like kidding around about a hijacking within earshot of airport security.

I am taken up in an elevator and when we stop, there is an attractive Latin lady waiting for me. She introduces herself as Chi Chi Rodriguez, Cassy Cochran's executive secretary, and she waves security goodbye. As she leads me to Cassy's office, through a hallway where framed portraits of all the DBS stars hang, I ask Chi Chi how long she has worked with Cassy.

"Almost twenty-two years."

"Really? Can I talk to you sometime?"

We are turning into a suite of offices and Chi Chi laughs. "Depends about what," she says, sweeping me through a doorway.

Suddenly I am in an expansive office with a glorious third-floor view of the park and the Hudson River. Straight ahead is a large wood desk with several chairs in front of it and a side desk with a computer terminal; over to the side of the office is a couch and three easy chairs; and off in the corner, up a step, is a kind of meeting alcove with a round table and four chairs. There is a TV console to my left, near the door, and the TV is on, but the sound is off and the closed captioning appears at the bottom of the screen. It is the new DBS house-and-home show with Alicia Washington. Apparently the host, a very bright and attractive young black woman, knows nothing about keeping house, and so the show tackles everything from cooking to laundry to decorating to diapering a baby. It's doing surprisingly well considering it's up against ABC's *All My Children.*

"Cassy will be here in a moment," Chi Chi promises. "Please have a seat." She indicates the couch. "Can I get you anything? Some water or coffee or tea or something?"

"Some water would be great," I say.

Chi Chi leaves and I am left alone. I immediately walk over to Cassy's desk to look at the pictures that surround it. Cassy's husband, Jackson Darenbrook, has great eyes, almost cornflower blue. Another frame shows a young, fair-haired man and a brunette woman—her son, Henry, and a girlfriend? Wife? Another picture shows a little boy, maybe four years old. Clearly Henry, for in this photo he looks a lot like his mother. Beside it stands a picture of Cassy and Jackson on a sailboat somewhere, looking tanned and happy. And there is a group picture of DBS personalities, for I recognize the network's anchorwoman, Alexandra Waring, and talk-show host Jessica Wright. And Alicia Washington and Langley Peterson, CEO. Who the others are I have no idea. There are a ton of other pictures on the far wall of all kinds of people doing all kinds of things on the sets, in the newsroom, receiving awards at company picnics.

"Sally!" a voice says from behind me, as if I am some sort of long-lost friend who has unexpectedly turned up.

I turn around.

"At last." Cassy Cochran walks toward me with her hand out.

Although I've seen her retouched press photos, I am still taken back by this woman's good looks. She is older than her pictures let on—there are a lot of lines in her face, though I suspect she may have had a good eye-and/or face-lift—and even her handshake is graceful, comfortable, confident *and* welcoming.

"It's wonderful to meet you," I say truthfully.

I like her already. What can I say? From everything I've read, my conversations on the phone with her, and now meeting her in person, I simply like her. Of course, the journalist in me is screaming not to arrive at this decision because this is exactly what my subject no doubt has in mind—to disarm me from the first so I will take her side when it comes to the conflicting stories I will no doubt hear. For there are *always* conflicting stories about successful people.

Chi Chi comes back in with water for both of us and we settle down, me on the couch, Cassy in the chair across from me, the tape recorder that I've tested on the coffee table in the middle. She is wearing an elegant, cool-looking pale gray suit, matching heels, a darker gray silk blouse, a strand of pearls and matching earrings. She has several bands of diamonds on her wedding finger. She crosses her legs and sits back in the chair, holding her glass of water. "So, where do we begin?"

"With you telling me a little about yourself," I say.

She smiles, looks at her watch and then back at me. "I thought maybe you should tell me a bit about you."

In the emotionally weakened condition that I am as the new Sally, the two-timing one, I find myself somewhat at a loss.

"I was curious why you left Los Angeles," Cassy says. "From what I hear, you had started a very promising career at *Boulevard*."

"Oh, that. Well, my mother was ill and I came back for just a little while and then I was, uh, offered a job at our paper."

She frowns slightly.

"I'm sorry?" I say.

"That doesn't make any sense. Why didn't you go back? Or come to New York?"

I feel the anger starting to rise because I know what she is doing. She is reminding me what it feels like to have my life scrutinized and then be cornered when what I say fails to make narrative sense. It is a warning shot.

"I didn't intend on staying in Castleford as long as I have," I finally manage to say. "And so now I am just starting to move on, as it were."

She is studying me. She smiles then. "Ah, I sense a hometown romance."

It happens before I know it. Maybe it's the lack of sleep, maybe it's the guilt I feel about Doug, maybe it's the fact that I am nervous. Whatever it is, tears spring to my eyes and I am forced to look away, covering them with my hand. I swallow, frantically trying to regain control.

Suddenly there is a light touch on my arm. Cassy Cochran is squatting down next to me. "I'm sorry, Sally. Can I get you anything?"

"No," I say abruptly, shaking my head. "I'm fine. I'm afraid I'm just not feeling terribly well today and I didn't want to cancel."

She reaches for my glass of water on the coffee table and hands it to me. Then she rises to retrieve a box of tissues from her desk.

"Thank you." In a moment, I am back in control. Perhaps more in control than in the past two days because I am so utterly embarrassed that the feeling overwhelms everything else. "I don't know what to say," I begin.

"Say nothing," she insists, sitting back in her chair. "We should have done as you suggested, I should tell you a little about me." She sits back in her chair and crosses her legs again. "You know the basics, I assume, my birth date and schools and things."

"Yes," I say, reaching for my pen and pad. The recorder is on, but I always feel more comfortable taking notes. It's easier to arrive at follow-up questions.

"So you know I was born in Cedar Rapids, Iowa," she says. "What you may not know is that my father had a drinking problem that caused him to float from job to job, and my mother was a secretary, an excellent one, and she essentially supported us. For all of his problems, I adored my father. He was wonderful. Of course I didn't see him much when he was drinking, because my mother would put him out. Anyway, he died when I was eleven. My mother and I, I'm afraid, have never gotten along very well—but I am her only child, so obviously we still have a great deal of contact. Anyway, we didn't have much money when I was growing up, but mother saw to it that I never missed out on anything. She really is a hero. I got to go to dances in pretty dresses. I got to be a cheerleader and I was encouraged by her to win scholarship money for college. And through a connection of her boss, I was able to go to Northwestern, which was not an inexpensive school."

So the mystery of her father is cleared up right away. I was right, there was a story there; he drank. She is throwing that right out there and I cannot help but wonder if she's doing so because after my little minibreakdown she thinks I'm a terribly sensitive—and neurotic—soul who will surely understand the delicacy of it all.

"I understand you went to UCLA," she says.

I nod and look up from my notes. "I know what you mean about your mother. My father died when I was nine. And like your mother, she supported us and really pushed me."

"It's a whole different generation, isn't it?" Cassy asks me. "Of course your mother is probably my age," she hastily adds.

"No," I smile, "she's older. Not much, but she's older."

"I suppose I should thank you," she laughs. "Did your mother go to college?"

I nod. "Yes. University of Rhode Island."

"My mother didn't," Cassy says. "I've tried to get her to go back—because she always wanted to." Her eyes drift away. "I don't know why, but she just doesn't seem to want to do anything like that."

"Perhaps she's not much of a people person," I suggest.

She turns back toward me. "That's exactly right," she says softly.

As Cassy resumes talking, I realize she is sharing this information about her father and mother because it is key to who she is today. She intimates that as a young person she may have developed an unhealthy tendency in relationships that was not very productive. She is politely managing to convey that her parents screwed her up, big-time, setting her up for future "difficult" relationships. She married young, to a man who would ultimately develop a terrible drinking problem like her father, and she eventually got sick and tired of reacting to his behavior and decided to change hers. She talks of the son she had with Michael Cochran, what a good boy he was and how, finally, years later her dream came true, her husband got sober. The only problem was that after two years of sobriety and twenty years of marriage, *he* left *her*.

I am somewhat stunned at this revelation, but manage to hide it. I merely continue to listen, acutely conscious that the tape recorder is running smoothly. In a matter of minutes, Cassy Cochran has managed to take a run-of-the-mill puff piece

and, with a thumbnail sketch of her life, transform it into a portrait of a fiercely bright, beautiful, impoverished young woman
who has spent her entire life trying to get over the death of her
father and the constant criticism of a very bitter mother.

"Do you think your mother's bitterness," I finally venture to
say, "stemmed only from difficulties in her married life?"

"Lord, no!" Cassy nearly cries. "Mother was born unhappy.
My uncle used to talk about my grandfather building her a tree
house in hopes she'd move out." We laugh, but then she looks
vaguely horrified. "Oh, Sally, this isn't good. Please, you
cannot—"

I've raised a hand. "No. Don't worry. I'm not interested in
causing your mother any more grief. It's just that I find it interesting she was so unhappy when, it appears, she remained in
the situation with your father by choice."

"Well if she hadn't, who could she blame all of her troubles
on?" Cassy clasps a hand over her mouth. "Oh, Sally." She
drops her hand. "*Really*, this is a minefield. And it *is* boring, believe me, the same old thing, over and over."

I smiled. Okay, off the hook for now. "All right. So why don't
you tell me about meeting Jackson."

"And then I met Jackson!" she begins, a light coming into her
eyes.

There is a soft knock on the door and Chi Chi's head pops in.
"I'm sorry," she whispers, "but Alexandra and Will say there's
an emergency. Can you come out?"

"Tell them to come in."

In a moment the DBS anchorwoman comes striding in and I
am very surprised at how slight she is. Tall but very thin. The
trademark blue-gray eyes are even more vivid in real life (there
is a Halloween mask of her that has been selling well the last
two seasons), and her thick black-brown shoulder-length hair
shines with good health. Unlike her TV persona, however, she
is wearing a DBS News T-shirt, tucked into blue jeans and secured with a belt whose buckle, if I am not mistaken, is in the
shape of the state of Kansas. Behind her is an athletic-looking
man with rumpled brown hair, who is shuffling through a
sheaf of papers on his clipboard.

Alexandra Waring looks at me. "*Expectations*, right?"

I nod. "Yes."

The anchorwoman turns to Cassy as much as to say, *Get rid of her.*

I stand up. "I'll wait outside until you're through."

"No," Cassy says. "Sit down." To Alexandra she says, "Go ahead." When the anchorwoman doesn't say anything, Cassy says, "The piece is not coming out for six months, for heaven's sake. Go ahead."

Waring shakes her head.

Cassy looks to the man. "Will?"

He looks up from the clipboard where he has been making notes. "She's right. This is not something—"

I save everybody some time and simply get up and walk over to the door. "I'll be outside." I close the door behind me. "Hi," I say to Chi Chi.

"Always a crisis," Chi Chi says sympathetically.

"That's what makes it the news department," I say diplomatically, waltzing over to a chair.

"Can I get you something?"

"No, thank you." And in that moment I remember that my tape recorder's in there, still running. I suddenly feel a little cocky. *Don't want me to know what you're talking about, eh?* I sit there for quite a while, almost forty minutes. Then Alexandra Waring comes out, followed by the man named Will. She stops in front of me. "I apologize for being rude, but you're in news, so you understand." She breaks into a smile and it transforms her face. She is suddenly much softer, approachable. "At least I *hope* you understand."

Alexandra Waring is one of the more interesting people in TV News. Rumors about her abound. Some say that, at thirty-six, she's unmarried because she's gay; some say she's unmarried because she doesn't have the time or inclination to be married; some say a widely publicized engagement a while ago to a TV producer devastated her.

Given her track record in TV news and her achievements during the last six years, I am not convinced this woman could have enough emotional energy left to be sexual in any capacity, but that's just me. Looking at her today I don't have any sense of what she might be. Strike that. I get the sense she is heterosexual, but I could be confusing class with sexuality. I've done it before. Exquisitely attractive women can be gay, they do not have to wear work boots. There are big ham-fisted "yous and me" kind of guys that are gay. There are terribly masculine women who are straight, and perfectly groomed, dapper men with a slight sway in their step who are straight, too. In other words, I have been so wrong so many times about so many people that I know better than to decide anything without actually consulting the person in question.

My sense, though, is that she is not likely gay. She is strong, intense, willful, but I don't sense the other. But then, what do I know?

"Anyway," she says to me, holding out her hand, "I'm Alexandra."

We shake hands. "It's an honor to meet you. Sally Harrington."

She turns. "And this is our executive producer, Will Rafferty."

We say hi and shake hands, but from his expression I can tell he is anxious to get back to whatever it is they're working on.

"Well, we've gotta go," the anchorwoman says. "But I'll see you soon, right?" She is backing out of the reception area. "Cassy said you want to talk to me."

"Yes."

"Oh!" she says, remembering something. She comes back. "I thought you might like to know—they've found the murder weapon in Castleford. It's a handgun that was reported stolen in a house burglary in Southampton, Long Island, last spring."

My mouth has dropped open. "How...?"

She is backing away again. "Smells like an organized-crime hit to me." And with that, she is gone.

I hear someone laughing. I turn around to see Cassy leaning against the door frame of her office, arms crossed over her chest. "We don't mess around. We check up on our interviewers."

"But how did she find out about the murder weapon?" I say.

"I've learned not to ask," Cassy says, waving me back into her office. On the way in she hands me my tape recorder, which is turned off. We resume our places and I set the recorder back up on the table and Cassy starts talking about her philosophy of life, how one can change one's thinking and live life differently at any point, and how people, like her, have to. "I used to think the goal in life was to have everything stay the same," she says. "I've learned the hard way that life is *about* change. Not the essential goodness in us, that should be a constant, but our relationships, our work, our goals should always be in a state of change, be a work in progress—" she shrugs "—otherwise we're dying, aren't we?" She looks at her watch. "Uh-oh. Sally, I'm sorry, but—"

"No, it's okay," I say quickly, reaching to turn off the recorder. "But we're still on for tomorrow, aren't we?"

"At two," Chi Chi says from the door that I did not hear open. "Cassy, Mr. Vandersall is here for his three o'clock appointment."

"So you'll be here at two tomorrow?" Cassy asks me, rising from her chair.

I hurry to get my stuff together. "Yes. That will be great. Thank you so much for making time today." I jam everything into my briefcase and walk with her to the door, where she turns to face me. "Eat a good dinner tonight," she advises, "and get some rest."

I look at her.

"You said you weren't feeling well," she reminds me.

"Oh. Right." I had forgotten. The fear and guilt kicks in again.

She turns her head slightly, in question.

"It's a romance thing," I hear myself explain.

"We've all been there," she says kindly. She gives me a slight pat on the back that I know means "good luck."

I think I'm going to need it.

17

I try to call Joe Bix right there from the reception area outside Cassy's office to find out if he knows the police have found the murder weapon in the Meyers murder. Not only do I not get a dial tone on my cell phone, but there is horrible high-pitched screeching sound that threatens to pop my eardrum.

"You're welcome to use the phone on the table," Chi Chi says. "I'm afraid no electronic signals can come in or go out of the complex without being encoded or decoded through our satellite band."

"Through your what?"

She smiles. "West End is one of the largest repositories of electronic information in the world. We have to take precautions against contamination."

I squint at Chi Chi slightly. "So you're saying it has nothing to do with security? After the Jessica Wright kidnapping?"

Chi Chi gives her head a little shake. "I wouldn't go there."

I sit down on the couch and scoot over toward the phone. "It's long distance," I warn.

"Dial two first," she tells me, nonplussed.

"Usually it's nine or eight."

"It's not the usual kind of phone line," she informs me. "Let me know when you're through and I'll have security call you a cab."

I call the *Herald-American* and page Joe Bix. I am patched through to him. What Alexandra Waring told me is true. The murder weapon, Joe says, was found this morning in a sewer on Ralston Avenue. It's a handgun that was reported stolen in a burglary from a home in Southampton, Long Island, the year before.

"Do we know why Meyers was in Castleford yet?" I ask.

"D'Amico might know, but he's not saying. He got a ton of calls after our story ran this morning. It's great, wait until you see it. Listen, do you have anything on Crazy Pete yet? And by the way, when were you going to tell me that he was last seen sleeping over at your house again? Al's throwing a fit."

"Don't worry about it," I say. "Anyway, Pete's tucked away in a safe house."

There is a decided pause. "You're kidding. Who put him there?"

"The D.A.'s office."

He gives a low whistle. "He must know something. I think there's thirty thousand dollars in the state's whole witness protection program. So where'd you get this? Your boyfriend?"

Pang. "What does it matter?"

"Yeah-yeah-yeah," he mutters.

"What are you getting from your friend at *Newsday?*"

"Not much at the moment," he admits.

"Well, we need to get an inside line on the Island. I say go to Royce, better yet, go to Royce Senior—"

"No way!" Joe says.

"Listen to me, Al Senior used to play golf down at Augusta with that whole Locust Valley lockjaw gang. Get him on the phone to find out what people know about Meyers, his business, his government contracts, whatever. Because one of those guys will know somebody who does know, and they'll jump for Royce Senior when asked."

"Good idea, I never even thought of that."

I hang up and look at Chi Chi. "I don't suppose it would be possible to reach Alexandra Waring, would it?"

"We can always try," Chi Chi says, picking up the phone. In a minute, she rings her call through to the phone next to me. Some man is holding on the other end and when I speak, he says, hang on, and then Alexandra comes on the line.

"I don't suppose there's any chance you'd tell me how you found out about the murder weapon being found in Castleford this morning," I say.

"Not a huge chance," she agrees. "But maybe."

"Well, let's put it this way," I say, "might there be other information available to you that we might find useful?"

There is a knowing chuckle. "Where are you?"

"Outside Cassy's office."

"Let me send someone up to get you. We'll talk about it."

Within minutes I find myself being led through the labyrinth of floors below ground to end up in the DBS newsroom, a massive place—full of people and machines—that is located off the main studio that's used for the nightly broadcast. My escort points to Alexandra Waring, who is standing in the doorway of a video-editing booth, reading through some papers. She glances up and pushes off the doorway. "Hi."

I say hi.

I follow the anchorwoman down a long hall, through a security door—activated by her handprint, for heaven's sake—and through another labyrinth of hallways. Then we go through a door to find an older man sitting at an old-fashioned oak desk, scribbling with a pencil on paper. This, Alexandra says, is the mastermind behind the entire electronic operations of the Darenbrook Communications empire, Dr. Irwin Kessler.

Dr. Kessler appears to be something between Sergeant Schultz on *Hogan's Heroes* and R2D2 in *Stars Wars.* I have no idea what he is explaining to me as he hands me a form that swears I will not duplicate anything in the computer banks. The paper also advises me that what I do on this computer terminal will be monitored and recorded. I sign it and Alexandra leads me to yet another room and closes the door behind us. There is one computer bank and two chairs on wheels. She gestures that I should take the one in front of the terminal, and she sits on the edge of the other chair beside me. While she does something to prime the computer for me, I look around. It's as though we are in a hermetically sealed space capsule.

"The question is," the anchorwoman says, squinting at the screen, "what is this information worth to you?"

"Name it," I counter.

She glances over. "Well..." Her eyes return to the computer. "I could ask for a peek at your piece on Cassy before you turn it in." She looks at me. "Just to correct the spelling, of course." Her eyes move back to the screen.

I consider this. "How about," I say, "I fax you a copy of the article at the same time I turn it in to *Expectations?*" She looks at me. "Just so you can correct the spelling *with* Verity and leave me out of it."

"How about," she says, bringing up a search engine on the screen, "you fax it to me one hour before you hand it in?"

I think about this. What do I care? Actually, I should care a lot. If Verity found out I gave anybody an early copy, she'd hit the roof. Any editor would, because it would mean the subject could descend with a team of lawyers before the story ever got on the stands. The editors want the lawyers to descend *after* the issue is out, the more publicity then the better. So if I say I will do this, I could kiss goodbye any future assignments from Verity or anyone else.

"I'm sorry, but I can't do it," I say, standing up. "I can't fax you a copy of anything at all."

"I see," Alexandra says, typing "Anthony Meyers, Riverhead, New York" into the search engine before hitting Enter. Within seconds the screen is covered with information. "Did you know he has a younger brother, John? And that there's a missing-person report on John in Tampa, Florida?"

"What?" I exclaim, sitting down and scooting next to her. "That's Johnny Boy," I say. "He worked for my father when he was a teenager."

The screen goes black. "What's wrong?" I cry, looking at her.

"We don't have a deal yet," the anchorwoman explains.

"But what can I do? You expect me to hang myself professionally?"

"If you want to write for magazines," she says, "then why do you care so much about this murder story?"

"Because it's news and it's my town and my beat and what the hell business is it of yours, anyway?"

At this, she bursts out laughing. She hits a key and the screen illuminates. She gets up. "You have fifteen minutes. Study it carefully, you can't write anything down."

I don't bother answering, there is too much to read. The database or whatever it is that I'm looking at is some sort of combination of the wire services, credit services, the Darenbrook newspapers, affiliate station newsrooms and some kind of government system that probably shouldn't be accessed. Not only do I have a bio on Anthony Frederick Meyers, but I have his social security number, his driver's license number, a list of bank accounts, credit cards, mortgage agreements and on and on.

A blinking line indicates breaking news, which is his murder; there is also a blinking cross-reference to his brother John. As Alexandra said, the Tampa Police Department has issued a missing-person report on John. I key into this. He was last seen four days ago in Tampa.

Huh. The day before his brother was murdered in Castleford.

I go back to the victim's dossier and into the cross references about his business. I try to memorize as much information as I can, and note how most of his assets are under his wife's name. There are no numbers on the business itself, just a list of current contracts, which mean nothing to me, nonetheless I try to memorize them.

What else? I scan and read. Three kids. He's a registered Democrat, belongs to Spring Glen Golf Club, handball champ men's division 1986, owns 1962 left-wheel Jaguar, got a ninety-seven-dollar rebate on a Sears refrigerator.

This is certainly an eclectic database.

Before I know it, Alexandra Waring is back. "I'm afraid time's up."

I want to look at one more thing, but the computer has seemingly shut itself down. I stand up, looking at her in awe. "This is really something."

She smiles. "I'm glad you think so."

She escorts me outside, where I thank Dr. Kessler, who says, "You haf never been here, remember that."

Alexandra winks at me and waves me on to follow. In the elevator I thank her. "I don't suppose—" I begin, wondering if I might ever get on that machine again, but she is shaking her head.

"Like Dr. Kessler says, 'you haf never been here.' I just wanted to give you a jump on your story. The missing-person angle on the brother should make a good headline for your paper tomorrow."

"But I didn't promise you anything," I say, mostly to reassure myself that I didn't.

"Just write a fair story on Cassy," she tells me. A security guard is waiting for me when the elevator doors open. I get out, but Alexandra does not. "Bye."

The elevator doors are not even closed before I'm fumbling

for my pen and paper, determined to write down everything I saw on that computer. "Just a minute, okay?" I ask the security guard, moving over to write on his countertop.

I write and I write and I write. Then I reread my notes and add some things. Satisfied, I thank the guard and go out to the cab. Then I scan my notes again after we start driving. I don't care if I get carsick; this is great. I can hardly wait to get to my room; I race down the hallway and burst in, grabbing the telephone to find Joe Bix.

"Joe! Get this. There's a missing-person report in Tampa, Florida, for Tony Meyers's brother, John. He was last seen in Tampa the day before Tony got murdered." And then I go into details, moving on all the information I can remember from the database.

When I've finished, he says, "Damn. I can't believe it. How did you get this?"

"A good reporter never reveals her sources," I say.

"Damn," he says again. "Well, girl, you just got yourself a shared byline for tomorrow's front page."

"Gee, thanks a lot," I say. "I could dictate the whole thing and get it all to myself if I wanted to."

"But you don't want to because you're a big-shot magazine writer now," he tells me.

I am distracted now, hoping against hope the flashing message light on the telephone signals a message from Spencer.

I get off with Joe and fax him my handwritten notes as follow-up. Then I listen to my messages. "I can't believe I might be able to see you," Spencer's voice says. "I've cleared the deck on my end, and I'm just sitting around here in my office waiting for you to call." There is a pause. "I'm so very glad I've found you, Sally."

I call his office. "I've cleared the decks here, too. I'm free until tomorrow around ten."

"You're kidding!" Spencer cries in a way that makes me feel weak. "Can we meet now?"

My heart is pounding. "Yes. Right now."

I have no defense except to say that physically I have never responded like this to anyone before. Never this free, never this easy. Somehow Spencer has unlocked something in me that I had no idea existed at all. Passion. I know that when I read certain books sometimes, or see certain movies, I can be intensely aroused, but somehow that passion always seems to dissipate when trying to carry it out in reality. I hate self-help stuff, but I must confess I have looked at some of it, wondering if maybe what some professionals hint can happen has something to do with me—that I have a lack of trust, that I hold back because...

Oh, hell, I don't know; all I know is I want to have sex with this man again and I want it this minute, I don't care, I don't want to think, I just want to be there.

He gives me an address on the East Side.

Within twenty minutes I have showered and changed and am downstairs getting a cab. I feel like I'm some sort of crazy person. My heart is pounding and I am excited and happy and terrified and feel like I'm floating outside of myself. As we arrive at the address, it's as if I'm watching the cab pull up beneath the awning of the building. I pay the driver and the doorman opens the door for me and I feel a slight tremor in my shoulders as I get out and look up and realize that I am here. I know what I am about to do—I'm stone-cold sober—and I float into the lobby and tell the concierge who I am here to see. He calls up and he smiles and tells me to go right up, 17B, and I walk through the hallway and stand by the elevator. I smile at a little girl holding her mother's hand and we all get in the elevator and I push seventeen. The little girl says hi to me and I say hi back and we arrive at seventeen and I walk out into the hush of the thickly carpeted hallway. I see Spencer at the end of the hall, smiling, waving to me, and I hurry down and in a moment I am in his arms again, and my mouth feels normal now, because the pressure is back on my lips. I don't see anything of the apartment because we go right into the bedroom and fall on the bed and start taking off each other's clothes, and I only feel right, I only feel good, and when he is inside me I feel normal again, I feel at home. *This is where I belong,* and he tells me, "Sally, I love you," and I think it's crazy, but I believe him, and I feel like I'm being lifted to another world, where all feeling is exquisite and all heartache has been left far, far behind.

18

I blow off everything to stay the night with Spencer. Now, in the light of morning, I am riding in a cab back to my hotel and I am scared again. I didn't call Doug at all yesterday.

Going up in the elevator of my hotel, I realize this is ridiculous. I have never made love so many times in my life. I suppose this is what a honeymoon is like, and that very topic came up in passing—around midnight last night, when we got up to make scrambled eggs for dinner.

Until this morning I have never been able to imagine myself married. Curious that when it should happen, I should visualize marriage with someone who is practically a stranger.

I know I have a lost my mind and yet I don't care.

Well... Yes, of course I do, but I have the strangest sensation that I am saving my own life. As if Spencer is a lifeline, and until now I have been drifting away, slowly dying.

There are no messages for me and I am both relieved and curious that there is no message from Doug. I remind myself again that we are not in a committed relationship. (I'll say.)

I order coffee and yogurt and Danish up to the room and hit the shower. When I come out, I sign for breakfast and place a call.

"Hi," I say.

"You sound funny, dear," Mother replies.

"Funny? What do you mean?"

"I mean we've talked more on the phone in the past two days than we have for a month here in town."

I laugh. "Well, I was just calling to see if you are, by chance, free for lunch this weekend?"

"I thought you sounded funny."

"Mother, I just want to talk, get your advice, maybe."

"I knew it. I heard it in your voice."

"Mother! Please, it's no big deal."

She decides not to argue the point. "Let me know when, darling, and I will make myself free."

"Sunday?"

"It's a date. Brunch at my house," she says. "By the way, Sally, that was quite a piece this morning. I'm afraid to ask how you manage to co-write articles when you're not even here, but I thought it was very good. Explosive. I worry about Johnny Boy being missing. He was such a nice young man and your father was fond of him. You don't suppose…"

"I don't know. He may just be in hiding because of what happened to his brother."

"Then I should think he would have taken his wife and children with him."

"Good point, Mother." When I get off with her, I reach for my pen and make a note. Maybe Johnny Meyers was in on the murder. But why? I saw on the computer yesterday that he's a builder in the Tampa area, nothing big, private homes, an independent contractor.

I check the time. Ten-thirty. I've got a few minutes before I need to review yesterday's tapes of Cassy Cochran. I call Buddy D'Amico.

"How the hell did you know Johnny Meyers is missing?" he says as a greeting. "I thought you were supposed to be working on your fancy schmancy magazine piece."

"Between the fancy and the schmancy I had some time," I say.

"So what do you want, Sally?" he sighs.

"I want to know if you think Johnny killed his brother."

"Now, what makes you think that?"

"Well, if he's in fear of his life," I say, "wouldn't he have taken his wife and kids into hiding with him?"

"Who's to say they aren't?"

My mouth parts. "Really?"

"I'm not saying anything."

"Well, you're saying something, I just want to get it straight."

"Goodbye, Sally." He hangs up.

Oh, well. I make my next call.

"Attorney Wrentham," Doug says gruffly.

"Hi."

Pause. "Hi. Where have you been?"

"Writing the story of the century," I say.

"I saw."

I realize he is referring to the *Herald-American*.

"I'm impressed that a glamorous New York writer like yourself can still get around out here."

He is being obnoxious and I decide it is because I didn't call.

"So how are you?"

"Fine."

Yeah, he's mad. "So how's Crazy Pete?"

"He's fine."

"Well, I just wanted to touch base. I'm coming home tonight."

"I've got something on for tonight," he says.

Okay, so he's going to be like that. Unbeknownst to him, it only sends a huge wave of relief.

When I replay the early part of the interview tapes with Cassy from yesterday I want to die. I cannot believe I sat there and nearly burst into tears within the first five minutes of meeting her. Some big-shot journalist! I sound like I'm in junior high school. I can't imagine what she must think of me.

Well, it can't be helped. All I can do now is make sure I am professional from here on in.

When I reach West End I am focused. Today, I have decided, I am going to ask the questions that will give me a framework of her life, a framework that will hopefully show me what angle I should take on this piece.

"Good afternoon!" she says brightly, coming out of her office with her hand outstretched. "We've cleared everything off my schedule, Sally, so it's just you and me. Come on in."

It is a gorgeous day outside and the view from Cassy's office looks particularly beautiful. A Circle Line cruise ship is chugging up the Hudson. "That's where we should be," Cassy says, following my eyes. "Not cooped up in here."

I shrug. "If you like—"

"No, I really shouldn't. I need to stick around here for a while." She is dressed in white slacks today and a blue cotton pullover blouse. She is wearing the same strand of pearls as yesterday, but today her earrings are gold hoops. Her hair is neatly piled on the back of her head again and I wonder what she looks like with it down. And when she wears it down. Or if she ever does, for I have never seen a picture of her like that.

This time I deliberately take the chair she sat in yesterday and start setting up my gear, explaining that, if she doesn't mind, I would like to ask questions today. What I don't say is that I hope she'll sit on the couch, so I can look down on her this time.

"I do better that way, anyway," she tells me, dropping down on the couch, crossing her legs and resting an arm along the back.

I start the tape recorder and sit back in the chair, crossing my legs.

We talk a little bit about how she has set up DBS, who reports to whom. We trace some of its early history, how she was hired originally as the executive producer of DBS News and very quickly found herself recruiting affiliates to form the network. She explains how desperately they wanted to get on the air early, during the summer reruns, when they had a much better shot at attracting viewers. Then she tells me how she suddenly found herself in charge of *The Jessica Wright Show,* too, and then the whole darn network.

She runs down the divisions of DBS beginning with DBS News. Alexandra Waring is managing editor and Will Rafferty is executive producer. Under the news umbrella is the international news division in London, headed by the division's former executive producer, Kyle McFarland; two news magazine shows that are both produced out of New York; and a documentary and video distribution unit, also run out of New York.

DBS Talk is headed by Denny Ladler, executive producer of *The Jessica Wright Show.* The division also includes the new Alicia Washington vehicle, *Hopeless in the House,* and a morning talk show originating from the West Coast.

Cassy freely admits that DBS Sports, the network's newest division, is covering everything no one else will, which means the lesser tennis and golf tournaments, a lot of soccer and minor league baseball and hockey in local markets. The division has even covered its share of fishing tournaments. "It's making money," she is quick to add.

"But the bread and butter of the network remains *DBS News America Tonight with Alexandra Waring,* Monday through Friday at 9:00 p.m., followed nightly by *The Jessica Wright Show,* at 10:00 p.m. These two hours of programming are broadcast, in English, around the world over the Hargrave World Communications Network to eighty-three countries," Cassy says proudly.

She gets up to get me a complete list of network officers. "Which brings me to one of the more interesting aspects of DBS," I say, scanning the list.

Her eyebrows go up.

"At least half the significant players at this network are women."

"Yes," Cassy confirms.

"Which is very unusual."

"Very," she agrees, smiling.

I gesture. "Well? Any comment?"

She shrugs. "I don't know, I guess we simply make use of the best people we can find, and we've found a lot of great women. And since we're successful, it has obviously been the right decision."

"So you're going to tell me your executive in charge of sports is a soccer mom, right? That's why you guys cover it?"

She laughs. "Well, she is, as a matter of fact. But if you're number four or five in town, why *not* cover soccer? It's wildly popular with some demographic groups, so for that coverage we go to different sponsors. Trust me, Sally, if it doesn't work, if we can't make money, then we're not doing it. If we are, then you know it's working and we're making money."

"But you don't have a *Jerry Springer*-type show."

"No."

"Why not?"

She shrugs. "We don't want to."

"But it would make money."

"Not enough to get me to put it on the air!"

We move into her relationships with the staff, who's been here from the beginning, who's new, what she saw in each. After about a half hour, it is clear that her favorites happen to be the network's two biggest stars, Jessica Wright and Alexandra Waring.

"To all reports, Cassy, you seem to have a genuine friendship with both Jessica and Alexandra."

"Oh, yes. We're very close."

"You socialize, shop together—"

She is nodding, smiling. "I know they're significantly younger than I am, but I—well, in all honesty, I consider them two of my best friends. Next to my husband."

"Really?" I say, making a note. "Won't that make it rather difficult if you have to fire them someday?"

"Good grief," she says, frowning.

"And what about contract negotiations? Aren't you trading on a certain amount of goodwill when you do that?"

"Aren't you the hardhearted Hannah," she says.

"Well, it's not exactly normal for management to be that close to the talent," I point out.

Cassy shrugs. "I don't know how we could be otherwise. We've been through so much together." And then she launches into a description of what it had been like building the network, inventing as they went along, the terrible pressure—the hours, the pace, the underfunding in the early days. I get the picture: they are like soldiers struggling to gain ground and then hold it.

"In Jessica Wright's autobiography," I say, "she makes no bones about having had a bad drinking problem when she first arrived at DBS."

Cassy nods once, as if to acknowledge that she knows what I'm talking about.

"And then she stopped," I say. "She says that if it hadn't been for the people at DBS, she would never have gotten help. Did you have something to do with that?"

"You'll have to ask Jessica."

I make a note. And star it. The answer might as well have been yes.

We talk awhile about Alexandra Waring and she tells me how it was her former husband, Michael Cochran, who originally "discovered" Alexandra anchoring the news in her hometown of Kansas City. Michael brought her to New York to his station, WWKK. I am familiar with the story but listen politely as Cassy talks about Alexandra's ratings taking off, her move to network news as a Washington correspondent and how she came to Jackson Darenbrook's notice when she was shot on the steps of the Capitol building. It is quite a story. The part I didn't know was that after Jackson signed Alexandra as the face to launch his new TV news network, it was Alexandra who urged him to lure Cassy back into news as their executive producer. Alexandra had been playing the hunch that Cassy was bored being a station manager, even if she had been the first woman to achieve the position at a New York station.

We circle back into the early days of DBS.

"Um," I say, biting my lip slightly in apprehension of bringing up this next topic, "yesterday you mentioned that it was only after your husband, I think you used the phrase, 'got sober,' that he separated from you."

Cassy nods. "Yes, that's right."

"How did you feel? I mean, presumably the years he was drinking couldn't have been so great."

She meets my eye directly. "How did I feel about what exactly, Sally?"

"That once he stopped drinking, your marriage wasn't working."

"Who said it wasn't working?" she asks quietly.

I hesitate. "Well," I say carefully, "since you got divorced, I am assuming that the marriage wasn't working the way it once had."

"You mean, like it was broken and we just threw it out?" she asks.

"I just wondered how you felt."

Cassy nods thoughtfully, her attention leaving me and drifting to the wall of windows. She waits a full minute before speaking. "Let me put it this way," she says, bringing her eyes back, "I took my marriage vows extremely seriously. When Michael stopped drinking, he came to realize that the drinking had held him back in many ways. And quite naturally, I think, he wanted to see the world." She pauses. "He wanted to go— and I didn't want to go—and we decided it would be better if he went on to see the world without me."

"I would have killed him," I blurt out.

She looks startled. "Excuse me?"

"I said I'd have killed him."

"Sally!" She says this in a warning tone, letting me know that my opinion is not a factor. I'm to merely take down what she's so carefully and tactfully phrasing.

"I'm sorry," I say, and I mean it. But I still had to say it. You have to provoke people sometimes, to get them to further explain themselves. It's rotten, really, but you do what you have to do in this line of work.

"Michael and I shared a long period of our lives together," she says. "And we have one very terrific son to show for it. And if you talk to, or meet Henry, you'll see that there must have been an awful lot that was right in our marriage to have produced such a man as he."

"Truly, I apologize," I say again. "It's just that so often it seems like the guy, when he stops drinking, leaves the woman who's propped him up all those years. And the situation is rarely reversed."

She does not respond to this, but simply looks at me, waiting. There is tension in her jawline that warns me to back off. But I don't.

"You must have been upset when he left. For California, wasn't it?"

"California, yes."

"So you and Michael were separated before you started working for Jackson Darenbrook?"

She nods. And finally she smiles. "Yes, I was separated from Michael and we were getting a divorce. The thing is," she adds, "Jackson didn't know, so when we started working together, he thought I was happily married and acted accordingly."

"So when did you get interested in each other, before or after he made you president of DBS?"

She decides not to take my obnoxious question personally. _"After."_ She laughs. "Actually, Jackson and I did not get along in the corporate suite, not at all. If the truth be known, we fought all the time. Langley was the one who promoted me. I think that if Jackson had his way, he would have fired me."

Suddenly she jumps up. "Come on. I'm getting cabin fever in

here." She strides over to the door and opens it. "Chi Chi, I'm taking Sally for a tour."

She is off and I hastily grab my tape recorder and try to catch up. She leads me downstairs into Studio A, where the sets for the news and now for *Hopeless in the House* are located; she takes me through Studio B, where *The Jessica Wright Show* is taped; we go into makeup, the Green Room, the staging areas. We walk through the newsroom, upstairs to the electronic research division where we run into that funny Dr. Kessler, who slips and says, "Ah, she ees back," referring to me.

Cassy is utterly astonished.

"Alexandra brought me here yesterday," I confess.

"Into *here? When?*" Cassy says.

"After our interview." I add, "You'll have to ask her about it."

"Trust me, I shall," she says. Then she turns around, squinting. "Is Alexandra trying to make some sort of a back-door deal? What is she trying to do, get a look at your article?"

I laugh. She obviously knows the anchorwoman well.

We continue our tour, and she shows me the breathtaking view from one of the complex's "inner" offices, which looks out, not to the outside, but down into the cavern of Studio A. It is neat.

Then she whisks me over to B Wing, which houses the offices for DBS. The wing across the park is A, where the executive offices of the print divisions of Darenbrook Communications are found. As we walk, Cassy waves to a lot of people. On the third floor, we turn into one of the outer office areas where a young Asian woman is seated.

"Hi, Marianne," Cassy says. "This is Sally Harrington, who's writing that article on me for *Expectations*."

She stands up and shakes my hand.

"I was wondering what Jessica's schedule looks like next week, if she has time to talk to Sally."

Marianne makes a groaning noise and flips open a huge date book. "It's pretty crazy," she admits.

"Well, Sally will call you directly and see if you can work something out."

"Will do," she promises.

We walk on to the next office where there is a young man seated. This is Trevor, Alexandra Waring's secretary, and we go through basically the same thing with him about Alexandra's schedule next week.

Cassy then leads me back to the middle section of West End, but takes me downstairs to pick up a bottle of water from the cafeteria and then down another floor to the day-care center. Cassy is greeted with an enthusiastic "Hi, Mrs. C!" from the little ones who can talk. Then we walk outside, into the square.

"The setup of the complex," she explains, leading me along, "was based on the model my mother-in-law used for the Darenbrook newspapers and printing plants years ago. That's Jackson's mother, who is no longer living, Alice May Gaines Darenbrook. So if you sense a woman's hand at West End," she says, "it is Alice May's, as learned by her son." She is smiling now. We are standing underneath a maple tree. The breeze is blowing, the sky is blue, the clouds are moving slowly over the Hudson. This is a very beautiful, serene place.

"Sometimes," Cassy says, looking around, "I walk out here and wonder how many blessings can I have in this lifetime?"

I look down to the recorder in my hand. I'm getting all of this on tape.

"And I thank God, Sally, for all that I've been given in this life. I am very, very lucky." She pauses. A bird is chirping overhead in the tree. "So whatever has happened to me in the past, no matter how painful it might have been, it has led me here— to a place where I am profoundly happy."

Her smile is sentimental. "I am so grateful that Michael is alive and healthy, and that our son loves us both. And that we will be, no matter what, forever a family."

I don't know quite what to say. Except, perhaps, that she should not repeat this sentiment too many times to her current husband.

We talk for almost another hour and I am getting hot. Now that I've got her talking, I'm beginning to wonder how I will get her to stop. She seems unfazed by the heat. She is cool, confident now, yet her tone is sincere. Sometimes she talks about her life in such general terms that it sounds like a philosophy lesson.

Do I dare say it? I'm getting bored.

A shadow suddenly falls over us and I whip around to see an athletic-looking man, in his fifties or so, with the friendliest blue eyes I've seen in quite some time. Of course I know who this is.

"Well, hi there, gorgeous," a deep Southern drawl says, addressing Cassy. He moves around the bench to slide in beside her and places his arm around her shoulders. "What I want to know is, why the heck are you giving an interview to Schroeder's wife and not to one of *my* magazines?"

"Because that would be nepotism, dear," she laughs as he proceeds to give her a warm kiss hello. "Jack, this is Sally Harrington."

He gives me an energetic handshake. "Hello there, Sally. No offense about Verity's magazine. It's just she's got lousy taste in men."

"Jackson!" Cassy says, pointing to my tape recorder.

"What? You think Verity's going to print in her magazine that I said her husband's a total jackass?" He leans over to address the tape recorder. "Hi, Verity! How are ya? How's the boy? He's a nice kid. Your husband's a jerk!"

"*Jack,*" Cassy says.

"That's the real story, Sally Harrington," he says to me. "How Corbett got so rich. You should ask him how many people's work he's chopped up like firewood and sold by the roadside like it was just so much junk."

Cassy turns to me. "Sorry."

"Oh, no," I protest, "I'm interested."

"I bet she is!" she says to her husband.

There is a little beep signaling that it's time for me to change cassettes again, which I do while Cassy and Jackson talk about the trip to Georgia he has only just returned from. Although the couple do not touch each other, I suspect they long to. I wonder if Darenbrook's boyish charm is a characteristic Michael Cochran shares.

It's clear that our interview is coming to a close, primarily because Jackson is now standing up, fidgeting, wanting to know when they can leave for the country. "We've just got that one monkey-suit winging this weekend, right?"

"Just that one," she confirms.

Cassy tells him she'll pick him up at his office in a little while and then they will go. He goes bouncing off to the building and Cassy waits until he is inside before speaking.

Her eyes are twinkling. "So you've met Jackson."

"He's got a lot of energy."

"He's a powerhouse, all right," she agrees. "I apologize for his cracks about Corbett."

"That's all right. I don't really even know him. My dealings have been with Verity."

"I'd invite you to come over to our house this weekend," Cassy says, "but I promised Jackson it would just be us this weekend. We're just over in Cornwall, you know."

"I know."

She shakes her head. "I'm still a little amazed Verity thinks I'm worthy of a story like this. I'm doing a shoot with a fashion photographer, if you can believe it. I'm a nervous wreck."

I can see that she's serious. "You'll do fine," I tell her.

19

"Listen," Spencer says to me a bit breathlessly when I call him, "I've got to go out of town, but I think I can get back to the city tomorrow. Can you come in? And stay over at my place?"

Go home tonight and come back tomorrow, on Saturday?

My body reacts viscerally before my weary brain can even think about it. My body wants to be with him. But I can't do it. I have to go home and think about what has happened; I need to shake this. After two nights I feel like an addict, sick without Spencer—this man I scarcely know—and I'm only perking up at the thought of being with him. Alone. And what is that about? Wanting only to be alone with Spencer, touching him, not wanting to waste time going out, eating dinner or even seeing a movie. In other words, getting to know him.

"I wish I could," I say, "but I have to stay home this weekend."

A pause. "Are you going to see *him?*"

It hurts to hear that. It hurts because Doug doesn't deserve it and after two days Spencer's hardly in a position to lay claim over me.

What a mess. I've been acting like a lunatic. Actually, there is another word for what I've been acting like, but that profession usually gets paid money for doing what I have been doing.

"I doubt it," I say.

"Can I call you?"

"Sure."

"When are you coming back in?"

"I'm not sure."

"Will you stay with me when you come back?"

"I don't think so, Spencer," I say softly. "I have a lot of work to do. I need to have all my things organized around me."

I hear something that sounds close to panic. "Sally, you *are* going to see me when you come back."

"Yes." Although I suddenly feel sickened, because it doesn't sound like such a bad idea, simply not to see him next week. To just get my work done and let my head clear and see if there is really anything to see. Even in my dazed state I know damn well this sexual obsession and attachment has little or nothing to do with who we are as people. In fact, maybe that's why I feel sickened right now, because I suspect it is the unhealthiest part of me that is responsible for it.

"Of course I will," I say. I could be lying, but I feel compelled to at least placate him. I know Spencer is a little off; I mean, he is kind of, well, swoony. But he's also told me he used to have a bad cocaine habit and since he kicked it, a little over five years ago, he hasn't been the same. "Us," he says, is the first thing that has made him feel flush with energy and excitement.

"Spencer, we'll talk this weekend," I promise. "But we both need to get some sleep, a little time to think things over."

"If you sleep with him or something just don't tell me, okay?"

Sleep with Doug? Suddenly I am angry, angry enough to bring up what I should have brought up to Spencer at the beginning. "I couldn't possibly sleep with Doug, even if I wanted to. I can't do it until I know for sure I haven't made some sort of a—a medical mistake. I never even asked you about your sexual history."

There is a silence. "You mean like herpes."

I feel sick at the thought. I can't even mention AIDS. "Yeah."

"You think you might bring something home to him?" He is upset.

"I have no idea, do I?" I am upset, too. "It's not you, Spencer, but your ex. How do I know where she's been, what she's given you, or what you've passed on to me?"

"Or what your blond Adonis in L.A. gave to you," he says.

"I know where he was and that's why I broke up with him!" I say. "And I know where Doug's been and what precautions he took, and I know what my gyn has confirmed, as recently as six weeks ago—that I don't have, and never have had, any sexually transmitted diseases."

"So now you're asking me."

"Yes." I wish I hadn't gotten so upset, because if Spencer

does have something it's unlikely he's going to tell me about it when I'm yelling at him.

Damn it, this stinks. Five minutes and it's gone from bliss to problems. I want to go home, I want to forget about the whole thing.

"The truth is," Spencer says quietly, "I was treated for VD in grad school. I have had no trace of anything like that since." He pauses. "And I have had several follow-up checkups. Nothing. The last was not even three months ago."

I feel slightly better, but not great. Spencer and I have been fools. Lucky fools, maybe, but only time will tell.

"Sally," he says, "can't you just stop by my apartment on your way out of the city? Just for fifteen minutes or so? I could leave the office now and meet you. I swear I won't hold you up." He pauses. "I can't let you leave town feeling this way. I want you to leave knowing that maybe we were crazy to give in to what we did, but that we did it together—and I am not a total loss. I mean, you may find—and I hope you do—that there is a pretty good guy here. Who certainly means well because, well, I've been around, Sally, and I swear to God I know I've never met anyone like you. And I can't just let you slip out of my life because I screwed up the beginning."

"It wasn't just you," I murmur. And then I sigh. Although I find his words are making my heart pick up again, I still have a headache, my stomach doesn't feel great and I long for the sight of my little house and Scotty. "We'll see each other next week," I promise. Now I mean it. "I need to go home, Spencer. I need some time. And I need to talk to Doug. Because even if it turns out we don't—you know. Whatever. I can't let Doug go on thinking that everything is fine. Because obviously it's not. Or I'm not."

"There's nothing wrong with you, Sally Harrington."

I wish I could laugh, but I can't. Because something *is* obviously wrong with me. Why else would I be sitting here, thirty years old, telling a stranger that I've been having sex with for two days, that I need to tell the man I know I love that something's wrong with our relationship?

Spencer lets me go. I check out of the hotel and get the Jeep and start the drive back to Castleford. I have only gotten to the

East Side, near the entrance to the FDR, when I pull over in front of a delicatessen on First Avenue. I go inside and get a bottle of lemonade, get back into the car and drink it. And think. Then I pick up the cell phone and call Spencer's office. He has left. I call his apartment.

"Hello?" He almost sounds afraid.

"Hi, it's me," I say, my heart pounding.

"Where are you?"

"About three blocks from your building."

"Really?" Wisely he does not say anything else. He knows I'm on the fence.

"I want to see you," I finally say.

"Oh, Sally. Thank God. Come right over. I'll meet you in the parking garage."

I start the Jeep and drive over. As promised, Spencer is waiting in the garage of the building. I hand over the car, take the ticket. "It'll be about two hours," Spencer tells the attendant, and he puts his arm around my shoulders and leads me into the building. "I have to leave in a couple of hours," he says to me. "I can't get out of it."

I don't say anything. I'm too scared to say anything.

We take the elevator up to the hall that seems very familiar to me now. We go into his apartment and I lean over to pet his cat, Seela, and say hello. She is an orange tabby.

"Best bargain I ever got," he murmurs, taking my bag and briefcase and putting them down and coming back to me. He gently picks up the cat. "She cost five bucks and came with her own can of cat food." The cat purrs and rubs her head under his chin.

I close my eyes. Spencer puts the cat down and wraps his arms around me, holding me tight. "I'm so scared," I whisper.

"I know, I know," he murmurs back.

III
Appearances

20

The telephone is ringing and I am trying very hard not to hear it. Finally I give up and surface through the pillows. Scotty, eyes bright and tail wagging, is creeping toward me like G.I. Joe. He's trying to come up and lick my face in such a way that I won't consider him a nuisance and send him back down to the foot of the bed. He can't help it. He is so happy to be home. And, frankly, so am I.

I glance at the clock. It is nearly eleven in the morning! Poor Scotty. He has patiently let me sleep for ten hours.

"Hello?" I say, picking up the phone and sliding out from under the covers.

"Sally, it's Cassy Cochran calling."

"Oh, hi," I say, walking through to the living room to let the now-dancing Scotty out the front door.

"I'm so sorry to bother you," she says, "but I thought I should let you know as soon as possible. I have to go out of town for a few days next week and I'm not sure when I'll be back. With any luck, maybe Wednesday. Chi Chi will call you as soon as we know."

"That's all right," I say. "I've got a lot of other interviews to do."

"And Chi Chi's helping you set them up, right?"

"Yes, she's been great."

When I get off the phone, I wander into the kitchen to start some coffee. The long stretch of sleep has done wonders for me. That horrible heavy feeling in my head is gone and I don't feel so rocky. I don't even feel particularly guilty, perhaps because I took a long, hot soak last night when I got home and feel like the evidence is gone.

I haven't talked to Doug. And it is strange that he has not called.

I call his apartment. His answering machine picks up. "Hi.

It's Sally. I just woke up after ten straight hours of sleep. Give me a call when you can."

Next call. "Joe," I say to his answering machine. "I'm in Castleford. Let's get together and go over what you've got and what I've got."

Next call. Buddy's house. I get his wife. "Alice? Hi, it's Sally Harrington."

"Sally, how are you?"

"Great, thanks."

"Buddy tells me you're writing an article for *Expectations.* That's so exciting!"

"Yeah, well, we'll see. I just hope I'm up for the job."

"Oh, Sally, you are always so good at everything," she says good-naturedly. "Remember when you said you couldn't play golf? And you beat everybody?"

"Well maybe after I finish this piece," I say, "we can go for a round. Take the baby. Put the car seat in the golf cart. And I'll walk. Heaven knows, I need it."

"There's Buddy," she says. "Let me get him for you."

"This is a low blow, Sally Harrington," Buddy says when he comes onto the phone, "calling me at home on a Saturday."

"I just wanted to let you know that I'm here," I say innocently.

"Okay, thanks," he says.

"Wait a minute!"

"What?"

"Well, what's going on?"

"I'm coaching a girls' soccer team and we've got a tournament this weekend, that's what's going on." He hangs up.

It's okay. I'm used to it. Guess he hasn't caught the murderer yet.

"Hi," I say to my mother, "did you get my note that I took Scotty last night?"

"Are you joking?" she asks me. "If I came home and found Scotty gone without a trace, do you think *anyone* in Castleford would have slept last night?"

I laugh. "So where were you? Out gallivanting after midnight?"

"We went to a party, if you must know."

I hear someone in the background on mother's end of the phone and I am stunned. I know it is Mack. He couldn't have stayed over last night, could he have? With Mother?

"Mack says hello," Mother says. "He just arrived to help me stake out the new greenhouse."

Phew. I don't think I can handle two loose women in our family. "So you're really going to build it?"

"After all these years, yes, I'm really going to do it." She laughs a lighthearted laugh and I wonder how long, if ever, it's been since I've heard it. She sounds so young. "I'm doing it because Mack is going to build it for me. He's trapped some poor engineering student from the university into making this his senior thesis or some such thing."

I thank Mother for baby-sitting Scotty and we reconfirm our date for brunch tomorrow.

Scotty and I are getting ready for a run when the phone rings.

"I wasn't sure you were coming back," Doug says.

I feel a truly dreadful pang. "Well, I'm here."

A pause. "So what's up? How did it go? I figured when I didn't hear from you things were going well."

"She's quite a person," I say to him. "In fact, she reminds me of Mother."

"No one is like your mother."

"Well, I think if Mother had gone into broadcasting, she might have been like Cassy Cochran."

"Is she really that beautiful? Like her pictures?"

"She looks older in real life, but somehow it works to her advantage. Don't ask me how."

We continue to talk in a stilted kind of talk, as if it's been years, and I ask him if he wants to have dinner and, much to my relief—and then to my slight dismay—he tells me that he can't, he's made plans. He isn't volunteering what his plans are, either, which lets me know he is very angry.

"Let's meet for coffee this afternoon," he says. "Can you come into New Haven? Meet me at Barnes & Noble?"

This is even weirder. He doesn't want me to come to his apartment; he wants me to meet him at the bookstore at Yale. What could he possibly know?

"Sure. Four's fine."

When we get off, I know he knows. And it's weird how part of me realizes we have to break up, and another is absolutely scared at that thought. But how could Doug possibly suspect something already?

After Scotty and I go for a run, Joe Bix surfaces and tells me he'll have dinner with me—at my house—at seven-thirty.

I feel rested and much better after my run. Without showering or anything, I sit down at my desk and start playing my interview tapes with Cassy and transcribing them onto my computer. It's interesting to listen to us. The material is good. The only new interesting angle is at the end of the tapes of the first day, where there is a little bit left from when I left the recorder running in Cassy's office when Alexandra and Will Rafferty barged in.

"So that's the *Expectations* writer," Alexandra's voice says, as if I am a new species of animal.

"She seems very nice," Cassy insists.

"Pardon me if I find it a little hard to believe that Verity employs any 'nice' writers."

The three laugh. "But I think she has," Cassy says.

"Well this one is so nice," Alexandra announces, "she's left her recorder on so she can find out what we're talking about." And there the tape stops.

I turn the recorder off and sit back in my chair.

It is a great chair. It belonged to my father. It is walnut and has five legs on wheels, arms and spring action that lets me recline. Whenever I lean back to think, I smile because I can see my father.

I wonder what he would think of Spencer.

21

I see Doug sitting at a table for two in the café area of Barnes & Noble. He is wearing dress slacks and shirt, blue blazer and loafers. Cocktail party clothes, I surmise, but I vow not to comment on it. He kisses me hello on the cheek and has trouble meeting my eyes. I go up to get my café mocha and sit down.

"So are you ever going to tell me where Pete is?" I ask him.

He shakes his head.

"Even if I already know he's up at Carmella's cabin?" Carmella is an officer of the court who has helped out the D.A.'s office before with a "safe" place to stash a witness. I have no particular reason to believe Pete is at Carmella's, except that I like Carmella, and she's the only other person—besides me—who would take pity on Pete.

From the stony look Doug gives me I think I might have guessed right. "Anyway," I say, clearing the air with my hand, "is Pete being helpful to you guys?"

Doug suddenly looks very tired. He runs his hand through his hair and drops it on the table. "I warned Carter that he's crazy."

"Well, we all know that. But if he happens to mention why I had to be the one to find Tony Meyers's body, I'd appreciate someone telling me."

"I'm sure George Bush knows," Doug says. "Why don't you give him a call?"

I frown. "What are you doing with him, anyway? You obviously don't think he killed Meyers—"

"They're letting him go," Doug interrupts. "He's probably back in Castleford already."

"Good, thanks. It gives me time to wash the guest towels."

This gets a rise out of him. "*Don't* let him back into your house, Sally."

"What am I going to do? Let him sleep on the woodpile? His father's not here, who's going to look after him?"

"He can look after himself."

"What, with all the Masons and the aliens after him?" I say, breaking up. I can't help it. Neither can Doug; he's laughing, too. "Oh, my," I sigh, covering my face with my hands. "How did I ever get myself into this?"

"The murder? Or whatever it is that you're doing in New York?" Doug asks.

Slowly I bring my hands down. "I'm writing an article in New York."

"That's not what I meant."

We just sit there, looking at each other, waiting for the other to say something.

"Doug, what is going on?" I finally say.

"You tell me."

"I'm not sure," I say, "but I do know you're acting very strangely."

"No, Sally," he says quietly, "it's not me that's acting strangely. A few days ago we were talking about the future and now..."

I lower my eyes to my coffee. "And now what?"

"I came in Thursday night to see you. You weren't at the hotel. You weren't anywhere, and I finally gave up at three o'clock in the morning and I came back to New Haven."

"Why didn't you call me?" I say, knowing that my face is getting red.

"I called your cell phone, Sally. It was shut off."

"I mean at the hotel. Why didn't you leave a message, so I'd get it?"

"You didn't tell me you were going out," he says. "You said you'd be working at the hotel. You went to the theater the night before. But you didn't say you were going out again, and the fact that wherever you were, you were there long after the bars and clubs closed, tells me that maybe you were doing something you didn't want me to know about. And that sucks, Sally. I feel like a complete and total asshole. I'm sitting out here thinking about looking for a job in New York if things work out for you, and you're not even gone twenty-four hours and you're already doing your best to forget me." He leans forward. "Where the hell were you?"

"I was at the apartment of a book editor named Spencer Hawes," I say, an image flashing through my mind of me *wanting* to climb on top of Spencer at one point, doing exactly what Doug always wanted me to do. "I met him through Verity, he invited me to his party, I got loaded and went to sleep until the party was over and he rolled me into a cab. I'm not proud of it."

He is studying my face. I have been as honest as I can be. He has a choice now. He can ask me how many other people were at this party or he can let it go and tell himself things might be okay after all.

He relaxes a little, exhaling through his nose. But he fools me, choosing something in between, something that indicates he knows things are not okay. "Just so you know," he says over his coffee cup, "I'm going out with Jane tonight to a cocktail party. And then we're having dinner."

Jane. This is the woman we broke up over last time. He used to work with her and was dying to sleep with her and I told him to go ahead and get it out of his system and while he was at it, get out of my life. I suspect Jane is a little bit off emotionally, because she is wildly attractive and yet Doug didn't sleep with her, but chose to come running back to me after a few dates instead.

It suddenly—*duh*—dawns on me in this moment that of course Doug slept with Jane. That he had talked about Jane to me as I had just talked to him about Spencer, with a bunch of short, distorted facts. And now that I think of it, Doug has never said he didn't sleep with Jane, he had only intimated that he hadn't, a fact that I needed to believe in order to get back with him.

I am rationalizing, of course, trying to make myself feel less guilty about my betrayal. And Doug is sitting here, asking me to tell him there was no betrayal. But I can't. And he knows it. And so I guess he's planning to betray me tonight with Jane and has decided to tell me about it up front, daring me to tell him something to stop him.

The point is, I guess, our relationship really has just blown up. And I guess it's better like this, breaking up at once, rather than dragging it out. It's curious how little emotion I feel.

But it will come later, I know, the regret. I have never acted rashly in a relationship and lived to be glad about it.

"I think you've made a mistake letting Crazy Pete go," I say, surprising Doug by abandoning the subjects of love, sex and betrayal altogether.

"Did you ever pay that ticket?" he asks, swinging the topic even further away.

"I'm contesting it," I tell him. My cell phone is ringing. "Excuse me." I fumble for it, praying it's not Spencer.

"Sally? It's Joe." There is horrendous noise on his end. "Listen, dinner's off. If you want to talk, you'll have to come downtown to Gleason's parking lot."

"Gleason's?" But the line has gone dead.

22

Gleason's is a downtown Castleford bar and grill, but the real action is taking place at the old Tranowsky's Auto Body shop that sits on the other side of the parking lot. There are no less than seven fire engines present. Main Street is shut down, ambulances are waiting and it is no mere fire burning in the old shop—it's an inferno. Half the firefighters are hosing down surrounding buildings in an attempt to save Main Street, while the other half are pouring everything they've got into the ball of fire.

I can't find Joe Bix and it wouldn't be appropriate to talk to him, anyway, if I did. Too much is at stake. I yank on my galoshes and run over to join the civilian line that is forming to take sandbags off the back of an O'Hearn Construction truck and pass them down, in brigade form, to the men who are attempting to make a sandbag fire wall in case the wind shifts and the flames blow toward the Mobil station. Someone hands me a surgical mask to wear against the smoke and fumes and soot. We work and we work and we work. I hear Devon calling my name. He is taking pictures.

What has frightened us all are the two burning carcasses of cars that were parked near the auto body shop. Tranowsky's has been closed for several years and I can't imagine how a fire of such immense proportions could start in a building that is essentially made of cement and steel. It's summer; the power's off in the building; the windows are boarded up to keep kids and vagrants out. But the fire is here and we're all scared because besides the businesses that have survived on Main Street, we've got a whole block of empty industrial buildings just around the corner, and heaven only knows what has really been left in them. If they are anything like the auto body shop, this fire will rage out of control until it's destroyed what's left of our downtown.

Insurance crosses my mind.

My shoulders are aching and I am thinking about my father while I continue to work. He would be here. Though Castleford has a truly wonderful fire-fighting force of five companies, there is always the small-town backbone that brings everyone out to help in an emergency. In a way, I think, it's pathetic that we are using these sandbags. They are designed for floods. But it's what we're used to doing here, building walls out of sand-bags, and I'm sure even if we're in the way, the firemen wouldn't dream of stopping us.

I miss you, Daddy.

The fire is finally under control. There are only a couple of steel support beams and part of a hydraulic lift left standing in the auto body shop. Even the cars parked around Gleason's have been damaged by heat and fire and chemicals. A few hours ago the bar was made of natural shingle, weathered gray. Now it is black. The tar roof has melted, hanging off the side of the building like lopsided cheese on a burger. Soot and ash are everywhere. The streets are awash with water, chemicals, gar-bage and muck. The crowd watching has grown very large.

We've quit the sandbag line and I think how ironic it is that several men promptly light up cigarettes.

I see a friend of mine, Maggie, resting with some other fire-fighters. Her gas mask is pushed up over her sooty face and she looks beat. Her husband is a firefighter, too, and her brother and her uncle and so was her dad. I pull down my surgical mask under my chin and saunter over. "Quite a fire."

Maggie kicks her head toward the remains of the auto body. "It melted the steel. I can't believe no one was hurt."

"How did it start?"

Maggie looks across the scene to the fire marshal's car. "You'll have to talk to Dean."

"How do you think it started?"

Maggie looks at her companions. One of them says, "That was no ordinary fire," and there are murmurs of agreement.

"What do you think happened?"

"Someone friggin' blew it up," a firefighter suddenly de-clares.

No one contradicts this statement.

"You better get a statement from Dean," Maggie says. She is a lieutenant; she knows the rules.

"Yeah, okay," I say, moving away. "You guys are wonderful, you know."

"Thanks for working on the wall," somebody says.

I wave an acknowledgement, looking around for Joe. The fireman didn't say arson; he said he thought someone blew the building up, which is a very different thing. To be honest, rather often in Castleford—during the dreadful, lingering economic depression that persisted in the Connecticut Valley for a good part of the 1980s and 1990s—people were caught torching their troubled businesses or homes or rental properties to get their hands on insurance money. We once even had a creature who torched his house in an effort to get rid of his wife and kids so he wouldn't have to pay alimony and child support payments—so he could live the good life with his girlfriend. I assure you, he was not from Castleford.

But explosives. In Castleford? To risk this kind of investigation for an old auto body shop? Why on earth would someone do it? What insurance could possibly be outstanding on such a wreck of a nothing?

Which, of course, makes me wonder if perhaps there was something *in* the auto body that needed to be burned....

I finally find Joe sitting on a stool at Clancy's Saloon, drinking beer. This bar, a little farther down the street, near the courthouse, caters to a pretty rough crowd and is usually half empty. Given the luck of the draw tonight, however, just about everybody in town is stopping in for a drink. "That was nice of you," Joe says to me as I slide in to stand next to his stool, "to work on the wall."

I let the comment pass. Some people are brought up a certain way and others simply aren't, and I am frankly too tired to try and explain to Joe—who is obviously not from Castleford originally—why working on the wall is not "nice," but just what you do.

"Did you file your story yet?" I ask him.

He nods, sipping his beer. Then he sighs, looking at me out of the corner of his eye.

"What?"

"I'm waiting for you to tell me something I should have filed in my story."

I laugh and look at the bartender and order a glass of seltzer and a glass of white wine. "Who owns that building now, anyway?" I draw the basket of burnt popcorn toward me and then think better of it, pushing it away.

"Something called Tergar Inc."

"That's Bob Castile. Terry's his daughter, Gary's his son."

"Damn," Joe says, looking into his glass, "I knew you'd do that."

I smile. "You've got time to add a detail or two." When he just nods but continues to look at his drink, I say, "So what's wrong?"

The bartender brings me my drinks. I chug the seltzer down.

"The Meyers story's dying," he admits. "I got your notes and everything, but I can't get anything to gel."

I finish swallowing, put the seltzer glass down and reach for my wine. "It's not you, it's the police." I take a large swig of wine and it tastes good. "They're stuck. They've let Pete Sabatino go."

"I thought you didn't know where he was," Joe growls.

Now I take a polite sip of wine. "I just know he's out."

"Out from where?"

"I don't know—out. Anyway, I'm going to see Buddy tomorrow and I'll let you know if I find out anything."

He squints at me. "How are you going to see D'Amico on a Sunday?"

"The point is, I am." I know the timetable of the soccer matches tomorrow in Cheshire and I know which team Buddy is coaching.

Joe looks miserable. "I wish you'd cover this story. Al's driving me crazy."

"Did you talk to old man Royce? Get any Long Island contacts?"

"Oh, yeah. I got to talk to some old congressman who's got Alzheimer's."

I resist the urge to biff Joe one. There is something about this conversation that is annoying me. I don't know whether it's

Joe's lack of progress on the murder—and his sudden fatigue about it—or my suspicion that if Joe is sitting here drinking, then he has probably not written more than a couple of lines for tomorrow's edition about those firefighters who risked their lives tonight.

I'm not sure Joe has ever really gotten the local angle of the paper, that "local" means the people we know, and that our readers are hungry for news about them and *that* is the only edge we have over the *Courant*, the *Register* or the *New York Times.*

On the other hand, I am supposed to be going national writing for *Expectations* magazine, so why am I sitting here in a hometown bar, thinking I should be at the paper knocking out a firefighter story? Why do I want to spend time pursuing the solution to a local murder when I should be in New York working on my opportunity of a lifetime?

I must be tired, I decide. I must have smoke in my head. I must be a local. After my behavior the last couple of days, I know for sure I've lost my mind.

"So what do the Long Island papers say?"

"There's a question about how well his business was doing," Joe says, perking up a little. "One of my contacts says he lived way beyond his means."

"But it was his business. It wasn't a front for someone else?"

"According to the stuff you gave me—which was correct, by the way, thanks—the business was in his wife's name. Evidently he had some sort of bankruptcy a couple of years ago and did it to shelter his assets."

"Huh." I drain my wineglass. "What about here? As a kid in Castleford—what do people say about him?"

"Not much. He was quiet. C if not D student—"

"Really? Any sports?"

He shakes his head.

"Did he work?"

"Yeah. He did some odd jobs."

"Where?"

"Um, I don't remember."

I am getting mad again. "Did anyone see him here in town?"

"No."

"Well, stay on it, Joe, and keep me posted."

"Where are you going?"

"You've got my cell phone number." I walk away, think of something and come back. "And for God's sake, find out if there was a body in the auto body shop, will you? It's the first thing we should have thought of, that someone might be getting rid of Johnny Meyers's body."

Joe's eyes bug out. "I know there was an explosion, but no one said it was intentional. Someone said it was an old natural gas connection under the building that somehow got sparked."

"I would say that qualifies as someone blowing up the building," I tell him. I better get out of here before I tell him something else since Joe is the only person I have at the paper to follow up on the Meyers murder in my absence. I don't know what's wrong with this Meyers story, but what should be run-of-the-mill information here locally seems to be strangely hard to gather.

I drive over to the paper, let myself in through the back and climb the stairs. The city-desk editor and art director are with Devon, reviewing an amazing array of photographs Devon took at the fire. "Need any help?"

The city editor looks at me gratefully. "We sure do."

"I've got a list of the companies and commanders that were there tonight," I say, waving my notebook. "Get your best shots and I'll do my best to identify who is who."

"Write something, too, will you?" my editor asks. "Something descriptive. Joe's got a bad case of *Dragnet*, if you know what I mean."

Just the facts, ma'am, just the facts. Dry, bare-bones copy.

And so for the next three hours we work up an extra half-page special on the fire and I am very glad I stopped by. This is what working for a newspaper is all about.

When I finally reach home, Scotty is glad to see me. Since I was too lazy to turn on the circuit breaker to turn the lights on in the ladies' room at the paper, I had used the facilities in the glow of the Exit sign. And so when I go into my bathroom and look into the mirror, I can't help but burst out laughing. I can't believe no one said anything to me. I look like a chimney sweep, a *bad* chimney sweep, who has destroyed her blouse, slacks and nails, to say nothing of giving her hair a complete filth makeover. I strip down and jump into the shower. Then I get out, put a towel around my head, slip on my terry-cloth robe and go out to my desk.

I hit the play button on the answering machine and the sound of Spencer's voice surprises me. Frankly, I had forgotten about him. "Hi," he says softly. I become slightly mesmerized by his message, of how he misses me, until he gets to the part about maybe driving here tomorrow on his way back to New York. Part of me is thrilled by the idea and the better part of me dreads having to tell him no. I've got work to do. Besides, it is too soon to completely overrun what had been Doug's exclusive territory.

But I would love to see him.

The next message is, of course, from Doug, who sounds awful. "Please," he says, "can I see you, Sally? We've got to talk and I did a miserable job of it today."

I sigh. I don't know what to do. And I'm too tired to figure it out now. I walk through the kitchen to the back door to call Scotty. I need to feed him. He comes across the yard but then stops about three feet away, standing there, half smiling. He growls in play. He is tired of being ignored for days on end. *I am your best boy*, he is reminding me.

"I know, baby," I say, sitting down on the step and holding out my arms. Scotty loves to be hugged. I used to put him in my lap and hug him when he was a tremulous little stray. He trots over and I scoop his seventy-two pounds into my lap. I hug him and can still smell the traces of a skunk that got him a couple of weeks ago. "What should I do about Doug?" I ask him.

He makes a sound of pleasure in his throat.

"Okay," I say, putting him down and giving him a scratch behind the ears. "You're right. Talk to Mother."

He tries to lick my face. He may have teeth like a junkyard dog, but his delicate pink tongue seems as thin as paper, a very collie trait.

We go inside and I give Scotty dinner. I make myself a large bowl of yogurt and grapes and resume transcribing the Cochran interviews into my computer. It is peaceful, productive and quiet. Scotty and I both feel tired, but good.

And then Crazy Pete shows up.

23

"Before I offer you something to eat, Pete," I say, pulling the sash of my robe a little tighter and knotting it, "I'm telling you that you are not spending the night here tonight. I am taking you home. Doug says you'll be perfectly safe."

"How would he know?" Pete says, following me into the kitchen.

I turn around to frown at him. "Convince me otherwise."

"I know a *lot*, Sally," he whispers.

"Right," I mutter, directing him to a chair at my breakfast table. I am not in the mood for this.

"Sally!"

"Listen to me," I say, swinging around and putting my hand on my hip, "I know you *know* a lot of things, Pete, but I don't think you know anything about this murder. I think some people thought you did, but it's not George Bush and the Masons and the aliens!"

Slightly stunned by the ferocity in my voice, he sighs and sits down in resignation. "All right. I'll go home. If they're going to get me, they're going to get me."

I walk out to my desk to get my tape recorder, pop in a new tape, check the batteries and come back to the kitchen to thump it down in front of Pete.

"Once and for all," I say, walking over to open my freezer door to look inside, "you are going to give me the straight dope on what you know. No runaround, no innuendo, no weirdness."

"No weirdness," he agrees, eyes widening slightly as I pull a rib-eye steak out of the freezer.

"Okay, first off," I begin, throwing the steak into the microwave to thaw, "did you ever speak to Tony Meyers?"

"No."

"You never told him, for example, you knew a reporter who might be interested in something he had to say?"

"No."

I look at him. No runaround, no innuendo, no weirdness apparently leaves Crazy Pete with a very limited vocabulary. "Why was Tony Meyers at Kaegle's Pond?"

"I don't know."

"Well don't you think it's strange that you left a message for me to go there, and when I do, I find his dead body?"

"Yes."

"And you don't have any explanation as to how he got there?"

He hesitates. "No."

I rub my forehead, trying to be patient. "Surely you must have some thoughts about it, Pete. Or at least about who killed him."

He looks afraid to answer.

"Go ahead, it's all right. Say whatever you want," I encourage him.

"I think the Masons sent him," he says quietly, as if saying it that way will offend me less. "I think someone told him he should go there, and I think they know I told you to go there, too, but he was dead when you got there." He's beginning to tremble.

Oh, brother, I can't do this. It's like picking on a little kid.

Okay, one more time, I will play along with him to see if there is anything I can make any sense of. "Pete, why is it the Masons in particular? Why do you fear them?"

"Because the Masons are the primary group the inner circle uses to control the world."

I look him in the eye. "Are there other groups? That this 'inner circle' uses?"

"The Council of Foreign Relations."

"A great many influential people belong to the CFR," I comment.

He nods. "That's why they're successful, the inner circle promotes their careers in their plan for world domination."

"Like who?"

"Like all our presidents, the media—"

"The media?"

He nods. "The women can belong to the CFR but not to the Masons, so that's why no woman has been in the inner circle."

"George Bush is in this inner circle?"

"Very close to it," he says, eyes narrowing.

"What media people are in the CFR?"

"Barbara Walters. Diane Sawyer. Henry Kissinger. Dan Rather. Peter Jennings. Tom Brokaw. But the other organization the inner circle uses is the Trilateral Commission. And when a man belongs to two or more of these groups, you know he is at the top of the chain, the closest to the inner circle you can get. George Bush is all *three*, a Mason, CFR and TLC. Bill Clinton is in all three, too."

"But one's a Republican and one's—"

"That's just a pretense, the political parties. The inner circle is a master of creating conflict to hide its presence. Ross Perot is a Mason. Imagine their power—Bush, Clinton, Perot—three left-handed Masons!"

I opt to skip the "left-handed" part of the conspiracy and put a frying pan on the stove and turn it on. I put a little bit of butter into it. "So who else?"

"Gerald Ford is a Mason and CFR. So is Newt Gingrich. So are the Rockefellers, David Senior and Junior, and John D."

I salt and pepper his steak. I find a Dole salad in one of the produce drawers in the refrigerator and fix that, too. "So how does this plan for world domination relate to poor little Castleford?"

"There are chains of commands. And just like how the Masons killed John F. Kennedy for straying, for defying their dominance, the Masons here in Castleford killed your father."

I sear the steak without responding and turn down the heat. I stick two slices of bread into the toaster and push them down and then get out the garlic powder. "You think my father defied someone's dominance here in town," I finally say.

He nods vigorously. "And I think they killed that Tony Meyers for the same thing."

"Pete," I say, coming over to stand in front of him and putting a solemn hand on his shoulder, "this is my father you're talking about. So don't mess with me. If you know something definite that makes you say these things, you must tell me."

He looks down. "It's just that I've heard things, Sally."

"Heard them where?"

"Around." He is uncomfortable and is looking around, as if for an escape.

The toast pops up and I walk over to butter it and sprinkle a little garlic powder on each slice. I flip the steak on the plate and bring it over to the table with the salt and pepper. I give Pete a napkin and fork and knife. I bring over the salad. I pour him a glass of seltzer. "Would you like some onion?"

He shakes his head no, mouth full. He is smiling. "Very good," he says while patting his mouth with his napkin.

I sit down across from him and watch him eat. So does Scotty from the floor. Scotty doesn't beg; he just breaks your heart. When Pete's gotten deep into his supper, I say, "You really don't know how Tony Meyers knew you were going to Kaegle's Pond?"

He stops chewing. Then starts again. And shakes his head.

He's definitely lying. Earlier Pete was convinced Tony Meyers was waiting at the pond to kill him.

"Who are you protecting, Pete? I won't tell anybody. I know you won't tell me because you're scared someone might get hurt. Isn't that right?"

He's stopped chewing again and is breathing heavily through his nose, watching me.

"Is it the waitress at Casey's diner? The one who told me to meet you? Are you afraid she'll get in trouble?"

He shakes his head.

"Who?"

He struggles to swallow and when he does, he drops his knife and fork onto the plate with a clatter and then just sits there, like he's waiting for the electric chair to be turned on and end his misery.

"Who is it, Pete?" I coax. "You know you can trust me."

A tear falls from his left eye and it makes me so sad, for I am reminded that in his poor, tormented mind, this world is such a dangerous place. And this murder has confirmed it for him.

"Papa," he whispers. "Papa told the man to go there."

"But you told me before that your father was at the seniors center that day, for War Day."

His face starts to screw up. It's so hard to know what is going on in his mind.

"Not Papa," he finally says, dropping his head.

Poor guy. He is so confused and so scared. I go over and give him a hug. "Everything's going to be okay," I tell him, patting his shoulder. I step back. "We'll talk another time about it."

"The cops think I'm crazy," he says, starting to look more like himself. "I heard one of them say it when I was at Carmella's."

Ha! So he was there.

"Did they treat you okay?"

He nods. "Except the cops kept saying I was a nut. Carmella didn't."

"Eat your dinner, sweetie," I say. And, as if there is a great weight off his shoulders now, Crazy Pete does.

After dinner, when he starts talking about the sign of the X, I have had enough for one day. Scotty's been given the little scraps of fat from Pete's steak already, and now even he wanders away, bored.

I get dressed, put Scotty in the back of the Jeep and drive Crazy Pete home. Scotty and I go with him to unlock the front door and make the rounds inside the house to make sure all is well.

All is well.

Instead of going home, like most sane people would at nearly 2:00 a.m., I drive back to the paper and let myself in. Scotty comes along. I want to see if there is a way I can access a membership list of the Castleford Masonic Lodge of twenty-one years ago.

You just never know.

24

The phone rings at eight-thirty and I remember I never called Spencer or Doug back last night. I take a breath. "Hello?"

"Somebody did set off explosives at Tranowsky's Auto Body yesterday," Joe Bix announces. "But it doesn't look like a pro, since he blew up half the parking lot with it."

"Did they find anything inside? Anything left?"

"If you mean bodies, no. The fire marshal says to all appearances, the building was empty, save a few old pots of paint and the lifts."

"That's weird." I think a moment. "Are we sure there are no plans to build anything downtown? Someone who'd want to clear everyone out of there?"

"Downtown? Hell, Sally, the city would give it to anybody who wants it."

True. The city still owned a lot of real estate downtown because of the run of bankruptcies, tax repossessions and abandonments after the mall was built.

"What about insurance? How much did Tergar have?"

"Only personal injury. The building itself wasn't worth five bucks, and the land has been appraised at less than ten thousand."

"Huh." I climb out of bed and pad through the house in my bare feet to let Scotty out the back door. "Why would someone want to blow it up?"

"Nobody seems to know, but they did blow it up."

"What kind of explosives?"

"They're not saying."

"Of course not. It would be all they have to go on," I say to myself. "Well, thanks for letting me know."

"That was a pretty good piece you put together last night," Joe slips in.

"Thanks. I just swung by and found the gang trying to fill space."

"Yeah, right."

I make some coffee and call Doug. He's not there, so I leave a message. Then I call Spencer. He's not there, either.

I look at the clock and know I have to hustle. I promised Mother we'd "do" church before brunch.

"You look..." Mother is searching for a word.

"Tired?" I suggest.

"Worried," she decides.

We are sitting on the back deck of Mother's house and are about to eat. We have already been to the Congregational Church where the minister said to me, as he always does, "And how wonderful it is to see *you* here this morning."

"Yes," Mother confirms, "you are worried."

I make a sound indicating she may not be far off in her observations, but I am too determined to eat my eggs and bacon and potatoes and biscuits while they're hot. And so I do. It doesn't take long.

Mother is eating fruit salad, glancing through the piles of sections that make up the *Herald-American* and the *New York Times* on Sunday. She is on "The Week in Review" of the *Times* when I finally say something.

"Mother?"

"Hmm?"

"Who was in charge of the investigation of Daddy's death?"

There is a decided pause on my mother's part before she slowly lowers the paper into her lap, making it crinkle. "What do you mean, investigation?"

"I mean, who determined his cause of death? The police? The fire department?"

"Well..." Mother looks off into the distance, toward the lake. "Let me think..." Her eyes narrow slightly. "The police, I suppose." She meets my eye. "Why?"

"I just wondered."

Mother is suspicious. "Does this have anything to do with Tony Meyers's murder?"

"No, Mother, of course not. I was just wondering. Last night at the fire at Tranowsky's, the fire marshal was conducting the investigation. I just wondered who does it if a building falls down in a flood."

"I should think the city engineer would have been responsible," Mother says. "Try City Hall. I'm sure the records are readily available." She resumes reading her section of the paper, but then brings it crumpling back down again in her lap. "Why would you be interested in that after all this time?"

I shrug. "I was on the fire line last night, passing sandbags near the Mobil station. It made me think of Daddy."

She pours fresh coffee for herself, sips, and then says, "There's something else, isn't there?"

I look at her innocently.

"You were acting funny during the sermon this morning."

"I wasn't acting funny."

"You were paying avid attention," Mother says, "which in my book, when it comes to you, is acting funny."

I shrug again and pretend to read the paper, feeling Mother's eyes still on me. The sermon was on monogamy. Slowly I bring my eyes back up. "I met someone in New York this week."

"A man," Mother adds.

I nod. "And I really, really like him."

Mother nods, waiting.

"Enough that I know I don't want—that I can't—well, you know, be with Doug in the same way right now."

Mother waits, but I don't say anything else. I go inside to use the bathroom and come back. After I sit down, she says, "Does Doug know?"

"I think so."

"What does that mean?"

I sigh. "It means we met yesterday and he went out with someone else last night, but then he called later, saying he wanted to see me. He said he thought he had acted badly. But when I called him this morning, either he went out or he's not answering, and I strongly suspect the latter."

Mother sips her coffee. "Your relationship has never been simple."

"Tell me about it," I sigh, petting Abigail, who has come up on the deck with Scotty to hunt for scraps.

"So you want to see this man in New York."

I nod. "Very much."

"But if he turns out to be nothing—which he very likely could be, since you don't know him—"

"I obviously don't feel committed to Doug the way I should be," I interrupt, irritated. I have a feeling Mother is somehow going to make me feel awful.

"So you're willing to let Doug go. And I mean *really* let him go, Sally, let him move on?"

I look at her.

"And not change your mind if this new fellow doesn't work out? You won't come back to haunt Doug when you're lonely?"

I know what she's saying. She's been through two breakups of ours already, when I vowed it was over, only to see me go right back to Doug.

"Sally," she says with that special tension in her voice that means she's trying her best not to lecture me but feels compelled to, anyway, "please take this the right way—"

I'm waiting.

"You *have* to grow up."

She's caught me off guard with this one.

"You cannot go on playing around with people anymore, Sally. You're thirty years old—not twenty, not fifteen. You can't do and say things and then not mean them. You've got to learn to bite your tongue and hold yourself in check until you're certain how you feel—until you know to what lengths you're prepared to go in order to make good on your word."

"But Doug—" I start.

"Doug needs to grow up, too!" she nearly cries. "Both of you! Sometimes I swear the two of you think you're still in high school and just haven't noticed that everybody else has grown up, made decisions and moved on to the next phase!" She offers a quick smile to lessen the impact of what she has just said. "Sometimes I think you and Doug will still be hanging out like you did in high school when you're in wheelchairs. And heaven forbid one of you wakes up, because each of you has to have the other in order to keep this fantasy going, that you have all the time in the world."

What she says is painful, but true. It has something to do with the sex life Doug and I have shared and the fact it began when we were teenagers. And the way I have acted this week doesn't reassure me much that my relationship with Spencer, if it can even be called that, is rooted in maturity, either.

The thought makes me feel scared. Anxious. I don't know, I just don't know.

"Perhaps it's because you've been living in Castleford again," Mother says. "But whatever it is, Sally, I don't think your relationship with Doug has been very progressive for either one of you. As for your new friend—he is single, I hope."

"Of course he is, Mother."

She nods once, as if saying, *Well, at least you got that right.* "What does he do?"

"He's an executive editor at Bennett, Fitzallen & Coe."

Her eyebrows go up. "How old?"

"Thirty-five."

"Divorced, I take it."

I shake my head. "No. He's kind of like me."

Mother sighs, shaking her head. "Thirty-five and never married—"

"Mother!"

"I just want you to be careful."

"Oh, so Doug being married and divorced by age twenty-seven is some kind of excellent credential?"

"Darling, let me explain something to you," she says, leaning forward to place her hand over mine. "I love you and your brother more than life itself. I think you and your brother are two of the most wonderful human beings that ever walked the face of the earth. I think you are kind and generous and hardworking and, heaven knows, bright—too bright, I often think. And you're lucky, too, Sally, because men find you attractive—despite, well, you know, the way you can be."

"And what way is that, Mother?"

"Difficult."

I wait for her to elaborate and she doesn't.

"Difficult," I repeat.

She nods. "Yes."

"How so?"

She withdraws her hand and sits back in her chair. "In what ways do you think you might be difficult?"

"Okay." I think. "I have an erratic schedule—"

"The problem is not your erratic schedule," Mother hints to me, "it's the fact that you prefer it that way. That you're always running around like a chicken with its head cut off."

"Well, thanks a lot!" I can't help but laugh.

"Well, it's true, Sally, your life is just in chaos all the time!"

"It's not chaos to me."

"And that's part of the problem!"

We both giggle.

"All right, all right, all right," I mutter, surrendering. "What else? Okay—I've got kind of a problem with authority."

"Yes, like any authority who is not you."

"How long have you been waiting to beat me up, anyway?"

"Go on. I promise you, it will be worth it."

"Okay. I've got a control thing, I guess."

"But not too much," she says encouragingly.

"And, I don't know, I'm impatient."

"That's not a fault, honey, that's genetic—you're just like your father."

After a while, I say, "Sorry to disappoint you, but at the moment I can't think of any other major faults I have."

"You're loyal to a fault," Mother tells me. "And it's that, well, shall we call it excessive sense of loyalty that has kept you with Doug. He's seen other women, and yet you've remained loyal."

I avert my eyes. "Not anymore, Mother."

She is silent for several moments. I glance at her and can tell this is not a confidence she particularly wants. "Darling, listen to me. Knowing you the way I do…" She sighs. "I'm just going to tell you the way it is."

"Please do," I say glumly.

"If, in the next year or so, Sally, you don't figure out what it is you're trying to do in your personal life, you won't know for at least another ten years. And by that time, if you want children, it will be too late."

I roll my eyes and fall back in my chair. "Oh, brother!"

"I'm just telling you the way it is. So if you don't want to have children, fine, then keep this up."

"Keep *what* up?"

"Carrying on like you're a schoolgirl instead of a thirty-year-old woman who has a major career decision to make."

"My career? How did my career get into this?" I suddenly feel hostile, and Mother or no Mother I am sorely tempted to *fwang* some leftover biscuit at her with my fork.

"Because your career is part of the problem," Mother says. "You've got to stop diddling about and focus on what it is you really want to do."

Now I am just sitting here, dumbfounded.

Mother softens slightly. "You have brains and talent. And you and I both know that coming back to work at the *Herald-American* was not your great career goal in life. And yet, you seemed to want to settle back down in Castleford, and since that was the case you obviously thought the *Herald-American* would do. But clearly it hasn't been enough. And now you've been given an opportunity of a lifetime—"

If I hear that phrase one more time I'm going to scream.

"And you go off to New York to see if this is, perhaps, the assignment that will lead you back to your original dream. So what do you do?" She pauses. "You're gone two days and now you're home, telling me you've met someone in New York and you want to break up with Doug."

"But I've already broken up with Doug."

"Sally, that's not the point! You've got to focus!" Mother rushes on, "You've got to make some decisions about your life! You cannot take an opportunity like this—this article for *Expectations,* one of the largest, most popular magazines in America—and use it as an excuse to play around with some man who clearly has a few problems of his own, when you know you should be working!"

"How can you say he has problems?" I blaze. "You don't even know him!"

"Well what *was* his last girlfriend like?" she wants to know, her voice rising. "Undoubtedly she was some good-looking gal who was as unfocused in life as the two of you obviously are!"

"Mother!" I am genuinely shocked. Mother is *never* like this. At least, not since I was fifteen and stole her car in the middle of the night to go joyriding.

Suddenly Mother drops her face in her hands. "You are so much like your father." When she looks up, there are tears in her eyes. "I love you so much. And I loved your father like no man I will ever love again." A tear spills down her cheek. "But I will not stand by, Sally, and watch you throw your life away on some second-rate relationship and some second-rate job simply because you can't make up your mind about what you want to do."

"Are you saying Daddy threw his life away?"

"Sally," she says, leaning forward, "he was a *man*. It's different for men, you know that. He found me—he had *me* to run the rest of his life *for* him. There is no way he could have gone out on his own if I hadn't helped him. He wasn't meant for cookie-cutter architecture, he would have been miserable. Certainly he would have made a lot more money in the corporate world, but that wasn't who he was—or who we were as a family. He needed to be who he was, and so I made it possible. I told him it didn't matter how much money he made. No man is going to do that for you."

"I hope you're giving this same lecture to Rob," I say. "I don't see him beating a path down the aisle anytime soon."

"Rob's difficulties are different," she says, sniffing. She wipes her eyes.

"Oh, what's his problem?"

"He's terrified of loss."

I look at her.

"He is. You'd do anything to avoid being responsible for your life, Sally, and he'll do anything to avoid being attached to anything or anybody who can ever be taken away from him." She takes a deep breath. "It's true. You react instead of act, your brother runs away." She sighs, rubbing her neck. "I just don't know. I've tried my best." She looks at me. "I'd like to see you two happily settled, that's all."

I count to ten. "So what do you think would be best for me? To move to New York? Something like that?"

"I know I don't want you writing for the sake of a paycheck, Sally. You'll go mad."

"There is nothing wrong with working for the *Herald-American*."

Mother looks at me. "For Al Junior?"

"You've got a point. Well," I say, standing to pick up our plates, "I'm not going to make do anymore, Mother. I can promise you that." I take the plates into the kitchen. The dogs follow and I give them their long-awaited scraps—Mother has a fit if anyone feeds them from the table. When I come back outside, I find her looking off at the pond again.

"I didn't really mean what I said about you and Rob. You made me angry."

"Why are *you* angry?" I ask, sitting down.

"Because I don't want you to waste this opportunity." She looks at me. "And I resent you trying to use me to assuage your guilt."

"What guilt?"

"Your guilt over having slept with a man you obviously don't even know. It is rather self-destructive, Sally, and I can't pretend not to be shocked." She pushes her coffee cup. "Although I suppose it was the only way you could break it off with Doug."

I'll be damned if I'll show any evidence to support or contradict what she has just said, but this in itself seems to verify what Mother wants to know.

"Oh, Sally," she says, "don't be like this."

"Damn it, Mother!" I jump up. "How am I suppose to react when you say things like that to me?"

"Don't raise your voice."

As much as I hate her in this moment, she is my mother and I respect her. Sort of.

"Did it every occur to you," she continues in that same quiet voice, "that the reason why you've 'met someone' so quickly in New York is because you've been absolutely starving out here? For the life you were always destined to have?"

"And what kind of life is that?"

"Bigger than Castleford, Sally."

I sigh, shaking my head. "You seemed so happy that I was back here, that I liked living here again."

"It's not about *living* here." She leans forward again. "It's about the difference between *choosing* to live here, and *staying* because it's the easiest thing to do. The same principle applies to Doug." She stands up and pushes back her chair. "Don't let yourself run away with your emotions, Sally. No more making-do with what you happen to find on the side of the road."

My mouth's open, ready to scream. *Something I happen to find on the side of the road?*

"And for heaven's sake," she adds, picking up the coffeepot and her cup, "be careful of your health."

Buddy D'Amico is standing on the sidelines of a tournament soccer field in Cheshire. He is shouting and jumping up and down. He is wearing pleated shorts and a polo shirt that has the logo of the Castleford public golf course on it. When the referee whistles the action to a stop, Buddy stops jumping and catches sight of me out of the corner of his eye. He groans, turning away. "Not fair! Not here!"

"Hi, Bud," I say, sidling on up next to him. "Your team looks good."

He can't help it. He smiles. "Yeah, they are. They work hard."

I point. "Look, I've brought Devon. He's going to take some pictures for the paper."

A couple of the parents come over when they hear this. "Steve, Angie," Buddy says, "this is Sally Harrington of the *Herald-American.* Steve Bernstein and Angie Manardo."

We say hi and I ask which girls are theirs and dutifully take down their names. I get a soda for Buddy from the concession stand and sip one myself and watch the game and cheer and whistle. (I like sports.) Only after the game is over (Buddy's team won) and he has talked to the girls, before they go running off to leave with their parents, do I approach him.

"Anything on the murderer?"

"No. Here, make yourself useful." He shoves an equipment bag in my hand.

"I think Pete Sabatino knows something about why Tony Meyers went to Kaegle's Pond," I say.

"Tell me something I don't already know." Buddy sighs, hefting his bag over his shoulder and leading the way to the parking lot. "Unfortunately, his story sort of bites its own tail, doesn't it?"

"So does anybody know what kind of explosives were used to blow up Tranowsky's yesterday?"

He looks at me. "I didn't hear anything like that."

"Well, you will. Someone blew it up."

"Well thanks," he says sarcastically. "Just what I want to hear on my day off."

"I think it's cool you're coaching girls."

"Well I've got to practice for when Ceil gets bigger," he said, referring to his baby daughter.

"Buddy? I need to ask you a favor."

"What a shock." He swings his bag down next to his car.

"No, I mean it."

He glances at me, and then pulls his keys out to open his trunk. "What kind of favor?"

"It's about my father's accident. I wondered if you could find out if there's a file on it."

"There should be something," he says, taking the bag from me and tossing it into the trunk. "Why, what's up?"

"I'm just curious. I'd like to see it."

He closes the trunk. "Sure." He gives me a pat on the arm. "Everything okay?"

"Yes. Mom and I were just curious about something."

He cocks his head slightly, studying me. "What about?"

"I'll tell you when I find it," I promise.

25

Driving home from the soccer game, I feel exhausted. And I feel sad.

Having Mother yell at me like she did this morning makes me feel terrible. I guess it was supposed to. Well, there's not much I can do but try and do what she said—put my nose to the grindstone and get this piece finished, don't be emotionally rash, grow up and figure out what I want to do with my life.

So that's why I tracked Buddy down and asked him for the police report on my father's death.

Mother's right. I do prefer chaos. I don't call it that—I call it keeping busy—but I keep myself hopping because I don't like a lot of downtime to think.

Because when I have a lot of downtime to think, like now, I get sad.

There's nothing worse than thinking you were robbed as a child. Because if you think that way, part of you will forever long for what you missed. And yet you know you can never get it. And so you get sad. Like I feel right now.

No cure except to work and drown the sadness in a sense of achievement.

My friend Morning from UCLA landed in both Cocaine Anonymous and Alcoholics Anonymous a few years back, which in this past year has led her to Adult Children of Alcoholics, Sex Anonymous and Emotions Anonymous. Morning never does things half-assed, not even recovery, it seems. Anyway, Morning sent me a meditation book for Christmas, which of course I just stared at for a while, wondering if she had finally flipped or what.

The point is, I opened that book and read a couple of chapters and I tried to meditate, which the author called "listening." I couldn't do it. I literally have too much, what he called "noise," in my head. The author talked about people like me, people who have to keep the radio or TV on, or who are forever talking to themselves, or who are on the phone, or working or whatever—never just sitting, listening to the universe. When I try to meditate, my head fills with thoughts and lists of things to do and within seconds, I am up and doing something. Morning said it's the sign of an undisciplined mind, which I know she knew would drive me up the wall.

After what Mother said this morning, I can't help but think Morning is right, but it is not just my mind. It is my emotions, it is my career, too.

Before we're around the big bend of the driveway, Scotty has begun to bark and whine and jump around in the back of the Jeep. When the cottage swings into view, I see why. There's a blue Miata parked in the driveway and, although it is cloudy now, the top is down.

Now what? I think, pulling in. No one seems to be around. I let Scotty out the back and he goes racing off into the woods, barking his head off.

This is weird. Where is whoever drove this car here? I walk around the back of the house. No one.

Scotty sounds like he's miles off, still barking.

Huh.

I unlock the kitchen door and let myself into the house and go to the answering machine. First message is from Doug. Sorry he missed me; he has some work he has to do. He'll call me later.

My brother Rob, wanting to know why Mother sounds so pissed at me today, what's going on.

Spencer. "You can't hide from me," he laughs. "I hope you're working hard. Talk to you soon."

Mother. Apologizing for being so hard on me. She loves me. I am the greatest thing since sliced bread.

Spencer. "Maybe you *can* hide from me," he says this time. "Where are you?"

I pick up the phone and call the number he left. There is no answer. I walk into the kitchen to let Scotty in and nearly jump out of my skin because Spencer's waving to me through the kitchen door. He is shirtless and glistening with perspiration, wearing a pair of white tennis shorts, belt and sneakers. Scotty is holding his T-shirt in his mouth, tail wagging. I can't help but smile.

"What are you doing here?" I say, flinging open the door.

"Looking for you. I decided to take a little run while I was waiting. I'm pretty sweaty, but can I get a kiss?"

He does. And he smiles. "Wow. I found you." He gestures. "Nice house! Nice dog!"

"He'll put a hole in that," I say, making Scotty hand the shirt over while Spencer comes in. I turn around. "I can't believe you're here."

"Me, neither."

We're shy. At least I am. It is so strange to see him standing here. This is my house, my town. I suppose I should be annoyed he just came, but I'm not. I'm glad. Nervous, but glad.

"I was on my way back to the city." He crinkles up his face. "Would you mind if I had a glass of water?"

"Oh, sure!" I say, jumping to it and getting him one.

"Anyway, I looked on the map and found Castleford, and then I got off at a gas station and looked you up in the phone book. There was a number, but no address. So I called and you weren't here. So I'm standing there, wondering what to do, when I think of calling the paper. So I ask the lady behind the counter what the name of the paper is and she says, 'Who are you looking for?' and I say, 'A reporter, Sally Harrington.' And she told me how to get here." He takes the glass from me. "Thank you." He gulps it. "Mmm, is this the famous well water?"

I smile. "Yes. But who was that lady, I wonder?"

"Oh," he says, lowering the glass, "she said to tell you hi from Bernice from choir practice." He polishes the water off and then walks over to the sink to help himself to some more. "I didn't know you were in choir."

"Not since fourth grade. I remember Bernice. She's working at a gas station?"

"Evidently. Anyway, I drove around a little. It's not much of a city, Castleford, is it?"

"You should have been here last night," I tell him. "Part of it blew up."

"Really?" He is drinking water again, muttering how good it tastes. A little hard, but good, which is an apt description.

For a book editor in New York City, Spencer looks pretty fit. He's told me he goes to the gym a lot—he has one in his apartment building. And this weekend, unlike me, it appears he's gotten some sun.

I tell him a little about the fire last night, the sandbag line, and how late I got in, and then how I had to meet my mother this morning, that's why I hadn't called. I give him a little tour of the house and in the living room he makes a beeline for a picture of Rob and me when we were kids, standing with my parents in front of our house.

"This is your father?" he asks, picking it up.

"Yes." I come over to stand next to him.

"He was so young."

I smile, looking at Daddy. He was.

"Your mother is a knockout, Sally," he says, putting the picture down and picking up another, a more recent one. "Wow."

"Yes, she is," I agree.

"You look like her."

"But I'm not *like* her," I sigh.

"What's the matter?"

I drop sideways into one of my armchairs. "She told me this morning I have to grow up. I've been fooling around too long."

"She doesn't want you to marry that Doug guy, does she?" he asks, coming over to kneel next to my chair. "I mean, part of me is hoping you told her about me," he continues, reaching for my hand, "and part of me is freaking out because she might want you to stay with that guy."

"It's not about any guy," I answer him. "It's about me and my rash decisions and my habit of creating havoc in my life."

He kisses my hand. "I missed you. I know it's ridiculous, but I have."

I feel that tingle between my legs. It doesn't take much.

"I was hoping I could talk you into letting me drive you into New York for the week," he continues. "And stay with me. Set up your stuff in my living room—there's a desk and phone, and there's a fax downstairs—"

"Spencer," I whisper, putting a finger over his mouth and shaking my head. "It's too fast."

"I don't care," he says, looking into my eyes. He pulls himself up to sit next to me in the chair, cradling me in his arm.

I see he has an erection in his shorts and I feel a falling sensation in my lower body, a hopeful anticipation. I am a disgrace. He is kissing my neck, lightly touching my breast through my T-shirt. "Come with me," he whispers. "There's no reason why not to. You need to work. I'll be at the office all day. The doorman will get you cabs, take messages, send faxes, whatever you want. You can order coffee, food. But then at night—" he is kissing my chest through my T-shirt "—we can eat dinner, talk about our day, crawl into bed. You and me." He kisses me for a long time. "Just you and me. All night. All week."

"It's crazy," I sigh, closing my eyes.

"It's wonderful," he breathes into my ear.

I don't know what we're doing; we're just sort of kissing and touching each other, and the next thing I know, I have my shorts off and I am undoing his belt and unzipping his shorts and he is pulling my legs up around him. He lowers himself to his knees, pulls me to the very edge of the chair where he carefully, skillfully, enters me.

"God," I groan into his shoulder.

I feel him pull back a little and I open my eyes. He smiles, his eyes narrow, as if he's bordering on pain. Then he presses his mouth to mine, firmly holding my derriere, and pushes himself all the way in. And pulls out. And in. And out, each thrust gracefully sliding deeper inside me, and then all the way back up, and then down, and then back, and then down, and then back.

"Oh, Sally," he breathes, pulling his mouth off mine. Now his eyes are closed, and his head is falling back, his movement starting to falter. He is about to come and I can't stand it, I don't want him to yet, and I find myself easing him back down on the floor and I slide down onto his lap. My breasts are in his face and I start to move against him, trapping him inside me, and I move, riding him, moaning, and he has completely stiffened, and I feel something and I know he is coming, but I have to keep going, and then there it is, it's coming, and I say, *"Yes, Spencer, yes,"* through my teeth and I am over the top, having spasms around him. "Oh!" I finally shudder, collapsing on his shoulder.

Oh, it's good. So good. So very, very good.

I can't move. But I have to because Spencer is laughing quietly, saying something about the fact his legs are either broken or asleep, and so I have to move and I finally just fall back on the carpet and say, "Ah!"

Scotty comes over to sniff around a little.

Suddenly he barks and charges for the front door.

"Oh, my God!" I whisper, sitting up. Someone's driven up. Scotty is barking his head off, jumping up on the window to look outside. I leap up and scurry to the window, wearing only my top. "Oh, my God—it's Doug! Get into the bedroom!"

"I can't walk!" Spencer gasps, trying to stand. "I told you, my legs are asleep."

"Go into the bathroom!"

He staggers over and crashes against the wall. I grab his shorts and my underpants and throw them into the bedroom, where Spencer is trying to stagger. I push him into the bedroom and tell him to turn on the shower.

Doug, thank God, knocks on the front door instead of just coming in like he usually does. But then I hear the living room door open. "Hey, Scotty boy," I hear him say.

I have grabbed a blue-jeans skirt and slipped it on. I poke my head out the bedroom door. "Doug? Can you take Scotty out? I just got back and he needs to go out!"

"We'll be outside!" Doug calls.

I wonder, panicked, if Doug got far enough into the living room to smell the sex in the air. Good grief, semen is running down my leg as I'm standing here. I go into the bathroom, where Spencer is standing near the shower. "It can't be your boyfriend," he whispers.

"Oh, yes it can," I say, grabbing a washcloth and wetting it and proceeding to pull up my skirt to wipe myself off. So ladylike. Right. I rinse it out and then do my legs.

"Someday this will be funny," he says, kissing me on the cheek and climbing into the shower.

There is *nothing* funny about this, I think, yanking a brush through my hair. I drink some Listerine and then swallow it by mistake, I'm such a wreck. I put on some mascara and dash out and through the kitchen out the back door. "Doug?" I call, coming down the steps.

"Hi," he says, coming around the house. "Who's here?"

"A friend from Kent," I say. "He went hiking on the farm and he's taking a shower." The Listerine is burning down into my stomach.

Doug stops walking and gets this horrible stricken look on his face. "It's him, isn't it?"

"Who?"

"Whoever you met in New York. He's here, isn't he?" He lurches off around the house and I go after him. Doug is standing at the front corner of the house, resting his hand on the stone, looking at the ground as though he is about to be sick. "I can't believe you'd do this to me. I thought we were going to talk things out." He hits the stone, saying, "Goddamn it!" and strides to his car.

"Doug," I say, "he just stopped in on his way back to New York. It's not like he was staying here or anything."

"Staying here?" He clutches his head and takes two steps before wheeling round. "Just what have you done with this guy?"

"He just stopped in, I didn't know you were coming over."

"Does he even know I exist?" he yells at the house. "Does he know you were about to get engaged to me?"

"Yes."

"Is he sleeping with you already?" he yells. "Goddamn it, Sally!" he cries, and he smashes the hood of the Volvo with his fists, leaving a dent. Then he yanks the door open, gets in and starts the car. I want to say something, but I don't know what. He guns the motor and lays a patch, backing up. He doesn't even look at me as he floors it, dirt and gravel flying as the Volvo swerves out.

When the car disappears around the bend, Spencer opens the front door. He is wearing his shorts and T-shirt and sneakers and comes down the stairs. "I can go after him and explain."

I am crying. "Explain what?"

"Whatever you want me to," Spencer says. "If you want him

back, Sally, I'll tell him nothing happened. I'll tell him whatever you want me to say."

I look at him, sniffing, wiping my eyes.

"But I hope you don't want him back. That you'll let him go."

I hold my face in my hands, trying to think.

"Give us a try. Sally, please. Trust me. I know there is something quite wonderful here, something between us that I have every reason to believe is different from anything you and I have ever experienced."

My head still down, I turn to Spencer and he puts his arms around me. I hide my face in his shoulder. He kisses the side of my head.

26

Spencer stayed the night.

Considering all that had transpired, I slept amazingly well. So did he. I am up early, just after six, to fix him a bowl of cereal and a cup of coffee before he drives into the city. He is at the front door, saying goodbye, when he looks at his watch, shakes his head and says, "Can't we sit and talk awhile? You could show me something—like a photo album or an old report card or something. Or we could go outside and take pictures of Scotty, or go for a walk and pick flowers, or sing songs or something. We could go over to the gas station and sing hymns with Bernice!"

I laugh, shaking my head. "Darling, you have to go." Five days and I'm calling him darling.

Reluctantly, he agrees and I wave goodbye as he pulls out.

Scotty and I go for a run in the fields. It is a beautiful morning.

I feel badly for Doug, but I also can't help but feel that in a way it was good the way things transpired. If nothing else, it bore no resemblance to how we've broken up before. And different is better, isn't it?

Of course I'm the one who feels that way because *I* have met someone wonderful.

Chi Chi calls, promising a major interview for me today, although she says I may live to regret it. It is with Cassy's mother, Catherine Littlefield, age seventy-one. Chi Chi says Catherine would die before seeing me in person. So we're doing a phoner.

Mrs. Littlefield answers the phone in Cedar Rapids, Iowa, and already I think she sounds like a bitch. Truly. There is something in the pitch of her voice that feels, well, hateful. Spiteful? Well, unhappy for sure. Or maybe she's just irritable, I think, trying desperately to cut the lady some slack; it could be she is nervous or hates talking on the telephone.

I introduce myself and thank her for making time to speak to me.

"I'll give you *some* time, I told that Spanish woman. I'm very busy."

"Yes, I understand that and I appreciate your cooperation."

"That woman said you wanted to fly out here," she says. "Told her no! Waste of time, waste of money, the phone is the lesser of two evils, I suppose. Why on earth are you writing about Catherine? Because of the rich second husband, I suppose."

If I play my cards right, I suspect Mrs. Littlefield can conduct both sides of the interview by herself. Interesting that she calls Cassy Catherine. And it's almost even morbidly fascinating that she named her only child after herself.

"I'm writing about your daughter's incredible success," I say. "Things have changed a great deal in recent decades, but Mrs. Littlefield, your daughter is one of the few women who has genuinely reached the top of their profession."

"I've never read your magazine" is her response. "I don't waste my time."

I start to explain my status, that I'm a freelancer on leave from a local paper, but I sense there is little use—I'd be wasting her time!

"Well, let's begin, shall we? I should tell you, Mrs. Littlefield, that I am going to record this conversation, on a tape recorder, so that I can make sure any quotes I might use are absolutely correct."

She snorts.

I've got to win her over on something. "Mrs. Littlefield, Cassy has told me what an enormous influence you have been on her life. She's told me about how you supported the whole family, how you raised her, helped her get to college—"

"Did she tell you her father was a drunken bum? And that the first thing Catherine did after leaving home was to go and find another one?"

"Uh, not in those exact words," I say.

To my surprise, Mrs. Littlefield cracks up. She sounds like a witch. "No, I'm sure she didn't!" she cackles. "Catherine's always had a soft touch when it comes to making excuses for the men in her life."

That's actually not a bad line and I make a note of it on my pad.

I ask her to tell me about Cassy as a child and when she does, it is painful to listen to. What I hear is a woman who is obviously proud of her daughter, but who also harbors bitter jealousy over the attention her daughter always drew. I can easily see how this woman browbeat her only child, how she constantly belittled Cassy in an attempt to neutralize the attention Cassy got for being so beautiful, so smart and, evidently, so good. (If this woman had been my mother, I would have killed myself.)

The most interesting thing about this interview, I find, is what Mrs. Littlefield doesn't tell me, things that Chi Chi mentioned this morning—that Mrs. Littlefield has always refused to come East, even for a visit, and that Cassy has always gone there to see her; that Cassy built her a house; that Cassy has been sending her money ever since she got her first big promotion twenty years ago. Mrs. Littlefield also does not mention that she was arrested two years ago for trying to run down her neighbor with her car.

But there is one fact Mrs. Littlefield does see fit to mention to the national press. "I don't suppose Catherine told you I was carrying her before I was married."

Oh, boy. Poor Cassy. "Uh, no," I say.

She sighs. "He got me liquored up at a church dance, don't you know. Next thing I knew... So there I am with a baby I didn't want and a drunk for a husband I *certainly* did not want."

"But you stuck it out," I venture to say.

"We took sacred vows." She tells me how hard she worked, how hard it was to save face with the husband she had, how hard it was to bring up Cassy and "watch her like a hawk, so she wouldn't take the path of her father."

Or her mother, I think.

This is the worst interview I have ever sat through. I hate this woman; I don't want to listen to her; I certainly don't want to quote her. But this is my job, right? To gather as much information as I can to develop a profile of Cassy Cochran.

And, I suppose, to that end, this interview is extremely helpful. If I don't start yelling at this bitch.

"Make them use a picture of me when I was young," she suddenly says. "Catherine knows which one. If you don't, I'll sue, I swear I will. You can't run pictures of me without my permission."

She's wrong, but I let it go. "You certainly are a very beautiful woman, Mrs. Littlefield."

She makes a choking noise. "Oh, but you *should* have seen me. I was the most beautiful girl in the county, everybody said so. I had gentlemen callers lined up all the way down the block and around the corner."

"I'm not surprised."

"It could have gone to my head, you know," she confides. "I was very lucky to have the mother I did. I didn't have airs, not like some people."

"Do you think your daughter has airs?" I can't resist asking.

"Catherine? She has the airs of a cat burglar, always sneaking around, poking her nose into everything."

I introduce the subject of her grandson, Henry.

"She named him after her father, can you believe it? We're lucky he wasn't born with a pint bottle in his mouth. Honestly, have you ever?"

I can't take it. We talk a little bit more and then I thank her profusely.

"Remember, Catherine knows the picture you can use!"

I hang up the phone. "Oh, *my*," I say to Scotty.

I pack my bags for New York and Mother calls to say she has found another last-minute deal for me through her cheapo-hotel line. "Am I forgiven for Sunday?" she asks me.

"Yes, of course," I respond, wondering what she would think of Sunday afternoon's little scene with Spencer and Doug. Then I am distracted by the telltale beep of my fax machine and move over to see what's coming through. It's from Buddy D'Amico. I tell Mother I'll be dropping Scotty by and hang up.

Sally,
　　Scan this and call me, okay?

Buddy

I pick up the next sheet. It is a scratchy copy of a Castleford police report, dated the night of the my father's death. The few lines of information are handwritten on the form.

Responded 9:02 p.m. North wall Castleford High gym col-lapsed in floodwater. Found Dodge Harrington's body un-der debris. Confirmed dead. Officers Smith, Calve joined us. Sanderson's ambulance took body. Came back to sta-tion to tell chief. He went to tell family. Back on patrol 12: 17 a.m. Flood continues.

The next sheet is a coroner's report. Wilbur Kennett Harring-ton died from head wounds sustained in a building cave-in.
　　I call Buddy and he immediately comes on the line. "Thanks," I tell him. "But it's not much, is it?"
　　"No, it's not," he agrees. "I took a walk over to City Hall and they don't have much, either. One of the guys is going to look around for me. He said so many buildings came down and there was so much damage in the flood that no one had much time for paperwork."
　　"Yeah. Well, thank you."
　　"I'll let you know if we find anything else."
　　"Thanks, Bud."
　　I stick the papers in my briefcase to take with me to New York. I don't know why, but I want them with me.
　　Strange.
　　Well, it was my father and I frankly haven't had the courage to ask much about his death before.
　　I drive over to Mother's and unload Scotty's stuff in the kitchen. I fill Scotty's water bowl and put it beside Abigail's on the floor. "Mother, why didn't you sue the city when Daddy died?"
　　She looks utterly perplexed and puts the bottle of Windex that's in her hand down on the counter. "What an extraordi-nary thing to say, Sally."

I shrug. "I don't think so."

"But why on earth would I sue the city?"

"Because a city building fell down on Daddy and killed him!"

"Your father designed it," she says softly, pulling off her rubber gloves.

"Are you saying the building fell down because Daddy designed it?"

"Certainly not! But the city wasn't responsible for the flood—it was an act of God. Why would I sue the city for something that was no fault of theirs?"

The conversation has ended as far as Mother is concerned, but all I think of is how much easier our lives would have been had Mother gotten some money after Daddy's accident.

I wonder if Mother is thinking back to when she took Rob and me into the gym after it was rebuilt? Every trace of anything that had killed Daddy was long gone, but she knew that every time we went into that gym, we would look at that wall, at that place where our father drew his last breath. So she took us, by the hand, to get us through it the first time.

Poor Mother. I can see by her eyes this is painful to her. "I suppose you're right," I sigh, walking over to her. "Thanks for taking Scotty. And getting me the hotel room."

She gives me a hug. "I love you," she says.

"I love you, too."

She holds me by the hands and looks at me. Then she shakes her head a little, laughs and releases me. "Go on. Go see your new beau."

I start to protest but she waves me away. "Don't even try, baby. I know you too well. Go on. Have fun. Good luck."

As I'm getting into the Jeep, Mother opens the front door. "And try to do some work!"

My new last-minute hotel is a lovely one on Columbus Circle, the Wyndham. I unpack my stuff and call Spencer's office. He is, his assistant tells me, tied up in a meeting. "Please leave me your number so he can call you," she says. "I know he wants to talk to you."

I leave my number and proceed to organize my notes and

materials for tomorrow's interviews. Spencer calls about an hour later and we agree on where to meet at seven for dinner. Now I'm humming, enjoying myself. At six-thirty I put on a little makeup, run a brush through my hair and go downstairs to walk up Broadway, through Lincoln Center and over to Columbus Avenue to a little Italian place. I stand just inside the door and read a giveaway paper until Spencer arrives.

"I brought you a present," he says, handing me a two-foot-long, strangely flexible, gift-wrapped package. "It's very romantic," he adds as we are seated. "Go on, open it."

"I can't imagine..." I say, tearing the paper. Then I laugh. It is a thickly braided pull rope to play tug-of-war with Scotty. I look at him and think, *Am I lucky or what?* "Thank you," I murmur, leaning over to kiss him. "We'll love it."

We have a delicious dinner and Spencer tells me a little about his frustrating day. "We've got a writer who hates to write and an editor who doesn't know how to edit, so we've got a five-hundred-thousand-dollar book that reads like—I swear—the first draft of a high-school history paper."

"What are you going to do?"

"The only thing I can do—I've sent it to a professor friend at Columbia who is going to do a quick read and laundry list for me. You know, what's messed up factually, flag the footnotes that I swear make no sense, stuff like that, and then I'll sit down and go through the manuscript and write a long editorial letter to the author, telling him exactly what needs to be done."

"If the editor's already released the money for a satisfactory manuscript," I say, "does the author have to do the work?"

"Legally, no. Therein lies the problem. He thinks it's a masterpiece the way it is." He shakes his head, sighing, but then suddenly brightens. "My dad called today. I told him all about you."

I smile.

"He wants to meet you." Then he cocks his head slightly. "Have I explained to you about my mother? I mean, that she's my long-term stepmother, not my biological mother?"

I shake my head. "No."

"I didn't think so. Well, she is. See, my real mom died when I was twelve, of cancer."

"I'm so sorry."

"Hmm, yes, thanks. Well, it was very sad. But my dad re-married the next year—I guess he felt like he had to, with my little sisters and all. Anyway, he married Trudy and I've called her 'Mom' ever since. She's been wonderful. And my little brother I've told you about, Sam, he's really my stepbrother."

As Spencer continues talking about his family, our over-whelming pull toward each other is starting to make more sense to me. It's a difficult thing to explain to people who did not lose a parent when they were little. To put it simply, a sense of loss becomes a defining factor in your character. I learned early that the storybooks lied, the world offers no protection; one day I had my big strong dad, who took care of me, and the next day I didn't. He was gone forever. It's not as dramatic as all that, except that I have become increasingly aware—certainly of late—of how the absence of my father has quietly dictated a great deal in my life.

Spencer is smiling at me. "You know what my dad said? He said you sounded a lot like my mother, my real mother. In the most flattering ways."

I could have told him that because I know that Spencer is, in some ways, like my father.

We walk to my hotel, chatting, swinging hands. We decide he will come up for a little while to my room but then will go home; we both have a lot to do. Tomorrow we will spend the night together.

It has been a near perfect day.

I am falling in love.

27

Tuesday begins with an interview with Cassy Cochran's old boss at WST. After an amusing account of how they *begged* her to go on the air as the station's first woman co-anchor, which she adamantly refused, the interview is not particularly enlightening. It does, however, give me enough superlative quotes about Cassy to, say, wage a congressional campaign on her behalf. "Financially responsible." "*Excellent* supervisor of workers." "Strong but never offensive." "Creative and hardworking." "Detail oriented." "*Absolutely brilliant* at long-range planning." And, it says a lot about Cassy that he would say all these things about her after she jumped ship to DBS. On the other hand, when she joined WST it was an insignificant independent player in New York and by the time she left, Cassy had turned WST into the first "super station" to be carried on cable networks across the country.

One bonus of the interview is a cherished photo her old boss agrees to loan me. It is of him and Cassy some twenty-three years ago, when she was a producer in the news department and he had come on board as an accountant in payroll. He was, he admitted, "Head over heels in love with her at the time, but then, everybody, *everybody* was." He looks at the photograph again before handing it to me. "Everybody is in love with her still."

Looking at the photograph, at least from a physical viewpoint, one can see why.

I ask him if he knew Michael Cochran and he says, yes, of course he did, everyone did. When he adds nothing further, I ask him what he thought of him. "As a news producer?" he asks, sitting back in his chair. "An ace. Absolutely first-rate."

"And as a husband?"

He frowns and vigorously shakes his head. "No comment."

After a moment, though, he adds, "But I'm glad she's not married to him anymore."

As I ride over in a taxi to West End for my big interview of the day, with Jessica Wright, I make some notes. It has become very clear, very fast that Cassy could have easily strayed along the way, that her beauty had attracted all kinds of offers. It has also become increasingly interesting to me how rigorously she insisted on staying behind the camera, preferring instead to slog her way up the production side of the business.

There was, of course, the mother. With that woman screaming at her for so many years, Cassy no doubt came to view her looks as synonymous with hell.

The cab stops at the front gates and I am checked in. We drive down into the reception circle. Today I am met at the driveway by a woman who says she's DBS security, but I think she looks more like a recruiter for the Junior League. Her ID reads Wendy Mitchell. She is somewhere in her thirties, I guess, and has a calm, laid-back look.

"You don't look like security," I say, attaching my security pass to the lapel of my blazer.

"Which is exactly why I am," she says with boarding-school ease. "This way." She gestures. "I'll take you up to Jessica's office."

I follow her into the complex. In the elevator I ask, "Do you mind me asking how you got into this line of work?"

"Not at all. I was a private investigator, and after Jessica had her incident—"

This translates, I assume, into "After Jessica Wright was kidnapped and nearly killed..."

"The network offered me a job to supervise the security on the talent."

"Just here, or elsewhere, too?"

"Oh, I travel with them. Like when *The Jessica Wright Show* was taping on the West Coast a few weeks ago. Or if Alexandra goes overseas, I usually go."

"So you're kind of a bodyguard as well."

She laughs a little, holding the elevator door for me as I get out. "Yeah, I guess."

I don't know why she finds that funny, but I don't have time to ask. We are already walking down the third-floor hallway of Darenbrook III, the north wing of the DBS broadcast center. We stop outside Jessica Wright's office where Marianne, the young Asian woman I met last week, is furiously typing into a computer. She glances up and then stands to stick out her hand. "Hello, Ms. Harrington. It's nice to see you again."

"Hi, Marianne." From her expression I can tell she is both surprised and pleased I remember her name. No need for her to know that I have drawn a chart of DBS with everyone's name filled in.

"May I get you something to drink?"

"No, thank you."

A loud wail comes from the inner office. Marianne smiles. "Jessica's on the phone with her agent. She said for you to go right in."

Wendy leads me in and I see the talk-show hostess standing behind her desk with the phone at her ear. She is something. First off, she is not much older than I am. I don't know why, but while she looks great on TV, she "feels" as old as the hills. Here, though, in real life, there is a vitality that is undeniable. While I found everything about anchorwoman Alexandra Waring sleekly battened down, everything about Jessica Wright seems softly right out there, physically and emotionally. She is wearing a short blue-jeans skirt, cotton top and clogs. Her legs are bare and tan; she has little makeup on but her eyes burn fiercely green; and her auburn hair seems much lighter than it is on TV. She smiles at me as I come in. At Wendy's direction, I take a seat on the couch that runs along one wall and start setting up my gear on the coffee table in front of it.

"No-no-no!" Jessica Wright is half yelling into the phone. "I don't care how much he's offering! Tell him he can burn in hell before I'll ever lift a finger for him—and even then it will probably be to fly him the bird." Her eyes have lowered slightly—and she is focusing on the chair across from me, listening. Her voluptuous mouth suddenly pulls horizontally into a line and her voice drops to a low rush. "I understand you have to deal with him on other projects with other clients. But I don't want you soft-soaping my reaction. I don't want you saying any 'As much as Jessica would like to, *but*—' crap. The message you are to convey to him is—" her voice is beginning to boom "—that he's a total fucking sleazebag and Jessica says back off before she really gets mad."

I have to choke down a laugh. Wendy mouths "goodbye" and backs out of the office, closing the door.

In a few moments, Jessica Wright is off the telephone, we've shaken hands and she is seated across from me, deftly crossing her legs at the knee. There is a knowing wariness in her expression. This gal's done a lot of interviews. "You certainly don't look like one of Verity's regulars," she observes.

I smile. The tape is running.

"She usually sends us some angry overeater, or undereater, or something not very healthy. You know what I mean? With a lot of suppressed rage coursing just below the surface? You know the kind of writer I'm talking about?"

I'm laughing. It is true. I don't know what it is about magazine writers, but on the whole they tend not to be a very happy lot.

"A little bird told me you got this assignment because you found Verity and Corbett in the woods," she says next. "It sounds like your big career break is as bizarre as mine was," and then she launches into a short history about how substituting on a community affairs TV show in Tucson ultimately led her to becoming one of the best-loved TV personalities in the nation.

I find Jessica Wright absolutely charming. She is funny and bright and slightly wicked, but I get the sense she is only slightly wicked about people she thinks deserve it. Like the producer her agent had just asked her to do a special for, a man who years ago had tried to blackmail a friend of hers. I'm dying to pursue this, but she sweetly refuses and instead launches into how Jackson Darenbrook discovered her "little" syndicated talk show out of Tucson and gave her a contract with DBS. She's quite comfortable admitting she arrived in New York "pretty much an alcoholic basket case. Three-tenths a drinking problem, seven-tenths just neurotic and on the verge of a nervous breakdown." Jessica rolls her eyes as she claims she was unceremoniously dumped into Cassy's lap as the only hope for a strong lead-in show to the nightly news.

"You know, of course, that Cassy was only hired to be the executive producer of DBS News, don't you?" When I nod, she races on. "But you know, everything was up for grabs here. We were literally inventing the network as we went. Old Alexandra Eyes was sneaking around, trying to wrangle a merger of our budgets—news and talk, can you imagine?—in an effort to get the staff she needed and get her people on the air months ahead of schedule. It was a wild time."

And then the talk-show hostess's expression dims slightly, and she looks thoughtful.

She is a terrific-looking woman. I can see why she is such a favorite with the people who have appeared on her show. There is something that is so alive, and yet gentle, about Jessica. A kind of vulnerability that surprises me enormously.

She raises her eyes to meet mine. "It's no secret about how I stopped drinking during that time."

I nod. "I read your autobiography—which was very good, by the way."

She beams.

"You wrote a great deal about Alexandra Waring and how you guys became friends—and how Alexandra helped you stay away from alcohol in those early days."

"Mmm," she nods, looking as though she is remembering those days.

"But you didn't say anything about Cassy."

Jessica's smile widens. "That's because she made me take it out."

My ears perk up. "Really?"

She nods. "Really. And it was funny because what I had written was basically how wonderful she was, that it was Cassy, in fact, who arranged for someone to take me to my first self-help meeting. That's AA, but you know, we're supposed to be anonymous so please respect that, okay? Don't say AA or I'll have a fit." (I nod.) "She rearranged my work schedule, suggested a good therapist, got me a nutritionist who specialized in people in recovery, she…" She laughs. "Oh, she did everything. Cassy wanted me to have every chance of getting into recovery, including offering to sacrifice the launch of the network with the suggestion I should go away to a rehab for a month or two."

She shrugs. "But I didn't. I went to the Alexandra Waring rehab instead."

"Right." All this was in the book, how she had stayed with the anchorwoman until she was more stabilized. "But why did Cassy have you strike that from your book?"

"Because that's Cassy. She sees herself as part of DBS. And unlike the rest of us egomaniacs who need our names in lights—" she laughs "—she believes the whole team should be credited for what she does. So I said 'the network' did this, did that. And in a way, she's right, because Cassy can only be who she is here because the CEO, Langley Peterson, and the whole board of directors of Darenbrook Communications, support her completely and totally and rely on her judgment in everything."

I find it interesting that as Jessica starts feeding me Cassy stories, the talk-show hostess doesn't realize they tell me a lot more about her than they do about Cassy. A big part of their relationship, it seems, has been Cassy mirroring Jessica's strengths back to her and pushing Jessica to develop them. While Jessica clearly adores her mentor, I'm not sure how well she actually *knows* Cassy.

Of course, Jessica just may be refusing to transgress an imaginary line in the sand.

She mentions her recent highly-publicized marriage to Will Rafferty, the executive producer of the news division. I ask if Cassy came to the wedding.

"Of course she did!" she nearly cries. "And she would have been *in* it, if she hadn't thrown such a fit. She said she just *couldn't* be a bridesmaid, that she's a million years old or some such nonsense, so I finally let her off the hook."

"Alexandra was your maid of honor."

She nods. "And Georgiana Hamilton-Ayres, the actress, was a bridesmaid. And Alicia Washington, who has her own show now. And then an old friend of mine from out west."

And so the interview continues, and we talk through almost three hours of tape until Marianne comes in to tell Jessica that it's time to start prepping for that night's taping. "Which I hope you'll come to," Jessica says. "I think you might find it interesting."

When I hesitate, she says, "But of course you've got work to do."

"No, I was just thinking. I'm afraid I'm supposed to meet a friend—"

"Say no more! We'll get this friend of yours a pass. Marianne will make all the arrangements."

And so I call Spencer and he says great, he'll be at West End at six.

Marianne escorts me up to the company cafeteria and has lunch with me, confessing that she's been told to keep her eye on me. And then, at two, Chi Chi comes to pick me up and take me to see Langley Peterson, the chief executive officer of all the electronics companies in the Darenbrook Communications empire.

Langley Peterson is tall, quiet and patient. He is the perfect cop in the henhouse, as it were, and judging from the photographs in his office, his wife Belinda—Jackson Darenbrook's sister—is not an unattractive woman. Still, I have to wonder if he has ever been tempted when working with women like Cassy, Jessica Wright and Alexandra Waring.

"So you're writing an article about Cassy," he says, sitting behind his desk. The fact that he's returned to his seat is always telling. But I don't think it's a power play with Langley Peterson; I think he is simply shy.

"Yes," I say, placing the tape recorder on his desk.

"I must admit, I was very surprised she went for this. Cassy is not big on personal publicity."

"I think she views it as an opportunity to promote new areas of DBS programming."

He lets out a gentle laugh, shaking his head. "Now, *that* sounds like Cassy." He sits back in his chair. "So what would you like to know?"

I read back to him some of what Cassy's former boss said about her this morning.

"Yeah," he nods, "that all still applies. All that's missing in those comments is that she is, without a doubt, the best-loved person in this company. And she inspires a kind of personal loyalty to our network that is without peer in the industry." He nods. "Cassy's the best. Really, like that song, better than all the rest. She's the one."

"Surely she must have some unpleasant tasks to perform. I mean, she can't possibly do her job and be nice all the time."

"Oh, she's not," he hastens to assure me with a laugh. "She and I—Cassy and I have gotten into such arguments, you cannot believe. One time Adele, my secretary, sent security in here because she thought for sure something bad was going to happen." He laughs. "Really. I mean, neither one of us is a pushover, and when we disagree, it can be quite a struggle. And if we lose our tempers, which happens maybe once a year, it's always with each other, because that's also Cassy. She knows I can take it, and not take it personally, whereas other people might not be able to get over it."

We talk about this aspect of her personality, that she does have a temper hidden in there, and then I ask him if Cassy has ever fired anyone.

"She's fired lots of people," he says. "This is TV. People come and go and if they can't handle the pace or the work, they've got to move on."

"So there are people out there who aren't particularly fond of her?"

"She couldn't possibly be a good executive and not have some of those people out there."

"A couple of names?" I ask hopefully. "People she's had to fire?"

"Oh, great," he mutters. "Corner me to be the bad guy and cough up names. Well, I can't do that. First of all, we almost always let the people say they quit. Oh, hell!" he cries, hitting the side of his head as if it is an uncooperative old TV, "You can't put that in! That'll hurt a lot of people."

As an answer I reach for the tape recorder, rewind the tape and erase that last part. "Just a few names," I coax.

He gives me two. One is a producer at a cable news network, the other a weekend anchor of a morning show here in New York.

After we finish, Adele books interviews with both.

28

I return to the hotel whistling. I've got some good stuff.

I order a pot of tea up to my room and start transcribing tapes into my laptop computer. Spencer checks in to see if we're still on for West End at six. I go back to work, laughing a couple of times through the Jessica Wright interview. I lose track of time and lurch away from my desk at five-fifteen and jump into the shower. I am just getting the last of the conditioner out of my hair when the phone rings. There is a phone in the bathroom and I wonder about getting electrocuted as the water from my hair streams into the receiver.

"Hey, Sally." It's Buddy D'Amico. "Sorry to bother you." Pause. "Where are you, Niagara Falls?"

"I have a phone in the bathroom. I was taking a shower."

He sighs heavily. "How will we ever get you back on the farm, Sal? A phone in the bathroom, la-di-da-di-da."

I wrap myself in a towel. "So what's up?"

"Actually, that's what I was going to ask you. I heard through the grapevine that you're looking for a membership list of the Masonic Lodge from twenty-one years ago."

"And who might be in this grapevine with you?"

"A detective has his sources," he jokes. "Look, Sally, no kidding, why do you want it?"

"Why are you asking?"

"Because I'm conducting a murder investigation."

"And what could it have to do with that?"

"That's what I'm asking you."

Interesting. If I say my request for a membership of the Masonic Lodge from twenty-one years ago has nothing to do with his investigation, that I'm just curious since Crazy Pete thinks my father belonged to something akin to a Satanic cult, then Buddy will be relieved. On the other hand, since he's asking, he must perceive there could be some kind of connection. "I wanted to see if Tony Meyers belonged."

"Liar," Buddy says. "You know darn well he wouldn't have."

I do? I better read up on my Masonic Lodges. "I meant his father."

"You are so full of it, Harrington," he says.

"Okay, if you're so smart, Buddy, you tell me why I want that list."

"No way," he says. "If you play dumb with me, I play dumb with you."

Now I'm getting irritated. "So what else is new?" I mean it as a rhetorical question, but Buddy takes it literally. He must be tired.

"The Preston Roadhouse went up tonight."

The roadhouse was built a couple of decades ago as the "sporting man's bar" in north Castleford and in no time became a big biker's hangout, drawing gangs from all over the state. A crackdown on the gangs in the past decade changed its clientele somewhat; now it's mostly frequented by employees of the new electric plant down the road and lost fishermen looking for the hydrothermal cooling discharge pipe from the plant that apparently lures fish of mythical proportions.

"Was anyone hurt?"

"No, thank God. But we've all been over there. We had to close 691 for a while, the smoke was so bad. It looks like a short in some kitchen equipment started a fire and then it hit the gas lines and the flame backed up into the tanks and blew out the whole side of the building."

"Huh," I say. "Funny how everything's blowing up around town this week, isn't it?"

"That's what I was thinking. Got any ideas?"

"There wasn't any real insurance on Tranowsky's Auto Body," I say. "There was no value to the land, really. We thought, if anything, maybe someone was trying to get rid of something in the building." I put the lid down on the john so I can sit. "To tell you the truth, Bud, the first thing I wondered was if Johnny Boy Meyers or somebody was in there."

"Great minds think alike," he tells me. "But he wasn't. Nothing was in there."

"What about the insurance on the roadhouse?"

"Oh, heavily insured, actually. The owner will do fine."

"Who is the owner?"

"Some guy in Norwalk."

"Norwalk? Who would commute from Norwalk?"

"He owns a bunch of stuff around here. He got the roadhouse and a lot of other parcels at one of the auctions." During the recession, about twenty percent of Castleford business properties changed hands this way due to the domino effect of bankruptcies. It was hard to keep track of who owned what anymore.

"Do you think it was deliberate?"

"I'll wait until Dean files his official report," he says, referring to the fire marshal. "They had the dogs there."

The dogs that worked for the fire department were amazing. They could get past any smell imaginable to zero in on the one they had been trained to find. One dog was trained to find gasoline and derivatives like kerosene; another, explosives. I've seen the gasoline-trained dog go through the charred remains of what had been a two-family house and point out six different places to the fire marshal. When the lab tested those spots, they tested positive for kerosene. And so they knew that someone had poured kerosene in six places on the ground floor to get the fire started.

"Keep me posted, will you?"

"Yeah, right, Miss Glamour Girl. I'll call you on your bathroom phone."

I hurry to dry my hair and get dressed. I grab my cosmetics bag to put my makeup on in the cab. I feel like a New Yorker now.

When we arrive at the West End gate, I realize Spencer's in the cab in front of me. I throw some bills at my driver and run to join Spencer.

"Hey," Spencer says appreciatively, sliding his hand into mine and kissing me hello. "I was going to apologize for being late, but..."

We are dropped off at the circle where security is waiting. As we are processed and taken inside to Studio B, Spencer is impressed with how many people I seem to know: Wendy the security gal; the receptionist; Jessica's secretary, Marianne. As we approach the studio doors, Alexandra Waring comes up the hallway and waves to me. "When's our interview?" she calls.

"Next week."

"Great! See you then!"

"This is some company you keep," Spencer observes.

"They're such a nice bunch, you can't imagine."

"I can, actually," he says as we file into the studio. "We published Jessica's autobiography, remember? I met a lot of them at her party."

I turn. "You were at the party where she was kidnapped?"

He nods.

"Then you know Cassy?" It is amazing to me that we have not had this conversation before, but then we really haven't talked about the piece at all. I don't like to discuss what I'm working on.

"I've met her—briefly. I don't *know* her."

Marianne shows us to two seats in the front of the studio audience. The place is full and the audience members are raring to go. It reminds me a lot of *The Tonight Show* studio in Burbank.

A man comes out to warm us up. He tells us, "We have a positively bizarre show tonight—Jessica thought of it. The producers have chosen five people who think they are coming to West End to simply watch the show, but are, in fact, set up to witness an accident, which we set up, outside the complex. The accident was videotaped. Now each of these people is going to, separately, describe what happened. Also appearing on the show are three famous attorneys who will critique the testimony of each 'witness' and choose the one they think will make the best for court and why. After all is said and done, the video will be played to show what actually happened at the scene of the accident."

The show comes off brilliantly. One attorney, a defense attorney, rouses boos and hisses from the audience after he insists the witness he has chosen as the best—a white, good-looking mother of two who is proved to have the most dreadfully inaccurate recollection of the accident—still makes the best witness because jurors will believe her.

When the show's over, Marianne takes us to Jessica's dressing room to say hi.

"Oh, my God," she says, rising from her dressing room mirror, where she is wiping off the worst of the TV makeup, "this is your *friend?*" She laughs, shaking her head. "Hello, Spencer, how are you?"

"Very, very good, Jessica," he says, coming over to kiss her on the cheek. "It was a wonderful show."

The talk-show host is still clearly taken back. She points first at me, then at him and then back to me. "How do you two know each other?"

"We just met last week."

Jessica smiles, nodding, looking at both of us. "Cool," she finally says, going back to her dressing table.

"Why did she say 'Cool'?" I immediately ask when we get into a taxi.

"I don't know," Spencer says.

"Do you think she knows we're more than just friends?"

"I don't know," he says again, putting his arm around me.

"Why don't you know anything?" I demand.

"Oh, I'm a very lucky man," he murmurs, kissing me.

We go to his house and order some Indian food. We eat it at the dining room table and talk awhile. Then we curl up under an afghan on the couch (we have to keep the air-conditioning on, Spencer says, because it's too noisy with the windows open) and we watch a movie.

Then we go into the bedroom and make love. Quietly, tenderly, a first for us.

I fall asleep in his arms.

But not before I hear Spencer whisper, "Thank you, God."

29

The alarm goes off at six and Spencer is out to the world. I just get up, reset the alarm for seven, slip on my clothes, kiss him softly on the forehead and go back to the hotel.

I've got a very busy day. I shower and do my room service thing and review my notes. At nine-fifteen I've got an interview with Bonnie Kirk, a news producer who was fired from DBS last year. I take a cab down to Eighth Avenue, nearly across the street from Madison Square Garden, and check in with the reception desk of a competing network. I am cleared to go up.

Bonnie Kirk has that stressed-out look everybody in news has on a bad day, although I strongly suspect she may have more of these than most. She asks me if I mind talking in "a special hideaway," and when I say no, I find myself being ushered into a concrete stairwell where she immediately lights up a cigarette, drags heavily and sits down on a stair to talk.

"I find it very strange you're writing about Cassy," she tells me. "She will usually do anything to stay out of the limelight." She drags again. "Does she *know* you're writing about her?"

"Oh, yeah," I acknowledge.

"Huh," the news producer says, "then maybe they're in trouble."

My eyebrows go up.

"That's the only reason Cassy would do this. If she thought there was no other way. To, you know, boost the ratings." She squints, chin resting in her hand, cigarette next to her face, smoke drifting up.

"I think she wants to help promote the network's new programming," I offer. "Now then," I say, tapping my papers together to signal we are going to begin. I am sitting on the first step below the landing, twisting around to address this woman above me. I am acutely aware of my muscles. I have used muscles with Spencer I know for a fact haven't been used in years, if ever. I smile to myself. It was a wonderful night. Spencer is a wonderful man. I have a wonderful job assignment.

Life is good.

"Maybe we should start at the beginning. What job did you hold at DBS?"

"Features producer, the nightly news."

"And your responsibilities?"

"To oversee every nonhard news feature story we developed either in New York or through one of the affiliates."

"And how long did you work at DBS?"

"Oh, ten months."

I look up. "Not long."

She cracks a smile. "Not long," she agrees, dragging on the cigarette and then mashing it out on the landing with her shoe.

"And you left...?"

"I left, all right." She laughs. "But not without letting people know what I thought."

"And what was that?"

"That Alexandra thinks she's God and she's not." She lights another cigarette and hastily exhales smoke over her head. "That you can't do anything at DBS News without Alexandra looking over your shoulder, screwing around with your stories, criticizing stuff and then, if the story is great—and a lot of our stories were—she gets all the credit."

"Did you say she *takes* the credit or she's *given* the credit?" I ask, trying to get this right.

"Given," she admits. "She's not that bad, not yet. She's not like the guys. The credit's given to her—she doesn't try to take it—but in the end, what does it matter? Either you become an extension of Alexandra or you're out."

I nod. "Well, she is the managing editor, right?"

"More like Evita Peron, managing dictator. And you can quote me on that."

I smile, making a note although the recorder is running. "This is not a piece about Alexandra Waring," I remind her.

"Oh, right, Cassy." She pulls on the cigarette. "Cassy was all right. If she has a fault, it's that she lets Alexandra get away with murder. Jessica Wright, too. They bend and break the rules left and right—"

"What kind of rules?"

"Oh, you know, they just hire and fire people at will, they really don't give everybody a chance. I mean, it's such a little club there, either you're in or you're out and it depends on their moods most of the time. And they have such fucked-up personal lives, who knows what their moods will be."

"Jessica's married—"

"Yeah, to my old boss, Will Rafferty. What does that tell you about the inner circle there? It's practically incestuous."

"And you think Cassy has allowed this—what would you call it, nepotism?"

"Ha!" the producer cries. "Come *on! She's* married to the guy who controls the whole shebang, Jackson Darenbrook! Langley Peterson, the CEO, is married to Jackson's sister! Jessica's married to the executive news producer of her best friend's newscast."

"And Alexandra?"

"Oh, Alexandra," she says in a conspiratorial voice, mushing out her cigarette. "Well, you know she's a major dyke, right?"

I choose not to respond but look interested. And I am.

"She's been messing around with Georgiana Hamilton-Ayres for like three years. So if you want to know what I think Cassy's most valuable asset to DBS is, it's been handling the spin on *that* story. For God's sake, they're photographed in the *Inquiring Eye* every week as 'gal pals' and the network pretends it's not happening."

"But don't you think that's Cassy's job, in a way?" I ask. "To develop strong programming and financial stability for DBS, and foster and protect those people who can make it happen?"

Bonnie Kirk stares at me a moment and then shakes her head, letting out a husky, bitter laugh. "Boy, have you bought into it big-time, I can tell."

"Bought into what?"

"The Inner Circle. The Daisy Chain. You think Cassy's just great, don't you? And the others? You buy into that whole 'We are family at DBS' shit. Come on, admit it."

I'd like to admit that if Bonnie Kirk worked for me, I'd fire her, too, her attitude is so annoying. But I don't. I suffer the rest of the interview wondering if she'll ever say anything substantive about Cassy, but she never does. Her ax to grind is with Alexandra Waring and that is all she wants to talk about.

I find that interesting, though, the angle on Alexandra Waring and Georgiana Hamilton-Ayres.

By twenty to eleven I am racing to get to West End, scanning another set of questions I have prepared for Jackson Darenbrook. Chi Chi meets me at the security desk and takes me upstairs to his office. It is enormous, almost like a one-room house. There is an office area, a bar area, a living room area, a conference area and in the corner, a StairMaster. He jumps up from behind his desk and kind of bounces over. He seems to be in a feisty mood, but then I think he might always be this way.

"It's such a nice day," he says after we say hello, "maybe you'd like to do this outside."

I say that with all my stuff, particularly the recorder, it's probably better to work in here. He says sure and lets me choose where I want to sit. I opt for the conference table, where I set the recorder down between us.

"So what do you want to know about my wonderful, beautiful, thoughtful, kind, generous, brilliant, sensational wife?" he begins.

"I was going to ask you how you fell in love with your wonderful, beautiful, thoughtful, kind, generous, brilliant, sensational wife," I say back to him, "but I realize that is a rhetorical question."

He kicks back his head and laughs. He is a cool guy. Likable. Something between Harrison Ford and Ted Turner. "I see why Cassy likes you," he tells me. "You're bright. Maybe you want a job here."

"Sounds good to me."

"I bet it does." He frowns. "How did you get mixed up with Corbett Schroeder, anyway?"

I look at him. "I didn't. I'm working for his wife."

He grunts, still frowning, and mutters something about Verity getting her head examined.

"I'm sorry," I say, "I missed what you said."

He sighs, deflated. "I promised Cassy I wouldn't say anything."

"Say anything about what?"

He flashes a grin. "You *are* a tricky one. We *should* hire you. I've got three hundred newspapers and twelve magazines."

"Is that a bribe, Mr. Darenbrook?"

"Well, it could be." He winks.

I laugh.

"Okay, so let me tell you about my wife," he says, looking at his watch as if he has timed this presentation. He looks back across the table at me. "Cassy has given me life. I swear. After my wife—my first wife—"

"Barbara," I say.

He nods. "After Barbara died so suddenly..."

His wife, I know, had been participating in some sort of diving contest at their country club. The Darenbrook children were on the swim team and it was an annual Labor Day weekend event, where the parents goofed around for the benefit of the kids. Barbara Darenbrook had hit her head on the bottom of the pool and died instantly.

"I didn't think I'd ever connect with another human being. 'Cause Barb and I were so close..." He smiles to himself. "But then I met Cassy—gosh, it was like ten years later—and, well, I love her more than anything." He examines my face carefully. "Sounds like bull, doesn't it? But let me tell you, Sally Harrington, I've been around. I mean, *around*—around and around and back again—if you know what I mean."

"I know what you mean," I assure him.

"When I first met Cassy," he continues, "I couldn't stand her and you know why? Because she represented everything I had been running away from since my wife's death. Love, responsibility, family, *myself*. When she came into my life, she called me on everything, demanded I snap out of it."

He looks away for a moment. "Thank God Cassy arrived when she did." He looks at me. "When there was still time to reach my kids. Lydia and Kevin." He sighs. "Barbara's sister and her husband raised the kids after Barbara died." He looks away again. "I don't know what would have happened to us." His eyes come back. "As a family, I mean. If Cassy hadn't come along when she did." He smiles. "They're grown up now, Lyddie and Kev, with good lives of their own."

"Cassy said that you two argued a bit when she came here."

"A *bit?*" He roars with laughter. "Yeah, I'll say—we argued a bit, all right, like day and night. I'll tell ya, it was so bad, I thought I was going to have to fire her. I couldn't *stand* her."

"So why didn't you fire her?"

"Creepin' crickets, you ever gone up against Alexandra and Langley about anything? Separately they're bad enough, but together? Ha! Forget it. And then Jessica jumped on board the Cassy wagon and, you know, it looked like everyone was going to fire *me* and I ran the joint!"

We talk a little more about this and then I ask him why he hired her in the first place.

"Alexandra," he says. "It was part of our offer to her, that we would offer Cassy the job of executive producer for DBS News at a stated salary. And she wasn't cheap," he adds.

"And whose idea was it to promote Cassy to president of the network?"

"Langley's. Of course, we made her executive producer of both the newscast and Jessica's show."

"And whose idea was that?"

"Langley's." He thinks a moment, eyes twinkling. "No, it could have been Alexandra's. Originally. And I'll tell you why." And then he explains that at the time, Alexandra wanted to go on the air earlier than DBS had planned, to take advantage of the reruns on the other networks. Alexandra knew she needed to have Jessica Wright as a follow-up to the news, which meant DBS could offer at least two hours of prime-time programming to the affiliates. They also pooled some of the production crews—to cut costs—so it made sense for Cassy to oversee it all."

"What did the unions say?"

"Until we had, uh, I think it was eighteen hours of programming a week, we technically weren't a network yet, and so we were exempt for a while on some regulations. For a while, anyway, we certainly aren't now." He squints at me. "You haven't talked to Lang yet, I guess."

"Oh, but I have," I tell him.

"Well, he should be the one to tell you all this stuff."

"Who's to say he hasn't? I just like to hear your opinion." I glance down at my notes. "So, Mr. Darenbrook—"

"Jackson, please."

"Jackson. How did this office romance start? I mean, how did you get from being co-workers to lovers?"

He bursts out laughing. "You've got to be kidding! What kind of question is that?"

"Well, if you met Cassy at work, and then you married her, certainly there had to have been a moment of transition, when you realized that what you wished to pursue with her was not business."

"Gad, but you're a pain in the ass," he says congenially, rising to walk over to the bar. "You want some 7UP or something?"

"No thanks."

He's clinking some ice into his glass and then uses a bartender hose to squirt soda over it. "When she cried."

"Pardon me?"

"When Cassy cried. Here, in my office. She said I was driving her crazy and I realized I was falling in love with her." He walks back over to the table and sits down. "It was right after she threw a section of the *New York Times* at me and screamed that I was driving her crazy. And then she burst into tears and I knew that was it. I was falling for her."

"When was this?"

"The Friday before we went on the air."

I make a note. "And were your feelings reciprocated?"

He shrugs. "I have no idea. Actually, I've never asked her. Because nothing happened that day—except that I knew. I'm not sure I wanted to know—it was kind of like someone throwing the lever that makes the drawbridge come crashing down over the moat, you know?" He thinks for a moment. "I think I was just a lot nicer to her after that. I stopped trying to make her so crazy, anyway."

This is very good. It will be interesting to read some of this back to Cassy for her reaction.

"And when," I ask, "did you know that Cassy had feelings for you?"

His smile broadens and those eyes twinkle again. "I think you should ask Cassy that. After all, a gentleman *always* defers to the lady's version of events."

* * *

I have to skip lunch to make my two o'clock with Glenn Mortimer, the political analyst, who was also fired from DBS news. He is now the weekend co-anchor of the morning show of a rival network. His office is near Lincoln Center and I am shown right in.

We shake hands and he tells me I can set up my tape recorder right there on his desk. As I set up, we chat and I sneak looks at him. He must get his hair done. I mean really done. Poofed, practically. But he seems nice enough.

"So you're doing a story on Cassy," he says, sitting back in a chair and bouncing his fingertips off one another. "I'm rather surprised. She usually ducks that sort of thing and pushes it on one of us on-air types."

"You're not the first to say that," I comment.

"What's she pushing?"

"Some new programming, I think."

"That's the only reason she'd ever do it," he says. "And if I know Cassy, it's probably connected to feeding children or bandaging wounded animals."

"Why is that?"

He shrugs. "That's the way she is. Looks like a goddess, but acts like Mother Earth. That's her thing, taking care of people, places and things. The more control she has, the happier she is."

Not a bad quote, I think.

He smiles, lofting an eyebrow. "Some might consider it a problem."

"Consider what a problem?"

"Being a control freak, you know."

"Do you consider it a problem?"

"Me? No. I like Cassy. I wouldn't call her a control freak. But I would say she has a strong desire to control everything she can."

Oh, brother, people with this kind of double-talk drive me nuts. No wonder he likes politics.

We move on to his role at DBS as their political commentator. He worked there two years and then his contract was not renewed.

"Who broke the news to you?"

"My agent."

"Ouch," I say.

"Ouch is right."

"Why didn't Cassy tell you?"

"Oh, she did, in every way she was allowed to. But, you know—" he shrugs "—none of the brass are ever allowed to tell talent anything. It's all really supposed to go through your agent. When the time for renewal was coming up, I tried to talk to Alexandra about the changes I thought we needed to make to my segment, but she wasn't really listening, I could tell. But I didn't think I was getting fired, I just thought Alexandra wasn't very interested in changing the format. That's what she's like. If she agrees with you, it's like the Fourth of July, everything all exploding in beautiful colors, but if Alexandra doesn't agree with you, she just gets very quiet and polite and you feel like she's merely tolerating you—you, way out there in Siberia."

"And what about Cassy?"

"Oh, Cassy was great. She sat me down about a month before contract negotiations and, thinking back—" he stretches and yawns before continuing "—I realize now she was trying to forewarn me of what was coming."

"Why, what did she say?"

"Just that political coverage was changing drastically at the other networks, that the general feeling was that our segment was a bit static and needed more pizzazz."

"How did you react to that?"

"I thought it was showbiz and told her so. That they hired me—make that Alexandra hired me—because she wanted more of an intellectual angle on politics. More like Bill Buckley and less redneck screaming and yelling like my successor does now over there."

I must say, the DBS political commentator surprises me, too. While the rest of the news hour is known for its integrity and fairness, the guy they have now is better known for his borderline insanity on the topic of red tape in Washington than for anything he actually says.

"How much did Cassy have to do with you while you were at DBS?"

"Oh, I saw her all the time. She's a hands-on kind of person.

Of course, she's been in news since forever, so she loves being around the newsroom and the studio. We used to think we would always be her favorite part of the network...."

"But?"

"She loves the news division, but keeps it at arm's length because of Alexandra. It's Alexandra's domain. Now *there's* the control freak, Alexandra—and you can quote me on that."

"Unfortunately I'm not doing a piece on Alexandra," I say, making a note and then looking up. "I'm doing it on Cassy."

"You can't write about one without mentioning the other," he says. "Certainly Cassy is a good executive on her own merits, but everybody knows part of her success comes from successfully handling Alexandra and all of her problems."

"And what kind of problems might those be?"

"Well, her control problems, like I said before. She drives any normal person up the wall."

"It's my understanding that her crew has been with her quite awhile."

"You mean Will Rafferty," he says, practically sneering. "Yeah, well, look who he's married to—Alexandra's best friend. She's even got that under control."

"I see," I say, nodding, writing. "What other problems does she have?"

"Well she's gay, let's start with that."

"Do you want to be quoted on that?"

"Go ahead and see if *Expectations* prints it. They won't. I don't know what it is in this town—everybody knows it but *nobody* wants to say it."

"I think the tabloids do." I recross my legs and try again. "Let's get back to Cassy, though. How do you think she 'successfully handles' Alexandra?"

"If I knew that, I'd still be there."

"So your ax to grind is with Alexandra, not Cassy."

"I don't have an ax to grind!" he says.

"I see." I take a breath, glancing at the wall of awards behind him. "Is that why you agreed to talk to me?" I'm trying to keep my voice light. "To talk about Alexandra?"

Suddenly he's pissed. "No. You called me, remember? What do you want to know about Cassy? She's frankly not very interesting—that is, beyond her looks." He considers this. "Well, I suppose it's kind of interesting. She's still a looker." He shrugs again. "I suppose it is kind of interesting that she ended up with the biggest playboy in the Western Hemisphere."

"Yes, that is pretty interesting."

"Jackson's nuts, you know," he confides. "At least the other husband drank and got nuts. This one's just nuts."

"Nuts?" I repeat, giving him a chance to retract this comment.

"All right, eccentric," he says.

I look up. "Why do you think Cassy married him?"

He looks at me as if I've got three eyes. "You're asking why the president of the network married the guy who owns it?"

"Yes."

He decides not to call me stupid. Instead he says, "Security."

I nod. "Don't you think she might have sought such security with a man with a little better track record? Someone who was not, as you said, 'the biggest playboy in the Western Hemisphere'?"

"Compared to her first husband, Jackson's a dreamboat. Michael humiliated her time and again. Besides, Jackson's got a couple hundred million in the bank, so why not take a chance?"

When I do not say anything, he adds, "Think about it. She's married for years to a jerk who drank and screwed around on her, left and right, and stands by him. So then he straightens himself out, right? And what does he do? He starts fucking around on her again and leaves *her.* Talk about *Beauty and the Beast* with a twist! So, you tell me... The creep finally takes off, you've been humiliated in the industry for years, so what are you going to do if Jackson Darenbrook starts making eyes at you?"

I only smile. He's giving me good stuff. The only problem is, I think I hate him.

"Did you know Michael Cochran?"

"Yeah, I knew Mike. I worked for him." He nods. "That's right. At WWKK here in New York."

"How long did you work with him?"

"A year."

"And what was it like?"

"Geez, he was such a drunk. Smart guy, but what a drunk."
He rolls his eyes. "I mean the first time you went out with him,
it was okay, but then it was like every night he wanted to go out
and then he'd get blind drunk and fall down and pass out. It
was awful." He chuckles. "That's how I met Cassy the first
time. She had to come down to a bar one night to get him before
they called the police. I helped her take him home. He threw up
out the window of the cab. Yeah, great night. And the next day,
I swear to God, he didn't have a clue about what happened, no
memory at all. And then I knew that's how he kept doing it, he
never remembered what he did. So why not? Particularly if
you've got a wife who'll bail you out all the time."

"Did you ever meet the Cochrans' son?"

"Harry?"

"Henry."

"Henry! Yeah, that's right, Henry. He was a good kid. He
came to the office once in a while. He was a lot more like
Cassy—lucky for him. But not a pretty boy, if you know what I
mean, which is good because Michael always had to be the big
man on campus. So the kid had to be submissive but not a fairy,
you know? He knew how to handle his dad, too, which was
more than I can say for Cassy."

We talk on in this vein and I am amazed Glenn Mortimer
isn't more guarded about his language. He's *supposed* to be the
wholesome friendly face in the morning, not the foulmouthed,
angry man he is. I also have the impression that he was offered
a wonderful opportunity at DBS but didn't cut the mustard.

He has given me a lot of interesting things to think about, certainly.

I take a cab back to the hotel and stop at the desk to cash a
check. I am going through cash in this city like water. I go upstairs, order a sandwich and large bottle of water and set to
work while today's interviews are fresh in my mind.

It feels great to work.

30

Spencer has to work until nine, so at eight I knock off and soak in the tub. About eight-thirty, as I am finishing the *Times* crossword puzzle, the phone rings. Now that I am a woman of the world who is used to such convenience, I am annoyed when I realize I can't reach the phone from the tub. I'm going to have to get out.

"Sally," Doug's voice says.

I am caught by surprise. "Doug, hi."

"I hope I didn't catch you at a bad time. Your mother gave me your number."

"I'm in the tub, actually."

Pause. "So how's it going?"

"Very well. I had some good interviews today." Normally I would share something about them with Doug but now I only feel resistance.

There is an awkward silence. "I just wanted to see how you're doing."

"I know," I murmur. "I've been wondering about you, too."

"Have you?" He sounds hopeful and that hurts.

"I'll always care about you, Doug," I say carefully. "It feels strange for us to be like this. And yet it never works. Does it?"

He sighs heavily. "I don't know what's left to try, Sal."

"I know."

"Can I see you? This weekend?"

"Sure," I say. "Let me call you when I know what's what, okay?"

"Okay." He sounds relieved.

"I'll call you when I come home," I promise.

I dry off and start putting on body lotion. The phone rings again and apprehensively I pick it up. "Red rover, red rover," Spencer says, "will Sally come over?"

"You bet," I laugh.

* * *

When I get off the elevator in Spencer's building, I find his cat, Seela, wandering around. I shift my bag over my shoulder and pick her up. I hear Spencer say hi and I look down the hall to see him coming to meet me. "Seela never lets anyone pick her up but me," he says. "So what is she doing in your arms?"

"I don't know," I murmur, lightly kissing the top of the cat's head.

"We're all falling in love with you," he sighs, kissing me on the cheek and sliding my bag off my shoulder to carry it for me.

"It feels so normal now for you to be here," he says, closing the door behind us. "It felt strange to come home and not find you here."

He's tired. He's been running around with an author who's starting his promotional tour. He opens a can of vegetable soup and makes a salad and some toast and serves us both at the table I've set, and he tells me about his day. Then he asks me about mine. I mumble something about the interviews going well, I think I'm starting to get a picture of what Cassy is really like.

Spencer clears the dishes and asks me if I'd like some herbal tea.

I look at him. Herbal tea. This is one of those moments where no matter how much we pretend to know each other it is blatantly evident that we don't. "No, I'm fine, thanks." While he is putting the kettle on the stove, I hear the faint sound of my cell phone ringing.

I excuse myself and run into the bedroom where I retrieve it from my bag. "Hello?"

"Still in New York?" Buddy D'Amico says.

"Yeah." I look at the clock. It's almost ten-thirty.

"You got a fax machine around?"

"I think so, hang on." I run out to ask Spencer and he gives me the fax number of the front desk downstairs. I give it to Buddy.

"Are you still at the office?" I ask, amazed.

"Yeah. Okay, so look, Sally, I'm sending you that membership list of the Masons. Don't say I've never done anything for you."

"Well, thank you." I am baffled. "Um, am I allowed to ask what I've done to deserve this?"

"Oh, I'm just in a good mood," Buddy says. "Because I've just caught Tony Meyers's killer, and I'm going to put him away."

"You're kidding! Who is it?"

"No one you know," he says cheerfully. "See you back in town!"

I try to raise Joe Bix on the telephone, but he doesn't seem to be around. So I call into the city desk and give them the news so they can sneak an item into the morning paper.

When I come back into the living room, I find Spencer stretched out across the love seat, his feet on the coffee table, watching the news. "Do you mind?" he asks.

Now we're getting to know each other. When the guy starts turning on the TV instead of fooling around, I know we are.

Eyes on the TV screen, Spencer holds an arm out, indicating the spot where I am to sit. "The doorman will bring up your fax."

"Oh, great," I say, sitting down next to him.

In a couple of minutes the doorman rings the doorbell and I get the fax from him. While Spencer watches the news, I look it over. For a town like Castleford, which has a diverse, heavily Catholic population, I see few ethnic names. As a matter of fact, this looks like a phone book for the United Kingdom during the reign of Henry VIII. Adams through Young. I recognize almost every surname on this list.

If I were Crazy Pete Sabatino, I'd think there was a conspiracy to be feared with the Masons, too.

An awful lot of these people, though, I notice, have either moved away from Castleford or have passed away. Certainly most of the children and grandchildren of these guys—my contemporaries—are no longer around.

The next pages cover the more recent membership roster, and although it is dramatically shorter, it at least resembles something from the twentieth century. Interesting. One Black man. One Hispanic. And the Masons are obviously a Christian thing.

Well, whatever this Masonic Lodge was that Dad belonged

to, it's either losing its appeal in Castleford, or it appeals to a group that no longer thrives in Castleford. Or in the area, either. The second list is annotated to say that the lodges of the four surrounding towns have, in recent years, been folded into the Castleford Lodge.

"What's that?" Spencer asks during a commercial.

"A list of the members of our Masonic Lodge in Castleford."

"My dad's a Mason."

"Really? How come?"

He shrugs. "I don't know. It's a club. You know, it's just guys sitting around."

"But only Christian guys, right?"

"I don't know." He thinks for a second. "There's the Ancient Order of Hibernians for Irish Catholics and Knights of Columbus for Italian Catholics, right?"

I shrug. "So what do they do at these meetings?"

"It's a civic group, like Rotary or the Elks or something."

"Rotary has women in it," I point out.

"Then it's like the DAR," he counters, referring to the Daughters of the American Revolution. "Anyway, they give scholarships and stuff."

"Do they have secret handshakes?"

He smiles. "Yeah, I think they do. That's why I wanted to join when I was a kid. I thought they had code rings."

"Do they have hoods and robes and stuff?"

"That's the KKK, Sally," he says, kissing my forehead.

"I don't know," I say, "I have a hard time believing my father belonged to such a group."

"Your father was an architect!" Spencer says. "The Masons were originally a guild in England somewhere, of all the stone builders—masons, get it? And so if you've got an English name, like Harrington, and you've got an architect, I think you've got someone who's likely to be a Mason."

I think about this while Spencer returns his attention to the news. I put the list away. "I'm going to crawl into bed and read a bit, okay?"

Spencer nods, smiling, eyes on the sports scores.

A week ago we were tearing each other's clothes off in the

hotel lobby after knowing each other for only a few hours; tonight we are an old married couple.

Whatever, I think, sliding under the sheets. One thing I love about this apartment is that Spencer has lamps with brighter bulbs in them than regular people. This is an apartment meant to curl up and read in and not go blind.

I start reading through the background material I have for tomorrow's interviews and I doze off.

I awaken when Spencer comes in after *Nightline*. He turns off the light and slides into bed, the two of us getting settled into a sleeping position on our sides. We are going to sleep.

I feel something. And I smile. I roll over and whisper, "I thought you were exhausted," and Spencer laughs, he thought so, too. "But I guess you're too much for me, Sally."

We make love.

31

When I get back to my hotel the next morning, I find a voice-mail message from Chi Chi Rodriguez. Apparently Michael Cochran is in town and Cassy wants to know if I'd like to see him while he's here. They can fix something up for this afternoon if I have any time. I call West End and leave a message for them—great, I'm at the hotel, let me know what his schedule's like.

Joe Bix calls at eight-thirty. "How the hell did you find out they made an arrest?"

"Buddy told me."

"And why didn't you tell me?"

"Joe, I called your home and left a message. I left a voice mail at work. You didn't respond to your beeper, what more could I do?"

There are some voices in the background on Joe's end and then he says, "Al wants to speak to you."

"Sally!"

"Hi, Al."

"What the hell is this? You called in a two-sentence story for the front page?"

"Al, I'm not even there. I should think you'd be grateful to have any kind of reference to the arrest in this morning's edition."

"The first part of that statement is key. You are not even here. That's what's screwing everything up."

"Why, what's going on?"

"Why are you looking for the membership lists of the Masonic Lodge?" he says next. "You took a leave to work on that magazine thing, so why do you have time to work on something else in town if you can only call in two-line stories to your own paper?"

I'm missing something here. Clearly I have a part in a drama that no one has remembered to send me a script for. "You're a Mason, aren't you, Al?"

"You're not doing one of those white-supremacy pieces, are you?" he says.

"Yeah, that's you, Al, a white supremacist. Leave me alone and let me talk to Joe, please."

The man they have arrested, Joe tells me, is no one anyone knows. He's from Russia and is employed as a warehouse worker in Queens. Nobody knows anything else.

At exactly nine-fifteen, I place a call on my credit card (hotels kill you with toll charges) to Chicago to reach Cassy's son, Henry Cochran.

He gives me an enthusiastic hello and we go through the preliminaries and I tell Henry that the conversation is being recorded. It is during this chat that I learn that he is sitting in the conference room of one of Chicago's largest architecture firms. He's there, he says, to get the basics down before one day going out on his own. What would he like to design? Buildings. What is he working on now at the firm? He sadly tells me the air-duct system in a new department store that is going up in Evanston.

"Did you go to Northwestern like your parents?" I ask.

"No, I went to Yale."

"Really?" I can't contain my surprise. "My Dad went there. He was an architect, too." And I tell him a little about what he did and Henry says he was lucky and that he hoped he could afford to do what he did, too. "But I've sort of got some upcoming obligations. I mean, well, I'm getting married next year and I'm not sure how messing around on my own can contribute to supporting a family."

I think of what my mother said, about the kind of wife my father needed to be able to risk what he did. I don't even know this young guy, but I have to resist lecturing him on the importance of marrying the right kind of woman if he wants to be a happy architect.

Then I remember how well-to-do his mother is, to say nothing of his stepfather. "Did you ever consider allowing your family to invest in your own firm?"

At this, Henry laughs and I like him. "You really just want to know why I haven't let my rich parents support me?"

"Well, no, I mean, really, invest in your business."

"Oh, come on," he says. "What would the point of that be? What would that prove about my abilities?"

"You want to have a family."

"I don't want handouts!"

"But if you're talented—"

"Then I'll have clients," he finishes for me. "No way, Sally. Come on. You know my mom's story, you know my dad's story. They made it on their own, why shouldn't I?"

This is Cassy's kid all right.

I ask him how he got to Chicago.

"It's where I got the best job. And I have an uncle here, and a cousin I used to visit all the time, so I thought, why not? And then I met Marie, my fiancée, and well, I love Chicago." He pauses. "So what do you want to know about Mom?"

I don't know why, but it is very strange to hear someone call Cassy Cochran Mom, even after hearing how much she mothers people. Is it an age thing? Or a beauty thing? Or a power thing? That a woman like Cassy is actually somebody's mother? Like mine has been to me, like anyone else's has been to them? This is a very important side to her—I hope Henry's talkative.

He is. When I ask him to describe his mother, he says, "She is the wisest, kindest person I know," and then he launches into numerous stories about how she was always helping the neighbors or taking in strays—including people—or volunteering her time because she thought it would mean a lot to Henry, for example, at his school when he was young.

"It's not like Mom had a whole lot of time on her hands." He laughs. "I remember one time Dad figured out that it cost a hundred dollars an hour for her to man the PTO bake sale."

"Was your mother strict?"

"Oh yeah," he says, surprising me. "Yeah, she was. Mom is very big on schedules, very big on routines. I had a set time to start my homework and I had a specific place where I had to do it. So from like second grade right through high school, there I was—at seven o'clock—at the kitchen table and Mom was almost always sitting right across from me doing what she called *her* homework."

He talks about a childhood growing up on Riverside Drive along the Hudson River in Manhattan and spending some weekends in upstate Connecticut.

"And what was the address of the Manhattan apartment?"

"Oh, it's the same one—where Mom and Jackson live now. One sixty-two Riverside Drive. At Eighty-eighth Street."

This surprises me. Usually couples start over in a fresh home if they can, and I mention this.

He laughs again. "Yeah, well, sort of. See, when Mom and Jackson were thinking about getting married, he was living in a hotel in New York—his house was down south. Mom loves the Upper West Side and they didn't see anything they liked any better than where Mom already lived. But of course neither one of them really wanted to hang out where Mom and Dad lived together for so long, so Jackson ended up buying the rest of the entire floor—it was two other apartments, big ones. They made the two other apartments into their living area and then they made a kind of guest suite out of my room, the old guest room and my parents' old room. They use our old living room as a dining room. It's complicated, but really a wonderful place. Kind of an urban mansion, which is what they need because, you know, Jackson has kids who come for holidays and he has what seems like a hundred relatives."

I am more curious, though, about how Cassy juggled a full-time job and a son and steer him back to that.

"Mom always had me in some kind of after-school camp. Sometimes it was sports, sometimes art or computer stuff. When I was really little, she used to run over to school and bring me back to WST. She used to pay the janitor to let me hang out with him while he was cleaning and doing repairs around the building. Then she met another lady in the building who had a kid my age. Mom worked out some kind of deal with her—you'll have to ask her, but I think she paid Roddy's tuition at my school—so then Mrs. Steinberg took charge of us both after school."

When Henry mentions their cleaning lady, Rosanne Di-Santos, who used to pinch-hit for Cassy in any matriarchal crunch, I ask, "Do you have any idea where she is now?"

"Oh, she's still at Mom's. At least, during the day. She's been

Mom's full-time housekeeper since she and Jackson opened up the whole floor. They do a lot of entertaining, for his business and hers, and Rosanne does everything."

I make a note. I want to talk to this Rosanne DiSantos who has been working for Cassy for over fifteen years.

Henry has lots of stories about his mother: how she never had time to exercise so she used to make Henry stand on the landing on the building's staircase and read to her while she tried to run up and down a few flights of stairs; how she and Michael sat in Michael's den and ran tapes of their respective stations' newscasts and critiqued them; how she cooked mountains of food one Sunday every month and filled the second freezer they had in the pantry, and how Henry, when he was little, thought all food came out of plastic bags, frozen; how good his father was at making up stories at bedtime and how dreadful his mother was at it, borrowing heavily from real life. He cracks up. "I swear, Mom used to keep telling me these stories about unhappy subway trains that kept trying to run away, and of course later I realized it was because they were having a lot of problems on our subway line and it was weighing heavily on her mind. But that was Mom. Flights of fancy just were never her thing."

"If there's one thing you could have changed when you were growing up, what would it have been?"

I have asked this as a way of bringing up his father's drinking. But Henry fools me.

"I wish we had a dog."

"Do you have one now?"

"Two," he says.

We talk a little about that. "Henry, if your mother has one fault, what is it?"

"She tries to do too much," he says without hesitation. "So she gets overextended, stressed-out."

"Why do you think she tries to do too much? I mean, your mother is a very intelligent, very self-aware person, why wouldn't she have this under control?"

He thinks so long about his answer, I begin to think he's refusing to even acknowledge that I asked it. "I think," he finally says, slowly, "Mom is in some way trying to make up for my grandfather. It's like she's trying to live two lives' worth, to make up for what he didn't do, for his dying so young, for never fulfilling his promise."

This is pretty deep for a twenty-five-year-old guy.

I ask him about his father.

"I see him a lot here in Chicago. I like his wife all right."

When I ask him about his parents' marriage, he says that I should talk to them about that. I thank Henry profusely and we conclude our interview.

While I was on the phone, Chi Chi called and left a message asking if I could do a late lunch with Michael Cochran.

"I'd also like to talk to Rosanne DiSantos," I say when I call her back.

"Getting a little personal, aren't we?" she asks me.

"Well, the story *is* about a person."

There is a thoughtful silence. "You'll never believe it," Chi Chi says, "but until you just said that I've never thought of it that way. We think in terms of *public* consumption around here, day and night."

Great quote, I think, writing that down.

"I'll ask," Chi Chi says, "but I can't promise anything."

Next I put a call into Verity. I promised I'd touch base and now that I can see how the piece is starting to shape up, I don't mind. She takes my call immediately. "Good, I'm glad you called. I've been wondering where you are, what's happening. I said to Corbett just last night, when he asked me how you were doing, that you went off with Spencer Hawes last week and I never saw or heard from you again."

"It's going very well," I say, deciding to skip over the Spencer part. I tell her about the interviews I've had, and that I'm meeting Michael Cochran for lunch this afternoon, and may be able to talk to Cassy's longtime housekeeper.

"When do you see the mother?" Verity asks.

"Oh, she wouldn't let me. She gave me a phoner, though. She absolutely refuses to let anyone see her and there is a particular photo she wants us to use."

There is a quiet chuckle. "Well, we'll see about that. So what is she like?"

"She is—Verity, oh my—the woman is such a bitch it's unreal."

She laughs. "That is interesting. But listen, Sally, I'm glad it's going well, but I think we should meet. I don't need anything to read, but I want to know what slant you'll be using, talk it through."

Part of me can't help but bristle. This is not normal procedure; this is a signal that Verity feels she is dealing with a novice who needs supervision.

"Will you be in Connecticut this weekend?" she asks.

"Yes."

"Good. Look, Corbett's going to be in Dallas, so why don't you come over to my house in Litchfield, say one o'clock on Sunday? Can you do that?"

"Sure," I say. "But are you sure you don't want to wait a week until I have something for you to read?"

"Quite sure."

"Fine," I say, writing this down on my calendar.

"So you haven't used our facilities here at all," Verity says.

"I haven't needed to yet, but you never know."

There is a pause. The rustle of papers. I imagine that if Verity is like most editors I know, she is probably reading through her mail or messages while talking to me. "So," she says absently, "you never told me, how was your night out with Spencer?"

Oh, boy. I wasn't expecting that one. "It was very nice. The play was pretty good and he—well, you know, he can talk about anything and so I had a very nice time."

"Have you seen him again?"

I don't know when she might talk to Spencer or what he has told her if they've already spoken. I don't know why, but I don't want people in on this, particularly not someone I'm working for. Still, I have to say something, so I say, "Um, yes. I did see him briefly." (Like a hundred times, briefly.)

"That's nice," she says lightly. "It's none of my business, of course, but I'm curious. What about your friend Doug?"

"We don't have that kind of commitment."

"Ah," she says, with an inflection that makes me think of someone spying on an old acquaintance strolling in Hyde Park or something. *Ah, Lord So-and-So, how are you?*

I don't know what to say next, and perhaps she doesn't, either, because we're both hesitating. Then she says, "Spencer's a very nice man. He's very bright. Maybe something will become of it. Now, that would be something, wouldn't it?"

I still don't know what to say, except maybe *Leave me alone, I'm overwhelmed enough as it is.*

But Verity does not require a response; she has to go. We confirm we'll meet at her house on Sunday. When I get off the phone I have to hurry to make it on time to the St. Regis to meet Michael Cochran.

I walk into the restaurant and spot Michael Cochran immediately. He is a tall, big man, in his late fifties—until I remember this can't be; he's supposed to be nearer to Cassy's age, which is fifty. He is handsome, a little heavier than I thought he would be; his handshake is firm, his smile very nice, his brown eyes kind. There are the ravages of his drinking, though, a fine network of spidery red veins over his reddish nose and a permanent spotty blush on his cheeks. Still, he is attractive, more so when he speaks. Within two minutes I can see he's very smart and that he's charismatic, a leader, a swashbuckling teacher.

"You look very young and attractive and nice," he says right away as we sit down, "a combination I don't think I've ever attributed to one of Verity's writers before."

I shake my head in amazement. "I have heard more about Verity's writers than I have about Cassy."

"That's because they're infamous," he says. He waits until I get the tape recorder going and then leans in toward the mike. "They think we're bad in TV, but Verity's writers sit at home and sharpen their claws and contemplate the best ways to strip flesh off bones. Our stuff, it runs on TV once and poof! Gone forever. Verity's stuff sits on coffee tables and in waiting rooms for months and months and months."

"You sound as though you have been a victim of her writers."

He cocks his head, shrugging slightly. "Yeah. Twice I got slammed in pieces about other people. And I figure I'm really going to get it in this one. I really gave Cassy a hard time and everybody knows it."

The waiter comes with menus and asks if we wish to have

anything to drink. I order a seltzer with lime and much to my surprise, I hear Michael order a glass of white wine.

So he's drinking again. That's news. I know Cassy doesn't know, nor does Henry. They both made the point, several times, that Michael had stopped completely after his rehab stay and so all the nightmares were in the past, too.

We talk a little about Henry and the other people I've talked to. When I mention Jackson Darenbrook, Michael murmurs, "Yes, the new husband," and I realize he is upset by it. But is this because Michael is drinking, which no doubt signals that he is not in a very good place in his life, or simply because he regrets having left her?

"Okay, so what do you want to know?" he asks after the wine arrives and he takes a large sip. "I was a lousy husband and a pretty good father. A so-so provider. Did I love Cassy? I loved that woman like no other, past, present or future. It's all right, you can put that in. My present wife knows. Everyone knows."

This is when I realize that he's had some drinks before arriving at the restaurant.

When he looks at me I see an old sadness in his eyes and I don't know what it is or where it comes from. I know that old Mrs. Potts, who lived near us in Castleford, had that same sadness in her eyes, and that she died a few years ago of liver failure. She was always so nice, but her eyes were always so sad, even when she was smiling.

When the waiter comes back, Michael orders a carafe of white wine and a chef's salad for lunch. I also order the salad. He tells the waiter to bring another wineglass and I know I am being instructed to join him. I don't have another interview until five and I think, okay, a glass or two.

It is around eight o'clock now and I am bombed, sitting at the downstairs bar of the "21 Club" with Michael Cochran. We are on our fourth tape. I have learned more about Cassy's past than I will ever get from her, that's for sure, but it is a dark, almost frightening version as Michael tells it.

He has told me about her deep insecurities, of her feeling unworthy, her terror of being alone. In detail he described how

Catherine Littlefield was one of the most fiendish monsters who ever lived—a woman who constantly screamed at Cassy about the day she would lose her looks and have nothing, just like her. She told her daughter over and over that her beauty was a sentence to unhappiness.

Michael used to periodically find Cassy sobbing, as if she had only just found out her father was dead. He says she misses him every day of her life. (I identify with that.) And yet, according to him, her father never accomplished anything in his life except breaking the heart of the little girl who adored him.

"And thanks to Monster Mom," he adds, "she's got a really fucked-up relationship with women."

"Really? How's that?"

"She has no friends—women friends, you know—never has."

"But what about, um, Alexandra Waring and Jessica—"

"She works with them, that's different," he insists. "She doesn't have any *friends*-friends, never has. Well, there's Sam Wyatt, I guess, but he's a guy." He takes a sip of his drink and makes a face like he's drinking battery acid. "She doesn't trust women."

From what I've seen, nothing could be further from the truth. But then, that's why you talk to different people who have known the subject in different ways for different periods of time; it allows you to see where great changes may have occurred in the subject's life. These changes, in turn, tell you where to dig, where to find the catalyst that caused each change. It almost always turns up an interesting angle.

I am making notes, but I doubt I will be able to read them later. I seem to have lost control of my pen a bit.

"She's been seeing a shrink, a therapist, for years, you know," Michael says, sounding much like a tattling brother. "She was fucking terrified she'd screw up Henry, hand down her neurosis. I was scared she was going to make him a wuss." He smiles suddenly, suppressing a burp. "But Henry's a great guy. And weller than well." He frowns. "It's not normal to be so content in life, is it? Is it?" he demands, leaning near me. He throws an arm out. "How can that kid be so happy?"

I tell him I don't know and try to steer him back to why Cassy went to a therapist.

"Oh, she just had all these *things*. She needed somebody to *relate* to, who could *communicate*. I told her she needed to learn how to relax, to let things go. But she's a control freak. She's got all this pent-up emotion inside—'cause you know how she's always really calm on the outside? Well, she's not. She's—she's teeming inside. There's all this anger and fear and all kinds of stuff in there, and she thinks the way to keep it all under control is to literally control every physical thing around her. It's enough to drive you nuts. One magazine out of place and she feels like the whole universe is going to blow apart."

"She's very neat?"

"Oh, God. Batten down the hatches, babe. She tries to organize everything around her, batten down everything so that, see, it will batten down the chaos inside her." He leans forward, hitting his chest. "And that's where the chaos is," he whispers, "deep down in her soul." He straightens up slightly. "You can't be married to someone so long and not know them. Because I'd get glimpses of the passion, Sally—a ferocity in that woman. Every once in a while I'd feel it when we had sex. And so it became a goal—could I coax it out of her? But then it would go away, sometimes for *years.* And then you know how she's always so calm and cool about everything? Well, all someone had to do was threaten one hair on Henry's head and you have never seen such rage. Absolute rage that would scare the shit out of Attila the Hun."

While he has been telling me all this, I have been trying to imagine what handling this six-foot-three alcoholic must have been like, and I'm also wondering if he ever hit Cassy or Henry. I'm pretty sure it must have happened. In what alcoholic home has it not?

Suddenly he's back rambling about his hour of glory when he brought Alexandra Waring to New York and she rose to the top of the local ratings. "And they fired me! Can you believe it? Because the fucking station manager wanted all the credit. I got Alexandra started! And look how well she's done! And who is responsible for that? Who started it all?"

(I refrain from saying "Alexandra.")

When he starts droning on about how grateful Alexandra is to him, I feel myself starting to nod off. It's versions of the same stuff we talked about at lunch, over and over, only now punctuated with more anger and profanity. I am feeling headachy and drunk and vaguely nauseous. I slip away to the ladies' room and call Spencer's apartment. Where on earth have I been? he wants to know.

On an interview, I tell him. 21 Club. Would he like to come to my hotel? In a half hour?

"I've got to get going," I tell Michael when I return.

"Ah, come on," he says from his stool, throwing an arm around me and trying to pull me between his legs.

Uh-oh. Knowing what I know about him, I should have expected this. "I'm sorry," I say, resisting, "but I have to meet my husband."

"Your husband?" He frowns. "Why don't you wear a ring?"

"Why don't you?" I counter.

"Ahhh," he says, reaching for me again, "I knew I liked you."

Oh, God, this is awful. And I have encouraged it, paying for the ten million drinks we've consumed all afternoon and evening.

"Listen," he whispers, nearly pulling me into his lap. People are looking at us. "We can slip over to the Hilton and have one good, quick fuck. You'd like that, wouldn't you?"

I try to pull away, but he yanks me close. "I've got one for you that's a block long. Ask Cassy. I've got the biggest one you've ever seen."

I get away by literally shoving off him like a boat stuck on a beach. "Sorry, but I don't have time." I scoot around the other side of my stool to use it as a barrier. I hurl a wad of bills on the bar, grab my stuff and hold out my hand to him. "Thank you very much for the interview."

He's mad now. "You fucking bitch!" he snarls. "Who do you think you are? You're *nothing*, hear me?" He waves me away. "Get the fuck out of here! You're a whore. You're a dog."

So much for my gracious debut as a high-profile journalist at the 21 Club. I carefully pick my way out of the restaurant and the doorman helps me into the cab.

Spencer's eyes grow large when he sees me slightly zagging across the hotel lobby toward him. "Are you okay?" he whispers, taking my arm.

"Do you mean am I drunk? Yes," I laugh, leading him to the elevator. I drop my bag and tapes go flying. "Oh, my interview."

"This is from one interview?" he asks, bending to pick up the cassettes and stuff them back into my bag.

"Great interview!" I declare, placing a hand on Spencer's shoulder to keep my balance.

We go upstairs and Spencer suggests I take a shower while he orders some room service since I haven't eaten.

"I ate," I protest as he unzips the back of my dress.

"Yeah? When?"

I let my dress drop on the floor and I turn around to kiss him. Spencer frowns slightly, bending to pick up my dress before going to the closet to hang it up. "I ate lunch."

"It's almost midnight, Sally."

"Midnight! It can't be midnight! It was just eight o'clock."

"Shower," he says, taking me by the shoulders to the bathroom.

It helps. When I come out, wrapped in the terry-cloth robe, I'm rubbing my wet hair with a towel.

"Who were you with?" he asks me.

"Obviously an alcoholic lunch date," I say, sitting on the edge of the bed.

"So which one of you is the alcoholic?" he asks.

"Not me!" I protest.

He's just looking at me and I panic, because I can see he is upset. "Oh, Spencer, I'm not—" I say, going over to him. "I mean, I'm drunk, yes! I know all alcoholics say they're not alcoholics, but I'm not. You didn't make a mistake, I'm not like that!"

He smiles slightly, pulling me into his lap. "I know," he murmurs.

"But you're upset."

"Not about this," he says. "Truly." He combs my hair back with his fingers off my face. "Not tonight. We'll talk about it another time."

"Is it bad?"

"Sally," he whispers, pulling my face down to kiss it, "not now. Don't worry."

"Okay," I decide.

Room service arrives. Spencer has ordered me French onion soup, a baked potato and a salad. He has a cheeseburger. "Eat," he says. I do.

Suddenly I am very, very tired. I know I should go and brush my teeth, but I can't seem to move. Spencer's helping me into bed.

And that's the last I remember.

32

The telephone is ringing. I pick it up, thinking I must have the flu. But then I remember what happened the night before and I thank the heavens that I packed Alka-Seltzer because I am going to need it.

"Hello?" I whisper.

"Sally?" a voice says. "I just got back, so if you'd like to come over and talk for a while, you can."

"Great," I say, trying to sound enthusiastic and sit up at the same time. "Who is this?"

There is a pause. "Cassy Cochran. Ever heard of me?"

"I'm sorry, Cassy," I say, "I just woke up."

She is laughing. "If you'd like, I can also get a good friend of mine to stop by. He's a neighbor as well. Sam Wyatt."

"Great," I say, wondering where the Alka-Seltzer is.

"I hear Mike was in town," she says then. "And Chi Chi set you guys up."

"Yes, she did." I sit up, clearing my throat. "Um, Cassy, I wanted to talk to you about that. Off the record."

"Oh, no," she groans, "what did he say?"

"It's not that," I say quickly. "It's just that—well, he's drinking again. And I know Henry has no idea he is, so I figured I'd better pass word on to you."

"Oh, God, no." She says this in such a quiet voice I'm not quite sure I hear it. "No, no," she says softly. Another sigh. "Well, I suppose that's his business. But it will hurt Henry terribly." Pause. "You were right to tell me, thank you."

I'm not going to tell her I went on a bender with him.

"Good Lord, it must have been some interview," she says. "Was he slightly buzzed and charming, or did he break the furniture and call you names?"

"Oh, he was all right," I say. "It was just very sad. He's not a happy man right now. He has a lot of regrets."

"Poor Lil," she sighs. Lil's the new wife, some eighteen years younger than Cassy.

We make our arrangements and I decide I'll check out of the hotel and drive the Jeep over to West End.

I also decide I must find that Alka-Seltzer. My head's not that bad, thank heavens; it's really just my stomach. I wander off to the bathroom and that's where I find the note. On the sink.

Sally, my love,
   I got up early and skedaddled home before going to work. Call me when you get up. I really, really would like to see you before you go back out to Castleford.

S.

How can you not love a man who is so cool he can say *skedaddle?*

When I call Spencer's office, I'm told he's in an editorial meeting. I smile, because I remember him saying that holding the meeting on Friday was his idea. If editors are going to fudge a day around a weekend, he prefers it to be Mondays. He has a theory that Mondays have hit-or-miss productivity because it takes people a while to switch over from their weekend mode.

I leave a message that I called, drink my Alka-Seltzer, hit the shower and get dressed. Just before I am to leave for West End, Spencer calls back.

"I owe you an apology. I was in no shape to see anyone last night, much less you."

"I wanted to talk to you last night about something," he says. "But it obviously wasn't the appropriate time."

Something's wrong. Something's off. I take a deep breath. "Spencer, what's wrong?"

"Nothing's really wrong," he says. "It's just that we need to talk about some stuff." He offers a little laugh, but it is not convincing. "You know, things are getting pretty serious."

I feel a pang of dread. I can't imagine what it is he has to talk to me about. But he did say we have to talk because things are getting serious, so it's not that he's changed his mind.

We decide I should call him as soon as I'm through at West

End. Spencer tries to sound cheery at the end of our conversation, but I know something not terribly good is on his mind.

When I see Cassy sitting in her office at West End I am amazed at the rush of protection I feel toward her. After listening to both Michael Cochran and Cassy's mother, Mrs. Littlefield, I am in awe of how she has become the person she is, when any lesser soul would be angry and bitter and, well, hard. But there does not seem to be a hard side to Cassy Cochran. There is a tough side, but that's vastly different.

She is on the phone and I take a seat. When she gets off she smiles. "Well, well, well, you've been giving everyone the third degree, I hear."

"It hasn't been that bad," I assure her.

"Yes, but now," she says, rising from her seat to come around her desk, "I hear you want to talk to Rosanne."

"I sure do."

Cassy sits down in the chair next to me and leans forward slightly. "If I have any hesitation at all, it is in how you would portray Rosanne herself."

"I'm only interested in her in terms of her relationship with you."

"That's what I mean. There have been some things in her life that are no one else's business. And I have been involved with some of them. So, what I'm trying to say is that I'm going to ask you to strike anything that pertains to her child. Because, you see, Rosanne doesn't understand the media. She'll like you, Sally, and she'll know that I wanted her to talk to you, so she'll be very eager to please and will probably tell you everything she can think of. And I don't want to see her portrayed in any other light than the true one—which is far different from a nervous woman doing her first interview with the press."

"No, I get it, Cassy," I say, nodding my head.

"I don't want you to take advantage of her naiveté," she says seriously, looking me directly in the eye.

"I won't. I give you my word."

She looks at me a moment longer and then looks at her watch. "What do you say we go to the cafeteria? No offense, but you look like you could use some juice or something." When I look at her, she shrugs, rising from her chair. "You've been out with Michael, what can I say? Except that everybody looks like you after having 'a drink' with Mike."

We go into the cafeteria and sit at a table by the glass wall that looks out over the park. This is a wonderful room, large and airy, with a fantastic selection of food and beverages. The employees who have stopped in here look like central casting, they are so diverse in dress, in manner and, according to Cassy, in skills. Everyone from news anchors to cleaning staff to computer technicians to gardeners share this room.

I have a bowl of soup and some coffee. Cassy drinks water and talks freely to the tape recorder about everything from hobbies ("sleep") to sports ("tennis, skiing, skating, in-line skating, swimming, a little sailing, a little horse-back riding") to religion ("Freelance Protestant, I guess. In New York we attend a Presbyterian church, in Connecticut, a Congregational church, and in Georgia, the Methodist church of my husband's childhood.").

At close to one-thirty, a tall, graying, distinguished-looking Black executive approaches our table. He has a security pass on like mine that reads Sam Wyatt.

I shake hands with him, trying to cover my surprise. It never occurred to me Cassy's longtime friend would be Black. (Strange how subtle our biases are.) Sam was, Cassy explains, a division marketing director of Electronika International but has recently been promoted into the corporate suite as vice president, public affairs for the whole conglomerate.

Cassy excuses herself.

"Is it okay to talk here?" Mr. Wyatt asks me. "Sometimes reporters don't like the background noise."

Ah. Of course. He's in public affairs, which means he talks to the press all the time.

It turns out to be one of the more enlightening interviews I've had. Sam originally met Cassy "a million years ago, when our children were little." They had both been recruited to work on the Riverside Drive block party. Area residents did this in the darker financial days of New York City, when private dollars were desperately needed to supplement the upkeep of the park and when they also felt the need to employ private security guards at night to patrol the neighborhood.

"I knew I liked Cassy at that first meeting," he says, "because when I said I wanted to set up a china-break booth—you know, where the kids and parents throw baseballs and smash stuff to smithereens—everybody freaked out. They said there was too much violence in New York and suggested I try a booth where people dropped clothespins into a milk bottle." He laughs. "What I wasn't getting was that all these white folks were terrified of some big Black man running around breaking things."

I have to laugh.

"So then Cassy stands up and says, 'Question. Do we want people to have fun and pour money into the coffers, or do we want to have the same old wimpy stuff nobody wants to do?' She looked at this one gal, who I knew was freaked the minute I showed up, anyway, and Cassy says, 'Come on, Rachel. Which do you think young Bernie *really* wants to do? Smash china with a baseball or drop clothespins in a milk bottle?'"

He throws his head back and roars. "Oh, man, you had to have been there. It was the way she said it. Everybody laughed and by the end of the meeting, Cassy and I were co-chairs of all the activity booths." He looks out the window, smiling, thinking back. "That was—well, my daughter Althea just finished her master's..." He looks at me with mock horror on his face. "It's got to be twenty years."

We talk more and he says they really didn't become such close friends until about seven years ago, when Cassy used her crew at WST to expose a stock fraud scheme at his company, Electronika International.

"The thing was," he explains gravely, "that I had been set up to touch off a firestorm of public controversy, which the bad guys hoped would drive our stock down—"

"The violation of the boycott in South Africa," I say, excited. "I remember that! That was you?" I slap my head. "Of course that was you! Sam Wyatt! The Black marketing director. I remember that!"

"It was really touch-and-go," he says. "If I was a whistle-blower, I could be finished in corporate life, but if I didn't blow the whistle..."

"And so Cassy moved in."

"It was pretty neat," he says. "Although at the time I was pretty scared. She brought in the FBI and, well..." He shrugs.

We talk about the fallout of that case and what happened to all the players. Then I switch topics. "Cassy mentioned, rather mysteriously may I add, that you were instrumental in helping two people she is very fond of."

"You don't want to write about any of that," he tells me.

Which of course only makes me want to. "Why not? What kind of help did you give? And to whom?"

He reaches over to turn off the tape recorder. "I helped her get Michael into a rehab, that's all."

I doubt this. "But you helped Cassy, too," I say. "By her own admission, she says she hadn't been able to deal with the situation, not for years."

He lowers his voice. "I'm a recovering alcoholic. In AA for years. That's all. Cassy knew it and we talked and that's all."

I have a thought. "Do you know Jessica Wright?"

He smiles a little. "Yes."

"You helped Cassy with her, too?"

"I didn't do anything," he says quietly, "that hundreds of thousands of other AAs don't do every day. I took her to a meeting, that's all."

"You're her AA sponsor, aren't you?" I say. "I talked to Jessica, you know, and she told me—off the record, too—about this mutual friend of Cassy's who's her sponsor or advisor or something—"

He is drawing his finger across his throat to get me to stop.

I do.

"Sally, honestly, this is not something you can write about. It goes against every tradition that AA has about anonymity."

I reach over to turn the tape recorder back on. "So as I understand, Mr. Wyatt—"

"Sam, Sam!" he insists.

"So as I understand it, Sam," I say, "you have been a great friend and confidant to Cassy for the past several years."

"I don't know about that," he says, wondering what I'm driving at on tape.

"In other words, she's been able to turn to you as a sounding board in her private life. Like when her husband's drinking got out of control."

He gets it. "Yes. And vice versa. The thing is, in these days and times, between work and family, there's not much time to cultivate friendships. Cassy and I were very lucky—we were neighbors, we got thrown together in community service, and then we just found ourselves becoming close friends. It's certainly convenient since she lives just two doors down and our spouses are wild about each other, too."

"All *right*," I say, signaling success with a fist in the air. We're on the right track now.

When I leave West End later in the Jeep, I am flying high. The interview with Sam was just wonderful, and it is almost enough to stop me from worrying about whatever it is Spencer wants to talk about.

While I'm stuck in traffic on Fifty-ninth Street, I put a call in to Joe Bix. "Hey there. It's me. What do we have on the murder suspect?"

"Not an awful lot," he says. "He's a Russian guy, been in the States for over two years, lives in Queens and works part-time for that warehouse. There is no connection between him and either Tony or Johnny Meyers that anyone can find."

"Except that Tony Meyers was in the toxic-waste-disposal business in Long Island, and maybe this was a mob hit."

"Give it up, Sally," he sighs. "You're worse than Crazy Pete. If it was a mob hit, then why do it in Castleford?"

"That's exactly what makes me think it was a hit," I say. "How would some Russian guy even know where Castleford was unless someone sent him there to specifically knock off Meyers? It would be much better to kill him in Castleford than in Long Island, where all his competitors are."

"Geez," Joe says. "I need a new job. I want to cover the governor's bill in Hartford and you want me to get killed by the mob."

"How did Buddy get this guy?"

"It was a nice piece of work. He got a description of him from some guy near the park who saw him and put it together with what a gas station attendant remembered about a guy in a car with New York plates the same morning. The guy bought a map and was sitting outside looking at it for a long time, evidently. That same car was found abandoned in Bridgeport; it had been reported stolen in Queens. Buddy got the prints and they matched the prints the Southampton police sent over from their burglary last year, the one where the gun was taken. Buddy turned all of this over to the FBI, who came back with a computer hit on this Stefan Bulgizt, arrested two years ago in a Kennedy airport luggage scam, and they picked him up in Queens."

"Wow," I say.

"Yeah," Joe says. "With computers, it's a whole new world. The police also think he may have been the one following you in the stolen car the next day."

"Comforting thought," I sigh. "Okay, gotta go. I'll be back in town tonight."

I find a parking spot right in front of Spencer's and load four quarters into the meter. The doorman nicely offers to take the rest of my quarters to feed the meter as needed, and also to keep an eye on the Jeep. "Oh, I don't think anything will happen to it out here," I say.

He laughs, rolling his eyes at the awning. "Yeah, that's what we all say when we first move to New York."

The concierge waves me right through the lobby, saying Spencer is expecting me. It is a nice building and a nice group. Spencer pays through the nose for all this niceness, though, far more than I could ever allow myself even if I made a lot of money.

When I walk into Spencer's apartment, I am slightly reassured by the look in his eyes. He does not look like a man about to break up with me. To the contrary. I drop my purse and kiss him hello and apologize again for being smashed the night before.

"It's okay," he murmurs, holding me around the waist, looking into my eyes. We kiss again.

"So what's up?" I ask, picking Seela up on my way into the living room.

"I've got some Amstel Light," he says, "and a bottle of chardonnay."

"I'm driving, darling," I say, dropping down on the love

seat, "so water will be fine." I look over at him, suspicious. "Unless you're trying to get me to stay."

He glances through the open partition of the kitchen. "Nice idea," he says, "but you said you had to get back."

"I really do now," I say. "I've got to get a jump on these transcripts. And I've got to meet Verity this weekend."

"You do?" He comes around the partition to hand me a glass of water and sit down next to me. He has a bottle of Amstel for himself.

"Yeah, she called me yesterday and asked me to come up to Litchfield. She wants to 'talk' about the piece, which means, I assume, she doesn't trust me enough to know how to write it." I expect Spencer to say something, but he doesn't.

Something *is* wrong. And the queasy feeling in my stomach confirms it. I sip my water and ask in a low voice, "What's the matter?"

"I don't really know how to explain this to you," he says, dropping his eyes to the coffee table.

I put my glass down and lean forward to take his hand.

His eyes come up for a moment. He looks so tired and discouraged. Miserable. Maybe even scared. He releases my hand to rub his eyes and then his whole face. He drops his hands to look at me. "I got a call from Verity yesterday, too."

"And?"

"She said she had talked to you."

"And?"

"And she also told me that you said you had seen me again, after the theater last week."

"Yes," I confirm. "I didn't feel like embellishing on it, though, so I didn't. I didn't know what you might have told her, or were going to, so I just said yeah, I'd seen you. I certainly didn't make a big deal out of it."

He nods, biting his lower lip slightly. "That's good. I wondered. I didn't think you'd broadcast what's been going on." He looks at me. "It's probably a good idea to keep our relationship to ourselves. Until you've finished the piece and she's paid you and everything."

A flag goes up. "Why? What would she care? She's the one who introduced us."

"Yeah, she did," he says. "She wanted my take on you, Sally. She asked me if I would take you somewhere to get a better sense of you, to see if I thought you were cut out for the assignment."

"She asked you to spy on me?" I say, getting angry.

"No," he says quickly, looking at me. "No! Sally, no, she didn't, nothing like that. She just wanted to make sure you could handle it and wanted to make sure you'd have someone in the city who knew something about writing to call in case you couldn't."

"Screw her!" I say, reaching for my water. "I don't need a baby-sitter."

"No, no, I'm not explaining this right," he says, miserable. "Sally. Look. There's something I have to tell you. I don't want to, but I have to. I can't let this go another day, not for another hour."

Now I am scared.

"The thing is, Sally," he says, almost in a rush, "Verity and I have been having an affair. For a long a time." He grimaces. "For over two years."

IV
Reality

33

Verity and I have been having an affair. For a long a time. For over two years.

I have to admit, I need a glass of wine after this announcement. I feel winded, stunned, utterly blindsided. I want to slug Spencer.

I get myself a glass of wine and drink it down in Spencer's kitchen, asking him, from the other side of the partition, "Why are you telling me?"

"Because you have to know," he says, rising.

"And why wasn't I to know before we did anything?"

He comes around the partition to stand in the doorway, looking at me as though he couldn't understand what I was saying, or why. "I didn't know we'd—" He gestures. "I didn't know I'd feel—I was scared to tell you until I knew you felt something for me."

I close my eyes and hear the voice of that bitchy Sally Harrington people in my past used to complain about. "So you waited." I open my eyes. "Until you knew I was on the hook, right?"

"Sally," he says softly. "Put yourself in my place."

"I am," I say. "And I told you about Doug right away."

"And I told you about my ex who moved out."

"Don't even get me started on that!" I cry. "You were living with one woman and having an affair with another—"

"The point is, Verity's giving you the professional opportunity of a lifetime!"

I put the wineglass down in the metal sink. "So why the hell are you telling me now?"

"Because," he says, moving closer but not touching me, "Verity wants to know what's going on, what's wrong with me."

I look at him. "Oh? She thinks something's wrong with you? So do I, as a matter of fact."

"Because I won't sleep with her," he explains. "And that's been pretty much our whole relationship."

I nod, staring off past him, feeling like dying. I can't believe it. But I am also sure I deserved it. "And when were you supposed to sleep with her?"

"Last weekend," he says quietly. "Verity usually comes over on Saturday afternoon if she can get away from Corbett. She came over last week and I pretended I had the stomach flu."

I look at him.

"And then I canceled on her Monday afternoon."

"Afternoon?" I say, taking a step back. "Where do you meet her in the afternoon?"

He sighs. "Here, sometimes. Sometimes at a friend's."

"Two *years?*" I cry, slamming my hand on the counter. Then I lower my voice, glowering. "You've been sleeping with her for two years and waited to tell me until now? After pretending that you've been so tragically alone?"

"I have been alone," he says flatly.

"It sure as hell doesn't sound like it."

He concedes that, nodding, dropping his forehead into his hand. "Yeah. It's a mess."

"I don't know why you should think it's a mess," I say in my high-handed voice. "She's only married to someone else— someone who could squash you like a bug, Spencer," I can't help but say.

"I know."

I pace the kitchen once and then whirl around. "Surely she knew someday you'd meet someone!"

He looks at me, sick. "You don't know Verity."

"Clearly," I say coldly, "I don't know you."

"Look, we haven't known each other that long—I'm falling in love with you," Spencer says, sounding a little desperate. "And I think Verity suspects."

"So *what?*" I demand.

"So—" He can't seem to come up with an answer.

So I get my purse and get the hell out of Dodge.

*   *   *

I drive back to Castleford in some kind of shock.

It's a little after nine when I arrive at Mother's and start the dogs barking. Too late I put two and two together about what it means when the lights are off inside the house and Mack's car is parked in the driveway. If I could leave, I would. I don't have the strength for this. But Mother has already looked out the upstairs window to see who it is and she is probably dying a thousand deaths because she realizes it's me.

She meets me at the front door in her robe.

God, I cannot believe it. Mother is having sex.

"Sorry to disturb you," I whisper, avoiding her eyes—actually, not looking at her at all—just reaching past her to signal to Scotty that he is to come out without Abigail. He does, nuzzling my hand. "Hi, babe," I say, dropping on one knee to kiss his snout. "I'll talk to you tomorrow," I whisper, turning away. "Thanks for looking after him. I'll pick up his stuff tomorrow." I am hoping I sound sort of normal, because I cannot deal with this right now.

Neither can Mother, for all she does is softly call, "I love you," and close the door.

I start to imagine her going back upstairs to face Mack, but I banish the scene from my mind. I don't want to think about anything anymore, all I want to do is to go home with my dog.

We reach the cottage, I let Scotty out and drag my bags out of the car. Scotty takes kick-aim at a bush and then dashes up to the porch, barking, activating the motion light.

"Scotty, quiet!" I say. "What the heck is that?" I say aloud, coming up the stairs. Sitting in front of the door is a large hunk of concrete and brick, with a metal cable coming out of one side. Now what? I wonder if in my absence part of the basement's started to fall apart. Scotty and I pick our way around the thing and go inside.

As Scarlett would say, I'll think about it tomorrow.

Before I go to sleep, I actually get down on my knees next to my bed, like I did when I was little, and say my prayers. I ask God to help sort out all this stuff with Spencer and Verity and, well, Doug. Because I can't help but think of Doug right now and I'm not sure what that means, either.

34

I call Buddy first thing Saturday morning and catch him at home making pancakes. I flatter him profusely on the work he did to catch Tony Meyers's killer, which keeps him on the phone. "I was also just wondering," I say, "what the story was on the Preston Roadhouse."

"Don't you read your own paper?"

"Yes, that's why I'm calling you. It says squat. Just not the same paper without me, is it?"

Buddy curses quietly, muttering something about not being able to flip properly while on the phone.

"Just tell me if there is anything suspicious about the road-house explosion," I say, opening the front door to look at that hunk of building debris on my front porch.

"There is something suspicious about it," Buddy says.

Huh. So somebody's left me a clue, something to write about. Too bad I wasn't here to see who brought it.

"Okay," I say, "that's all I wanted to know. Thanks."

"That's it?" he says suspiciously.

"That's it," I say. "Thanks."

Next I call Crazy Pete Sabatino. "Hey, Pete, it's Sally."

"Hi, Sally," he says, sounding terribly depressed.

"Have you by chance dropped anything off at my house this week?"

"No."

"Are you sure?"

"Yes."

"Okay, thanks. I just wanted to check."

After I get off, I go outside to look at this thing, and discover that Scotty has left his mark on the side. Rascal.

I have the good sense to call Mother before going over to her house. "Mack's just getting ready to leave," she says quickly.

"Actually, that's why I was calling. Mother, can you ask him to wait until I get there? I need his help—professionally. Really. So could you please ask him to wait?"

"Of course, darling!" she says, the relief and happiness in her voice saying it all. No doubt she thought I was coming over to confront Mack. Mother may not know it, but I am a complete coward in this regard. I just wish they'd go away somewhere, say to France, to explore this part of their relationship. Actually, she'll never know how much I wanted to exclaim, when she answered the phone this morning, *"Mother!"* the way she always says, *"Sally Goodwin Harrington!"* whenever she is shocked at my behavior.

"I'll be right over," I promise.

Mother and Mack are walking around the pieces of the greenhouse Mack is undertaking to build when I arrive. Scotty bounds around the corner of the house to find Abigail, and then the two go off into the cornfield. (What exactly they do out there, we don't know.) Carrying the load of concrete that was left on my doorstep, I stagger over to the ancient picnic table under our old maple and set it down heavily. Mother and Mack are walking toward me, looking puzzled.

"Good morning," I say cheerfully.

They say hello and gather around to look at this thing. "Mack, I have an enormous favor to ask of you. I need someone who knows something about construction materials to analyze this thing and, well, frankly, there's nobody around here in Castleford I can trust. I don't suppose you might have a colleague in engineering or architecture who might be able to tell me what this is and where it likely came from?"

He looks at me, a little perplexed.

"I think it might have something to do with the Preston Roadhouse," I explain. "Someone left it on my porch this week. And if I know what it is or where it's from, I might be able to figure out why someone left it for me."

"And you can't trust anyone?" he asks, glancing at my mother.

"I need someone from outside the loop. When it comes to construction, everybody's connected in this town."

Mack can't help but smile. "You lead a very exciting life, Sally, don't you? Murder here, arson there."

He is a bit short, but Mack is an attractive man. Quiet, yet manly. I suspect he will be very good for Mother. He's nothing like my father, but I suspect that is also a good thing. And he's just that much older than Mother that I don't worry about him dumping her. She's still way out in front for her age group and he'd be a fool to do anything but commit himself totally.

I think of Spencer and feel the wind leave my sails. *But he hasn't slept with Verity since,* I remind myself.

Verity. God. I have to see her tomorrow.

"Are you sure this isn't something that should go to the police?" Mother says, reaching out to touch it but then drawing her hand back.

"Not until I know what it is." I point. "Scotty whizzed on this part, don't touch it."

"I know what it is," Mother suddenly says. "Or what it's part of." She points. "That looks like part of a cement buttress. Where the cables, like that thing, are run through the cement when it's wet, and then when it's dry, they take the mold away." She looks to Mack. "Don't you think?"

He shrugs helplessly. "Sorry, Belle—I could write out a formula to calculate how much weight a buttress can take, but I'm afraid I don't know very much about construction. But I do know someone who does."

"Do you? Could that someone look at it for me?"

"I'll go check now," Mack says, starting for the house. "I'm just afraid he might be away over the summer leave."

We go inside and I have some coffee with Mother while Mack calls around. We're in luck; his friend, a professor of engineering, is at his home in Middletown. He invites Mack to bring the sample over to his lab at the university tomorrow. I help load the concrete debris into Mack's trunk and whistle for Scotty. I've got to get home and get to work.

After all, I have a feature article to write for *Expectations*. I have to get ready to meet with my boss tomorrow, the woman my lover has been having an affair with for over two years.

It is terrible of me, I suppose, but when I turn into my driveway and see Doug's Volvo I want to scream. Regardless of how

I may have felt last night, the last thing I feel like doing today is facing him. Although he still has a key to the cottage, he has not used it, but is sitting in a chair in the backyard throwing a tennis ball on the roof of the house.

"Hi," I say.

"Hi," he says. He looks terrible. His eyes are swollen with fatigue; he needs a haircut. Otherwise the Docker shorts show off his great thighs, the polo shirt shows his dedication to the gym and his smile, the dedication his parents had to orthodontics. He stands up. "I'm sorry, Sally, but I love you."

He says this simply, holding his hands out, palms toward me. "I know you've met someone new, someone you're crazy about, but I can't just let you walk away. I can't do it."

He does not sound like a lawyer in court. He sounds more like the Doug I fell in love with a long time ago, unsure but determined, a little shy but with an objective.

"Come inside," I murmur, leading the way into the kitchen. "I'll make us some iced tea." While I get things ready, Doug sits at the kitchen table. It's as if he has never been here before. "Doug," I say matter-of-factly, "I don't know what I'm doing."

He doesn't say anything.

"And it's true, I have met someone. But I have no idea where it might go." I crash the ancient ice trays in the sink. (Someday I'm going to break down and spend a dollar on plastic ones instead of sticking with the metal ones that came with the refrigerator in 1812.) "The one thing I do know," I say, looking down into the sink, "is that I've done something that may be irreparable in our relationship. I'm not sure you'll ever trust me again."

I stand there, with my back to him, waiting. His answer comes easily enough. "Oh, I will. Because you'll never do it again. I know you. You can't even look me in the eye, you feel so guilty. And Sally, we didn't have a firm commitment."

I turn around. "I had a commitment to you."

"And clearly you shouldn't have. Clearly there was something you were not getting that you needed to get from someone else."

I turn back around to put the ice in the pitcher. I wish Doug would stop being so nice.

"It's a lot like when Jane and I were working together," he says. "I wanted to sleep with her, remember?"

How could I forget? I hated him for it and yet I didn't blame him, because our sex life had been in a funny phase. The passion had vanished, leaving only tiredness in its wake. I'm still not sure what was going on. It wasn't just ebb and flow; it was something else. Like our feelings had moved into a serious zone and our bodies were like, uh-oh, back up, this is getting too close. It was as though I couldn't give him everything I had, even if I had wanted to.

"The question is," he says quietly, "is whether you will ever find me as sexually attractive as you once did. Or if there is something about me that simply isn't what you want."

That's not what this is about; there is nothing about Doug I don't want and yet I know if I try to explain it—which is what he wants me to do—then I'm going to end up discussing the depth of the love I feel for him. And if I talk about that love, he's going to know that he still has his claws in me because that is what I always talk about when we're about to get back together again.

And, of course, this would be the easiest course, wouldn't it? To simply be grateful that Doug wants me back, to bask in that comfortable love I have felt for years and ignore the sense of failure I always feel when we get back together.

But I don't want to do it this time. It's not fair to Doug. It's not fair to me. Perhaps he doesn't really get it, the depth of my betrayal to our relationship. That I left it with nary a glance backward, and just for sex. I didn't even know the guy!

Of course I feel like killing Spencer, because yesterday I could have had this talk with Doug, no problem, and told him we shouldn't try again. But today, now that I know Spencer's been having it off with Verity, that he's scared of her, I'm finding this exchange with Doug difficult; the appeal of falling back into our old ways is there. But I cannot do that, because I know I am genuinely at sea.

I know I love Doug like a lifelong friend. I know I like sex with him. I know I am utterly enthralled with *that idiot* Spencer, and feel as though I have discovered a whole other kind of person I wasn't sure existed.

I also know that I will very likely end up losing both men, because the whole situation is so indicative of what my mother has been trying to tell me—that I have to grow up.

It is said that complicated people have complicated problems. I have decided I must simplify things, even if just for today.

I pour two glasses of iced tea and come over to sit at the table with Doug. Scotty is nosing me, trying to say something, but I can't pay attention to him now. "All I can tell you," I say quietly, "is that I don't know where I am headed, but I'm pretty sure it is not back to where we've been."

"I know."

I look at him. He smiles a little ironic smile and takes a sip of the iced tea. "I came to tell you that I'll give you six months. That would be January. After the holidays. We'll leave each other alone until then, and then we'll talk to see how we feel. If we feel as though we want to be together, then I'm going to insist we get married. As to whether we live here, or move to New York or elsewhere, we'll figure that out."

I don't know where the tears come from, but they're falling. Is it exhaustion or stress or simply that I cannot believe Doug is saying this. In the past, he'd always indicated that the thought of getting married again was something akin to contemplating being seared with red-hot irons.

Of course, by January, a man like Doug is going to have any number of good candidates to fill the void I've left. More and more I'm beginning to realize that my void will not be a big one. Friend, confidante and Saturday night sleepover partner does not a wife make.

At any rate, I am crying because this makes me love Doug the way I did in the beginning—and the way I did when we made up before.

You must grow up, Mother's voice says. *It is not good that adolescent behavior makes you feel comfortable.*

Oh, pooh, Mother, I think as I take Doug's hand to thank him. A short while later, we are hugging at the front door. And then he is gone and I am crying again, this time with Scotty trying to lick the tears away.

I finally wash my face and pull myself together and move to my desk in the living room to get to work. The telephone starts to ring and like a fool, I pick it up.

"Oh, Sally, thank God you're there. It's me and I'm a mess. I've left you a hundred messages."

I glance at the machine and the light is blinking, although it says there are eight messages, not a hundred. I'm beginning to realize that Spencer gets kind of dramatic.

"I had to tell you about Verity," he rushes on. "And surely you can understand why I was scared to after—well, after we had just been together that one night and scarcely knew each other. I thought for sure it would send you running away, never to come back."

The contrast with Doug an hour before is not flattering to Spencer. He sounds like a gangly teenager. His mother, I think, should tell him to grow up.

"Look, you've got to let me see you in person. I can't leave things this way, not for another day."

"Maybe it's not me you should see," I say. "Maybe you feel guilty because you know Verity's in Litchfield, waiting to see you."

There is a decided pause and then Spencer's voice grows deep. "I did not ever, and would not ever, meet her in her family's home. I know you think I'm a scumbag, but I'm hopeful someday you'll understand how this started. It's not about love, it's not about breaking up her family—it was about sexual release for both of us."

I wish I hadn't heard this rationale a hundred times when I lived in Los Angeles. I wish I didn't know that in Spencer's circles, this behavior is pretty normal. I certainly wish I didn't feel as though I have hopelessly dirtied my soul by succumbing to him and, by association, joined this merry band of sexual hobbyists.

"What I don't understand," I say, "is how you could betray her so easily. Two years is a long time."

"How did I betray her?"

"You were supposed to find out how my article was going, not sleep with me."

"I don't think Verity could care less if I slept with you," he says. "What will set her off is the idea that having you in my life means I want to cut her out of mine."

"Hasn't this woman ever heard of sexually transmitted diseases? She could care less who you sleep with?"

"Sally—" He sighs. "Will you just calm down for a minute?"

"I am calm."

"Just listen to me, all right? The last time Verity and I were together—"

"When?"

"Um, about two weeks ago."

"Where?"

He sighs again. "Here. At my apartment."

I wonder if I'll ever even see this man again. "How do you know she doesn't have another young stud around, Spencer? How do you know she hasn't picked up herpes or VD or AIDS or something?"

"There is no other stud. And I'm clean, I've told you that. Verity is a maniac on the subject. She's terrified of Corbett—you must have suspected that, and yet their life together sexually is abysmal for her—"

"My heart goes out to her," I say sarcastically.

"You've got me so upset, Sally—"

"I've got *you* upset!" I am furious. "How dare you feed me such bull about your sordid love life! Do you think for one second I would have gotten involved with you if I had known you were servicing Verity Rhodes? Are you crazy?"

"That's why I didn't tell you. I knew you wouldn't. And I knew I had only a small window to get through to you, that you had a man in your life. Verity told me that, and I knew you'd be back in Connecticut, and that night we went to the theater and we talked and talked—remember? How we talked about everything that night and how we both knew, we just *knew*, there was something big going on between us, something that needed to be explored, and I'm not talking about sex—"

"But that's what we did, didn't we?" I say, trying to remind myself of reality as I quickly pull myself out of the dream of that first night, for that first night had been magical, there *had* been a connection between us. We had discovered we were intellectually similar, that our hobbies and tastes and interests were similar, that our disasters in relationships had been similar, too, and that our dedication to work was unhealthy, in ways, and that our moods, that all-or-nothing kind of attitude, was not good....

I remember so clearly stopping on Fifth Avenue in front of the Barnes & Noble windows, where he pointed out a book he had edited, and told me stories of other books in the window. And then he had turned to me and taken both my hands in his and said, "I feel so wonderful being able to tell you this, because it's not so interesting to most people. I mean—you get it, Sally. That the glamour is fleeting, the work is long, long hours and it doesn't make a good story. That work is really the only story there is in publishing—long hours and a lot of disappointments and then that one breakthrough, every great once in a while, that keeps you going."

"Sally, please," Spencer urges, sounding hoarse, "let me drive out tonight. Not to do anything but talk. I've got to see you."

"Don't you think it's Verity you should see?"

He is debating how to respond to this. "I can't talk to Verity about what has happened, Sally, because I'm afraid she'll try to hurt you."

"So you're going to wait until my article is published?"

"I think I have to," he says quietly.

"And how are you going to duck her until that time?"

"I don't know," he says honestly. "But I'm going to have to."

"Not if you're not seeing me anymore. In fact, you'd be doing me a great favor by sleeping with her and keeping her happy until I'm published in her magazine," I say meanly.

"Sally, listen to me—"

"I don't want to. I'm tired, Spencer. I'm tired of all this."

"Sally, I'm never sleeping with Verity Rhodes again! Meeting you only confirmed what I knew before. As long as I was doing it, I was avoiding my own life. And then I met you and I knew what I wanted."

"It hasn't even been two weeks, Spencer!"

"At least let me talk to you later," he says. "Please. Just to know the lines of communication are open." He might as well have said, "Just so I know you haven't gone running back to Doug."

"Sure," I say. "Maybe around eight. I've got things to do."

"Great." If I wasn't so angry, the relief I hear in his voice would strike a small pain in my heart.

When I shut out the world, I am always amazed at how much work I get done. By seven in the evening I have finished transcribing a draft of each interview and have settled in at the kitchen table to highlight quotes. The piece is shaping itself rather vividly in my mind, because the shape of Cassy's persona has become stronger and stronger. This is a very special person; worth celebrating, certainly. She has taken a not terribly promising hand and played it into an incredibly productive life.

Around seven-thirty I let Scotty out the back door and notice that Crazy Pete is sitting on my backstairs.

"Hi," I say. "You're not on the lam again, are you?"

"No," he says. "I just stopped by. I drove over but you were working. You didn't even look up."

I vaguely remember Scotty barking and my decision to ignore him. I walk out to sit down in a beach chair facing him. "So how are you?"

He shrugs. "Okay, I guess."

"Are you working?"

Looking down at the ground, he nods.

"That's good."

"Papa doesn't want to come back to Castleford," he says. "He wants to sell the house."

Poor Pete. Except for that brief sojourn at college that time, he has never lived away from his home in Castleford. This announcement from his father has to be turning his world upside down—if for no other reason than his satellite and ham radio equipment and hundreds of books and videos and cassettes will have to be moved somewhere. And working for minimum wage is not going to get him a very big place, not unless he gets into one of the complexes underwritten by HUD that offers affordable housing. But somehow I doubt any landlord is going to be eager to take in the town's conspiracy nut and his sixty-foot antennae.

I wonder if maybe the library would accommodate his equipment if he shared it with other patrons once in a while, though I don't think City Hall across the street would be so wild about looking at the antennae and monstrous satellite dish, either.

No matter which way you look at it, big changes are coming to Crazy Pete's life.

"I'm sorry to hear that," I say. "But I'm sure he'll come back up to spend Christmas with you. Maybe the summers."

He looks at me. "He says I'm crazy."

"He still loves you."

Dejectedly Pete looks to the ground again. "If Mom hadn't died, everything would be okay."

"Well, look at it this way," I say, "it will be wonderful to have your own home, your own hours, your own way of doing things."

"I have my own home now," he says.

"No, you have been living in your parents' home."

He looks like he might burst into tears. "I know I should have moved out."

At forty-something, he's at least on the right track.

"But Mom liked me at home. It saved money."

"You paid rent?"

He frowns. "Well, sometimes."

The poor lamb. I wish I didn't know there were so many equally lost, dependent children in this country, but there are. Study after study confirms it.

"I'll help you find a new home," I promise.

"The library's hooking me up with a housing organization."

"Good," I say. "And I'll help you with your budget."

He looks like he's going to cry again.

"You'll be a lot happier in the end, Pete, I promise you." No response. "I know it's very scary right now, but once you're settled and supporting yourself, you're going to know a joy and satisfaction you've never had before." I have a thought. "And you can get the dog you always wanted! We'll go to the Humane Society and get the best dog in the whole wide world—except for Scotty, of course."

At this, Pete finally smiles. Then bites his lower lip, thinking. "I hope they don't snatch him to conduct experiments."

I know better than to ask who.

35

I get up early Sunday morning not because I've set the alarm, but because of the sense of alarm my whole being has about this day. I hit my desk to work on the Cochran profile at four-thirty and by ten my sense of panic has disappeared. From a professional viewpoint, I am prepared for my meeting with Verity. I've got a good handle on how the piece will fall together; indeed, I've hammered out a structure this morning. The only question is the strength of my nerve. Can I sit down with my employer and see her as the person who has given me "the opportunity of a lifetime" in my career (how I've come to hate that expression), as opposed to the married woman who has retained Spencer as a trained stud for two years?

He's done the same things with Verity he's done with me. But over and over and over and over and over for two straight years.

Ten days, Sally. Get over it.

Since I'm going over to Litchfield, anyway, I decide I might as well zip over to Cornwall first. I've got the address of the Cochran-Darenbrook country home and I'm curious to see it. My street atlas of the whole county pretty much pinpoints where Cassy's house is.

To actually see the house, though, is proving a little more difficult than I thought as I drive around Cornwall. It's on a private drive that stretches at least a mile back into the hills. At the end of it, as if that is not remote enough, an unassuming gravel drive begins, which trails back even farther into the woods. I know it is the Cochran-Darenbrook house because I recognize Jackson's sense of humor on a small sign next to the drive that reads Reckless Manor.

Do I go up the drive or not? If I do, I will be invading their privacy when all I wanted to do was see the house. Well, when all else in my imagination fails, truth becomes an option. I call the house on my cell phone and tell Cassy, who answers on about the seventh ring, that I just happened to be in the area and was curious about their house. I tell her I can't stay more than fifteen minutes because I am expected at Verity's within the hour.

"Just the kind of guest we love," Cassy laughs, "one that can't stay. By all means, just follow the drive."

I bounce up the drive, ascending the hill, thinking you'd have to have a four-wheel-drive vehicle in the winter to make it. I wind this way and that, finally coming onto a small clearing. At first I think I am looking at the caretaker's cottage, but since this is the end of the road I quickly realize that this *is* the house. It is a simple, weathered, cedar-shingled home with a porch on two sides, a peaked roof, a large stone chimney and large windows that look old-fashioned, but up close I discover are those very expensive new ones. A navy blue Mercedes sports coupe is sitting near the house.

Across the drive is a barn that doubles as a garage. I park near it. The double doors are open and I can see a massive, forest-green four-wheel-drive Lincoln wagon parked inside. I can see a lot of other things as well—a Harley-Davidson road bike, two snowmobiles, a canoe, two sculls, a kayak, tennis rackets, cross-country skis, downhill skis, life preservers, backpacks, a tent, Coleman lanterns, fishing rods, a creel, hip waders, water skis, a folded up trampoline, a folded-up Ping-Pong table and what I think is an old cider press.

To the side of the house, just down a slight grade, I see a large swimming pool with a brick-inlay terrace around it and a cedar picket fence around that. The house, I realize, is on top of the hill I drove up, for I can see quite a distance in three directions.

"Hi!" Cassy greets me, coming off the front porch. Her hair is wet, slicked back flat against her head, and she is wearing a cotton skirt wrap over a one-piece bathing suit. Her face is a little shiny, no doubt from sunscreen. This is about as vulnerable as any subject can be. No makeup, wet hair, bathing suit. She looks every bit her age and is absolutely beautiful.

"I had just finished my laps when you called."

"I've got no excuse for disturbing you like this," I say, feeling embarrassed over my intrusion.

"Come on in," she says, leading the way into the house,

pausing only to remove a pebble from the bottom of her bare foot. "Jack!" she calls.

We have walked into a vaulted living-room-kitchen area that has a tremendous stone fireplace. The windows are all open and a breeze is blowing through. All that separates the two rooms is a counter. A plain hardwood table in the corner serves as a dining table.

This house is very different, needless to say, from the country home maintained by the Rhodes-Schroeders. Interesting. Particularly since Jackson Darenbrook is on roughly the same financial footing as Corbett.

I hear someone bounding down a set of wooden stairs and then Jackson appears from around the corner. "Hey there!" His hair is wet, too, and he is wearing swimming trunks and a T-shirt that, I bet, he had just run upstairs to put on because both are dry. As a matter of fact, looking back at Cassy, I note that while she is wet, her bathing suit is not. So I get it. They were swimming in the nude when I called.

I find it wonderful.

"Hi, Jackson," I say. "I'm so sorry to disturb you. It was just that I had some time to kill before going to Verity's—"

"I was going to have you come here, anyway, at some point," Cassy says.

"It's beautiful."

"We love it," Cassy says simply.

"Yeah," Jackson says, going into the kitchen area to open the refrigerator door, "it's great after New York. And in case you don't think we keep up with the neighbors," he adds, pulling out a bottle of Snapple, "we have a fancy-schmancy ancestral mansion in Georgia with seven bedrooms."

"Ancestral, right," Cassy laughs. "Your father built it and your sister and brother-in-law live there."

"That's what makes it ancestral," he insists, smiling. He holds up the bottle in his hand. "How about a shot of Mango Madness before going over to the Marchioness de Sade's?"

"Jackson!" Cassy admonishes.

"No thanks," I tell him. The Marquis de Sade was jailed in the eighteenth century for combining torture with sex, among other things, so I find this comment rather startling.

"Let me tell you what old Corbie's up to these days," he says, leaning over the counter as a conspirator might. "He's muscling in on the Unibank-Mercantile Trust merger."

I frown. "I thought it was a done deal."

"That's what they thought, but Schroeder's threatening to mess it up. So they're going to have to pay him to butt out."

"Jack," Cassy sighs.

"He's after Bestro Cosmetics," he continues, ignoring his wife, "which Unibank holds title to under their reorganization. See, Sally, he's got this thing about models—and he figures that if he's the CEO of Bestro, then all the models will have to audition with him, if you know what I mean."

"Jack!" Cassy is genuinely annoyed now. "You don't know any of that."

"Everybody knows it," he insists. "The guy is a dick head."

"Out," his wife commands, pointing to the pool.

He laughs, pausing to give his wife a kiss on the cheek before going outside. "Nice to see ya, Sally!"

Once Cassy sees that her husband is safely out of earshot, she returns her attention to me. "So you're working on Sunday?"

"It was the best time for Verity to meet."

Cassy lofts one eyebrow. "You couldn't have finished the article yet."

"No." I shrug. "I think she's checking up on me. I'm not wild about the idea, but then again, I am new to the magazine."

"You'll do fine, I'm sure." She looks around. "There's nothing much to show you, I'm afraid. There're just two bedrooms and a bath upstairs."

"That's all right," I say quickly, moving toward the front door. "It was very good of you to accept my intrusion so gracefully."

"Not a problem," she says, following me. She stops in the doorway. "Good luck with your meeting."

"Thanks." I feel awkward walking out, like I'm a stalker or something. I turn around. "I really didn't mean to invade your privacy, Cassy. It was just that I was curious about the house. And now that I've seen it, I'm so glad I did. It's far different—and more wonderful—than I imagined."

She smiles. "Thanks."

After she closes the front door, I walk to the Jeep feeling more than ever like a boar, just crashing in from the woods. A husband and wife enjoying some precious time alone together.

I wish I could pretend that what Jackson said about Corbett doesn't alarm me, the implication that Corbett sleeps around, too. The number of sexual partners I need to be concerned about via Spencer and Verity is becoming alarmingly large.

"Sally, you're right on time," Verity says, kissing me on the cheek and pulling me into her house. She must be a size six I decide, following her to the glass sunroom. I guess it's a solarium. Anyway, the windows are closed, the central air is on, and Verity is dressed in linen slacks and a silk blouse. The glass-top table is covered with papers, magazines and photographs. There are not one, but three sets of reading glasses on the table.

"My art director just left," she says. "I want to show you something." I follow her into a den. Sitting on the back of the couch, on the desk and on the mantel over the fireplace are large color Veloxes, pasted on cardboard backings, on exhibit.

I am stunned.

"That's the cover," Verity says, pointing, and there is a close-up of Cassy Cochran that is so beautiful I don't know what to say. It reminds me of a studio portrait of the 1940s.

I know Cassy will be terrified by it—and perhaps secretly pleased, for while some of it has been retouched, they have left enough lines for anyone to know that she is not a young woman. It is the portrait of a great beauty, caught in the last moments of nature's full gift. But what makes the photograph so startling is that it captures so completely that special nuance Cassy possesses, that until this moment I couldn't put my finger on—an aura of kindness, graced with wisdom and intelligence.

The other photographs are great, too. There is one of Cassy and Michael (boy, did he look handsome back then), holding young Henry between them. There is one of her sailing with Jackson. There is one of her at maybe age two, sitting obediently next to her grimly beautiful mother. No doubt about it, the technicalities of Cassy's physical beauty came from her mother. There is a picture of Cassy on the set of what looks like an ancient TV studio in Chicago. And then there is a series taken recently by the same photographer who took the cover shot: Cassy in the newsroom with Alexandra Waring; Cassy watching *The Jessica Wright Show* from the control room; Cassy in jeans and blouse and Top-Siders, leaning back against a railing on the Hudson River; Cassy working in her office, half-glasses on, laboring over some kind of computer printout.

"Wow," I finally say.

"Wow indeed," Verity comments objectively. "She's very photogenic." Abruptly she turns to me. "So, dear Sally, this is what your words have to compete with." She smiles suddenly, and I see why Spencer would find her attractive. She's very powerful. At times Spencer can be very dominating in bed and I know he would love having a woman like this surrender to his control.

Stop it, I tell myself.

"Is everything all right?" Verity says, ducking her head a little, as if to see through my eyes into my soul.

"It's just the pictures," I murmur, looking back at them. "They are wonderful."

"Mmm," she says, leading the way back out. "I just hope the Darenbrooks' security is up to snuff. After this cover, every weirdo around will be obsessed with her." She glances at me over her shoulder. "How do you think Cassy will feel about them?"

"I think she'll be frightened, at first," I say.

Verity stops in her tracks and turns around. *"Really? Frightened?* What a curious word to choose."

I regret using it. I am starting to feel protective of Cassy. "What I mean is, she's downplayed her looks all her life. That's a big piece of the story. Her mother, as you can see, was just as good-looking, but she did such a number on Cassy as a child, about how her looks would cause her nothing but trouble and how she could only rely on her brain, that Cassy will do almost anything to prevent people from looking at her that way."

Verity and I go into the sunroom where she beckons me to sit. "So you think it's genuine, this aversion she has about her looks," she asks with interest.

"It's not an aversion," I explain, "it's more like an instinct to instantly dismiss. Like if someone meets her and says something about how beautiful she is, she'll get impatient and say, 'Thanks, yeah, I know, okay, can we please move on now?'"

Verity smiles slightly. I bet she's had her share of this, too.

"And something else I'm writing about is that since she's married Jackson, she seems to have become more comfortable with her looks."

"It may not be him," Verity says. "It's easy for women to discount their beauty while they have it. It's another situation entirely when you begin to lose what you've taken for granted all your life. She may simply be at that point."

I consider this. Then I pull a pad from my bag and make a note. "That's possible." I look up. "The only question is, how do you tactfully ask someone, 'Now that you're losing your looks, wouldn't you be more grateful about them if you could get them back?'"

Verity laughs. "Ah, I see you are the right one for this article, Sally."

"So we'll see," I say absently, writing down another thought I have. When I look up, I remember Verity's connection with Spencer and I hate it. Why can't I just be another writer today, learning all I can from someone at the top of her industry?

Damn it!

What did he say? Something about the fact if Verity knew, she would want to hurt me?

I shake it off. "Almost every person connected to Cassy through her work has mentioned how everyone has, or had, some kind of crush on her."

Verity nods. "I've heard that, too. Particularly about all the old guys, they would be in love with her and keep promoting her." She sits back in her chair. "So, did she sleep with any of them?"

"Any of her bosses?"

She nods.

"No," I say slowly, thinking. I make, then, my definitive answer. "No."

"Never?"

"Never."

"Are you sure?"

"I am sure," I say with conviction.

"Well that's sort of a drag, isn't it?" the editor muses, pulling a manila envelope into her lap.

"What Cassy would do," I say, "and I'm including this in the piece, is that she would have dinner with, for example, her boss at WST. And they would be romantic dinners, sort of. Like he would take her to a secluded table at the Russian Tea Room, the Carlyle or Le Cirque. It was as if she would consent to pretending he *was* something special to her, when, in fact, it would be more a father-daughter relationship than anything."

"So what about this father-daughter thing? Her father was a boozer, right?"

"Yes."

"And he died when she was young?"

"Eleven."

"So how does that factor into her relationships?" She's reaching back to the table to get her glasses.

It's rather awful to be conducting an autopsy on someone's life like this, particularly when it's someone as nice as Cassy, but it's the nature of the business.

"Michael Cochran's appeal was definitely wrapped up with her relationship with her father. It wasn't that they were so much alike, but Michael was a little older than she was, certainly more experienced, more confident, and he absolutely adored her. It was like a dream come true for her, I think. He was bright and funny and protective like her father, but worked hard and got a lot of recognition professionally, whereas her father never held a job for longer than a year or two. So she thought Michael was very different. It wasn't until maybe ten years into their marriage that the drinking and womanizing became an issue."

We talk on. I don't want to complain, but I'm starving and I don't even get offered water. Verity keeps asking questions and I keep answering them, giving her what I think are the interesting highlights to a very good story.

During one of my answers, she closes her eyes, and when I finish, she opens them to ask, "What is the most devastating thing you've found out that you will not put in this article?"

"That Michael Cochran is drinking again and cries over missing Cassy, but ended up lunging at the interviewer instead."

Her eyebrows go up. "And you're not putting that in?"

"Well, I might put the desperately missing Cassy part in."

Verity sighs, looking to the floor for a moment, before returning her eyes to me. "You're doing a good job of collecting information, doing interviews. I particularly like your valor in getting drunk with Michael Cochran—" She cracks a smile. "The man is vulgar. But Sally, the fact remains, this piece still has no bite. It has no—" She snaps her fingers. "Nothing that says, 'Wow! This is the hottest issue of everything on the stands!' I don't hear people mentioning it in the news. I don't see items about it in the newspaper. Do you know what I mean?"

I don't say anything. My heart is sinking. Is she going to make me twist this into something that it's not?

"We've got to make people desperately want to read the article. We want them to hear a little bit about it somewhere, just enough to let them know they must read the whole thing or they will miss out."

I nod. "But can't it be in a positive way? Does it have to be negative?"

"Of course it doesn't have to be negative," she says impatiently.

I am at a loss. I'm missing something.

Verity has slipped on her glasses and is opening the manila envelope that has been sitting in her lap. "Somehow, Sally," she says, pulling out a leather book and thumbing through the pages, "you have managed to completely miss a major event in Cassy's life. I don't blame you, but I do expect you to get up to speed on it." She abruptly closes the book and puts it back into the envelope. She peers at me over the top of her glasses. "You read shorthand, as I recall."

"Yes."

"Good," she says, taking off her glasses with one hand and holding out the envelope to me with the other. "Take this home and read it. You'll see that you're going to have to rethink your piece. Don't be upset by not finding this part out—Cassy's obviously very deceptive when she wants to be."

I blink.

"You're going to confirm the identity of the person that's written about in there. I know who it is and I'm sure you will, too. I realize you have become a big fan of Cassy's, but you're going to have to think of it this way—either this affair will be exposed by a tabloid, who will tear her apart, or we reveal the affair in your profile, where, at the very least, you will paint a sympathetic portrait of a great woman who had a moment of weakness. Considering what her husband was putting her through at the time, I certainly don't blame her."

I feel like I'm having an out-of-body experience.

Verity stands up, a signal that I am to leave. So I stand up, too. "Do your best, Sally," she says. "You can't quote directly from the book, you'll have to paraphrase. Make damn sure you can prove it happened. At the very least, witnesses and confirmation of the time they spent together. Truth is the defense against libel."

Now I'm in shock.

Verity escorts me to the front door. "When this article is published, Sally," she says, "you are going to be a big name overnight. To keep you," she adds, smiling, opening the door, "I'll have no choice but to offer you a contract. As a matter of fact, I've got a draft of such a contract for you sitting on my desk right now. One hundred twenty thousand for four personality profiles next year."

A contract?

Stunned, I thank Verity for her help and vote of confidence and walk out to my car. Mechanically I get in, turn on the ignition, put the car into gear and drive away. At the first opportunity, however, I pull over to the side of the road to rip open the envelope and take out the book. I open it and read a few lines of what someone has written in shorthand.

And then I feel scared and a little sick.

Because what I am holding is Cassy's journal.

36

The journal begins with an undated entry:

The only thing I understand about therapy is that I need it. Sometimes I feel like the tapes have been running in my head for so long I'm incapable of thinking for myself when it comes to Michael. Phoebe says I'm not supposed to keep a journal for her, but for me, even though all I want to do is forget.

Okay, me, here's your journal. Let it work miracles! Somehow. Please.

I feel so damn stupid. Why I think Michael will ever change. Why I think locking him out will do any good. Sam says to do it, and I am, but I don't think Michael will care, he will just keep drinking. I should only talk to Sam, and to Phoebe, but I find myself talking to her again. I shouldn't be. She told me that time she thought she was falling in love with me and now I'm blithely going ahead pretending that she never said it. I guess because she knows Michael and his problems firsthand. And I still think she's just lonely.

There's nothing wrong with being friends. Phoebe agrees. But something tells me that no good can become of it, that behind that facade there is a vulnerable young woman who shouldn't be dragged into this mess called my life.

Michael's run up over ten thousand already on the American Express card. Thank God she made me get my name off the account after Sam said something about it. It's strange how someone so young can know so much. She says her grandfather drank and she knows how her grandmother handled it.

She is incredible. I've never met anyone like her. Certainly not one so young that knows so much. We keep talking and I think maybe I shouldn't, but I always do.

Last night I missed Henry so much I slept in his bed. It is so lonely here without him. And Mike. But then I think about the American Express card and I think to hell with him!

This house is so empty. She called tonight and we talked for a long time. She made me feel better. I've got to talk to Phoebe about it.

Mike's brother called to see if it was true that I'd thrown him out. I said yes. He said he thought it was a good thing, that either Michael will get help or die in an accident.

Sam says I should change the locks on the door. I don't think it's necessary. He's not even in New York.

We talk every night now. I look forward to her calls. Tonight she asked me if I had many friends. Women friends. I said I have some family friends in the country, but in the city I'm so busy. I told her that Rosanne was a friend, and so was Chi Chi. I guess that says something, that my so-called friends are people who work for me.

I feel so confused. I want Michael to come back—and I don't want him to come back.

I would like her to come over for dinner. Or maybe I could go over there. At least do something other than talk on the phone every day, but I'm scared, too. It's so stupid, because I'm not the least bit attracted to her, and yet, part of me must be, I think. I can tell she still feels something for me, but it doesn't upset me. To the contrary, I feel deeply flattered.

Henry called this morning and said Michael showed up at camp. That he had been drinking but didn't make a scene or anything. I bet it was far worse than Henry let on. He did say Mike missed me so much, and was miserable, and Henry told him all he had to do was get some help and he could come home.

I wish it was that easy. Now that he's gone, part of me dreads having to deal with his moods again, and he doesn't have a job anymore. If for one second I thought Michael would go to AA like Sam, I'd feel differently.

Or would I? Like Phoebe said, sometimes it's hard to go back once you've tasted freedom. I feel so weird being alone here, but I also dread having to go back to the way we were.

I met her for dinner tonight. It was a quick meal near the station and it was very strange. It's one thing to talk to someone all the time on the telephone, but it's another when you see them in person. I felt so strange. I had trouble looking at her. She talked on like nothing in the world was unusual.

I wish I knew what was going on with me. Everything seems out of whack. I feel almost happy that Mike is gone. Phoebe says not to worry about it, but I have to, I have a family to keep together. It's not Henry's mess, it's ours, and we owe it to him to get our act together.

Or maybe we should just end it. I just don't know anymore.

She gave me a quick hug at the cab, after dinner. I looked at her and I nearly died because I almost kissed her, like I would Mike. You know, a see-you-later kiss.

I can barely write this. I doubt I will be able to talk to Phoebe about it. Part of me doesn't want to talk about her anymore. I want her separate, away from the rest of it. Being with her is simple. She gives and doesn't take much. What a phenomenon in my life!

Who am I kidding, this is trouble and I know it. Maybe I should just give this journal to Phoebe to read.

I had her over for dinner tonight after work. I could barely eat, I was so nervous. I can't believe what is going on with me, I don't understand it. But I feel it, I definitely feel it. I am drawn to her. And I know she is drawn to me.

But I didn't do anything. I couldn't even go near her when she left, and I think she knew that. I wanted her to leave but I didn't want her to leave. When she got home she called and we ended up talking nonsense for an hour, but I didn't care, I don't want her to think I don't care.

Mike's in Chicago, I hear. We're gearing up for the awards dinner. Things coming on Electronika mess. Yeah, Sam! I pray he gets through this with a career intact. It's the least I can do for all he's done—has tried to do—for Mike. For what he's done for me.

I'll see her at the awards dinner. That will be strange.

I hope people won't be too hard on Michael. He certainly won't be there to defend himself. If WWKK gets anything, I wonder if anyone will thank him.

There I was tonight, waiting in bed for the phone to ring. She called. I want to see her. I mean, I really want to see her. I know what that means, but I've decided not to analyze it. I like being with her and that's it.

She is doing so well in New York it's almost alarming. And yet it seems very natural to her—no swollen head, not even much of an acknowledgment of the sensation she is causing. All she seems to care about is how I am, what I am thinking about.

I think about her all the time now.

I don't know what I want. But then maybe I do. Phoebe isn't much help. She only asks if I think having feelings for another woman is more acceptable than having feelings for another man. In other words, do I think an affair with a woman doesn't count.

I can't believe I can even write that. Feelings for another woman. Yes, that's what they are. And there's more. I know I am attracted to her. Physically.

I had her over for dinner again. Nothing happened, of course. I'm beginning to think she won't let anything happen. We just talked about Michael and I sautéed some vegetables in garlic and olive oil, and I made some bread and tossed a salad. It was pretty good. She loves all the old movies and collects a lot of Garbo, Carole Lombard, Hepburn, et cetera. She'd never seen *Now Voyager* and so I

rented it and it was great, as always, although I felt depressed after.

I am married, mother of one child. What am I doing?

I had some wine. She doesn't really drink, she says. I
did, anyway, because I was nervous. Scared, I suppose is
more like it. Not of her. Of me.

Michael's in town, I hear, but I don't know where. Part
of me wants him in a rehab, part of me wants him dead, I
get so angry. He told the bank manager I stole all his
money.

Long conversation with Henry. What an incredible
young man. He has a counselor out there who had problems with someone drinking. Henry's giving me a pep
talk! Hang tough, Mom, he says. Don't let him come back.

Thought about flying out and surprising Henry, but
can't do it right now.

Stopped at sidewalk table on Seventh Avenue and
bought T-shirt because I don't want to feel so old. Is forty-
one old? I used to think so. Now I feel like life may be starting. Me in a T-shirt!

Found Michael in the apartment yesterday. He chased
me.

Got to awards dinner shaking mess and got ovation for
Electronika story. Felt so strange. Drank too much, saw
her—

I can't even write what happened. It's too new. I don't
know what I'm doing but I think I'm glad I've done it.

I did it. I made her take me home after the dinner and I
went to bed with her.

That sounds crude. It wasn't. It was, I don't know—different.

Who am I kidding? It was wonderful! I was scared to
death and she made love to me like no one ever really has.

There. I said it. Now, can I admit that to Phoebe? I don't
know, but I don't want to think about it, I just want to en-

joy it. It's as though she sees someone in me that I thought had died years ago.

Last night she came here and we went into the guest room. I kept thinking I should have changed the locks like Sam said, half expecting Michael to come home. I'm too old for this, I keep thinking, and yet nothing seems to faze my body. I don't know what she has unlocked in me but I feel as though I have never had sex before. I feel starved. I do love her, but I worry about what is to happen because I don't think this is going to last the way she hopes, although she has not said anything. She is too smart.

I am thinking about men. Sexually.

I should shoot myself for writing that. Look at what she has done for me. Look at all the love she has poured into me.

What am I doing? If I am going to sleep with her, I have to focus on her. I can't be drifting so soon.

Henry's coming home next week. Michael is heaven knows where and I'm not sure I care.

I'm beginning to see that she is thinking we'll just go on and I will go over to her place. I don't know how I'll feel when Henry is home. I realized how tired I was at work this morning. I guess my body's starting to come back to terra firma, hinting I cannot run around like this day and night.

Still, how can I do without her? Her support, her affection? How can I ever replace it? The idea of going back to that old existence is unbearable. Sleeping with her is a small price to pay for such comfort and support.

What am I saying?

Someday she's going to want someone with her. It's not going to be me, I know that. I'm not convinced it will be a woman for her, either. Strange to be carrying on the way we have and entertain the thought that neither one of us is really gay, but more and more it seems we found each other during an emotional crossroads.

I don't feel gay. But I don't think I'm in love with her, either. Not that way. Not the way I should be if I am.

I just read my last entry. I don't think I'm in love with
her. Certainly I love her, but it's not that bottom line. The
sexual energy is not what it was. I cannot say the same for
her. If anything, her desire seems to be increasing as mine
diminishes and I'm not sure what to do. I don't want to
hurt her.

She cannot lead a gay life. She must know this. I'm
scared to ask her what she is thinking. Every time I get near
the topic, she only sighs, kisses me and says all she cares
about is how happy she is in that moment.

And there the journal ends.

I am almost shaking. I feel as though I have violated every
right to privacy any human being can have. I might as well be
part of the Thought Police.

Verity's read this, too. And who else, I wonder.

How the hell did Verity get this?

I dig into my briefcase to find the chronology I've constructed
of Cassy's life. I find the period before Michael Cochran went
into rehab, when Cassy helped Sam Wyatt with the Electronika
International story.

I check another notebook to verify yet again what I have
known from the first entry. I know who Cassy had the affair
with. And then I wonder why I never suspected it before.

37

Cassy Cochran's housekeeper lives in what I suspect is one of the nicest buildings on the West Side of New York, on Riverside Drive and the corner of Ninety-first Street. As the doorman calls up to announce me, I have to wonder exactly how much this Rosanne DiSantos gets paid. If the average one-bedroom apartment in Manhattan goes for one thousand dollars a month, I cannot even imagine what living in this place costs.

Rosanne herself opens the door (I'm now half expecting *her* to have a housekeeper), and since I had pictured an older, heavy-set woman, I am very surprised to find a short, trim, Italian-American woman with long dark hair, large brown eyes and very effectively applied makeup. She is wearing designer jeans and a flattering T-Shirt that has Leonardo DiCaprio's picture on it.

"Boy, do you look like one of 'em," she says, eyeing me carefully and waving me in. "Are you really a reporter, or are ya just workin' for Mrs. C?"

"Excuse me?"

She gestures to my linen suit and heels. "You're one of them. You fit right in. I don't care what she says, I think the fix is in on this article."

"Is this a compliment?"

"Yeah, if you like being sort of conservative and all. I guess you've got that WASP thing going."

I guess I do.

Rosanne leads me through the large foyer into a spacious living room with a stunning view of the Hudson River and Riverside Park. "Have a seat. What can I get you to drink?"

As Rosanne goes off to get me a glass of water, I look around. There are lots of pictures in here. On the secretary is a large one of Rosanne, an old woman and a teenage boy. A cat comes sauntering in, matter-of-factly rubbing against my leg.

"That's Missy," Rosanne says when she comes back in.

"The cat or the lady in the photograph?"

"Ha! A smart-alecky one. You're a reporter, all right." She hands me the glass. "The cat is Missy, and belongs to Mrs. G.— Mrs. Emma Goldblum. This is her apartment. I sublet from her. And that," she says, pointing to the boy in the picture, "is my son, Jason. I'm a widow," she adds, "and so is Mrs. G. We decided to live together. It's been great."

I should say so, I think, looking out at the view. On the other hand, the woman in the picture looks like she's in her eighties and I should imagine having some young people in the house in New York City is a comfort. I know Rosanne works exclusively for Cassy and Jackson now; I wonder if Mrs. Goldblum was ever a client?

We sit down to talk and within an hour it is clear that Rosanne worships the ground Cassy walks on. For the sake of her son, Rosanne says, she doesn't wish to go into the circumstances of her husband's death, except to say it was quite sudden and horrible, and that had it not been for Cassy, Rosanne might have lost custody of Jason.

I turn my head slightly at this, because it does not make much sense. I turn off the tape recorder, put the pad and pen on the table and say, "Just for my information, completely off the record, could you explain?"

"My husband was shooting drugs," Rosanne says. "He was a Vietnam vet," she adds, as if this forgives him of everything. "I put my son into foster care for a while because I didn't want him exposed to the way his father was, and then his father died of an overdose and the foster parents tried to get custody of Jason permanently. Mrs. C. and Mrs. Goldblum helped me straighten everything out."

I nod. "I see." I turn the recorder back on. "If it's all right with you, Rosanne," I say, "I would like to say something like Cassy was there to help put your family back on firm footing after your husband's fatal illness."

Rosanne smiles, although I see a spark of pain in her eyes. "That would be great. So what else do you want to know?"

"I'm interested in what Cassy said to you about this interview."

"She said for me to say whatever I want."

"Anything?"

"She did say that if anything slipped and it was awful she wouldn't fire me," she admits.

"What kind of slip?" I tease.

"Oh, I don't know. Probably stuff about Mr. C. Jackson doesn't do anything that's very interesting. He does dramatic stuff, but it's not as interesting as the things Mr. C. used to do."

"What kind of dramatic stuff does Jackson do?"

"Once he brought home a baby ocelot," she says. "See, Mrs. C. said she wanted a cat, but wasn't sure what kind. And then another time he flew her to the wrong country. She said she wanted to go the Vineyard and he thought she said Finland, so he took her to Finland for their anniversary. That was pretty funny."

She tells me more about Jackson and his children, and Cassy's son, about how all the children come home for the holidays, who's doing what, how much they like their respective stepparents. When I steer our conversation back to Michael Cochran, Rosanne's face takes on that vaguely pained look again.

"Oh, Mr. C.'s all right. You know, he just had that drinking thing."

It occurs to me that Rosanne and Cassy at one time had rather a lot in common in regard to their marriages.

"But then he stopped, so that was good," she adds.

"But then he left," I point out.

Rosanne nods. "And then he left," she agrees. And then, as if she feels she owes me something, she relates a story about how Michael, when he was drunk one night, threw a TV set out the apartment window. "Nobody got hit or nothing," Rosanne says, "so it's a funny story now."

I wonder how funny she would find it if she knew Michael Cochran was drinking again. And that, from Michael, I already knew that Rosanne's husband had been a drug addict, that they had lived in an SRO—single-room-occupancy hotel—where they had shared a bathroom and kitchen with a great many people. None of this is going into the article, though. Still, it's helpful that I know it.

"Michael Cochran says one of the main reasons he went into rehab..." I begin, pretending to read from some old notes.

"Hey, you write shorthand like Mrs. C. She's always leaving me notes I can't read."

I smile. "Anyway, Michael Cochran says one of the main reasons he went into rehab was because Cassy finally threw him out."

Rosanne nods. "That's right."

"And for the first time, she wouldn't let him come home."

Rosanne nods again. "It wasn't easy for her."

"And he had been fired, so he didn't have his job to go to."

She shook her head. "No, he didn't. I think he went out west somewhere, bounced around. Mrs. C. was worried sick about him, but she had some good advice and decided to stick to her guns, that he couldn't come back unless he got help."

"And so he went into Hazleton in Minnesota."

"Mrs. C. flew him out there."

"What enabled her to be able to do it that time?" I ask, my heart pounding because I am being such a sneak. "To not take him back in?"

Rosanne shrugs, thinking. "Her friends, I think." She's beginning to look vaguely uncomfortable and I wonder if she had any idea what her employer had been up to at the time.

"Like who?" I ask, pen poised over paper.

"Um, Mr. W., Sam Wyatt. He lives down the street. He's been a friend of the Cs' for a long time. He and Mrs. W. knew what was going on with Mr. C. and they were very supportive. He and Mrs. C are good friends. She helped him on the stock scandal at Electronika International a while back, you might remember that."

"That was at about the same time," I say, jotting down a note.

"Yeah, I guess it was," Rosanne says vaguely. "I don't know,

I was so out of it around then, it was right after my husband died."

"Was there anyone else who helped Cassy?" I ask. "In helping her stand firm about Michael's drinking?"

"I don't know, maybe you should ask her."

"Henry was away at camp," I continue. "And I think by then she had met Alexandra Waring."

"Oh, yeah," Rosanne says, shifting slightly, "she was around. Mr. C was the one who hired her, you know, brought her to New York from Kansas City and made her a big star."

"That's right," I confirm. "And she and Cassy have remained close friends ever since."

"Mr. and Mrs. C went down to Washington that time she was shot."

"That was later," I say.

"Yeah, I guess that was a year or two later."

"But when Alexandra was working here in New York, she and Cassy became friends."

"Yeah."

"So maybe she was helpful in supporting Cassy. After all, she knew about Michael's drinking firsthand, right? Because he was fired from their station."

Rosanne shrugs. "I don't know."

"Was there anyone else around at that time?" I ask lightly. "Besides Sam Wyatt and Alexandra Waring?"

Rosanne shrugs again. "I really don't remember, you'd have to ask Mrs. C."

"Sam Wyatt and Alexandra Waring," I read back from my notes. "That's good, thank you. I'm seeing Alexandra this afternoon, as a matter of fact, so I'll ask her."

Rosanne doesn't say anything; she's waiting for my next question.

"I think that's about it," I say, turning off the tape recorder.

"It is?" She's surprised. "Don't you want to know anything else?"

"You mean besides…" I say, flipping back a page in my notes to quote to her, "that 'Mrs. C. is the kindest, smartest, most generous person in the whole wide world'?"

She smiles, coloring slightly. "Well, she is."

"I know," I say, standing up. "And I thank you for confirming it."

And so I leave Rosanne's apartment, knowing that in my next interview I will be talking to Cassy's ex-lover.

38

Alexandra Waring is reading something at her desk when I walk into her office. She looks up, smiles and stands before coming around her desk to shake my hand. "How are you?" she says. "I hear they caught the shooter in the Meyers murder."

"I'm afraid you probably know about as much as I do," I confess, having trouble looking at her. She is so friendly I feel almost sick with guilt.

"It's got to be a mob hit, don't you think?" she asks, gesturing for me to sit on the couch. She sits down in the chair across from me. "Why else would some imported Russian thug from Queens shoot a Long Island toxic-waste consultant over in Castleford?"

"God knows," I sigh, setting my stuff up. The image of the hunk of concrete left on my porch flashes through my mind. I glance over at her and Alexandra seems a little put off by my answer, and then I realize how flippant it must have sounded. "I'm sorry, what I mean is—" *She is a mesmerizing kind of person. Those eyes, that smile, the energy. The power. I can see what attracted Cassy.* "You're right, the murderer decided it would be better to do it somewhere other than Long Island, where people might immediately assume it was connected to his toxic-waste-disposal business."

"So you think it's a mob hit, too."

"Or something like it."

She watches me set up. "So how's the article coming?"

"Very well," I say. "People have been very insightful."

"That's good."

This is starting off stilted and it's my fault. But I can't help it. There's too much going on in my head.

Frankly, I'm rattled. I know too much.

"I love your office," I say, once the recorder is on. There are so many plants in this office it smells like the outdoors.

"Thank you. It drives the building people crazy, though. They say I'm giving off too much moisture in here and it's doing something to the ventilation system." She laughs. "I told them that was exactly the point, to do something about the ventilation system."

"That's what's so different in here," I say. "There's fresh air."

"I'm spoiled rotten," she says, crossing her legs. They are terrific. The blue silk blouse she is wearing only intensifies the color of her eyes and I am having a hard time concentrating.

"So," I say, "why don't we just start off with how you first met Cassy." I hope my voice does not betray me; I am so nervous. This whole thing is too big for me. Verity, the journal, DBS, *Expectations,* the whole thing.

"Cassy's former husband, Michael Cochran," Alexandra says easily, "hired me to work at WWKK here in New York. He had been looking for a new anchor, a woman, and he saw my tapes from Kansas City."

"How old were you?"

"Twenty-seven."

"So Cassy was forty..."

She does not take the cue, so I finish, "Forty-one."

"Why is that important?" she asks, curious.

"I'm just trying to keep my time line straight."

She studies me for a moment and decides to let it pass. "Anyway, shortly after I arrived, the Cochrans had a party at their home. That's how we first met."

"And you guys became friends?"

"Well, she was at a competing station, so we became friend-*ly,*" the anchorwoman says. "For example, I sat in a booth at Cassy's neighborhood block party." She laughs. "The things we do for publicity."

"So the three of you were actually friends."

"Well, yes. I guess so. I worked for Michael. And yes, we became friends after a time."

I make a note. "I talked to Rosanne DiSantos this morning," I say, looking up. "And she says that during that difficult time for Cassy, when she finally told Michael he couldn't come home until he got help, that you were a good friend to her."

Our eyes have locked and I know she suspects something.

"It was exactly what you said," Alexandra says, "it was a difficult time. Because I was working with Michael, I just happened to be there."

"He was fired from WWKK."

She nods. "And I was concerned about him."

"Did you talk to him while he was on his, well, drinking spree?"

"He called me at work once." She frowns. "Is this really necessary? I should think Cassy would be the best source for this."

"What I mean is, did you help Cassy to get him help?"

She pauses and says, "I really think you should talk to Cassy about it."

She has successfully stared me down and I look at my notes, trying to regroup. I don't know what I'm doing. I want to move to Mexico, anything to get out of here. I swallow. "If you had five words to describe Cassy, what would they be?"

She relaxes a bit, then settles back in her chair, and so do I. She looks to the ceiling for a while and then back down to me. "Regenerative."

I write this down and look up.

"Resourceful. Loving, kind and gentle," she finishes.

I write it all down, nodding. "*Kind* and *gentle* are two words almost everyone has used."

"For good reason."

"She commands a great deal of loyalty," I say, "even from those she has fired."

Alexandra's eyebrows go up. "Oh?"

"I talked to Glenn Mortimer last week," I say, referring to the former political analyst for DBS News.

"Oh, him."

"Do you care to make any comment about him?"

"No," she says simply.

"Well, he had quite a lot to say about you."

"I'm sure he did."

We're sitting here.

"He was still very appreciative of Cassy," I say.

No response whatsoever from Alexandra.

"And I also talked to Bonnie Kirk."

"Uh-huh," Alexandra says, nodding.

"Actually, she talked more about you than she did about Cassy."

"Since I'm the one who had her fired, I'm sure she did."

"Well, um," I stammer, trying to figure out how to say this, "aren't you curious about what she said?"

"No."

Now what?

"She was pretty angry," I offer.

Alexandra nods once, as much as to say, yes, that sounds like the same Bonnie.

"Um," I say.

The anchorwoman leans forward in her chair. "What is it that you want to ask me, Sally?"

"It was about a comment she made." My face is burning.

"And you want to tell me what she said. Even though I'm not interested in hearing it."

Oh, God, there must be another line of work I can get into. This is awful. "Well, it was kind of an interesting comment."

"And what could this possibly have to do with an article about Cassy?"

There, she said it, daring me to try and link the two. She does suspect me.

"Well," I say, "if what Bonnie Kirk said about your life-style is true, then I wondered what role Cassy may have played—or plays—in enabling you to engage in it."

It is impossible to read the anchorwoman's expression, but I know I have crossed the line with her.

"So, in effect," Alexandra says carefully, "you're asking me if you can spice up your article about Cassy at my expense?"

God, I just want to die.

"That if Verity can't get any dirt on Cassy, she's told you to come after me."

"No," I say truthfully, shaking my head.

Alexandra takes a deep breath, shaking her head. Then she curls forward, placing her elbow on her knee and resting her chin in the palm of her hand. "If there is a living example of goodness and integrity, it is Cassy Cochran. You may quote me on that. In regard to my personal life—and I'm glad you have that tape running—I have to caution you, Sally, when it comes to that little square of ten minutes I *call* my private life, I am fiercely private and voraciously protective." Then she straightens back up.

I'm not absolutely sure of it, but I think I've just been threatened.

"But," Alexandra continues in her normal tone of voice, "you're entitled to know what everyone else does: I am not married. I will get married only if I decide to have children."

"And Georgiana Hamilton-Ayres?"

"Is my best friend in the world."

I can't take those eyes on again. I simply nod and make a note. I've got to get out of here. At least, change the subject. I look up, smiling. "Tell me the worst thing Cassy has ever done to you."

Instead of this taking her aback, Alexandra's face immediately crinkles into self-deprecating laughter, and she launches into a story that goes back to when they were trying to assemble the pieces of the newscast. She wanted it one way, and Cassy wanted it another, and Cassy sat back and let Alexandra run with her ideas, even though she knew they wouldn't work.

"But why?"

"Because I wouldn't listen. And the network brass was too scared to say no to me. I was their big hope at the time. They wanted me to get on the air."

"So what happened?"

"We did a dry run of my format for the newscast and I think it was Jessica who suggested we change the name of it to, *Snooziola City and the Narcoleptic Sandbaggers.*

We laugh. The tension is clearing. "So that's the worst thing Cassy has ever done to me," Alexandra finishes. "Let me hang myself in front of the entire network."

I chuckle, making a note. I no longer feel suicidal.

"Actually, it was a very good thing," Alexandra continues. "I was thirty years old by the time I moved to DBS. I was scared to death and thinking I had to know how to do everything by myself. And that little crisis proved that I didn't, that I had to learn to work as part of a team. And as a result of that teamwork, we have a very successful news division."

"What defines 'successful' to you?"

"If something happened to me," she says, "would the news division survive, would it still attract viewers? The answer is a resounding yes, it would. We may have started out as a personality-driven network—" She laughs. "Never underestimate the power of being shot live on national TV. It was that whole TV episode, you know—my being shot, my being in the hospital, my recovery—that carried over to attracting so many initial viewers to DBS. They were curious to see how I was. Everybody knew me because the shooting had been rerun so many times on every newscast in the country."

This is true. It was very dramatic footage. The whole country watched in horror as the young network reporter, conducting an interview in front of the Congressional Building, was suddenly shot.

We go on to discuss the history of DBS and Alexandra happily recounts every step of the way—how Jackson approached her, how she knew Cassy was the one to oversee the development of the news division and then *The Jessica Wright Show,* and then the entire network. She talks straight for almost forty minutes.

She balks, however, at talking about Jessica's drinking days. She won't even react to the statements Jessica has made. "No," she says quietly, shaking her head, "it's not appropriate. You'll have to go with whatever she's told you."

As things are winding down, her secretary, Trevor, comes in to tell Alexandra it's time for a meeting downstairs in the newsroom. I say that was about it, anyway, and start packing up my gear. I am acutely conscious that Alexandra has not moved but is sitting there, watching me.

"I imagine this article is going to pay very well," she says.

"For me, certainly," I concede, putting the cassettes away.

"And it will probably lead to other assignments from Verity."

"I don't know." I finish putting my stuff away and stand up. "I really appreciate you spending so much time with me."

She does not get up. Instead, she says, "Sit down for a second, Sally, will you?"

I sit down, nervous.

She looks at me for a long moment and then crosses her arms over her chest. "You've changed." A moment passes. "In less than two weeks you've changed."

What am I supposed to say to this? I say nothing and simply sit there, feeling my face grow warm again.

"Don't let this assignment change you," she nearly whispers. "It's not worth it. I know the money and the excitement is alluring, but understand that with *Expectations* you are no longer covering the news, you are trying to make it. It's a distinction you need to think about." She stands up and claps her hands once, like a teammate might after a huddle. "But who am I to tell you what to do with your life?" She extends her hand. "Good luck."

Driving home to Castleford, I have an awful lot to think about. One thing I do know. I can't deal with Spencer or anybody until I sort this article out. I call Spencer's answering machine at his apartment because I know he will not be there.

"Hi," I say. "Listen, I know I said we could keep on talking, but the truth is, I need a few days to clear my head and focus on this piece. I think you, of all people, can understand that. So I wanted to tell you that I'm shutting off my phones, that you are not to take it personally, that I have not given up on us and that you are not to worry. And if there is some kind of emergency, you can reach me through my mother." And I leave him Mother's number.

That's the best I can do.

I pick up Scotty at Mother's and learn it's going to be a day or two more before Mack's friend can look at that hunk of cement for me.

"Fine with me," I say, "because I'm shutting off the phones and working straight through."

Mother's reaction is almost instantaneous. Her eyes light up and her smile explodes. "You're really going to do it, aren't you? Write a brilliant article!"

I don't know how brilliant it's going to be, but at least I will do some serious work on it.

And so I go home and write. And write and rewrite and scrap it and start it again. For two days I work fifteen hours straight and by Thursday morning I know I'm going to have a major piece for *Expectations*. I also know that Cassy is awfully lucky to have me as the writer on it. With any luck, I can talk Verity into believing I can't verify the identity of the woman in the journal. And the best I can do is to tell Cassy, face-to-face, that I know she had a brief affair with another woman and give her a chance to comment.

That's the best I can do.

I'm sitting here, tinkering with this draft, dressed in gym shorts and an athletic bra (it is hot), drinking well water. I read a paragraph out loud and then I hear a tapping sound at the window. It is Mother and she is crying.

39

"What's happened?" I cry, rushing outside to her.

She pushes my hand away, refusing to let me help her inside. I'm alarmed at her appearance. She looks older, pale, extremely upset.

"Sit down, Sally," she says in my living room in a horrible voice. She sits in one of the armchairs.

Astonished, I sit in the chair across from her.

Her eyes are red. "Why did you really bring that thing to my house and ask Mack to look at it?"

"What thing? The cement thing?"

"I've been thinking and thinking about it since he called me this afternoon," she says, ignoring my question, "and for the life of me, I can't believe you would do it to hurt me."

I am frantic. "Do what, Mother? What are you talking about?"

"You know how many years it's been since I've been able to have—" She sniffs. "A friendship, a relationship. With a man other than your father."

"Mother!"

"And now you bring all of this up, and you pull Mack into it—I just can't believe you would do it, Sally. It's a mean and dirty trick and it's hurt me terribly."

I rush to my mother's side, sliding down on my knees next to her chair. "Mother, I don't have any idea what you're talking about."

"That piece of debris. You *knew* it was from the high school, you *knew* it was from where your father died. And you *knew* how much it would upset me." She covers her mouth with her hand as tears fill her eyes again. "If you wanted to cause trouble—"

"Oh, Mother, no!" I wail, throwing my arms around her. "No, no, no! Dear God in heaven, I swear to God, Mother, I had no idea." I pull back to look at her. "I would never do anything to compromise your happiness, Mother. I only gave it to Mack because I trusted him—I see him as a member of the family."

She wants to believe me so badly.

"That cement is from the high school?" I ask her. "Castleford High? Are you sure?"

She nods.

"How does Mack know that?"

"He doesn't know it. But I do," my mother says, starting to lose it again.

I take her in my arms and rock her. "Mother, whatever it is, you must tell me."

"It was too strange to be a coincidence," she explains tearfully. "You arriving Friday night—I was so embarrassed, I didn't know what to say—"

"You didn't have to say anything," I tell her. "Mack is a wonderful person, and he cares for you and you for him, and I only care that you two can be together."

"Oh, Sally," she sobs, "I miss your father so!"

At this, I start crying, too. Gradually the storm passes and I get up to retrieve some tissues. We blow our noses, wipe our eyes and feel better. Mother now knows that I did not intend to cause a rift between her and Mack. I also realize how vulnerable Mother is and how difficult she might be finding it to "be" with Mack in the intimate way she had been with my father.

Poor Mother. I love her so much.

"What exactly did Mack say?"

"He took that thing to his colleague, and his colleague recognized immediately that the brick was local, from New Britain. It was probably made in the end of the 1970s or early 1980s. He needs to do some checking on the cement and cables, but he said the piece was from part of a buttress that is primarily used for some kind of performance center or large warehouse-type of building."

"So how do you make the connection with the high school?"

"What other brick building was built in 1977—one that was some sort of large performance center that has already been demolished? And who else do you know, Sally, that was so proud of the cement buttresses in his designs in the late seventies? That debris is from the gymnasium, Sally, I'd bet my life on it."

I call the police station and ask that Detective D'Amico call me back. Within two minutes, I have him on the line. In less than twenty minutes, I am meeting him in a parking lot in Middletown on the Wesleyan campus. We go into the building to find Mack, and I can see from down the hall that the expression on Mack's face is grave. "I've upset your mother terribly, Sally," he murmurs when he reaches me. "And frankly I'm at a loss as to why."

"It's not your fault," I say, taking his arm. "Mother seems to think that that cement thing is from the building where my father was killed. I had no idea, Mack. I've brought Detective D'Amico with me. I thought it was debris from an arson case. I never would have brought it over otherwise."

"She was so upset," he murmurs. Clearly he is, too.

"A lot of crazy thoughts ran through her head," I explain. "One of them was that I brought it over to deliberately upset her and drive you off."

He looks horrified.

"It was just a wild thought, but she's got it all sorted now. She knows how much I want the two of you to be together. I know how much she loves you, Mack."

He lunges to hug me. He is not a very big man, but his hug is strong. Just as abruptly, he lets me go. "Thank you," he whispers. "I love her very much."

Buddy clears his throat, pretending he's not listening to any of this.

Mack leads us to an office on the second floor and introduces his colleague. "If you don't need me, I'd like to go and see your mother now."

"Go," I urge.

Professor Marrietto takes us into the classroom that is connected to his office, where the hunk of cement is sitting on one of the lab tables. He reiterates what Mack has already relayed to us, that the brick is from a factory in New Britain, made in the late 1970s, and the cement is from one of two local cement facilities. He explains how he knows this from the components of the formula used to make these building materials and that, just as Mother had repeated to me, this hunk of debris was from a cement buttress in a brick building, probably near the corner of some kind of auditorium or warehouse—

"Like the corner of a brick gymnasium built in 1977?" I ask, interrupting him.

He looks at me like I am a genius. "Yes! That would be consistent. Was this gymnasium recently torn down?"

"No," Buddy says, speaking for the first time. "We're talking about the gym at Castleford High. One wall crumbled in the big flood in 1978. Then they took a wrecking ball to the rest of it. We think this piece is from that debris."

The professor looks slightly puzzled. "A wrecking ball? Are you sure?"

"Actually, I'm positive," Buddy says, "because I've just recently been reading the reports on it."

I look at Buddy.

"Why do you ask?" Buddy wants to know. "About the wrecking ball?"

"Because there are traces of a demolition charge," he says, pointing. "These smudgelike marks. There."

"Professor, thank you," Buddy says abruptly. "If you don't mind, I'll take this with me."

"Certainly," the professor says, turning to reach for a folder. "Here, I've made some notes you may find helpful."

Buddy opens the folder to scan the contents and the color, I swear, drains from his face. "Thank you, sir," he says then, tucking the folder under his arm before I can get my hands on it. "And I'd appreciate it if you kept this confidential. I may need to call you later with some more questions."

"Yes, that would be fine," the professor says. He looks at me. "I hope I've been of help. Mack's been a great friend for years and years."

"Yes, Professor, you have," I say, feeling a terrible sadness starting to come over me. I don't know what is going on, exactly, but I suspect there is some dreadful new wave of grief coming my family's way about Daddy.

Professor Marrietto helps carry the building debris to the trunk of Buddy's unmarked police car. We thank him again and he goes inside. In the meantime, I have swiped the folder from Buddy and am reading the contents.

The composition of the brick...

The composition of the concrete...

The composition of the mortar...

The composition of the co-axial cable...

The chemical composition of the flashing from a demolition charge...

The professor's even made a sketch of a corner of a large building, with an arrow pointing to where this sample most likely came from. Another arrow points a little ways away, where, he has written, he thinks the demolition charge was set in order for this piece to break off in the proportions it had.

Buddy puts his hand out for the folder. I give it to him. He hits his other hand with the folder, eyes on mine. "Do you get it?"

I shake my head. And then, in the next instant, I do.

V
Exposé

40

"Pete?" I call into the Sabatino's house. The front door is open, not a good sign for the home of a conspiracist. I walk inside. He is not here. Someone else has been, though, because the house has been turned inside out. The living room, den, kitchen and bedroom on the ground floor have been ransacked. So have the bedrooms and Pete's "library" on the second floor. Everything has been pulled out, turned over or ripped apart, all the way up into the crawl space in the attic, and all the way down into the basement, where I feel obligated to look behind a pile of snow tires for a frightened Crazy Pete.

No sign of him.

I leave through the front door and drive down the street to use the phone at a convenience store. I tell Buddy that I stopped by Pete's house, but he's not there. Someone else has been, though. The whole house is torn apart. I'm worried about him.

"I'll find him, Sally. Go home, let me handle it. You agreed you'd lie low."

"But I've got to do *something*, Buddy. I can't sit around. If I can find Pete, I can at least ask him if he knows anything about—"

"Do *nothing*," Buddy roars. "Do as I say, Sally, I'm begging you. Go home, better yet, pack your bag and get the hell out of Castleford until I tell you. Your presence is only a liability."

Every instinct I have as a reporter says to stay. But every instinct I have as the daughter who must know the truth about what happened to her father says don't interfere. One hint of what Buddy and I suspect, and any evidence—or people—may vanish. If they have not already. Obviously someone's already looking for something at Crazy Pete's. I can't help but wonder, at this point, if it might be the debris Buddy has sent on to the state lab.

"Sally," Buddy says quietly, "listen to me. If we have any

chance—any at all—of finding out what happened, and who is responsible, our ability to construct a case will largely depend on you staying out of it. If anyone in Castleford sees that you're interested in anything but your *Expectations* piece—"

"Okay, okay," I agree. "I'll go to New York."

When I arrive home, I half expect to find my house ransacked or at least that Crazy Pete is hiding behind the woodpile. No on both counts. There is only Scotty dancing around. I let him out the kitchen door, where I see that Mr. Quimby has been here; he's left his racing form on the table. I pick up the phone to call him, but there is no dial tone. "Hello?"

"It's Spencer," a solemn voice says.

"It didn't even ring," I explain. "I picked up to call somebody."

"Sally, I've been out of my mind!"

"Well, you've reached me, even though I asked you not to. What do you want?"

"Don't be like this, Sally, please. We need to see each other."

"No. Not now, I've got too much on my plate."

"I don't blame you," he says. Someone in the background says something to him and he raises his voice. "Just close the damn door, will you? And tell them to leave me the hell alone!" That voice says something else. And Spencer mutters, "Damn it, it's my boss, I've got to go. Sally, I've got to see you."

"Why?"

"*Why?*" he nearly yells. "Why do you think? Because I love you and we have to talk this out!"

I only sigh, packing Scotty's bowl and food and favorite pull toy in a bag to take to Mother's.

"I—I've got to go. I'll call you," he says hastily, hanging up.

I'm having a hard time remembering what I found so attractive about Spencer that I was willing to abandon my life for him.

I dial my mother's house. "Hi. Everything okay?"

"Yes, dear, quite." She sounds enormously better and I dread the day we may have to dredge up everything all over again about how Daddy died. "I feel very badly about how I acted. If I hadn't been so tired I wouldn't have…" She sighs. "I hope you can forgive me."

"Oh, Mother, there's nothing to forgive. But if you want to baby-sit Scotty again for a few days, so I can go back into New York, we would both certainly appreciate it."

"Wait until I tell Abigail," she says, sounding like herself again. "She'll want me to give her a bath and set her hair."

I put a call into mom's cheapo-hotel line and I am in luck. If I check in tonight, I can get two nights at a cheapo hotel with all the rest of the hookers in town. Unfortunately I have lost my taste for less-than-great hotels and decide to try to use my status as a writer for *Expectations*. I get the manager of the Claremont on the phone. I explain my situation to him and promise a plug for the hotel in my piece, how would that be? He's says they don't need any plugs, but he'll let me have a room for $150 a night instead of $260.

I pack up my recorder and tapes and computer disks and the draft of my article. After much hesitation, I wrap Cassy's journal in a bag and stick that in my suitcase, too.

I drive into New York with talk-radio blasting at me. My head is filled with so many unhappy thoughts it is a luxury not to think, but simply to drive and listen to people ranting and raving about politics.

When I hit the elevated roadway on the Bruckner and the skyline of New York swings into view, I remember how terribly excited I had been driving in to Verity's office that first time. The memory makes me sad. I feel sad about the turn the article has taken, but in the scheme of things, Cassy's problems pale next to the possibility someone might have killed my father.

My throat tightens as I think of the funeral, and I think of Mother and of Rob.

Rob. At some point, I should call him. He should be here if and when things break.

I check into the Claremont and order up a steak and French fries and a bottle of red wine, which I have no problem consuming while watching a series of those bizarre talk shows on MSNBC. Around midnight, half in the bag, I call Spencer. "You have messed up my life," I tell him.

For once it seems he has the good sense to keep his mouth shut.

"If you had just told me about *some* woman," I complained, "you didn't have to tell me *who*, just that there was someone—"

"I can't talk right now," he says. "Can I call you later?"

"No, you can't talk to me later—you talk to me now." I have a thought. "Don't tell me Verity's there. Your girlfriend. Or do you have another girlfriend I should know about?" I look at the clock. "Who the hell's at your apartment at midnight?"

"Well if it's midnight here," he says calmly, "then it's only nine out there on the West Coast. So, let's say around ten, your time? Good? Okay, great. Call me then." And he hangs up.

I am still sitting here with the receiver to my ear. I was calling him so that he would talk his way into coming over here and then say nice things to me and hold me and tell me he loves me and make up. It was not part of the plan for him to have someone there, someone he has to convince he's receiving a call from the West Coast.

Screw him, I think, snuggling down into the bed. I'm not waiting an hour.

I fall asleep with the talking heads on TV still arguing.

41

I sleep in. Then I breakfast in bed while reading the *Times* and the *Wall Street Journal* and watching CNN. I tell the housekeeper I do not need maid service today. I am trying to steel myself for this phone call.

Chi Chi's warm greeting makes me feel awful. Cassy's bright hello makes me feel even worse.

"So how goes it?" she says, sounding happy. "Verity sent over some copies of the photographs they want to run. I can't believe it. At first I wondered who that woman was, and then I realized it was me. And you know what, Sally? I like them. I don't know what's happened to me, but I like them. Really, I do. Maybe this whole experience is doing something good to my head."

I want to die before doing what I have to do.

"You and I need to meet one more time," I say.

"Sure. Do you want to come in tomorrow?"

"I think maybe we should meet outside the office," I say.

She pauses, no doubt picking up something in my voice. "If you prefer, you can meet me at seven tomorrow morning for a walk in the park, how would that be?"

"That would be fine."

She hesitates for a fraction of a second. "Has something happened, Sally? Is there anything I can do?" she asks. And then I realize she's wondering if *I'm* all right.

"You're very kind," I say quietly. "But there's nothing, thank you. In any event, I look forward to seeing you tomorrow." And as I say those last words, I feel, literally, a pang in my heart.

Dear God, I've got to think this through.

"Sally," Buddy says, coming onto the phone.

"Hi." I have worked out in the hotel gym for an hour and

have showered and am sitting here in a robe, my hair dripping wet.

"Where are you?"

"New York." I give him the number of the hotel.

"Who else knows you're there?"

"No one."

"Really?"

"Really."

"Good." I have a feeling he's reading something or making notes. "I found Pete," he says. "He was in the back of the storeroom on the second floor of the library."

"Doing what?"

"Hiding. But he's not talking. We swept the house but haven't found anything. No fingerprints, nothing. I asked him what he thought someone might want in his house and he looked at me like *I* was crazy. Then I asked him if he had any idea who might have broken in, and he said—"

"The Masons," I fill in, yawning.

"Exactly." He sighs. "Though, given what we're running tests on," he says, referring to the hunk of concrete, "I'm beginning to wonder if he's right."

I have the membership list with me. I suppose I could stare hopelessly at it again for a while. "Buddy, thank you. And let me know."

"Sure will."

I have gone back to the bed to lie down. I feel so tired. Not sleepy, but weary. I remember once, in my senior year of high school, I had been running nonstop for months when I finally crashed. I had, at the last minute, been doing sports and student council stuff while working a job at the mall in an effort to improve my scholarship chances. And then one night, a rare night I actually had off, I remember going up to my room and suddenly feeling as I do right now. Tired, overwhelmed—the goal simply impossible to reach if I stopped to think about it.

Only now I don't know what my goal is. I don't really know where I want to live, what kind of reporting I want to do or who I want to love.

So much of my life since Daddy died has felt surreal. Like my little family, my mother and brother and me, how we would act like we were a family, and not like the band of survivors we were, desperately missing Daddy but pretending we didn't hear each other secretly crying. I once even heard Rob, when he was nine, after he lost the game for his Little League team. I heard him crying in the potting shed, asking Daddy why he had to mess everything up.

I wonder how my uncertainty is related to the fact Mother has found someone I can plainly see wishes to take care of her. And, in all probability, will. With no Mother to worry about, what noble purpose do I have? Exposing some nice lady's love affair that even she, at the time, knew was a kind of desperate emotional measure to save her sanity? And how about my cheating on Doug? And having an affair with a man who's having an affair with the married woman who's paying me to sandbag aforementioned nice lady?

Surely there is an easier way to live.

There is one thing I want to know for sure, though. I will find out what happened to Daddy. And perhaps finding that out will take away the element of choice in my life, the element I seem to have so much difficulty in handling.

I roll over to pick up the phone. I call Spencer's office and I ask if I can be squeezed in to see him this afternoon. In his office. After checking, his assistant comes back to quickly say yes, whenever I can get there.

The offices of Bennett, Fitzallen & Coe are located on Park Avenue and Fifty-sixth Street. I stop at the security desk in the lobby and am given a name tag that reads BFC. I am then directed to the bank of elevators that will take me to Spencer's floor. When I get off, I find a simple but appealing reception area of bookshelves and books, and that inevitable little table with a phone on it that I am to use to call somebody somewhere to say that I'm here. It's not necessary, however, because coming around the corner in his tailored pants and white shirt, sleeves rolled up, is Spencer. He takes me in his arms and hugs me and refuses to let me go. "Thank you," he sighs.

When, over his shoulder, I see an attractive woman come striding around the same corner, toting a large leather briefcase,

I say, "Spencer," in warning, and he backs away, looking over his shoulder. "Oh, hi, Kate," he says as the woman smiles politely and pushes the elevator button as if she has not seen anything.

"Hi," she says.

"Kate, I'd like you to meet the woman I hope I can talk into marrying me someday," he says, pulling me forward, "Sally Harrington."

"Hi," the woman says, stepping forward to firmly shake my hand. "I'm Kate Weston."

"Our publisher," Spencer says, "my boss."

The elevator arrives but the publisher waves the occupants on. Clearly she's interested in whoever I am and where on earth I've appeared from. According to Spencer, they are good friends, have worked long, long hours together and have traveled many miles to sales conferences and conventions.

"So should I be congratulating you?"

I finally find my voice. "I met Spencer less than three weeks ago."

"Oh, my!" she exclaims softly, eyebrows rising at Spencer. "After all this time, you just met her and...?"

He nods. "She appeared," he says, "like a miracle." He takes my hand and looks at me, while saying to Kate, "She's very angry with me right now and rightfully so. I dragged her into my life before she had any idea how screwed up it is."

"You mean how *complicated* it is, Spencer," Kate Weston stresses, patting his back before hitting the elevator button again. "If you're going to change your life, you have to start by changing your language, which will change your thinking and your behavior, right?" She grins at me. "We're working on a self-help book that has some catchy stuff in it." Then her expression grows more serious. "All I can tell you, Sally, is that I've known Spencer for ten years, and worked with him for three. And he's right, his life has been pretty screwed up. But he is a wonderful friend and a gifted editor, and I'd hate to see him get pistol-whipped in some alley by some glorified thug who buys cosmetic companies to improve his social life."

This time she gets on the elevator when it arrives.

"Thank you," I say. "And it was very nice to meet you."

"I hope I see you again soon," she says, and the doors close.

I turn to Spencer, astonished. "She knows about Verity?"

He nods. "Yeah."

I consider this. Then I take his hand. "I want to meet some of your colleagues. That's why I came. I need to meet people who know you."

It is clear that Spencer is well liked. We stop in offices and in alcoves all over the floor, meeting everyone from a senior editor to an art director to a man in a closet who is in charge of supplies. The latter likes me because he's handicapping his bets in the back pages of the *New York Post* and I know how to do this because Mr. Quimby has taught me. We talk ponies a bit and I invite him to come up to Connecticut sometime to go to Mohegan Sun or Foxwoods.

There is an editorial assistant, a young Korean woman Spencer shares with Kate Weston, whose windowless office looks like a receiving station for a paper recycling center. She has the exhausted look that we all did at the beginning of our careers, that comes from the hours and the stress and the cramming, to say nothing of bad coffee and bad office air recirculating for the fifty millionth time. "It's very nice to meet you. You're the reporter, aren't you? The one writing for *Expectations?*"

I am very surprised. "Yes."

She smiles broadly. "Spencer talked about you. He says you're very good."

I look at Spencer "Oh."

"We have all your clippings," she continues, pointing to a file cabinet. "To be honest, I haven't read them all, but certainly Spencer has."

"I see," I say. "You have a file on me?" I ask him as soon as we're outside her office.

"I just wondered what your writing was like."

"What tear sheets do you have?"

"Everything from the *Herald-American*. I had to pay some bitchy lady in the newspaper's library for them. She kept saying, 'If you want her to write a book, why don't you just get them from *her?*' So then I started talking *dinero* and she started faxing them through."

"Why didn't you just ask me?"

"Because you're busy," he says. "Besides, maybe I just wanted to read them without you knowing."

"Huh," I say as we continue down the hall, wondering what he would have done if he hadn't liked my work. We arrive in Spencer's office and I love it. It's not overly large, but has a nice wall of windows. The best are the bookshelves, which are loaded with books and sketches of jackets and pictures with authors and all kinds of little toys and paperweights and memorabilia. It is chaotic but wonderful; all booky and fun and nice.

I'm beginning to look at him the way I did when I first met him. And then I notice something. "Have you lost weight?"

"Hmm," he acknowledges, picking up the phone. "About ten pounds or so, I think. I always do when I'm worried sick." He directs me to a chair. "I just have to return a few calls and then we can go."

"Where?"

"Anywhere," he says. "So we can talk."

While he's chatting on the phone, I wander out to where his assistant is sitting. Her name is Madeline and she went to Bowdoin College. That is all I know about her. "So how long have you worked here?"

She looks up from her computer where she has been working on a letter. "For Spencer, or Bennett, Fitzallen & Coe?"

"Both," I say, admiring the pictures on her desk.

"For Spencer, a little over a year. For the company, I'm coming up on two. I joined the training program after I graduated from—"

"Bowdoin," I say, leaning closer to look at a picture of a dog.

"How did you know that?" she exclaims, pleased, as people always are when I give the reporterlike impression that I've been researching them.

"Spencer mentioned it. Who is that?"

"That's my dog, Sharky," she says proudly. "He lives with my parents, though, in Pennsylvania. I can't bring him to the city."

"But you can see him at your parents' house."

"Oh, yeah. He goes nuts when I come home."

I smile. "I bet your parents do, too."

She laughs. "How did you know?"

I don't, but she seems so pleasant and Spencer says she's so good, that, of course, her parents love her. I don't think she's messing around with aspiring actors who work as bartenders like I did when I was her age.

"I hope he treats you well," I say, glancing at the office.

"Spencer? Are you kidding? He's wonderful. I mean," she says, dropping her voice in a whisper, "the workload's a nightmare in this office—some of his authors are absolute fruitcakes, too—but Spencer is so sweet. He's always doing things for me. He gave me a gift certificate to a bed-and-breakfast in Maine, where his parents are. And I went up for a long weekend with my boyfriend and Spencer's father let us use a sailboat for free all weekend."

"That is very nice."

"He did it because we have this hiring freeze here, and nobody's getting raises." She sighs. "Certainly not editorial."

That was very nice, to give his secretary a little vacation.

But, of course, it also makes me wonder what he's given Verity.

We leave the offices at a little after five and walk a few blocks up Park Avenue. New York is humming; the streets are streaming with people and cars heading downtown toward Grand Central Station, uptown toward the more residential districts, and simultaneously east and west across Fifty-seventh Street. I am fascinated by the concept that at 5:00 p.m. any given elevator in Manhattan will disperse its occupants to three states.

We walk up to Sixty-third Street and turn into the Park Avenue Café. It is a lovely restaurant that is new to me. It's one of Spencer's favorites. We are shown to a small table for two near the bar and each order a glass of wine.

After we have settled, commented on the decor and have sipped our wine for a while, he looks at me and murmurs, "Thank you."

I sip my wine as if I have not heard.

"I'm so glad you saw the office. It's where I spend more than half my time."

"I liked Kate very much."

He grins. "Yeah, I knew you would. You guys are a little alike."

"She seemed very surprised by my appearance, and by what you told her."

He laughs, grimacing slightly. "Yeah, I'm going to catch hell for not telling her about you before. Usually she knows all the sordid details." He panics. "Not that there's anything sordid about us! I mean before, about other people. You know."

"Why didn't you tell her?"

"Well, for one, I knew she'd yell at me because she knows about the situation with Verity."

"And what is that situation now, by the way?" I ask, reaching for my glass.

"I'll get to that in a second," he promises. "Anyway, I didn't tell Kate because I was so happy, it was so fast and new, I really just didn't feel like sharing it. Sharing it without you. You know? Because that's all I've wanted, to be with you. I didn't want any outside distractions."

I know exactly what he means. Well, we may be immature, but at least we are immature in the same way. Of course, that's the way Doug and I have been, according to Mother. "We barely know each other."

He shakes his head. "Not true. We just don't know each other very well."

"I'll say," I sigh, taking a sip. I've drunk more alcohol in the last three weeks than I have in a year.

"Which is why it is so important," Spencer says, "to meet people who've known me a long time." He leans forward. "And why you should let me come to Castleford to meet people who have known you a long time. Like your mother. Like your friends."

"I'll let you meet Crazy Pete," I offer.

"It's why we need to spend time together," Spencer continues, "to do things together, maybe travel a little, do some sports or something— Can we go sailing, for example? We can go up to City Island, if you want, or the Sound or the ocean or a lake. Or do you like to water-ski? Swim? Fish? Canoe? Play tennis? Bridge? Pinochle?"

"Tell me what Kate Weston thinks of Verity," I say.

The hopeful expression on Spencer's face vanishes. "She sort of hates her, I think."

I am surprised. "*Really?* Why?"

"Well..." He sighs. "Her infidelity, for one."

"Her infidelity with you," I clarify.

"With me," he confirms. "Particularly because of Corbie Junior." He lowers his voice. "Kate and her husband have been having trouble getting pregnant, so I think she's particularly hypersensitive on the topic of motherhood."

"What does Kate's husband do?"

"Actually, he's an editor, an executive editor like me, at one of the Random House companies. They worked together at Bennett, Fitzallen & Coe for years, and then they fell in love. There was a very unsuccessful takeover going on at the time, so after they got married they bagged publishing and moved to Los Angeles to do some TV production for a while. They did very well, financially—they were heading up a production company for Lydia Southland—but they hated the business, and so when Bennett, Fitzallen & Coe got sold again and the new owners cleaned house and started hiring, they called Kate and offered her the publisher's job, and they came back. To New York, and to our industry."

"Who hired you?"

"Kate. I was at Simon & Schuster then."

"I remember," I murmur. I smile slightly. "She'd be a very interesting person for me to talk to then."

"About me? Absolutely," he says eagerly. He reaches his hand across the table in a gesture asking for mine. I am a pushover for this man. I give him my hand.

"My love," he says quietly, "I promised someone I'd talk to you about your article."

"What article?" I say, stiffening slightly.

"Your piece on Cassy Cochran."

I withdraw my hand. "You still haven't explained what Verity was doing at your apartment last night at midnight."

"It wasn't Verity," he says. "It was Jessica Wright."

"*Jessica Wright?* The talk-show lady? What the hell was *she* doing there?"

"Asking about you," he says, signaling the waiter for a check.

42

As we stand outside the Park Avenue Café, Spencer says, "I told you before, we published Jessica's autobiography last year. That's how I know her."

"I don't buy it," I say sharply. "Kate Weston edited her biography, and that's hardly grounds for Jessica showing up at your apartment at midnight to talk to you."

"Okay, fine," he says, bowing slightly as he takes a few steps back. Then he comes back to me. "We slept together, years ago, when she first came to New York. The very first month she was here, as a matter of fact."

"You *slept* with her?" I say, amazed. I throw my hands up. "What is this, happy hands at home? There're fifty people in this city and you're all sleeping with each other!"

"There might be something to that," he says philosophically.

Now I take a step back to screech, "I can't believe you! Who *haven't* you slept with?"

A man, passing by on the sidewalk, laughs out loud.

"There is only one person I've slept with since I met you," Spencer says, following me as I keep backing away. "There is only one person I ever want to sleep with again."

"Ha!" I cry. Just then my back meets the wall of the building. I'm trapped. I'm also furious because it reminds me of that first night I met Spencer.

"Okay," I say, holding my hands up, "just back off a little." He complies. I'm losing steam rapidly because my curiosity is now getting the better of me. "So what did Jessica want?"

"She wanted to know if there was anything she could do to buy you off the Cochran piece."

I am floored. "Bought off? You mean like a bribe?"

He doesn't answer and I interpret this as a yes.

"Why?"

Spencer looks around to make sure no one's listening. "In

one of your interviews, and she wouldn't say with whom, you evidently said something that makes Jessica suspect you're about to sandbag Cassy."

"And?"

"And Jessica thinks you'd be hurting a lot of people."

"Did she say what it is that's she's so afraid I'm going to write about?"

"No." He draws closer again and I let him. "I told her you weren't like that, that you wouldn't do a hatchet job."

"And what did she say to that?"

"She said I should consider the person who assigned the piece, and then tell you that Verity would like to see Cassy get it."

I'm puzzled. "Verity?"

"Well, Verity's husband."

"Corbett. Why would Corbett want to see Cassy 'get it,' as you say?"

"Because he hates Jackson Darenbrook with every bone in his body."

I rest the back of my head against the building, looking up at the sky. Suddenly this whole assignment is making sense. Why it was given to me. Because Verity wanted to offer the "opportunity of a lifetime" to an out-of-town novice who had no ties in the city, someone with no connection to the vast network of people in the communications industry who practically revere Cassy Cochran. Someone who might do anything to make a name for herself. Of course Jackson Darenbrook wouldn't care what anybody wrote about him—they've written everything under the sun about him already, anyway—but he would care if Cassy was publicly exposed in some way. Perhaps he'd even be devastated if Cassy had not told him about her affair.

The nameless interviewee who is suspicious has to be Alexandra, of course. Jessica Wright's best friend. She must have sent Jessica on this mission to find out if there was anything they could offer me to stop the exposé.

"Sally?"

I lower my head. Then I lean forward and kiss Spencer lightly, once, on the lips. "Thank you," I murmur. I kiss his cheek and then move away, pulling my bag open to find my cell phone and address book.

"What are you doing?"

"Hang on," I tell him, looking for Cassy's home number. I dial her number, hoping against hope. When I hear her voice I feel a surge of relief. "Cassy, it's Sally Harrington. I'm sorry to bother you again, but it's extremely important I see you. Right now."

"Sally, I just can't," she says.

"You have to," I say. "Honest to God, Cassy, it's so very important. It has to do with your personal life."

Silence.

"It's regarding a relationship you had in the past."

"All right," she says then. "I'll fix it somehow. Come here. Now. Riverside and Eighty-eighth Street, number 162. I'll tell the doorman to send you right up."

I fold up the phone and stuff it back into my bag. "Get me a cab, will you?"

"Yeah, sure," he says, backing up to the corner and holding up his hand. "Do you want me to come with you?"

"No." I'm trying to think. I've got to go back to the hotel before going uptown to Cassy's. "I'll call you as soon as I'm through."

"Promise?"

"Yes." A cab pulls over and Spencer holds the door for me. I tell him not to worry.

This is not going to work out well for me, I know that already. As I ride up in a second cab, from my hotel to Riverside Drive, I realize the hardest part will be to keep my anger in check. There is a vindictive streak in me that is simmering dangerously close to the surface.

I could throttle Verity.

She chose me out of hundreds of writers for two simple reasons: my writing passed and my backwater career, she assumed, would make me an ethical retard and hungry for recognition.

The doorman at 162 Riverside Drive greets me by name and escorts me to the elevator. I go up to the top floor and although there are four different doors, only one is clearly marked as the one to approach. The whole floor, I remember from Henry's description, is now the Cochran-Darenbrook penthouse. However, when I ring the doorbell, Cassy opens the door behind me and quietly says hello.

She backs up to let me in. We are standing in a foyer that is lined from floor to ceiling with books. Cassy is dressed in a black silk dress, heels and pearls. Clearly she had been preparing to go out. "We can go in here," she says in that same quiet voice, showing me into a casual living room. She directs me to the love seat in front of the massive window that overlooks Riverside Park and the Hudson River. I sit down, sinking into the pillows. She sits on the edge of the chair next to me, crosses her legs and neatly folds her hands on her knee. When a single gold bangle slides down to her wrist, I realize that she is nervous and is desperately trying to control it.

"Well?" she says simply.

"Verity gave me this," I say, pulling the manila envelope out of my bag. "I have no idea how she got it."

I hold the envelope out to her, but she doesn't take it. She only looks at it.

"It appears to be a personal journal you kept," I explain.

Cassy's eyebrows go up slightly in surprise. "I've had several."

I'm still holding the package. "I believe this is the first. The one you kept between the time Michael left home and when he went into rehab."

"Oh," she says softly, her head falling forward slightly.

I place the envelope on the coffee table and leave it there. "Verity gave it to me."

Cassy looks up.

"She wants me to reveal both the affair and the identity of your lover." Cassy looks as though she might be trying not to throw up. "I will not do either one," I tell her.

She nods slightly, eyes moving past me to the window. "Thank you." A moment later she says, "But what would stop Verity from—"

"I will." I say it so forcefully, it makes Cassy jump a little.

"She won't do squat when I'm through with her," I say through clenched teeth.

"Sally," she begins to caution me.

"Don't worry about it," I say, standing up. "I know what I'm doing. That's why I'm here. To give you back your property and tell you what's up. And also to tell you not to worry. I just apologize for not coming to you sooner."

Cassy is now standing and follows me as I make my way back to the door in the foyer. "I'm not clear on how you will deal with Verity."

I turn around. "Let's just call it a little exposé of her own."

She shakes her head. "Be careful. Please."

"I'm out of this industry, anyway," I say. "It's not any nicer than I remember it being in L.A. Alexandra's right. You can report the news, or you can try and make news. And there is a vast difference between the two."

"That's very true," Cassy says quietly. "You'll do well, Sally. At whatever you choose."

I open the door and then close it again. "Just one thing." I turn to look at her. "What is it between your husband and Corbett Schroeder?"

She crosses her arms over her chest. "About twenty years ago—"

"Twenty years ago!" I cry.

She nods. "No joke. About twenty years ago, Corbett said something to Jackson's first wife, Barbara, that Jack didn't like. They were at a black-tie event in the grand ballroom of the Hotel Royale in Dallas. And so Jack got mad..." She's starting to smile. "And he picked Corbett up and he threw him over a pastry table into the reflecting pool. One of the photographers at the party got the shot and all the wire services picked it up."

I wait a beat. "And that's it? That's the source of the big feud?"

"That's it," she nods, smiling. I'm smiling and shaking my head, no doubt thinking the same thing, *Men are weird.*

When I get back to my hotel I call Spencer. "The deal is," I say, "we do not talk about anything—no Verity, no article, no boyfriends, no girlfriends, nothing! No booze, no weirdness.

Just come over and we'll order some cheeseburgers and ice cream and watch a movie. That's the deal and no negotiation, it's my last hurrah of hotel life and I'm inviting you to share it."

"I'm there," he says. And he was.

43

Doris Black comes out into the reception area shortly after nine in the morning. "We weren't expecting you, Sally," she says, half scolding me, "and I'm afraid Verity is tied up in a meeting."

"I'll wait until she's through, then," I say, sitting back down on the couch and picking up my book.

"I'm afraid that's not possible. In fact, it's impossible this morning."

"I'll tell you what," I say, ripping off a piece of my bookmark and scribbling a word on it. "Why don't you pass this to Verity and see if she'll see me after all?"

Doris frowns at me and doesn't dare open the note I've folded in my presence. I know she will as soon as she is around the corner.

In less than two minutes, Doris is back, motioning me to follow her. She is ticked but politely silent. She opens a door for me and tells me to go in, Verity will be there in a moment.

I am standing in a small conference room. Moments later, the door swings open and Verity comes in, closing it firmly behind her. She shifts her weight to one foot and crosses her arms. "What is this?" she says, holding my note in her fingertips.

I had written *Spencer*.

"I'm here to talk to you about setting me up to hurt Jackson Darenbrook by sandbagging Cassy."

"What are you *talking* about?" she says irritably. "You're writing about her life. The truth. What's the problem?" She narrows her eyes. "Scared of the big, bad anchorwoman, perhaps? The scorned lover?"

I narrow my eyes, too. "How did you get Cassy's journal? Aren't you the least bit worried about being prosecuted for theft?"

"I want to know what this note is about," she coldly demands, thrusting it toward me.

"It's about telling Corbett that you've been screwing Spencer Hawes for over two years," I say. "Unless, that is, you drop this whole exposé on Cassy."

I see Verity swallow. "I cannot publish some cream-puff piece in *Expectations*," she says, braving it out in a slightly nasal tone of voice. "I know you think you're the greatest thing since Nellie Bly, Sally, but frankly, we don't."

Oh, shove it, Verity! I want to say. But I'm the new and improved adult version of Sally Harrington, so for Mother's sake I won't. "I was going to suggest you just run a photo essay," I say, trying to keep my voice level. "I'll send you material you can pull captions from."

"I know you speak from unparalleled experience in world-class journalism," she says sarcastically, "but—"

"And you're going to get the Pulitzer prize." I walk over to the table. "Here's a check made out to *Expectations* for five thousand dollars," I say, tossing my personal check on the table. "Here is your credit card." I drop the six pieces I had cut the card into. "And here is another check for $2,411 of expenses I've charged on it to date." I toss this second check on the table, too. (She doesn't have to know that I've borrowed over four thousand dollars on my credit cards this morning to make these checks possible.)

"How terribly virtuous of you," Verity says. "But when you cool off, I don't want you coming back. Take the kill fee at least, the five thousand."

"No, thank you," I say. "There is only one thing I want and it's not money." She glares at me, curious, though. "I want Spencer. And I want you to leave him alone."

If there were a breeze, I do believe it would blow Verity over.

"You little country tramp," she whispers, her lip starting to curl. "So you *have* been fucking him." With that, Verity throws her head back and laughs. "Oh, my dear, really," she says, suddenly fleeing to the door, "you can have him."

I stop myself from following her so I can make some final nasty remark. But then I remember that I am now out of it, out of the slag track, as glamorously enticing as it may be.

44

—→ ←—

While waiting for the hotel car valet to bring the Jeep around, I call Mother to tell her I'm coming home.

"So you'll be wanting Scotty," she says.

"Yes."

"That's all right, then. Mack and I were just leaving to go up-state. For a hike and a picnic. So we'll just drop Scotty off on our way."

"That would be great, thank you."

"All right, sweetheart," she laughs. "And how are things? Is the piece finished?"

"Oh, yeah, the piece is finished," I say, thinking there's no reason to worry Mother about it now. "I'm going back to the paper on Monday."

On my way out of Manhattan, I start reviewing the complete and total disaster that currently reflects my finances.

My cell phone's ringing and I pick it up. "Hello?"

"Sally!" Spencer says. "Are you all right? What the hell happened between you and Verity?"

"Oh, she's called you, has she? What did she say?"

"That I'm lousy in bed, a juvenile delinquent, and to stay the hell away from her."

I burst out laughing.

"What the hell's going on?"

"I'm going home, Spencer, and you can't talk me out of it. I'm not coming back in for a while. This city makes me sick."

"Then I'm coming out there," he says.

"Do what you like," I say. "But you should bring Seela. You leave her alone too much."

He pauses. "I love you, Sally Harrington."

I wish he wouldn't say that.

By the time I am nearing Castleford, I have decided that if I think about my finances anymore I will shoot myself. Now that

I don't have the article to write, I decide I might as well bail out. I stop at the grocery store to load up on supplies and then hit Blockbuster for movies.

When I swing outside the cottage, I notice that Mr. Quimby hasn't mowed the grass. I also notice I haven't weeded or watered anything for a month and the gardens look like hell. Well, these are things I can do between videos. I lug my bags and the groceries and videos up to the front door and unlock the door. No Scotty. I guess Mother's gotten hung up. I drag my bags inside and freeze. The living room and office have been ransacked. I slowly put the groceries down and walk over to the telephone to call the police.

"Don't move," a deep male voice says from behind me. There is something sharp pressing on my spine and I assume it is a knife.

"I'm not moving," I say.

"I want the book," he says. "The brown leather book. Where is it?"

"Oh, a friend of Verity's," I sigh, turning around. He grabs my neck and yanks me back into position, facing away from him. The guy must be huge; his hand is almost all the way around my neck.

"Where is it?"

"I don't have it anymore," I say. "It's back with the owner in New York City."

"I will kill your dog."

"My dog?" I say, twisting around. He is huge and has a stocking pulled over his head.

He yanks me back around again. "Where is it? I'll kill that dog, I swear I will."

"I don't have it anymore, I told you. Where is my dog?"

"Get the book," he growls.

"I don't have it!" I cry, losing it. "Goddamn it, where is my dog?" I jerk away from him and get enough leverage to shove him back. Then I pick up my dictionary and hurl it at his face and dart around him to get to the kitchen, where I close and lock the swinging door. He easily smashes the door open, but I've grabbed a meat cleaver in one hand and a carving knife in the other, and this gives him pause for thought. But then I see Scotty lying motionless outside in the backyard and I run out.

"Scotty!" I yell, running to him. He doesn't move. I drop down and put the side of my face against his ribs. He is breathing but something is very wrong with him. A hand grabs my hair and violently yanks my head back, making me cry out in pain.

"Get the book and I'm out of here," he growls.

"I gave it back to the person who wrote it!" I say. I try to push his hand away; he smacks me on the side of my head and suddenly my face is down on the ground next to Scotty's.

I hear a weird *thunk* and suddenly the pressure lifts from the back of my head. The man's body crumples to the ground next to me. Another man is there, a stranger, standing over us, rolling the burglar over and yanking the stocking off his head. He uses it to secure the burglar's hands behind his back. Then he kneels down to try and help me sit up. It's not happening. I am in some kind of shock and the world is reeling. I close my eyes and he lowers me back to the ground. "I'll call 911," the man says, taking off for the house.

I open my eyes and see Scotty. I pull myself closer to him, trying to touch him. He is barely breathing.

The man comes running back. "He did something to my dog," I sob.

"Probably drugged him. We have to get him moving." He picks Scotty up in his arms—no easy feat, for he is over seventy pounds—and I watch as the stranger carries him over to the outside faucet where the hose is hooked up. He turns the faucet on and tries to revive Scotty by dousing him with water.

"Don't get it in his nose!" I call in broken sobs.

"I won't," he promises, and he douses Scotty again with what, by this time, must be cold water from the well.

"His eyes opened a little!" the man calls. After prodding and dousing and pushing, Scotty can sort of stand if the man holds him under the chest. His arms laced under Scotty's chest, the man straddles him and drags Scotty along. Scotty keeps going limp, but the man doesn't stop, forcing him to stumble along.

The burglar makes a gurgling noise and I don't want to say anything to the stranger because I don't want him to stop walking Scotty. I make myself sit up. When I do, I see that the burglar's head has a horrible gash in the back of it and that blood is streaming all over the place. This guy's not going anywhere.

I hear the sirens in the distance and the man cries, "He hears it! His ears moved!" and he keeps walking and dragging Scotty and soon I see a police car, and then another, and an ambulance not far behind. Soon we are surrounded by people in uniform. One paramedic rushes to the burglar and one to me. Moments later an unmarked car comes bombing across the lawn, stopping just short of where I am. Buddy and another plainclothes man jump out.

"Don't move," the paramedic says to me, "you've got a head wound."

"I'm all right," I insist. "Please help my dog. The burglar poisoned him or something." I lurch to sit up and push the paramedic. "Please." The paramedic looks up at the police officer who kneels beside me, touching me lightly on the back. "You've got to stay still," he tells me.

Buddy squats down on the other side of me, wanting to know what happened. I trip over my words, trying to explain that this has to do with something in New York. It's not about anything going on here in Castleford. "He was trying to get back some evidence I had for the story I was writing."

"Oh, great," Buddy mutters, looking at but not touching the side of my head. "Nice people you hang out with in New York."

"That man, the one with Scotty," I say, "he saved me, Buddy."

Next to me, they have shifted the burglar onto a stretcher. They have bandages on his head and an IV hooked up to him. Another policeman is hanging over him, nearly shouting, "What did you give the dog?" A policewoman is now holding Scotty up while the paramedic is looking at him.

"I don't know who that man is," I say to Buddy, "or where he came from. I don't know where the burglar came from, either. There weren't any cars, but he was in the house when I got here."

Another police officer runs over to tell Buddy there is a dirt bike in the field on the other side of the woods. No plates.

"Tell backup to swing over to Bafter's Lane," Buddy says. "See if this thug's car isn't over there somewhere."

"What was it?" the cop hanging over the burglar is yelling, then bending closer to hear him better. The cop straightens up. "Valium!" he calls to the medic. "He says he gave the dog Valium."

The medic already has a tube running down Scotty's throat to pump his stomach. I can't watch. The man who saved me comes walking over. He is in his thirties, late thirties, maybe, dark hair, dark eyes, nice build. He drops down next to Buddy and smiles at me. "Your dog's going to be okay."

"Thank you," I whisper.

Buddy's staring at the man. "Where the hell have you been?"

"Well," the stranger says, standing up, "I'm here now. That's all that matters, isn't it?"

I don't know what's going on; I am having a hard time thinking straight.

Buddy stands up, too. "Sally," he says, glancing down at me before looking back at the man, "meet Johnny Boy Meyers."

Johnny is smiling down at me. "It's been a long time, but it's good to see you, Sally. You look a lot like your mom."

There is a slight buzzing noise in my head and the light is starting to go yellow. In a moment, everything goes black.

45

They take the burglar and me to Midstate Medical Center and I have to have a CAT scan. The head is fine—I will only have a dreadful set of black eyes ("Why doesn't her hard head surprise me," Buddy says to the doctor)—but I have to wear a neck brace because the burglar yanked something out of whack. The burglar, it turns out, is a gentleman named Spiker Fetch from Waterbury, a small-time crook who once did time in the Cheshire prison. He has a very serious concussion, seeing as Johnny Boy hit him over the head with a shovel. We're all naturally very curious about the chain of command behind this attempted theft and assault (as if I don't know where it began), but Spiker's not talking. Yet.

Mother, of course, is completely freaked out. My brother, Rob, she tells me while I'm still lying on a bed in emergency, is coming home from Colorado. Mack comes back in behind the curtain to say there is a young man from New York in the emergency waiting room who is having a nervous breakdown.

This, I know, has to be Spencer. I ask Mack to bring him in.

"Sally!" Spencer whispers, running across the room and kind of elbowing Mother out of the way. "I drove out—I wanted to surprise you—and I went to your house and there were all these police officers and all they would tell me was that you were here. God!" he cries, hesitating over his attempt to guess what part of me is least likely to hurt and then diving to hug me around the waist. "Thank God you're all right. I didn't know what to think."

Over Spencer's shoulder, I can see that Buddy is listening with some interest.

"I'm going to be fine," I say quietly, stroking the back of Spencer's head once. "But I want you to meet my mother."

Spencer's head flies up. "Where?" He's got a hold on my hand but I don't have the heart to tell him he's holding it too tightly. He turns around. "But of course you're Mrs. Harrington! Look at you!" He lets go of my hand to take my mother's hand with both of his. "I'm Spencer Hawes, Mrs. Harrington, and I apologize for so rudely pushing my way in here—it's just I was so upset."

"And perhaps you know something about it?" Mother asks him. "Sally says the man was looking for some kind of journal, something she was using for her *Expectations* article."

Spencer's head whips around. "Does this have something to do with what Jessica was talking about?"

"I'm sorry," the head nurse of the unit announces, coming in through the curtain, "but there are too many people and too much noise in here. One person can stay, the rest of you—*out.*"

I know Mother assumes this means everyone but her. "Mother, could you let me just speak to Spencer for a moment?"

"Yes, yes," she says, taking Mack's arm. "I could use something to drink, anyway." She steps back. "I'll be right outside if you need me."

After everyone leaves, I focus back on Spencer. "Verity gave me a journal that Cassy wrote."

"Where did she get it?"

"I think she might have had it stolen."

He frowns. "No."

"Well then, you tell me how she got it. I took it back to Cassy last night. She didn't know it was missing, and she sure as hell didn't give it to anyone."

"It just doesn't sound like Verity."

"Does it sound like Corbett?"

"Yes," he says without hesitation.

"Then Verity's going to have her hands full trying to explain to him why the piece isn't running."

"It's not going to run at all?"

I shake my head. "I gave her everything back. Including a refund of the expenses I'd run up."

He sighs, brushing my hand with his finger. "Was it very bad, what you found out?"

"Not bad," I say. "Not at all, as a matter of fact. It was just private."

"So what's to stop Verity from getting someone else to write it?"

I narrow my eyes a little. "Take a wild guess, Romeo. I told her she might have a little exposé of her own to deal with."

"Oh, God," he says, looking away. "Sally, you can't mess with someone like Verity and—"

"The mistake I made with Verity was to ask her if she wasn't a little nervous about being linked to stolen property," I tell him. "If only I had thought to mention that I'd already given the journal back to Cassy, then none of this would have happened."

"You really think she—"

"Spencer—I *know* she did. And she won't be messing with me anymore, because you're going out there, right now, and call her and tell her what's happened. Tell her I already gave what she wanted back to Cassy, and that her thug screwed up and will be in the Castleford jail, and if she thought I was angry before, she should see me now. And then I want you to come back in here and tell me what she says."

He doesn't want to do this, but I make him promise he will.

Spencer leaves and Mother comes in with a box of orange juice, which she tries to get me to drink. We start arguing over whether or not I'm allowed to have anything and she goes off to find the doctor. Left alone, finally, and flying high on painkillers, I doze. When I open my eyes again, I see Doug.

"Hi."

"Hi," he whispers. "I heard at the office. Are you okay?"

"I'm fine. As soon as they sign off on me, Mother's taking me home."

He's looking down at my hand. "I hear he's here."

"Yes, he is."

"Nice crowd you run with in New York," he says, looking over my injuries.

"Nice crowd I live with in Castleford."

He lowers his voice. "So it's true, then? About an investigation into your father's accident?"

I would nod if I could, but I can't with this thing on. "I hope so. Talk to Buddy." My mind is clouding over. These drugs are making me feel loopy.

"I was hoping you'd burst into tears when you saw me," Doug blurts out. "I wanted you to say, 'Thank God you're here. I love you and I need you.'" He lowers his eyes again. "Like you used to say."

I lift one hand slightly. "I don't know what to say, Doug."

"No." He jams his hands into his pants pockets and takes a step back. "Okay. I just wanted to make sure you're all right, that you're taken care of. Call me if you need anything." He's moving quickly now. "I'll see you in five months and two weeks."

I close my eyes again, drifting.

"Sally?"

I open one eye. It's Spencer. "Verity says to send her the copy for the captions. She's running a photo essay. She says you'll know what that means."

I smile and let myself fall asleep.

46

"What I need to know, Mrs. Harrington," Buddy says to my mother on Saturday morning, "is what you remember about the night your husband died."

Mother is making green tomato relish while Buddy, another detective from the Castleford Police Department and I are sipping coffee at her kitchen table.

"You know about the flood," Mother begins. "The dam broke and the entire downtown was under three feet of water, and Dodge had been down there on and off for five, six days, sandbagging with the rest of the men."

Buddy nods. His father had been there, too.

Mother is holding a paring knife in one hand and a green tomato in the other, and is staring out the window over the sink. "That's why everyone was caught by surprise when the water started to threaten the high school." She looks over at Buddy, her face lined in concentration. "The school wasn't on the flood-plain, but when the runoff banks crumbled over on Juniper Avenue the train trestle came down and dammed up Wooliston Creek, and the main river started overflowing the banks upstream. And the rain kept coming and coming, the sewer system was backing up under the streets, and then finally the line burst up through the ground near the school, dumping water into Maple Brook, which had already risen over its banks. No one could have known it was going to happen."

"How did Daddy hear about the school? The flooding?"

"Everyone on the downtown line heard about the water rising toward the school. I know Dodge was there because he came home later and told me he had been up to the school to look for himself. He said he had to go all the way around, almost to Wallingford, to get there, that everything was going under in that part of town."

"And that was the day of the accident?" Buddy asks.

Mother nods. "I remember because that afternoon I fixed him a steak. Dodge loved steak and potatoes. His children are just like him," she adds as an aside to Buddy. "And that's what I gave him. Steak. Fried potatoes. Spinach."

"And what happened next?"

"Dodge tried to reach Phil—"

"Phillip O'Hearn," Buddy says.

"Yes. He built the gym with Dodge. And Dodge wanted to talk to him about it."

"But he couldn't reach him."

"No. I think he left a message with Gisela. Because we were all home with our children. Nobody could go anywhere."

"And then?"

"Well, Dodge ate his supper and slept for about two hours. I think it was about seven o'clock when Phil got his message and called him back. I woke Dodge up because he asked me to, if Phil called."

"Do you remember what they talked about?"

"Actually, I do. Phil said he had just been to the high school and was worried about the gym. He said he thought water was getting in under the foundation. Dodge was very surprised by this, I remember, because he kept saying to Phil, 'But we have the runoff under there, remember? I designed it because of what happened when the old pool cracked.' But Phil was obviously panicked about it, anyway. He said he was afraid one wall was about to buckle."

"So what happened then?"

"So Dodge got off the phone," Mother says, "and he was beside himself. He couldn't believe that within the last three hours, since he had visited the school, the gym was now in such trouble. He grabbed his gear and said he was going over there to check it out. I was worried and didn't want him to go—because at that point, the power in that area was completely shut off, there were all kinds of trees and wires down and the idea of Dodge sloshing around up there in the dark scared me to death."

To this day, a dark rainstorm gives me a chill. In my own way, I remember that night, too.

"And so he went," Buddy says.

"And so he went," Mother echoes softly, eyes falling to the counter. She puts the knife and tomato down and then just stands there, looking at them, as if waiting for them to do something.

"Did he go alone?"

"He left here alone," she says.

"Was he going to pick up anyone?"

"I don't know."

"Wouldn't he have picked up Phillip O'Hearn? Since he was the builder?"

She shakes her head. "I don't think so. Dodge wanted to check things out for himself."

There is something in her tone that catches our attention.

"He wanted to check things out for himself," Buddy says carefully. "Because he was having a hard time believing that what Phillip O'Hearn *said* was happening to the building, was really happening?"

"Yes," she says. "Dodge said there was no way that wall should be buckling."

"And did you hear from your husband after that?"

"No," she says quickly, as if trying not to think about this part. "At around eleven o'clock—the news was on TV—the police chief and the fire marshal came to tell me what had happened."

I remember the wail that reverberated through the house when Mother was told the news; I remember sneaking out of my room to the staircase and hearing the chief say, "Let me call someone, Belle, to be here with the children," but I couldn't hear what Mother said. I didn't know Daddy was dead. I didn't know what was going on. I did get sleepy trying to figure it out, though, and I went back to bed. Mother didn't tell me about Daddy until the next morning, about a half hour after Rob and I had finished eating breakfast. Years later she said she had wanted to make sure we had eaten something that day.

"Maybe you should sit down, Mrs. Harrington," Buddy says quietly.

Mother comes over to sit, her face pale beneath her tan. "There's something more, isn't there, Buddy? And it has to do with that debris Sally brought here."

"Yes, it does."

"Mother," I say gently, reaching to touch her arm, "the state lab's run tests on it, and they've found evidence of an explosive—a kind that was commonly used in building demolition then. And the tests prove that the charge was used in the vicinity of the northeast buttress."

"The wall that came down." She says this like a child reciting a lesson she doesn't understand but is dutifully trying to memorize.

"Buddy thinks someone may have set the demolition charge off when Daddy was there that night." I swallow. "On purpose."

She meets my eyes and her whole body slowly stiffens. She turns to Buddy. "Someone killed Dodge?"

I command my throat not to close up. It is too important. The neck brace is not helping.

"The lab also found," Buddy continues quietly, avoiding her question, "that the cable in the debris showed imperfections, Mrs. Harrington. At first they thought it was because of the blast, but now we know for sure that those imperfections were made in the manufacturing stage."

Mother turns her head slightly, as if to hear better.

"The cable used in the building of the gym was defective, Mother. It never should have left the plant where it was made."

Her head slowly turns back to me. "Why did it?"

"They think Mr. O'Hearn bought it under the table to save money. He had a lot of projects going on and he was overextended."

"Your father would never have had anything to do with that," she tells me.

"I know," I murmur, patting her hand. "No one thinks he did."

She nods, looking fearful now.

"Johnny Boy put the debris on my porch, Mother. He wanted us to have it. He wanted us to know what happened."

"Where did he get it?"

"From where his brother hid it, twenty-one years ago."

"Tony Meyers?" Mother shakes her head. "But why?"

"We think, Mrs. Harrington," Buddy says, "Tony Meyers had been blackmailing Phillip O'Hearn for quite some time."

Mother slowly rises to her feet, her face flushing deeply. I rise with her, ready to catch her if she should faint.

"Are you saying that Phil killed Dodge?"

"We don't know for sure," I say gently, moving to put my arm around her. "That's why we have to have this discussion, Mother. You're the only one who remembers things." I ease her back down into the chair and walk into the living room to pour a small brandy in a cordial glass. I bring it back into the kitchen and silently hand it to Mother. She needs no push; she takes a sip.

"We know now, Mrs. Harrington, that several years ago Phillip O'Hearn set Tony Meyers up in the hazardous-waste-disposal business in Long Island. And we know that Tony called his brother, Johnny Boy, in Florida about a month ago to say he was in trouble. The books on his operation in Long Island were a mess and he said he was worried that something might happen to him. He said he wanted to send Johnny Boy a key to a storage unit in Wethersfield. The next thing Johnny knew, he heard Tony had been shot dead here in Castleford, and so he played it safe, sent his family away and went off the radar, sneaking up here to Wethersfield to see what was in that unit."

"Why didn't he just come to you?" Mother asks Buddy.

"Because he took one look at that piece of debris and knew where it was from. He had worked on that building himself, remember, with your husband. Johnny Boy also remembered how, after the accident, O'Hearn's crew came in and razed the whole gym and carted it away before anyone ever even thought of analyzing the debris. Everyone just assumed that, like so many other buildings in Castleford during the flood, the gym had been a casualty of rising water."

Mother thumps her brandy glass, staring at it. "Hal Fields."

Buddy nods but I am taken aback. I had forgotten about him. Once a building inspector in Castleford, he was appointed city engineer not too many years ago, went from there to prison for accepting bribes. He's dead now.

"Hal Fields had to have been in on it," Mother says, her voice gaining strength. She sips the brandy and thumps the glass down again, making me fear it will break.

A funny light is beginning to shine in my mother's eyes, and I wonder if she is like me, feeling a strange exhilaration because after all these years we are beginning to realize that Daddy might not have been killed by one of his own buildings.

"So Johnny's Boy been hiding out, Mrs. Harrington, trying to put it all together. Finally he left the debris on Sally's porch to put us on the scent. He's been in the old cow lean-to by the strip-mining operation at Brackleton Farm."

"He was scared Phil might have him killed, too?"

Buddy nods. "He still is."

"I don't blame him," she says, finishing off the brandy. "Phil's the eighth richest man in New Haven county now, you know." She shakes her head. "But to kill Dodge? Over some cheap cable?"

"Well, that's just it, Mother," I say. "We think it may have been a lot more than the cable in the gym. We think he may have used bad materials in a lot of buildings, and he was scared Daddy was going to turn him in. Because if he did, it would have all been over before he had even started."

She hangs her head slightly. "Phil." She inhales sharply through her nose and kicks her head back up to face Buddy. "Now what?"

"Remember when Tranowsky's Auto Body blew up? O'Hearn built it two months after the high school gym."

"He also built the Preston Roadhouse the same year," I say. "Which has also conveniently blown up recently."

"He built the bowling alley around that time," Mother says, thinking out loud. She looks at Buddy. "Phil bought it back and tore it down last year and then sold the lot to Home Depot."

"That's right," Buddy says. "And that's the key. He bought it back, tore it down and carted everything away. Which means, after the auto body and the roadhouse were destroyed, there is nothing left in Castleford that O'Hearn built in 1977."

"In other words," my mother says dully, "there is no evidence."

None of us say anything.

Mother looks at me. "Your father would have hung Phil himself if he knew he was endangering the lives of the children using that gym."

"The thing is, Mrs. Harrington," Buddy sighs, "we have Tony Meyers's murderer in custody, but that's where the chain of evidence stops. We don't know who hired him. We think Phillip O'Hearn may have deliberately used faulty materials in the four buildings he constructed in 1977—which Hal Fields inspected and approved—but all we have is this one piece of debris from part of one building. And since everything else has either been destroyed or carted away somewhere, we have nothing to link the buildings."

"Oh, but that's not true," Mother says. "There is another building still standing. The grocery store in Wallingford. It was the same year, I know it was, because he won all those bids almost at the same time." She frowns. "Of course he underbid everybody. Now we know why."

"You mean where the dance club used to be, Mother? In an old A & P? Right off the Merritt?"

Mother nods.

"Are you sure, Mrs. Harrington? Because we don't have that building on our list."

"I know for a fact Phil started that building. I know because he was fired from the project before it was completed. He had spread his crews too thin on too many projects—one of which was the high school gym."

Cars are backed up all along Silver Avenue near the old A & P, the people inside them wondering what horrendous crime was being investigated by the battalion of police. I am here, too, standing with Buddy, my neck hurting under this stupid brace, watching as police techs take apart the walls. Mack is here next to me, standing in for Mother, who is at Bradley Airport picking up my brother.

We get word in less than an hour. No sign of faulty cables. No sign of faulty anything. They'll tear more of the wall and ceiling apart, but they're not confident of uncovering anything of importance.

"I suppose we should have known," Buddy mutters, turning away. "Or O'Hearn would have blown this one up, too."

*   *   *

"Well," my brother Rob suggests, yawning, "we can put Johnny Boy in a cage in the center of town and see who tries to kill him." It has taken Rob hours and hours to get home from the obscure northwest corner of Colorado where he lives, but there is no way he is going to sleep and miss a minute of this. He was only five when Daddy died, but when I first saw him at Mother's today I could see the same bright light in his eyes that had come into Mother's.

"Thanks a lot," Johnny Boy tells my brother.

Rob and Johnny Boy and I are sitting around in a conference room at the Castleford police station while Buddy comes in and out, trying to figure the next move he should make. The FBI doesn't seem very interested in anything but the possible connection between the hit man that killed Tony Meyers and a competing, Mafia-owned-and-operated hazardous-waste-disposal operation in Long Island.

"We could run a front page article about the findings of the debris," I suggest.

"And admit up front," Buddy nearly growls from the door, "that we have nothing to compare it to, even to confirm that it *was* a part of the gym?"

"I think we have to go public," I insist. "We need someone to come forward, someone who knows or saw something that night. Or anytime since."

"I agree," Johnny Boy says.

"Well you certainly can't go public," I say. "You're not supposed to even exist." Johnny Boy's staying up at Carmella's cabin. Buddy spirited him into the station for a brainstorming session.

"It's been more than twenty-one years," Rob says. "I mean, is it even a crime anymore? After all this time?"

"There is no statute of limitations on murder," Buddy says. The words hang in the air for several moments.

And then I get it. I get an idea. I know who to call. I know who can help.

47

William Rafferty himself, the executive producer of DBS News, arrives with a crew at Mother's at 11:00 a.m. Monday morning. Our family—Mother, Rob and I—sit down around the dining-room table with them, and we begin laying out the story. At around one, as Mother is trying to push sandwiches and salad on everyone, Abigail furiously begins to bark in the front of the house. I walk out to find Alexandra squatting down next to Abigail, getting the side of her face licked. A black limo is waiting behind her.

"Thank you so much," I say as she gives Abigail a final pat and stands up.

"It's a good story," she says. She winces slightly, looking at my black eyes and the neck brace.

"You don't want to know," I tell her firmly, ushering her into the house.

Alexandra introduces herself to my family, sits down and starts right in. At three, a news van from WSCT in New Haven arrives. At five, Mother is serving sandwiches again. At seven-thirty, the group disperses, fanning out over the county.

I drive home. I walk around to the backyard and find Spencer batting a tennis ball out in the field for Scotty to chase. Spencer's wearing ancient gym shorts and a T-shirt. I am surprised at how at home he seems dressed like this.

Seela is dozing on a towel Spencer has brought out to the yard from her carrying case. She likes security, he tells me.

"You're still here."

"Sally!" He smiles, hurrying over. "How did it go? I wanted to call but I thought I better not."

We kiss briefly. "It's just as well you didn't," I say, yawning. "It was long and complicated and went on forever. It's like NASA over at my mother's. Of course she and Rob love it. It's something to do, something to try."

"What do you think?"

Scotty has pushed his way between us to press the wet tennis ball against Spencer's thigh as a small hint. "You're such a rascal, aren't you?" I ask Scotty, bending slightly. "No, don't jump up. That's a good boy." I straighten up and toss the ball. "If anyone can do something, they can."

Spencer puts his arm around me and leads me toward the house. "So we just say a prayer."

"Yes. It's out of our hands." I turn to look at him and wince at the pain in my neck. "So what have you been doing all day?"

"I glued the leg back on the table in your office," he says. "That's some hardware store down the hill. I kept looking for the pickle barrel to sit around."

"Cracker barrel."

"Well, sitting down around some barrel," he says. "One guy was talking and I swear, I could have been right back in Maine. The accent was absolutely on target—*aye-yup*."

"A lot of people are from Maine," I say. "They came down after the war, because there were jobs."

Scotty drops the ball at our feet and barks. I smile. He is fine now. I barely feel like pressing charges against Spiker Fetch anymore. Well, except for this brace and my black eyes.

"Oh!" Spencer suddenly exclaims. "And I did that." He points to the woodpile.

Holy smoke. There is about a half cord of newly split wood. "Wow. Who would have ever guessed that executive editors could be so handy?"

He smiles, turning me to face him so he can hold me around the waist. "I love you."

"I keep telling you, it's very premature."

"Okay," he agrees, "I prematurely love you."

"Our track records are abysmal, Spencer," I remind him, resting my forehead on his shoulder.

"Yep," he says cheerfully, holding me.

"And you live in New York."

"Yep."

"And I live out here."

"Yep."

"So how do you propose to resolve this?"

"I propose to rent a house around here and come out on weekends."

"What about your house in Kent?"

"I won't rent it anymore."

I look up at him. "I thought you owned it."

"No. I don't own anything. Well, except Seela."

"What do you do with all your money?"

"I spend it living in Manhattan, that's what I do with it."

"Do you own the Miata?"

"Nope. Lease it."

I place my forehead on his shoulder again. "Darn. And I thought you were rich."

"Nope, not rich," he says. "My parents aren't, either." He thinks a moment. "If I lived somewhere like here, though, I'd be very well off. I could buy a place. And a car."

"You could probably buy half of Castleford for what you pay in rent."

"This isn't exactly a booming metropolis, is it?"

"It is if you like steamed cheeseburgers and drive-ins."

Spencer gasps, bouncing me off his shoulder. "You have a drive-in?"

"Not even a mile away from here."

"You're kidding!" he says, excited. "Can we go? I haven't been to a drive-in since I was little!"

"Sure. The movies start at sundown. We can go tonight if you want."

"And do they have a playground and stuff? And run cartoons?"

"No," I laugh, "those days are over. But they still have those slides of floating hot dogs and dancing Cokes and stuff during intermission."

He is so excited that I think, gosh, maybe he *would* like living out here. At least part of the time. I wonder if maybe...

Well, as Mother says, time takes time.

We go inside to shower and change. After feeding the animals, we decide to go to the drive-in in the Miata because there are restrictions about where the Jeep can park, it's so high. We are just getting into the Miata, putting the top down and debating which are better, Dots or Milk Duds, when a cloud of dust appears down the road, signaling the roaring approach of a brand-new Cadillac.

"Oh, no," I say, because I know who it is and what this is about. And I was so looking forward to forgetting everything at the movies for a couple of hours. "Can you please go inside and get my tape recorder off my desk, Spencer? There's a clean cassette in the right-hand drawer. Pop it in, will you, turn it on and bring it out here."

Spencer unlocks the front door and hurries into the house.

The Caddie comes to a sliding halt, skidding off the dirt and tearing into my lawn. With the motor still running, the door flies open and Mrs. O'Hearn, red-faced and wild-looking, hauls herself out and points to me over the roof of her car. "How *dare* you talk about us in this way, Sally Harrington! Your father is turning over in his grave!"

"I'm sure he is," I say from my seat in the Miata.

"Who are those people trespassing all over my property!" she demands. "They're down at the offices, they're at the sites, they're at my house!"

"Looking for Mr. O'Hearn, I presume."

She glares at me. "Mr. O'Hearn is out of town on business."

"Then tell them where he is," I suggest. "They'll go there, I know they will, and then they'll leave you alone."

She comes around the car and starts pointing at me again. "I've known you since the day you were born, Sally. How *dare* you implicate my husband in the misfortune your family suffered—"

"The gym wall did not fall down and kill my father by itself, Mrs. O'Hearn."

"The flood waters eroded the foundation!" she yells.

"The flood waters did not!" I yell back. "Someone detonated a building charge and brought the wall down on top of my father and broke his back!" I scramble out of the car. "And your husband sent his crews in to knock that building down and cart it away so no one would know."

"Liar!" she screams at me.

"I'm not lying!" I shout, coming around the car. "Tony Meyers knew about it and he's been blackmailing your husband for years! But now Tony Meyers is dead. So I don't know why you just don't talk to DBS News and be done with it. Take your money and your kids and your grandkids and clear out, Mrs. O'Hearn. If you get out now, at least you'll leave your family with some sense of honor."

She slaps me and the jolt to my neck makes me cry out. "You have no right," she says, voice cracking. Weeping, she runs to her car, guns it, slams it into reverse, and then swerves over the lawn and around the driveway to speed off.

"Wow," Spencer finally says as the dust cloud floats over us. He turns off the tape recorder with a click.

I burst into tears and he comes over. I hide my face in his shoulder. "Somebody has to pay, Spencer," I sob. "Somebody killed my father."

The telephone's ringing inside the house. I'm too busy sobbing and being angry to get it. Spencer calms me down and we go inside, bagging the idea of the movies, bagging the idea of everything. I hit the play button on the answering machine.

"Where are you, Sally?" Buddy's voice says. "We need you down here, Sal. Something—someone—important has come up. I need you. Call me. Come here, do something, but get here. Please."

"I'll drive you," Spencer says, opening the front door.

"Hi, who are you?" I hear Rob ask Spencer from behind me in the reception area of the police station.

"I'm the help," Spencer answers. "You're the brother from Colorado, I take it."

"And you're the new boyfriend from New York," Rob says.

"Maine, actually."

"No kidding," Rob says, interested. He holds out his hand. "Rob Harrington."

"Spencer Hawes."

"Sally?" Buddy's head has popped around the corner. We all start toward him, but Buddy says, "Just you, Sal, for right now."

I go ahead, leaving Spencer with Rob. Buddy takes me by the arm to the side of the hallway and whispers, "We've got a witness who knows something. But I need your help. I need you to talk to him."

"Sure. What do you want me to say?"

"Whatever you want. Look, Sal, it's Pete Sabatino."

I feel like bursting into tears. "Oh, Buddy."

"I'm serious, Sally," he says, giving my arm a shake. "And he wants to talk to you. He says he feels bad. He needs to tells us something, but he wants to tell you."

I feel like I'm at the end of my energy. The absolute end. "All right. Whatever. Let's do it."

Buddy takes me into the interrogation room and Pete looks glad to see me, but then sinks down in his chair, slowly falling forward to rest the side of his face on the table like a small child.

"Hi," I say quietly, taking the seat next to him and putting a hand on his shoulder. "Pete, is it true? Do you really know something more about Daddy?"

"I always did," he says quietly.

"I remember you tried to tell me something."

Slowly he sits up. He can't look at me. "I told you the Masons did it."

I nod. "I remember."

He looks away. When he turns back, he has tears in his eyes. "The man who did it needed money." He swallows. "He needed money because he'd been out of work for a long time. And he had a family, see? And a man said he'd give him a house, a job, a future. Respect." He struggles to swallow. "So he went out that night, the night of the floods. And he took his bag of tools. And then Mr. O'Hearn built us the house and gave Papa a job."

I look at him in disbelief. "Pete, are you saying your father...?"

He nods, a big tear rolling down his cheek. "I think Papa did."

In no time Buddy D'Amico has called a judge at home to arrange a search warrant, and tears off with a group of police officers to go through the Sabatinos' home. Spencer and Rob and I walk over to Dunkin' Donuts to get some coffee. We go back to the station and sit around, waiting. Waiting. Spencer goes out to get us some gum. We wait, not talking, just sitting there, the three of us, watching the desk sergeant go about his duties.

Finally, Buddy returns. They haven't found anything, except a deed to the house.

Unlike normal people, the Sabatinos had not taken out a mortgage to buy their house. Evidently, as Crazy Pete said, it appears that Mr. O'Hearn built the house and gave it to Mr. Sabatino. He never paid a dime.

Not in money, anyway.

Mr. Sabatino, we find out by midnight, has not been visiting his sister Rosa in Miami after all. Mr. Sabatino, it turns out, is long gone from the country.

48

On Thursday night, Rob, Mother, Mack, Spencer and I are with Buddy at WSCT in New Haven where DBS News has set up special telephone lines and operators.

Tonight *DBS News Magazine* is running a story called "Murder in Castleford." Will Rafferty produced the story and Alexandra is the reporter. I must say, even though I thought I knew everything in the case, I am fascinated by how they unfold it. They have covered all angles: the police, the FBI, Johnny Boy, Mother, me and Rob, the fire chief, the coroner, the whole nine yards for over twenty-one years.

Alexandra says more than once that the evidence against Phillip O'Hearn is only circumstantial. There is Pete Sabatino's testimony that his father, Frank, went out with a bag of demolition charges the night Dodge Harrington died—the same kind of demolition charges that the police believe were used to bring down the high-school gym wall that killed Harrington. There is the fact Frank Sabatino, three months later, received a new house from his new employer, Phillip O'Hearn. There is also the suspiciously quick demolition of the gymnasium by O'Hearn Construction and the carting away of the wreckage to a secret location. And then, too, Alexandra says, there is O'Hearn's inexplicable demolition of a profitable bowling alley he built the same year as the gymnasium; the mysterious explosion of Tranowsky's Auto Body a few weeks ago—also built by O'Hearn Construction in 1977; to say nothing of the recent gas leak and subsequent explosion of the Preston Roadhouse—"You guessed it, also built by O'Hearn Construction in 1977."

"But why would the man who would later become the eighth wealthiest man in New Haven County order the murder of the friend who gave him his professional start?" Alexandra asks on camera as she strolls in front of the high school. She gestures to the building. "Take a community-minded, passionately inspired young architect, father of two, and show him a builder using substandard materials in a place like a school..."

She explains that Hal Fields was the inspector who approved all the buildings O'Hearn Construction built that year: the gymnasium, the bowling alley, the auto body shop and the roadhouse. She recounts how Fields became city engineer, was arrested on multiple counts of bribery—many connected to O'Hearn's growing empire, and yet not directly tied to him—and went to prison for two years. Then Alexandra switches focus to Tony Meyers, an O'Hearn employee who police believe saw the unmistakable signs of blasting in the gymnasium rubble he was instructed to cart away. Tony hid a damning piece of debris, the police believe, and blackmailed O'Hearn. Documents show how O'Hearn set Tony up in a toxic-waste-disposal business in Long Island and continued to help Tony even after it became clear Meyers was no businessman and a loose cannon to boot.

Alexandra goes into great detail regarding the trouble Tony Meyers's company fell into. Not only was he under investigation by the feds for illegal dumping, but he had bookkeeping discrepancies, federal tax subpoenas and a very tough competitor trying to cut in on his turf. He came to Castleford, his brother Johnny is shown saying, to put the muscle on O'Hearn to bail him out again. Someone alerted Frank Sabatino to "the problem," Alexandra says. Pete overheard his father talking on the telephone about "the cement problem," or "the concrete problem" or "that old flood problem" several times during the week of the murder. One night Pete—"who has a history of paranoia" as Alexandra phrased it—overheard his father actually say to someone on the telephone that "Nobody knows anything about Dodge Harrington and nobody will, don't worry about it. I gave you my word and it's still good. Don't sweat it. I'll take care of it. Just send him to me."

"Him," Alexandra says, "was presumably Phil O'Hearn's blackmailer, Tony Meyers."

The next day was Pete Sabatino's once-a-week meeting at the *Herald-American* with reporter Sally Harrington, the daughter of the man killed twenty-one years ago. It was during that meeting Pete first blurted out to Sally he thought maybe somebody might have killed her father.

Two days later, Tony Meyers arrived at the Sabatino home, where Pete overheard his father say he—Meyers—would get paid at Kaegle's Pond at noon. Pete tried to get ahold of Sally. When he couldn't, he left a message that Sally should be at Kaegle's Pond at noon. So Sally went and found Tony Meyers, shot dead through the heart.

Alexandra goes on to explain that Pete Sabatino went into hiding until the authorities came to believe that he had nothing to do with the murder. His father, Frank, left Castleford, telling friends and family he was worried about the trouble Pete and his conspiracy theories had gotten them into, and that he was going to his sister Rosa's in Florida for a while. Instead, he caught a hopper flight from Hartford to JFK, where he boarded a plane to Milan, Italy, and has not been heard of since, except through the lawyer who told Pete his father was selling the house.

"And what about Phillip O'Hearn?" Alexandra asks, as they show a panoramic view of his estate from the air. "The impoverished young man who got his first big break in business from Dodge Harrington, twenty-three years ago, is worth some forty-six million dollars today."

They show Mr. O'Hearn sitting in a snappy blue blazer on an antique couch in his living room, holding hands with Mrs. O'Hearn. "There is not a word of truth to any of this," he says quietly.

"Not one word?" Alexandra says.

"Not one word," Mr. O'Hearn says.

"You mean you did not build a house for Frank Sabatino and give it to him three months after Dodge Harrington died?"

"No. He worked for me. He paid for the house in work."

"He did fifty thousand dollars' worth of work for you? In addition to his salary?"

"Yes," Mr. O'Hearn says.

"What kind of work was that?"

"Some demolition, some stonework. He is a certified stonemason."

"Did Frank Sabatino do any of the demolition work on the gymnasium where Mr. Harrington was killed?"

"Yes."

She looks at him then, as much as to say, *Did he by chance do a little demolition work just before Mr. Harrington died?* but she doesn't have to voice the question.

She moves on. "Why did you decide so suddenly last year to buy the bowling alley and then tear it down? It was a profitable business."

"I wanted to build a more profitable business."

"But you didn't build anything," Alexandra points out. "You tore a perfectly good bowling alley down and carted it away inside of three days and then sold the land to Home Depot."

"A very lucrative deal," he says.

"But area financial experts estimate a loss of at least four hundred thousand dollars on this deal you say was so lucrative."

"Then your area financial people should be fired," he says calmly, "because they don't know what they're talking about."

They move on. "Mr. O'Hearn," Alexandra asks, "why would so many people be bringing this up if there wasn't some evidence, some grave doubts out there, about why you moved so quickly to destroy the gymnasium and take all the wreckage away—a massive amount of material, may I add—to a location no one in your entire firm can seem to remember?"

"I have no idea," he says.

"I do," Mrs. O'Hearn pipes up. "Because they're jealous. They always have been, that's Castleford. There are still a lot of people around here who can't stand it when a poor kid makes it. How many of those people," she says eagerly, moving forward in her seat, "those people who are saying all of these horrible lies, how many of those people, Ms. Waring, are rich people?"

"Not many," Alexandra admits. "Actually, none. Not rich."

"I rest my case," Mrs. O'Hearn says.

"So that is the reason," Alexandra says, "that they're jealous of your husband's success? And so twenty-one years later they've all decided to—"

"Of course they're jealous! My husband can buy and sell this town and they hate it. And after all my husband has done for them! Why, that Peter Sabatino, my husband tried to give him a job, but he couldn't do it. The man is very nice, I'm sure, but he's a stark raving lunatic, going on and on about Martians and George Bush—just ask anyone in Castleford!"

"It's all right, Gisela," her husband says, patting her hand.

"And the Harringtons?" Alexandra says. "Why, after all these years, would they suddenly turn on you? When it was Dodge Harrington who started your husband's career, and your families considered each other friends?"

"I don't blame Belle," Mr. O'Hearn says quietly.

"It's that Sally who's behind it," Mrs. O'Hearn says. "And what's Belle going to do after Sally's dug up all this nonsense? Why, Sally Harrington gave up her life to come home to nurse her dying mother—"

At this, Mother visibly flinches beside me, and I hear her mutter something indistinguishable under her breath.

"So what is Belle going to do? Of course she's listening to Sally—and we all know Sally's never been right since Dodge died. But that's not my husband's fault!"

Rob elbows me like he used to when we were kids. "You is *bad*, girl," he whispers.

At this point, the attention moves to the man in prison awaiting trial for the murder of Tony Meyers. His story, as given to us by a Russian translator, is that Tony Meyers was messing around with his wife and that's why he tracked him down and killed him. The only problem is, as *DBS News Magazine* has learned, the suspect's wife is still in Moscow. Clearly, this is a put-up job.

"There is no statute of limitations on murder," Alexandra says, "but the same rules of evidence apply: if you don't have evidence, you don't have a case. And in the case of the murder of Dodge Harrington, there is motive, but no weapon, no evidence and no witnesses. And so as Phillip O'Hearn continues his life as a country gentleman and multimillionaire, Belle Harrington in the valley below continues to live with the uncertainty of who, exactly, was responsible for the murder of her husband twenty-one years ago."

At the conclusion of the piece, when the network cuts to a

commercial, we all stand around a moment, feeling vaguely stunned by what we have seen and heard.

Mother is the first to snap out of it. "Well if that doesn't stir the hornet's nest, nothing will."

Twelve minutes later, one of the telephone operators is waving frantically at us, and a call is put through the speaker system.

"I think I know where the old Castleford High gymnasium is," a man calling from Durham, Connecticut, repeats over the monitor.

"Where?" Buddy D'Amico asks.

"Under my house," the man says. "I paid a local guy two thousand bucks to fill in the ravine and he brought in truck after truck of brick and cement for me in 1978."

"What makes you think the debris was from the gym?" Buddy asks him.

"'Cause my boy pulled a slab out that had Hall of Fame chiseled on it. He put it on his bureau and put all his trophies on it."

Buddy frowns. "That's it?"

"Yeah, that's it. 'Cept my wife just went in there to look at the thing and she moved the trophies around and she says underneath it, clear as day, it says Castleford High School. My boy covered up that part because he went to Durham High."

There is another stunned silence. And then Mother bursts into tears.

49

"This is where Dad taught us how to swim," I say, pointing to the murky spot in the pond where there used to be a dock.

"It needs to be dredged," Spencer says.

"It sure does."

He looks around. "And this all belongs to the Calhouns?"

"Yes. They bought it from the estate." It is so very beautiful here. It's hard to believe Castleford is a city. There's nothing but trees and flowers and water and trails and mountains as far as we can see. I am particularly happy this morning because I've been freed of the neck brace.

"Do you think they'll ever sell?"

"Their kids will when they inherit it. They don't live around here anymore."

He puts an arm around my shoulder as we walk along the path. We are coming into the pine grove that my grandfather planted some sixty-five years ago, when the Harringtons were rich. The pine needles are soft under our feet, the air smells delicious and almost edges out the smell of the Cutter's we're wearing. "Do you think you could purchase an option on the property? For the day the kids do inherit it?"

"No," I say. "One, I have no money. Two, I doubt the Calhouns want to dwell on the fact their kids are never coming back to Castleford, and that they'd sell the land out from under them this minute, if only they could."

"It's not an unusual story," Spencer says, bending to pick up a dead pine bough and move it off the trail. "It's going on right now in my family. What will happen to the marina."

"What will happen to it?"

"I don't know. My sister's teaching out at Carnegie Mellon, I'm in New York, even my cousin's a lawyer down in Charleston. I mean, this higher education thing really backfired on my family—everybody's stuck in the books, nobody knows how to do anything practical anymore."

"You chop wood, you fixed my desk, you seem pretty handy to me."

He smiles. "Yeah. If anyone did anything, it would be me. I love the place. But it's not a part-time enterprise, not by any stretch of the imagination." He rubs his cheek. "But back to Maine, gosh." He shakes his head. "Some days it sounds good, others, unimaginable."

"Well, if you ever did go back," I say, "you'd introduce steamed cheeseburgers and build another drive-in."

He laughs, taking my hand and squeezing it. "Only if you come with me."

"Speaking of money," I say.

"Which we weren't."

"Are you ever going back to work? Because I have to."

He laughs. "Yeah, I do. I need to go back in tomorrow, actually."

We walk along. Spencer clears a few more branches from the path.

"Mother really likes you," I finally say, watching him. "I find that scary."

"Thanks a lot."

"She's been yelling at me for years to grow up and then I meet a guy who makes me act like a kid half the time, not even an adolescent, and she thinks this is great. Go figure."

He comes back to my side and puts his arm around me again. We have spent so much time together the last eight days it feels like his body is an extension of mine. "I've got something to ask you."

"Whatever it is, we don't know each other well enough."

"Hey—"

"Okay, ask me the question."

"Will you drive up to my parents' house next weekend? To meet them. Drive up on Saturday morning, early, spend the evening and stay overnight and then come home the next day." He pauses. "My mother wants to meet you. So does my dad. So does the marina."

I glance up at him. "Do they know how long we've known each other?"

He nods. "Uh-huh. And Dad told me to get you up there before I blow it. He saw the *DBS News Magazine* piece and thinks you're hot stuff."

"Oh, no," I groan.

He gives my shoulder a squeeze. "But it's Trudy who really wants to meet you, my stepmother."

"Really?"

"Yeah."

"Is that good?"

"That's very good," he tells me. "She says she has a feeling about you."

"Sally? Is that you?" Mother calls from the living room.

"Yes," I say, sliding the glass door to the deck closed behind us.

"Come in here, dear, I have something to show you!" She sounds very excited.

We walk into the living room and find Mack and Rob sitting on either side of Mother, studying the letter Mother is holding. "Look!" she cries, handing it to me.

Dear Mrs. Harrington,

After a brief discussion at our executive committee meeting this week, we have unanimously voted to make a contribution to the Wilbur Kennett Harrington scholarship fund that has been in existence in Castleford since 1980. (Sally inwardly flinched, remembering quite well the establishment of the Fund when *they* desperately needed money but her mother had been too proud to tell her friends they had needed help.) Please find the enclosed check for $50,000 and a matching donation from my husband, Jackson Darenbrook, for the same amount.

It is our greatest wish that the memory of your husband may further serve to inspire young people. I know, firsthand, of the numerous good qualities you and your husband have inspired in your daughter, Sally.

We are, in fact, hopeful we may entice your daughter to

join our staff at our affiliate station in New Haven, WSCT-TV. In that regard, Sally may expect to hear from us directly. On behalf of all of us at DBS, I send our sincerest best wishes.

Cassy Cochran
President
DBS Television Network

"Can you believe it?" Mother says.

I pass the letter to Spencer and look at the checks. Fifty thousand dollars, fifty thousand dollars—one hundred thousand dollars for the endowment of the Dodge Harrington Foundation. That just about quintuples it. "I have no idea what the WSCT reference is about," I say.

"Oh, she's waiting out front to talk to you," Mother says, taking the letter back from Spencer.

"Who is?"

"Cassy."

"Cassy Cochran?"

"She's right outside, dear. Go talk to her."

I look at Mother and then at Spencer, who's suppressing a smile. "Go on," he urges.

I open the front door. Yep. There she is, Cassy Cochran, wearing khaki shorts, a pale yellow T-shirt, Top-Siders and gold hoop earrings. She's on the other side of the driveway, throwing sticks for Abigail and Scotty. For a TV executive, she's got a pretty good side arm.

"Hi," I say, coming down the yard.

"Oh, hi." She throws one more stick for each before coming toward me.

"Mother's absolutely over the moon in there about the donations. Thank you so much. I hope one of you will come out when we award the scholarships next spring, because there are going to be an awful lot of grateful people."

"Sure, that would be great, that'd be fun."

As if they have nothing better to do! "And that was so generous of Jackson. We'll all be writing to him. And you. Rob, me and Mom."

"We're just glad to do it, Sally. Your family's been through a lot."

There is an uncomfortable pause.

Cassy clears her throat. "What do you think they're going to do about O'Hearn? Can they get him on anything?"

"Oh, yeah. We have absolute proof now, from that guy in Durham, that he purposely used faulty building materials in the school gym. And it wasn't just the cable. They found pipes that were defective, and air vents that had some sort of illegal construction, and evidently there was even a problem with some of the Sheetrock he used."

"But surely the statute of limitations—"

"On the building violations, yes," I explain. "So the way the D.A. has approached it is, okay, we can't prove who set off a demolition charge, but we can prove that the faulty building materials used in the construction of the gymnasium directly contributed to the collapse of the wall, and therefore, to my father's death. And there's no statute of limitations on that. They're charging him with murder in the second degree."

She shakes her head sympathetically. "I hope they get him."

I make a sound of disgust, walking over to Scotty to take his stick. "It'll drag on for years, and he's got all the money in the world, so who knows." I throw it. "But we'd have absolutely nothing if it wasn't for you," I add, turning toward her. "You have no idea the effect all this has had on my family. It's as if we're all waking up for the first time since Daddy died. You've given us a kind of release I can't begin to explain."

"You don't have to explain. I know what it's like."

"Of course you do," I say quietly. "With your father."

"You know, Sally," she says, "working on that interview with you has been a very good experience for me."

I slap a hand over my eyes, groaning.

"No, I'm serious, Sally." She touches my arm. "Really. It's been very good for me."

I drop my hand.

"In fact, I was wondering if maybe I could read what you wrote. What you would have written."

"Verity's running the photographs as a photo essay. Did you know that?"

"Really?" Cassy says. I can see that she is pleased. She's right, working on this piece has been good for her. A month ago she would have been trying to crawl under the car to hide from this.

"I'll put my stuff together and send it to you. I think you'll find it rather enlightening."

She is reaching into her pocket. Out of the corner of my eye, I see Abigail and Scotty sneaking up the hill toward us, each dragging what looks to be an entire branch from Mother's brush pile. Cassy pulls out a piece of paper, unfolds it and hands it to me. It's handwritten in ink, dated yesterday.

DEAL MEMO
   One-year contract
   investigative reporter, WSCT News, New Haven
   $75,000 salary
   full health benefits
   can still write for *Herald-American* or other periodicals
   perks to be listed in contract (clothing allowance, company car);
   401K
   In good faith I approve this offer in principle and hereby extend it to Sally Harrington.
   Alexandra Waring

   In good faith I accept this offer in principle to DBS News, Inc.

"You're supposed to sign down here," Cassy says, pointing. She slaps her back pocket, finds what she's looking for and holds out a pen. "It's not a lot of money for TV, even out here, Sally," she says, "but it is a trial job, and you can still do some writing to supplement your income."

Supplement my income? Thank heavens she doesn't know what I've been making at the *Herald-American.*

"I don't understand who I'd be working for."

"DBS News through our affiliate, WSCT. It's a trial training period. They want you, they want to try it, but we're footing the bill."

I take a breath and look at the paper again, trying to think.

"I'd love to, you know that," I finally say. "But this is just like what happened with Verity. I'm being offered an incredible opportunity for every reason other than the caliber of my work. I don't ever want to be in that situation again."

The dogs *are* dragging branches and they're looking at me and Cassy in hopeful collusion.

Cassy laughs. "Sorry, guys, those are beyond me."

As if they understand, the dogs release their branches and start playing, tumbling around together on the grass.

"You're wrong, Sally," Cassy tells me. "We're offering you a job based on the skills we've seen firsthand. There are two things we know about you, absolutely. No, four. You're smart, you can write and you have character. And as Alexandra herself said, the camera likes you. You saw yourself the other night, Sally. The lens likes you."

I did notice and she's right. I'm beginning to come around to this idea.

"And Good Lord," she continues, lowering her voice, "surely you've noticed the caliber of reporting we're getting out of that station. I mean, come on, Sally, talk about gobbledygook—needless to say it sure would be nice to have at least one literate person in the field."

Another good point. I *know* I can do better than most of the station's on-air talent.

"So, what do you say?" Cassy says.

"I say—I gratefully accept your offer in principle."

"Hooray!" Mother cheers from her upstairs window. "Oh, can you believe it, Mack? Sally's going to be on TV!"

"Hold out for a cool car," my brother advises from the bathroom window. "Don't let them stick you with a compact."

"You go, girl," Spencer calls from the same window.

Abigail runs over to bark at the men's voices.

"With audience demographics like these," I joke, holding a hand out to Cassy, "how can I possibly miss?"

"I don't think you will," she says, shaking on it. She looks down at Scotty, who's just sitting there, smiling, looking up at her. Cassy leans over. "And what about you? What do you want?"

Scotty raises his paw. And so Cassy shakes on it with him, too.

Now I know it's a good deal.